QUEEN OF THE UNDERWORLD

A GUARDIANS OF HADES PREQUEL

FELICITY HEATON

First printed January 2023

First Edition

Layout and design by Felicity Heaton

THE GUARDIANS OF HADES SERIES

Book 1: Ares

Book 2: Valen

Book 3: Esher

Book 4: Marek

Book 5: Calistos

Book 6: Daimon

Book 7: Keras

Book 8: Thanatos

Book 9: Hades

Prequel: Queen of the Underworld

CHAPTER 1

Hades was in a black mood and the Underworld shook because of it.

Crimson lightning struck around him, each bolt that connected with the obsidian earth making it tremble and spraying chunks of rock and gravel in all directions. A great jagged streak hit close to him, the heat and power of it buffeting his left side and knocking him away from it. The chariot pitched, the sudden movement shaking him with enough force that the cold, numbing darkness lost its hold on him for a heartbeat.

A moment he seized as fiercely as he gripped the leather reins to guide the horses to safety.

He gave a hard shake of his head, trying to dislodge the thickening darkness as it crept back in, as it whispered in his ear and shredded the fragile fragments of his humanity with sharp talons.

Before he could even begin to fight it, it pulled him back down into the abyss, stealing control of him once more, and all he could feel was hatred. At himself. At this world. At everyone.

His lips stretched into a slow, malicious grin as he raced through the dark lands on his chariot, carving the earth up in his wake as he thundered forwards, the shadows that clung to his shoulders streaming behind him like onyx wings. The light from the ribbons of lava that flowed down the cragged faces of the black mountains and formed rivers beside the road reflected off his obsidian plate armour, chasing over the talons of his gauntlets as he raised his hands and snapped the reins again, urging the four black steeds to run faster.

The thick air filled with the beautiful melody of screams of souls as the ground trembled and bucked, and a spiky mountain burst from a plain off to his left, like the fierce teeth of a beast that had circled beneath its prey from below to catch them within its jaws.

And devour them.

The fear of every soul in the village the mountain destroyed trickled through him, feeding the darkness within him.

His lips peeled back off his fangs as his grin widened. He savoured their pain. Their terror. Pleasure rolled through him, a drug he couldn't get enough of, one that only made him crave more as the darkness tightened its grip on him. He cracked the reins harder, demanding the enormous onyx horses obey him. They whinnied in response and surged forwards on a new wave of power, carrying him faster across the uneven land, up an incline towards an ancient mountain range.

Another fierce bolt of scarlet lightning struck close to him and his head whipped towards it. The brightness of it seared his eyes and he flinched, growling at the light. The cold receded for another heartbeat, and Hades was quicker this time.

He gritted his teeth and fought the darkness, refusing to let it rip control from him again. Sweat dotted his brow as he struggled against it, attempting to purge it from his soul to free him of its grip. His breaths shallowed and grew faster, his muscles clamping down on his bones with enough force to make his entire body ache as he waged war against himself. The darker side of his blood that he kept secret from all—a feral beast that lurked within him, constantly waiting for the right moment to strike, constantly trying to make that moment happen by whispering poisonous words in his ear to weaken him—fought back, clawing at his mind with wicked words designed to spread doubt and feed his fears.

Hades clutched the reins harder, trying not to listen to the truth it spoke, but it wouldn't be silenced. It purred at him, murmuring words designed to seduce and tempt, to draw him back into its arms and make him surrender to it.

He couldn't remember why the darkness had risen this time.

But he felt sure he had done terrible things while it had held him in its grip, numbing him and robbing him of any soft emotions he might possess, transforming him into a monster fuelled by rage and a thirst for violence.

He always did.

Hades looked at his realm as the lightning continued to rage across it, as the land shifted and mountains erupted. This catastrophic storm was his fault. It was born of him.

And he regretted it.

He tried to pull his temper back under control, fought harder against the darkness that slowly chilled his blood and shut down his feelings, those seductive words it murmured to him luring him back towards it. He couldn't give in to it. He glared at the black talons of his gauntlets and tightened his grip on the reins. He couldn't.

Whatever had plunged him into a black rage must have been powerful, so devastating that he had completely lost himself to the darkness.

If he let it take him again, he might not come back from it.

Fear of what he might do if he became the darkness, losing the last shreds of his humanity, was a potent motivator and had him fighting harder as he clamped his teeth together and growled. He could not let the darkness take him again.

But he couldn't remember why it had so easily stolen control.

If he could, he might be able to tame the darkness again and bring it back under *his* control.

Hades looked at his dark realm again. How long had he raged? So much felt different to him as his powers stretched outwards, connecting with the lands and funnelling through them to reach far from him. He swallowed hard, regret tasting bitter in his mouth. He hadn't meant to harm so many under his care.

But then, he never did.

His mood shifted, guilt twining with the regret, with the fear, dragging him back down. He didn't want to feel these things. Did he? He wanted them gone. Didn't he?

Hades lost focus as those desires snaked through him, the thunder of hoofs growing distant in his ears and his connection to his realm falling away. No. He didn't want to feel them. He didn't want to feel anything.

What was the point when it only led to pain?

The darkness purred again, wrapping cold arms around him that promised oblivion. That promised an end to his suffering.

It was better he felt nothing.

Then the betrayals didn't cut so deep.

He frowned at his hands as a flicker of a memory broke the surface, shimmering just beyond his reach—the reason the darkness had consumed him. It was there and gone in a flash, and he snarled as he cursed it, as he tried to make it come back. Lightning struck all around him, carving great pits in the black earth, and in the distance ahead of him, people screamed.

His grin slowly returned as one by one those screams fed the darkness and dulled his emotions, leaving him numb once more. Before it took him again, tearing awareness and control from him, a question echoed in his mind.

What was he so angry about?

The darkness purred an answer.

What did it matter?

Every day was the same. Nothing would ever change that. He woke in a black rage, consumed by something he could not name, his soul shrouded in darkness, and stalked from his temple to carry out his duties.

Over and over again.

Forever.

Hades pushed back the darkness, mastering it again, but not quite able to shed it completely. It hissed another question at him, another attempt to tear him down and make him give in, one that had him wavering and had anger spiking his blood.

How long had it been since he had seen the sun?

He gazed skywards, but there was blood red where he felt blue should have been, and thick plumes of black ash where white clouds should have drifted.

Hades curled his lip and shut down that line of thought, his mood darkening further as his black eyebrows knitted hard. He sneered at his realm, one made of ash and blood.

A realm of darkness.

Where Zeus, his youngest brother, had dared to banish him while he bathed in the light of Olympus, and allowed their brother, Poseidon, to rule another realm of sunshine and life.

While Hades ruled death.

They had betrayed him. Yes. His own flesh and blood. His own brothers. Even Poseidon, the one he had protected with his life countless times, had betrayed him. They always betrayed him. Always formed an allied front against him. Always sought to cage him here. To steal the light from him.

Another scream scraped in his ears like a broken symphony as he entered a village, his horses not slowing as they thundered down the narrow path that cut through the heart of the cluster of thatched black stone buildings. Males and females desperately scrambled out of his way, racing for cover to avoid being struck by his horses or the lightning that slammed into the ground.

Hades glared at the noble souls.

Souls sent to him by Zeus.

"Olympians," he growled.

On a sneer, he unleashed a fraction of his power.

Behind him, a great fault split the earth in two, and those screams became bellows of sheer terror, threaded with notes of agony as other males and females yelled names or cried for help.

Hades's eyelids drooped to half-mast and his smile grew lazy as his shadows seized those who were close to climbing free of the crevasse and hurled them into the dark depths. Pleasure rolled through him, fogging his mind and making him crave more.

He turned his sights on the road ahead of him, one that cut through a gorge.

The souls who were walking along it towards him all fell to their knees as he approached and clasped their hands together, raising them above their bowed heads as they murmured praise to him.

His shadows tore from the ground, rocketing towards them.

Hades clamped his molars together and growled as he shoved back against the darkness, subduing it in time to halt the shadows before they cut the people to ribbons. He breathed hard as he drew them back to him and wrestled for control of his own body, clawing it back inch by inch. The darkness within him writhed and snarled, battering the cage of his body and scraping at his mind, raking talons over it in a light caress as it poured honeyed words in his ear.

Kill them.

"No," he hissed and urged the horses onwards, before the souls could snap out of the haze of terror that had fallen over them when his shadows had launched at them. "They are not souls from Olympus. They were mortal once."

He cast a regretful glance down at them as he thundered past them, guilt twining with agony to form a sharp lance in his breast, and he turned his face away, despising himself for the horror he had unleashed on the village. Those souls hadn't deserved his wrath either.

His mood shifted again, his rage swift to rise as he broke out onto a large plain. He huffed and tightened his hands around the reins as thoughts of Zeus and Poseidon clouded his mind and the shadows encroached, spreading to blot out the light.

Because he had recalled why his mood was so foul and the darkness had taken him.

Poseidon had dared to interfere with Thanatos's duty to reap a female's soul and bring it to Hades.

The god of death had returned from the veil without severing her life from her body despite the fact the Moirai had dictated her time had come, and when Hades had asked him why he had dared come to him empty-handed, Thanatos had growled that Poseidon had struck a deal with the three Fates.

Sparing the female.

Because his brother had apparently laid claim to her.

She was to be his queen.

Hades snarled and cracked the reins as he glared at his realm. A mountain in the distance erupted, a cataclysmic blast of fiery light detonating to push back the darkness and fill the air with distant screams.

Zeus had his queen, and now Poseidon was to have his.

Where was Hades's queen?

His younger brothers didn't deserve a loyal female. Both were philanderers. They bedded their servants, and mortals, and any female who took their fancy. He knew it. He knew Zeus often left Olympus to seek out beautiful maidens in the mortal world, slaking his lusts with them.

While Hades spent his every waking moment working, ensuring that the dead found their resting place, and that the mortal world, Olympus and Poseidon's islands remained free of wandering souls that could cause unbalance and tip the realms towards an apocalypse if they were left alone.

A wide glowing orange crevasse snaked across the land ahead of him and as he reached it the black rock rose to form a bridge beneath the hooves of his horses. They galloped onwards without breaking their stride, their confidence in their master absolute.

At least someone in his realm trusted him.

Would not betray him.

That stray thought gave him pause as he crossed the lava-riddled plateau nestled in the heart of towering black mountains.

Did he desire others to trust him as these beasts did?

He shook his head and scoffed. "No."

His men feared him. Fear made them obey him. The souls feared him. Fear kept them in line, making his life easier. Fear was pivotal. It was key.

It brought all who stood before him to their knees and under his control.

But still the niggling feeling lingered, refusing to die despite his best attempts to kill it.

The darkness twisted it, distorting it into something else. Perhaps it wasn't a desire to have someone trust him, but rather a desire to simply have *someone*.

Hades growled and cast that wretched thought aside. He needed no one. Not his brothers. Not a female. No one. All he needed in his life were subordinates who obeyed him without question and his duty.

His mood darkened again, thoughts turning treacherous, refusing to leave behind the one that had struck him. It echoed in his mind, tormenting him, flooding him with a need to lash out at the lands and roar at the sky.

Where was *his* queen?

The Fates had made one for each of his brothers. His *younger* brothers.

He was the eldest. The most powerful. If anyone deserved a queen, it was him.

A female who would do his bidding. Who would warm his bed and satisfy his needs, and obey him.

His grip on the leather reins slackened as a feeling coursed through him.

He found the thought of having someone… *pleasing*.

Yet the Moirai denied him.

He bared his fangs at his realm, mentally baring them at the three females. He had been given the darkest realm to rule, had been betrayed and banished from the mortal world by Zeus, and had been charged with the task of keeping the titans imprisoned, no easy feat given their vast strength.

All he knew was death and darkness.

He was owed something for the centuries he had remained loyal to his duties.

He clenched his jaw until his teeth ached. He growled through them, the sound rumbling across the land together with the cracking of rock as more fissures opened across the plain, blazing bright orange.

He was owed someone.

A sheer cliff across the base of one of the mountains ahead of him snared his gaze and he frowned at it. It was no natural cliff. He peered at it, straining to make it out as he turned his horses towards it, drawn to it and unable to deny the urge to take a closer look. As he neared it, his eyes slowly narrowed, the black slashes of his eyebrows dipping low.

There were markings on the wall of obsidian rock.

Hades slowed the horses and brought his chariot to a halt before it. He hadn't been imagining them. Upon the chiselled surface of the cliff, markings had been inscribed, forming a circular pattern twenty feet wide.

He dropped off the back of his chariot, his black cloak swirling around his ankles, and cautiously approached the cliff, the pointed toes of his onyx metal boots scraping on the obsidian rock beneath his feet. When he was within forty feet of the markings, the circles and glyphs burst to life. Dazzlingly bright colours seared his sensitive eyes that had grown far too used to darkness and he flinched away, a growl leaving his lips as they pulled taut to flash his fangs.

A gate.

Hades squinted at it until his eyes adjusted to the brightness of the series of glyph-filled colourful rings, each of which rotated in the opposite direction to the previous one.

It had been so long since he had been near a gate that he had almost forgotten what they looked like.

Curiosity tugged him towards the shimmering circular portal despite the wary part of him that whispered to keep his distance.

He wasn't meant to leave the Underworld.

Not because his youngest brother had decreed it, but because he was well aware of how his power affected the mortal realm.

And this gate led to that delicate light-filled world.

It was one of only two in the Underworld. The other was leagues away. He looked off to his left in that direction, the great black mountains that surrounded him blocking his view but not stopping him from seeing the gate in his mind. Despite the distance between him and it, he could sense the constant hum of its power. He could always feel it if he put his mind to it. He was connected to everything in his realm. It was part of him and he was part of it. Bound to it.

Zeus had made sure of that.

After defeating the titans and overthrowing their father, they had drawn lots. Hades was sure Zeus had manipulated the sticks, ensuring he received Olympus to rule while Hades was cast into the darkness to rule the dead. Zeus and Poseidon had formed a fast bond during the war, one that had left Hades feeling like an outcast within his own family, despite how Poseidon had followed him as eldest while they had been trapped by their father.

How quick his brother had been to follow Zeus instead once he had freed them, shunning Hades.

So, it hadn't surprised him when Zeus had taken care of Poseidon, giving him the oceans to rule.

They were always taking care of each other.

He sneered, flashing fangs again.

Zeus hadn't just bound Hades to this realm. He had sowed the seeds that sprouted in his mind to whisper that he couldn't leave whenever he had the urge to walk in the light for a time to cleanse his soul. Zeus wanted him here, trapped, slowly losing himself. Each year he spent in this realm chipped away at the light within him, allowing more darkness to seep in.

Now, Hades wasn't sure there was any light left in him.

He couldn't remember the male he had been.

He could only remember the darkness.

The seething, unquenchable thirst for violence and bloodshed, and terror that was his constant companion, darkening his mind with shadows and whispering in his ear, seducing him into obeying it.

If he could shatter the gate between the Underworld and Olympus to allow the darkness to seep into that bright realm, he would do it.

He stared at the gate before him.

If he could shatter this one to make his realm collide with the mortal realm… His mood faltered. He would not do it. He sharply shook his head, dislodging the dark hunger that had spurred his terrible thoughts. He would not do either. The Underworld was his to protect now—his home. He would defend it and keep it safe until his last breath.

Hades stared at the gate, feeling the power of it humming in his bones. It was waiting for him. He looked back at his chariot, aware that he should leave, and then at the gate, aching to step through it. Drawn to it. Crossing the threshold felt like a vital need he had to satisfy, one that would kill him if he didn't go through with it.

A stray thought gave him pause.

Had the Moirai brought him to this place he hadn't ventured in centuries?

Hades gave another sharp shake of his head, angered by his foolish and sentimental thoughts. The Fates did not care about him enough to lead him anywhere. He was master of his own destiny. Poseidon's interference and declaration that he would have a queen by his side had caused a fault in Hades's armour, one he repaired as he hardened his heart and pushed out the weakness. He needed no one.

But he still couldn't convince himself to turn away from the gate.

If he stepped through it and into the mortal world, he would aggravate Zeus, perhaps almost as much as Poseidon had aggravated him.

Hades hiked his shoulders and stalked forwards.

His pulse raced, heart galloping as he closed the distance between him and the shimmering rings. The power the gate emanated grew stronger as he neared it and the rings shone brighter. How long had it been since he had visited the mortal realm? How long had it been since he had walked in the light? Whatever light there was on the other side of the gate, it wouldn't last long. His dark influence would blot it out in a matter of minutes, but they would be minutes in which he was no longer one with the shadows.

And if his disobedience angered his brothers, so be it.

He would show them who was the strongest and most powerful.

Hades drew down a breath.

And stepped into the portal.

And out into a cool, dark cavemouth.

Only he wasn't alone.

Ahead of him, beyond the cave, the barren land gave way to lush grass and verdant trees bathed in light and filled with life—a young forest that shouldn't have been there.

But it was the soft, melodic song of a female voice that snared his attention. And bewitched him.

CHAPTER 2

Hades strode forwards with purpose, no trace of fear in his steps despite the nerves that attempted to engulf him as curiosity tugged him towards the forest. The darker side of his blood writhed and snarled, battling him for control, and he used every ounce of his iron will to hold it back, denying it.

Deeply aware of the devastating effect he would have on this fragile world if he let it steal control while he was here.

He would not harm this realm. He would leave it as he had found it, but not before he knew the owner of that bewitching, delicate and beautiful voice.

He sucked down another breath, anticipation swirling through him as he approached the entrance of the cave and the edge of a young forest that stood in defiance of the dry, barren stretch of coastline that hugged the Aegean.

An impossible forest.

"This land should not be able to bear such life," he murmured as a distant memory of this place rose to the surface, one of dusty, arid dirt and tan rock under a stifling, hot sun, "and yet my eyes do not deceive me."

He arched an eyebrow and canted his head.

Feminine voices curled through the trees, a trio of them speaking while one continued her siren's song, luring him towards her.

Hades stilled where rock met grass and tried to pinpoint their owners with his senses. One was closer to him than the other three, who were all grouped together at a distance. He edged to his right, his focus on that single female, curiosity rising within him again to have him trying to catch a glimpse of her.

That desire to catch just a glimpse transformed into something else—something powerful and demanding—as her soft voice grew closer, her song growing clearer, and he smelled the faintest hint of lilies.

Heat curled through his veins, that scent rousing a fierce need that thrummed in every inch of his body and had the darkness writhing harder, violently attempting to wrench control from him and make him find the owner of it. He needed to see her. He couldn't remember the last time he had smelled such a delicate scent. His world was ash and smoke and blood, and death.

Everything about this female seemed to be the opposite of what he knew.

Her song teased his ears as her scent teased his nose, and his breath caught in his throat as he was swept up in her—a female he hadn't even seen yet. Not just the man in him either. The darker side of him burned with a desire to see her too. He needed to know if her beauty matched her voice and her scent. He loosed a low growl and took another step forwards, remaining just within the shadows of the cave, the powerful need to see her colliding with a wariness of disturbing her.

He inched further to his right and straightened to his full six-eight height, the hard black plates of his armour shifting as he strained to catch a glimpse of her. He felt as if he wasn't master of his own body as he tried to spot her, but it wasn't the darkness in control of his actions.

It was the pressing desire to see her.

She was moving closer, but no matter where he moved, the trees blocked his view. His claws itched with the need to attack them until they were nothing more than splinters of wood and his view was clear of the obstruction.

He moved the other way, tracking her with his senses, and discovering something intriguing.

She was strong.

Not mortal.

There were mortals near to her though. The other three females. Were they her servants?

What goddess had come to this place, so far from Olympus or Poseidon's realm?

Her power caressed his, grazing it lightly in a way that urged him onwards and made him forget about the mortals as it cranked up the desperation to see her.

Because he had never felt anything like her power.

It was light. Warmth. Goodness.

It was everything he wasn't.

Hades edged closer, a predator stalking his prey, his mind churning with dangerous thoughts that roused the darker side of his blood and brought it to the fore again. Perhaps the Moirai had brought him here after all, seeking to give him something he desired for once, an attempt to appease him. Poseidon had his new queen. Zeus had his. Hades hadn't even seen this female, but already his blood burned for her. The brush of her power against his and the delicate beauty of her voice were enough to entrance him and rouse his desire to an unbearable degree.

He wanted this female.

The thought of her warming his bed had his blood quickening.

It had been too long since he had taken a female, his duties keeping him too busy to indulge in such things as his brothers did. But he had the feeling it wasn't his ignored physical needs that had his body aching for this female.

It was something else.

He growled low, baring his fangs, and his breaths came faster still as he moved to his right. He glared at the trees that continued to deny him, blocking his view. There had to be a better vantage point, one that would allow him to see more than tree trunks and the leafy scrub that covered the ground in places.

He froze, his entire body locking up tight.

His breath gusted from him.

A striking scarlet-haired maiden stepped into view.

She was beauty and light wrapped in flawless pale skin and rosy cheeks and pink lips that beckoned him, awakening something fierce in him as her tongue poked out to wet them. His breath lodged in his throat as he gazed at her, his awareness of the world destroyed and something fundamental inside him changing from just the sight of her. She was perfection, and she roused not only the man in him, but the darkness. It growled at him, sharpening his fangs and his nails as it whispered a fierce demand that echoed the desire that thrummed in his blood and beat in his heart.

Take her.

Hades wrenched his eyes from her and glared at the sharp talons of his black gauntlets, deeply aware of his appearance. Obsidian irises that ringed fiery pupils. Pointed ears. Razor-sharp fangs. Wrapped in shadows. And the darkness didn't even have him in its grip right now.

He glanced at her again, her beauty a lance through his heart that made it ache and bleed. How different they were. He spread his left hand and gazed at his palm and his outstretched talons, feeling the vastness of the differences between them, and the wretched darkness he had courted and allowed to infect him.

Darkness that would be a barrier between him and this beauty.

One he might not be able to overcome.

The darkness murmured in his ear, spying an opening and slipping through the cracks to tease control from him.

He didn't need to overcome anything.

He only needed to take what he desired.

He needed to take her.

She would make a fine queen. He would bend her to his will, and she would obey him, and please him.

Hades crushed that dark desire and cast it away from him, and fought back against the darkness, fearing she might see that part of himself he could never quite conquer. She would never want him. No one wanted him. Shadows snaked around his soul, slowly closing to squeeze out the light.

He lifted his gaze to her.

And those shadows parted again, the darkness receding the moment his eyes landed on her and she bewitched him all over again.

Her glittering emerald eyes danced over the flowers she held as she lightly touched the blooms, a smile playing on her lips that spoke of pleasure—joy he wasn't sure he had ever felt in his long existence.

Certainly never over something as simple as some flowers.

She blossomed before him as she inspected the bouquet, her flowing crimson hair a striking splash of colour amongst the green of the forest. The layers of her soft jade gown swept around her bare feet as she slowly walked through a clearing filled with flowers of every colour, every step she made carried out with grace and care, her feet touching only grass and never once straying too close to one of the delicate blooms despite the fact she kept her striking gaze on her bouquet.

And she wore a crown of flowers that made her look like a queen.

His queen.

Not just a beauty to warm his bed and ease his loins. This graceful goddess was his queen.

Something deep within him knew it, and something dark once again demanded he take her and make her his.

Hades fought it, slowly subduing that wicked urge as he studied her, using the sight of her to tame the very feeling she had evoked.

The air seemed to sparkle as he watched her tending to the colourful blooms, as he lingered in the shadows drinking his fill of her. She was innocence and beauty as she spoke to the small animals that strayed close to her, trusting her despite how easily she could harm them.

Perhaps they could feel what he could—that this female would never harm another.

Perhaps she had been born of this forest. She looked as if she might have been, and appeared as if she wasn't quite of this world. She was something else. Nothing like the other goddesses he had seen and knew. His fingers twitched with a need to reach out and grasp her so he would know whether she was real or a figment of his imagination, conjured to torment him.

While at the same time, he wanted to remain where he was, observing her from a distance, overcome by the softer emotions that clashed with darker desires.

She was bewitching.

Enchanting.

Magical.

Alluring.

Hades wasn't sure he had ever seen anything so pure.

So perfect.

So damned beautiful.

His mind emptied of anything that wasn't her, his focus obliterated by her. She was all he knew as he watched her from a distance, struggling to comprehend the powerful and intense feelings she stirred in him, or the incredible pull he felt towards her.

And suddenly, he knew how the souls in his realm felt when they first came to him and why they often wandered to the far reaches of his lands, or remained curled up and sobbing for weeks.

Because he feared losing sight of her. He feared her leaving.

He feared her being taken from him.

The thought she might be stolen from him and he might never see her again was like a blade in his heart, twisting deep. Sheer agony rolled through him and his mood darkened, turning blacker than night. If anyone tried to take her from him, he would destroy them.

She was his.

Clouds gathered above him in response to his shift in mood and his dark power rising with it, blotting out the bright sunshine and plunging the area of forest where he was into shadows.

The darkness only gathered faster as one of the other females said, "My lady, we should return."

"I will be but a moment." The sound of the delicate redhead's voice was pure bliss but sheer torment at the same time as he realised something.

She intended to leave.

That fear she would be taken from him and he would never see her again was about to become a reality.

A desperate need to make her notice him grew rapidly within him, surging through him and stealing command of him as easily as the darkness could at times. He growled as he moved into a position where she would be able to see him and stared at her, willing her to look at him now.

Wild with a need for her to see him.

Even when he felt deep in the black pit of his soul that it wouldn't go as he desired.

Rather than wanting him, she would be terrified.

Such a delicate creature would never choose a beast like him.

That feeling clawed at him, shredding his insides to allow oily black to spill into the lacerations. It poisoned his mind, drawing up the darkness, until he seethed with a need to seize hold of her and take her, and had to fight to hold it back, waging war against it and aware that if he gave in to it, he would destroy everything.

She would never want him.

She crouched, her pale green dress pooling around her bare feet as she returned to picking flowers, a melody still playing on her tempting lips. The sound soothed the raging beast of his darkness, dulling the sharp edge of his mood enough that he could let go of the urge to grab her and entrancing him so thoroughly that he couldn't have convinced his feet to move even if he had wanted to carry out his plan to take her.

She plucked a bloom and added it to the bouquet before rising and moving on, continuing her walk through the forest.

Not leaving.

Warmth curled through him, softening the hard reaches of his heart and loosening the hold of his darkness even further. He frowned and examined the intriguing shift in his mood, and his eyebrows rose as he realised he was pleased. Not the usual kind of dark pleasure he took from his daily work, but a lighter kind, one that satisfied him almost as much.

And the source of this curious feeling was the female.

She had shown him she was intent on remaining rather than doing as the other female bid and leaving, and that had pleased him.

Her sweet song continued to soothe him as she meandered through the trees, drifting towards the next patch of flowers, and he soaked up the sight of her, an irritating feeling growing in the back of his mind.

He couldn't be here much longer.

His power was already affecting this world and it wouldn't be long before she noticed it.

And then noticed him.

He was torn by that.

Wrenched between wanting her to see him and not wanting it.

Hades glowered at her now. He wanted to say he wasn't a beast who would pounce on her if she strayed too close or made a sudden move, but he could not. There was a growing tightness inside him, one that felt as if it might snap at any moment and he might do something crazy. He pulled down a steadying breath and fought back against the rising darkness, pushing it down deep inside him and clawing back control, hyper-aware of his appearance.

If this delicate creature saw him now, she would bolt in terror. He was no fool. His appearance was monstrous and his reputation was the same. A female like this goddess would never want a male like him.

Even when he desperately wanted her.

He curled his fingers into fists that had his talons digging through the leather palms of his gauntlets and into his flesh. Drawing blood. He needed to appear gentler. He scoffed. If that was possible.

The darkness purred again to take her.

Hades clenched his jaw and denied it.

He didn't want to frighten her.

That desire was visceral, a living and breathing thing within him that had him at its wretched mercy. He didn't feel fully in control of himself as it gripped him. It felt as if something else had taken the reins and was making decisions for him, just like the darker side of his blood did, and he didn't like it.

But he also didn't fight it.

Because he wanted her to stay.

He wanted it with every beat of his black heart as it thundered and his limbs quaked, his entire body trembling as he fought to hold himself back until he had managed to make his appearance more pleasing.

More human.

And when he was ready, he would return for her.

His lips stretched in a slow grin as the darkness purred within him, his mind flooding with pleasing thoughts that awakened something ravenous and dark, and dangerously possessive. It consumed him, filling his head with a single thought.

She *would* be his.

He sneered as another thought punched through that one, shattering his pleasure with a cold dose of reality.

But how?

Hades lifted his hand to reach for her, rage and fear colliding within him as she turned away and began walking further from him. Anger that she meant to leave him clashed with fear that she might, and it was a ferocious storm within him, ripping him apart as he watched her leaving and desperately wanted her to stay.

Black thoughts snaked through his mind like jagged vines to crowd out the light, to banish his softer emotions as something within him—something feral and vicious—snarled that she would leave him if he didn't stop her.

She could not leave him.

Hades wrenched back on the reins, denying his dark need to take her. Awareness swept through him and his breath leaked from him as resignation chased on its heels.

But he had to leave her.

It beat inside him, drumming faster and faster as the clouds blackened and the wind picked up, and the darker side of his blood howled at him to teleport to her and snatch her now, before it was too late. He would lose her if he didn't grab her right now.

He would lose her if he did. He was soul-deep aware of that.

What did it matter? He had to take her and she would obey him. She would be his.

Hades growled low and shut down that dark line of thought. Resolve flowed through him, together with determination. He had a plan, and he would stick to it. He would leave. Right now. If he lingered any longer, she would notice the storm and then him. No good would come of that.

So he would leave, and somehow make himself more presentable, and then he would return to this place he was beginning to feel belonged to her.

She hadn't been born of these magical woods.

They had been born of her.

That was why she took such pleasure in the flowers and the creatures who had made it their home.

The confidence that she would return and he would see her again loosened the tight feeling in his breast and had him taking a step back into the shadows. His mind churned, plots forming as he continued to watch her.

She would be his, but he needed to ensure she would remain that way once he took her.

As the shadows grew thicker around him, the darkness grew stronger. His brothers had taken females they desired, making them their queen, and in time those females had come to accept their new life. So it would be with this goddess.

Hades eased further back into the darkness of the cave, towards the gate, before she noticed him and he ruined everything. To ensure she remained his, he would do something that would be both a pleasure and a torment.

He would speak with Zeus.

Partly to anger his brother and partly because he desired the male's blessing. If Zeus gave it, no one would be able to take the goddess from him.

She would be his queen.

Hades grinned, flashing his fangs.

Even if Zeus denied him as Hades expected, she would still belong to him. He would take her regardless of what his brother said and he would fight everyone in this world to keep her. No one would take her from him.

Rather than heading through the gate behind him, Hades teleported to the one in a remote dusty stretch of land near Athens. He stepped through the shimmering portal and out into the harbour of the bright white city that clung to the foothills of the mountain.

A city that buzzed with life, kissed by sunshine and the turquoise sea.

Olympus.

Darkness surged through his veins and crowded his mind, rage burning up his blood to have his talons flexing at his sides as he tracked the people coming and going along the promenade, dressed in fine white chitons and gowns, and adorned with gold.

Olympians.

His claws itched to rip through them as the darkness snarled within him, goading him into painting this fair city with blood and death to take what was rightfully his and had been denied him. All would tremble at his feet and beg for mercy. Even his brother. His grin stretched wider as pleasing images of Zeus on his knees before him filled his mind, spreading intoxicating warmth through his body.

Hades bit back a growl and eased back a step, away from the people, unable to trust himself to be near them now that the darkness was rising again, slowly devouring what precious little light remained in his soul.

He breathed harder, his chest straining as he fought it, battling to calm himself and clear his mind. He knew how the Olympians spoke of him, how they feared him and twisted the tales of him, turning him into something monstrous.

A monster he could easily be when the darkness took him.

A monster he would not become.

Hades fixed his gaze on the largest white temple that sat on a promontory of tan rock high above the others and teleported there, seeking the escape from the crowds and hoping it would help him retain control.

He landed in the heart of his brother's chambers.

Hades turned in a slow circle, surveying the bright white room that was open to a balcony overlooking Olympus on one side. Between two of the fluted columns that lined that side stood a gold chaise longue and beaten gold table laden with dark grapes and an empty goblet, and against one of the columns someone had propped up a fan with a long gold handle. He sensed movement in the other rooms beyond the white marble walls that enclosed three sides of the room, but only one of the people was approaching him.

He continued to stare out at the city, at terracotta roofs enclosing green gardens and the leafy trees that lined the broader avenues. So different to his realm. The contrast was marked, and undeniable. Hades hated it. He despised how he felt whenever he ventured here, how this pure, pale city tainted his view of his realm, making him see it as a grim, dark place.

A betrayal.

He betrayed his realm whenever he thought like that, whenever he compared it to this one and found it lacking. The Underworld was everything to him. He didn't want it to be like this city, and yet… he also wished at times that it wasn't so dark or so dangerous. Despite his efforts, his realm remained a bleak and savage land, one filled with bloodthirsty beasts and death.

And it was all his fault.

He kept his eyes on the city, cursing his weakness and how this city affected him, and how he let the darkness affect his own realm, as the person entered the room to his left.

His immense power pressed against Hades's own.

As if that would scare him away.

Hades crushed the fear and the anger his thoughts had stirred, destroyed the regret and the shame, and hardened his heart, drawing up the darkness like a cloak around it.

"What is this about, Hades?" Zeus said, his bass voice pitched low, a cautious edge to it that didn't quite cover the anger Hades could hear.

And sense in him.

Hades slanted his younger brother a dark look, but remained where he was, his body facing the chaise longue and that view of endless blue sky, white buildings and glittering turquoise sea, all bathed in bright sunlight.

Warm sunlight.

Clouds formed on the horizon. Black. Forbidding. A storm that would ravage this peaceful, pretty little city if he remained where he was for long enough and made him want to linger, so those under Zeus's rule would know their god-king's power was not absolute.

Zeus had come to him unprepared. His brother wore only a white knee-length chiton embroidered with gold, and leather sandals. The waves of his brown hair were damp, as if he had been bathing. Perhaps he had and that was the reason he hadn't donned his golden armour.

"Hades," Zeus demanded, his tone hardening as his golden eyes flashed.

Making his name an order to answer him this time.

Or what?

They would fight?

Hades turned the darkness into an impenetrable wall around his heart, welcoming the numbing cold as it obliterated his softer feelings, stopping them from reaching the surface so his face remained impassive.

Shadows shifted around the pointed toes of his metal boots as he pivoted to face his younger brother, seething with a need to make that fight happen. It would be glorious, and he would be the victor. The thought of crushing his insolent brother and reminding him that he wasn't the most powerful god—only the most powerful Olympian—was alluring, enough to have his mind growing hazy with pleasure that tempted him into striking first.

He clawed back control instead, because if he fought Zeus, then he wouldn't be able to tell his brother what he had come here to say, because Zeus would be nothing more than a bloody stain on the white marble floor. And the walls. And the columns.

And that precious gold chaise that his brother loved to rest upon, gazing out at his bright city.

Doing nothing.

Zeus acted as if being the god-king of Olympus was a difficult and demanding duty, but it wasn't. His brother wasted his hours lazing in his temple, allowing his subordinates to do everything, and not bound by any real duty.

Unlike Hades.

"Hades," Zeus said, softer this time as he sighed. "I will not ask again. What brings you here?"

Hades looked back at the horizon and the approaching storm, sensing the unrest spreading through the city as the citizens noticed it too. He savoured it, soaking it all up and feeding on it. They were right to fear. His gaze grew hooded. If he teleported to the harbour, or perhaps one of the busy squares, terror would snake through this city, throwing the peaceful streets into turmoil. He would shake Olympus.

Zeus's gaze drilled into him, and Hades sensed the warning. His brother was aware of the path of his dark thoughts and if Hades didn't answer soon, he would find himself removed from this realm before he could get what he had come here for.

"What brought me here?" Hades murmured. He saw the scarlet-haired maiden in his mind, an unearthly beauty whose memory was enough to have his heart pounding. He put force behind his words. "I have seen my future queen. You and Poseidon have your queens, the latter at great cost to myself and the balance of these realms. I have deemed it is only fitting that I have one of my own. A king should have a queen, and I have chosen mine." He sensed the shock that ran through Zeus, an emotion that grew stronger as Hades added, "She is a goddess of Olympus."

Hades knew that without a doubt. A beauty such as her could only come from this place of light and life.

He slid a look at Zeus, satisfaction rolling through him as he caught the stunned expression on his brother's tanned face. It morphed into another emotion before Hades could savour it. A look that could have been mistaken for tenderness.

But Hades knew his brother too well.

Any moment now, Zeus would tell him to return to the Underworld and forget the goddess, because she would never be his.

"So take her and make her yours."

Those words leaving his brother's lips had his gaze leaping back to him just as he was about to look at the city again. His eyes widened slightly as he reeled. He stared at Zeus, at his brother's flat expression that spoke of how serious he was, unsure how to proceed.

Until it dawned on him that Zeus had just given him permission to take the female he desired.

A dark need to claim her swept through him.

His heart laboured and his lips stretched into a grin as a feeling pounded inside him, one that clouded his mind and silenced the voice clamouring in his head, screaming at him to follow through with his original plan—to make his appearance more pleasing before he approached her.

He needed to return to her right now, before she left the forest and he was forced to await her return.

He would do as Zeus decreed.

He would take her.

And she would be his queen.

CHAPTER 3

The stretch of dusty land that formed a cape at the very edge of the world had beckoned her again this morning, within the first few minutes of her day. It was a place few dared to venture, which made it perfect to her.

Persephone had barely sat down for breakfast when her mother, Demeter, had begun talking about Aristaeus, the minor god she was determined to marry Persephone off to. Aristaeus was growing impatient and wanted to wed Persephone soon, and she had the feeling her mother wanted that too.

How much longer could she put it off?

She had managed to claw together several years of freedom for herself, but with each one that passed, it was growing harder. She had the terrible feeling that it was only a matter of days now before her mother and Aristaeus forced her into wedlock, stealing that precious freedom from her.

Persephone blamed the rumours that had run through Olympus years ago for her upcoming demise. Her mother had been more than content for her to remain a maiden before someone had started the whispers that had reached her household—a rumour that the god of war, Ares, meant to ask for her hand.

As if she would marry such a narcissistic oaf.

A few days after hearing the rumour, her mother had announced her betrothal to Aristaeus.

As if she would marry such a dull, witless male.

The more Persephone thought about the match, the more she felt her mother had picked Aristaeus out of all her suitors because if she married him, she would remain in her current position within the Olympian pantheon. Marrying Aristaeus would neither elevate her above her mother, nor shift her to a lower position in the hierarchy of the gods.

Marrying Ares would have placed her above her mother.

Persephone plucked at a flower. She didn't want that. She didn't want to replace her mother. But she also didn't want to marry a male she hadn't chosen; one she could never come to love.

Demeter was deaf to her protests, having heard them many times over the years, so Persephone hadn't bothered to argue with her this morning. As soon as her stomach had been full enough to see her through the day, she had made her excuses, had gathered her trio of maidens and had gone as far from Olympus as she could get.

As a goddess of several hundred years, she didn't need her mother to decide who she married, or whether she married at all. What she really needed was to escape the hold her mother had on her.

Persephone frowned at the flower in her fingers.

What she really needed to do was pluck up the courage to speak to a male, and then follow that up with being brave enough to steal a kiss, or let him steal one from her.

She was growing tired of hearing her servants, and her mother's servants, and even some of the goddesses she knew, talking about males when she had no experience of them herself and it was looking more and more like her first experience would be with her dreaded suitor.

Her future husband.

Persephone's lips flattened.

It wasn't going to happen.

She would speak to Zeus about it and convince him to persuade her mother that allowing her to find her true love was the wiser course of action. There were many goddesses who were older than she was and they still hadn't married.

Including the one who had given her the braided token that Mira, the oldest of her maidens, was in possession of so her mother didn't find out about it—a token that allowed her to teleport.

Unlike many of the gods and goddesses of Olympus, Persephone hadn't been born with the ability to teleport. It was only a minor inconvenience since her mother rarely let her out of her sight.

Persephone had been sneaking out more and more often recently though, striking out on her own to explore the world, savouring her freedom as she began to feel it was slipping away from her.

She had found this spot decades ago.

And she had decided to make it her own—her haven.

And by the gods, she had been glad of it when her mother had suddenly announced her betrothal to Aristaeus.

She gazed at the forest that surrounded her, one filled with life and colour. It had taken years of work to create this place, sneaking off whenever her mother wasn't looking. If her mother knew about it and what she was doing, she would be locked in her room and kept under guard for the rest of her days—or at least until her low position in Olympus was secured with her marriage. Sometimes, she had to make herself leave this forest and return to Olympus before her mother sat down for dinner and realised she was missing.

Persephone scoffed. "*If* she noticed I was missing. Sometimes I wonder if she would. If I made a home for myself here, would she even care?"

Her heart grew heavy at the thought her mother might not care that she was gone, that she might even be happy to be rid of her.

She huffed at that. "If I was gone, who would Mother order around? The servants certainly would not allow her to control them as she controls my every action."

Or they might.

Demeter had picked her servants from the lowest classes, selecting desperate females who would do anything to retain their position and scant wages.

It was tempting to remain here, but she couldn't do it. Her mother would notice she was gone, and the whole household would suffer for it. There was nothing quite like her mother when she was in a mood. She somehow managed to grow more tyrannical.

Persephone scowled and mentally berated herself for thinking of her mother in such a fashion. Her mother had her faults, but she felt sure that somewhere deep inside her, Demeter did love her.

She sighed as she took in the forest, deeply aware she couldn't stay here, even when she wanted it. Her mother would find her, and she would destroy this sanctuary in order to force Persephone to return to Olympus.

She didn't want to lose this place, and she knew it wasn't only because she had created it and enjoyed using her powers over nature when her life in Olympus rarely called for it. The only time someone asked her for help was when they wanted their garden improved before a feast. It didn't really help her confidence. Other goddesses went off to fight wars and she was called upon to summon flowers and maybe ensure the grain harvest was bountiful so those in Olympus could have bread and other things.

Another long sigh escaped her.

Lamenting her life wasn't going to change it.

Only she had the power to do that.

Maybe when she returned to Olympus today, she would speak with her mother and set her straight, informing her that she wasn't going to marry the dreaded Aristaeus.

And maybe the deer across the way that was eyeing her would suddenly sprout wings and fly.

The deer wasn't the only animal that had made a home for itself in the forest. Others had flocked here, shunning the bleak, arid lands that surrounded her pocket of nature in favour of sweet grass and berries. Birds had been swift to make their nests in the trees that were always heavy with fruit. The vast swaths of flowers that formed a patchwork quilt across the forest floor provided nectar for the bees and butterflies, and other insects.

This place was her haven. A place where she could be alone.

Two of her maidens erupted into giggles a short distance away, reminding her that she was never alone.

Wherever she went, they followed, but she didn't mind them. Unlike her mother, they didn't try to oppress her or marry her off to some halfwit god who happened to have offered the best price in exchange for her hand. As if she was meat in a market. She glanced at her maidens and smiled at their antics as they threaded flowers in Mira's dark hair, weaving them into the circle of plaits that formed a crown on her head. It was a comfort to have them around her. They were her closest confidants, and seemingly her only allies.

A bee buzzed past her and she tracked it with her gaze, savouring how alive with activity the forest was now, but how peaceful it was at the same time.

Around her, birds sang and insects chirped. Persephone breathed deep of the warm air, tasting dew despite the dusty lands that enclosed the lush pocket of green she had been working hard to create on the coastline. The mortals who lived near this place called it the end of the world, and it had been a barren place before she had decided to transform it into something the mortals would no longer fear.

Did they come here?

She liked to think they did, and hoped they wouldn't destroy it in their pursuit of wood and meat, and would enjoy it as it was. For once, she wanted someone to see what she could do and find it beautiful and special.

She paused halfway through picking a crimson flower and lifted her head to gaze at the bright green glade nestled among the verdant trees.

A breeze swept through the forest, carrying the scent of the sea, and she looked over her shoulder in the direction of the coast, catching a glimpse of the turquoise water. A vision of when she had first set foot in this place filled her mind, the woods disappearing around her. When she had seen the waves breaking against the rocks and the clear water sparkling in the sunshine, she had been bewitched.

There was such raw power here. Strength. But beauty too.

She had stood near the edge, as close as she had dared to get to the water, ignoring the pleas of her maidens as they had tried to get her to move back to a safer distance. The waves had pounded the rocks only feet from her, spraying her with salt water, but she hadn't been afraid.

She had been exhilarated.

She had raised her arms and welcomed the tempest, letting it break over her, letting it make her feel alive.

Free.

The forest came back into being around her and she took it in. She had never felt as alive as she did in this place. She couldn't be further from Olympus and she loved it.

She heard one of her maidens say, "To the shore?"

"I will follow." Persephone didn't want to leave. Not yet. Maybe she could convince them to let her linger a little longer. Maybe. They had already brought up returning to Olympus several times and the last time Mira had looked half-concerned half-anxious, leaving Persephone feeling that if they didn't go back soon, she would get both herself and her maidens into trouble. But perhaps she could delay a little longer. Her trio of maidens enjoyed lazing on the rocks as much as she did, soaking up the sunshine, and talking about the latest scandals, and she wanted to hear the gossip. "Meet me at our rock. I shall only be a moment."

Mira looked reluctant to agree, but the two younger females pulled her with them, their white robes blending together as they moved arm in arm.

Persephone crouched again, the layers of her pale green dress pooling around her bare feet as she went back to picking flowers. It was strange that a crimson one had grown. She didn't remember adding such a colour. She lifted her head. She couldn't see another one like it anywhere among the pastel-coloured blooms.

She plucked it and added it to the bouquet before rising and walking on, heading through the forest to reach the rock rather than following her maidens towards the path along the shore. The grass tickled her feet, cool against their soles, and sunshine streamed through the canopy, warming her skin.

A song played on her lips as she meandered through the trees, drifting towards the next patch of flowers.

"I just need something lilac and then my bouquet will be perfect."

The woods suddenly grew darker around her and she frowned and peered in all directions.

Had the sun gone in for a moment?

She had overheard one of the guards outside her home talking about approaching bad weather, and when storms swept across Olympus, they often did the same in the area around the Aegean in the mortal world.

She looked up at the sky through the leafy canopy and sure enough, clouds were gathering. She stared at them, her eyebrows slowly lowering. She had never seen clouds so dark before. They were black as night, and heavy looking, as if they would burst at any moment and cause a torrential downpour.

Persephone abandoned her quest for the final flower and turned away.

Froze as a feeling tripped down her spine.

A sensation that she was being watched.

Dread followed it, chilling her blood, and she wanted to laugh at how silly she was being. Nothing in this forest would harm her. It was probably just an animal watching her.

She turned in a slow circle, seeking the source of the sensation to prove to herself it was just that and she was being foolish.

Locked up tight again as her gaze snagged on a lone figure in a shadowy recess of a pale cliff just beyond the trees.

A man.

She couldn't make out anything about him other than his size. He was impossibly tall, but lean.

And he was watching her.

She swallowed and went to turn away, but he stepped forwards, into the light.

It chased over the hard plates of his black armour.

Armour that was not of mortal fashion.

Alarm bells jangled in her mind, but they quietened as her eyes leaped up to his face and her gaze collided with his. Her breath hitched as his cold blue eyes pierced hers and held her immobile. The ferocity of his sculpted features unsettled her, quickening her pulse until it beat like a warning drum in her mind. She edged her foot backwards and his black eyebrows knitted hard, his gaze instantly dropping to her feet, shattering the spell that had been holding her in place.

Persephone was quick to pivot away from him, her mind on hurrying back to her servants and leaving this place. In the distance, her maidens called for her.

"I am coming," she said, loud enough for them to hear.

Only something drew her gaze back to the male and she couldn't stop herself from looking over her shoulder in his direction. He hadn't moved. He lingered where the shadows seemed to have gathered, only part of his face in the light, and was staring at her as if the sight of her tormented him.

Why?

Curiosity kept her feet rooted in place in the grass.

Why did he look as if her leaving would destroy him?

Darkness swept across the land, spreading outwards from him, and the air chilled as shadows snaked through the trees like onyx ribbons and the forest stilled, growing deathly quiet.

And she knew.

This was no man.

This was a god.

And his power was incredible as it surrounded her, fierce and dark, and immense. Like nothing she had felt before. It seeped into her skin, heightening her awareness of him until her body vibrated with it as he stared at her, drawing all her focus to him. The forest around them fell away, until there was only her and this bewitching male, and the only sound in her ears was her unsteady breathing as it trembled from her lips.

Persephone recalled the stories mortals told about this place at the end of the world.

That it was the gateway to a realm that was grim and terrifying.

A realm of death.

Ruled by a dark and malevolent god.

"Hades," she breathed as she stared at him, at the pointed onyx spikes that rose from his thick black hair like a crown, one fit for a dark king.

Something crossed his features, something that made her feel… *powerful.* As if she had power over him, not the other way around. His fierce expression softened, some of the darkness leaving it as he gazed at her, the rigid line of his shoulders relaxing beneath his pauldrons. She wanted to speak his name again to see if she had imagined his reaction to it, and see if she really did have power over him. The thought she might had her body warming and strange sensations igniting inside her, ones that were as unsettling as his steady gaze.

Now that he didn't look so frightening, he was almost *handsome.* She felt wicked as she admitted that to herself. The god-king of the Underworld was handsome. Her mother would throw a fit if she heard Persephone say that. All of Olympus would be horrified. She stared at him, feeling a little bold as he remained where he was, at a safe distance, and just gazed at her.

As if she had bewitched him.

Her pulse steadied, her fear slowly trickling away as seconds ticked past and neither of them moved.

What would he do if she moved?

When she had gone to leave, he had stepped towards her, as if he wanted to stop her. If she moved a step in his direction, would more of that darkness lift from his handsome features? If she moved a step away, would that darkness return?

Did he find her as fascinating as she found him?

Crimson bled into the edges of his blue irises and his lips flattened, as if he was irritated by something. His fingers flexed, sharp black talons that sliced through the air in a stilted fashion, as if his body was too tense to move smoothly. She gazed at his wide shoulders and thought they might have lifted again, growing rigid once more. It was hard to tell with his armour concealing them, not only the vicious-looking black pauldrons that protected his shoulders but the folds of his black cloak where it was affixed to clasps on either side of his neck.

He looked nothing like an Olympian.

He was all wicked darkness.

From the sharp spikes of his obsidian crown that protruded from his black hair, smallest near his temples and largest at the back of his head, to the sharp talons that tipped his fingers and the pointed toes of his boots.

And that growing ring of crimson around his irises.

What did that mean?

She wanted to know.

Her maidens called again, piercing the spell he had cast once more.

Persephone tore her gaze away from him, turning to go to them and aware that if she kept them waiting much longer that they would come to check on her. She didn't want them seeing Hades and potentially running afoul of his infamous temper.

Darkness filled her vision, a wall of black armour that hugged a lean, masculine figure, and she gasped as a cool palm met her forehead, sending electricity arcing down her spine.

A thick, black fog instantly rolled through her mind, dimming it and sucking the strength from her.

She cast a stricken look up into his now-crimson eyes.

And sleep claimed her.

CHAPTER 4

Hades couldn't tear his eyes away from the delicate beauty he held in his left arm as his chariot thundered across the black lands of the Underworld, the four great onyx horses that drew it unerringly finding their way back to his temple without his direction.

She lay slumped backwards, her hips pressing to his thigh, his forearm against her shoulder blades and hand gripping her left shoulder to keep her in place. Her scarlet hair flowed in the breeze like ribbons of blood as her head tipped backwards, lolling and exposing the smooth pale column of her throat.

His fangs itched to pierce that creamy flesh.

To mark her so all would know she belonged to him now.

To claim her.

He gazed at her throat, his eyes growing hooded, his mind turning hazy once again as the darkness that had receded to leave him aware of what he had done poured back through his veins and demanded he mark her so no one would take her from him.

No one *could* take her from him.

She was his.

Despite the guilt that gnawed at him as he stared at her, as realisation sank deep into his soul to rouse fear. Fear that she would be taken from him. Fear that she would despise him. Fear that she would never truly be his.

This had not been the plan.

But what was done was done.

A quiet voice whispered that he could take her back.

Hades snarled and bared his fangs at it, and clutched her closer to him, his talons in danger of piercing her flawless skin. Crimson lightning struck across the land, a series of bolts that flowed in a line to overtake him, the final and most powerful blast hitting the side of a mountain and showering rock down the steep slope as it carved a crater in its face. He would not take her back. She belonged to him now.

He would somehow make this work, and he would somehow find the strength to deny the darker urges that wracked him and coaxed him into surrendering control to them. She was his, wasn't she? She would serve him well, whether she liked it or not. He gritted his teeth and fought back, struggling to deny that desire to bend her to his will. The darkness was strong though, used his fears against him and spilled tempting words in his ear, attempting to make him do its bidding as it filled his mind with images of this female beneath him, her bare curves pressed to his as he took her and her sweet cries teased his ears.

Hades screwed his eyes shut and growled, desperate to push the darkness back down and claw himself towards the light.

The light.

His eyes flicked open and darted to the female, and the hold the darkness had on him began to fade, just as it had when he had been fighting it in the forest while she had been looking at him. He had lost that fight when she had turned to leave, the darker side of his blood swift to consume him and have him teleporting to her and sending her into a deep sleep so he could spirit her away.

Hades stared at the delicate redhead, losing himself in her.

His heart galloped as fast as his horses, a tremulous and unsteady beat as he was swept up in a strange and powerful whirlwind of foreign emotions.

Anticipation he had experienced many times before, but never like this. He anticipated battle and bloodshed, but now he awaited far gentler things, ones part of him felt sure could even be more satisfying than violence.

Craving he knew well, but it was also different now. He didn't crave blood on his hands. He craved the feel of her soft skin beneath his palms. He craved her gaze on him, blazing like green fire with the heat of a thousand suns, as it had back in the woods. She had feared him, but then that fear had been replaced with something else, something he didn't dare believe he was right about.

But what if he was?

Claiming his queen might be easier than he thought.

They hit a bump, jostling her, and he pulled her closer as his chest constricted, the thought that she might tumble free of his grip and injure herself making his talons close over her shoulder more firmly, until their sharp tips pressed against her fair skin once again.

By the gods, she was beautiful.

They raced through a village, and he sensed eyes on him.

On her.

Darkness welled inside him, rising swiftly to have him tugging her closer still. He glared at any who dared to look at her, his shadows streaming out behind him as his mood blackened. It spread like an oily tide through his veins, one that smothered the softer feelings she had evoked in him, systematically destroying them to replace them with a seething need for violence. His shadows writhed and snapped at the land around his chariot.

The darkness grew stronger with each male who gazed upon her, stealing pieces of him as it slowly consumed him, and he bared his fangs at all who looked at her and tucked her closer to him, lifting her head and palming the back of it as he held it to his chest, concealing her from their wretched gazes.

She was his and only his.

Screams rang out behind him as he sneered and his shadows ripped into every male who had dared to look at her, the harrowing sounds cutting off abruptly as his shadows made fast work of them.

Setting an example.

No one looked at his female but him.

Ahead of him, the black temple loomed, the beaten gold dishes of flaming oil that sat before each column illuminating them with blue fire. The light reached the triangular pediment, revealing the frieze of him at war, riding his chariot as he was now.

A sharp feeling arrowed through him to have him turning his chariot away from his home as he catalogued the guards who patrolled the area around it, his servants, and the souls who came and went, offering prayers and gifts to him.

Too many males.

He clutched the slumbering female more tightly, almost smothering her against his chest, and urged his horses onwards, towards the mountains, to a stretch of empty land that stood at a distance from the temple and the large black barracks. When he was satisfied he was far away enough from any males, he pulled the horses to a halt. They reared and whinnied, kicking out and snorting as they shook their heads.

White froth streaked their glossy black coats and gathered at the corners of their mouths, and each of them breathed hard as they settled, struggling to recover from their race across the Underworld. He would see to their care once his queen was situated in her new home, safe from any prying eyes and unable to escape him.

Hades scooped her up into his arms, cradling her beneath her knees and against her back, and stepped down off the black-and-gold chariot. He carried her past the horses, heading towards the jagged onyx mountains that spewed ash and sparks of fire into the crimson sky. Shadows clung to his shoulders and streamed behind him, as agitated and restless as he was.

He gazed down at her. "I must construct you a home that is both safe and befitting of you, my beauty. Something striking."

Something that would strike fear into all who saw it, keeping them away from his queen.

A wide circular foundation rose beneath the pointed toes of his black metal boots and he kept walking forwards, never taking his gaze off her, transfixed by the sight of her and how the darkness grew quieter the longer he looked at her. A step rose beneath his left foot and then one beneath his right, and walls grew from the black ground, forming around the circular base and keeping pace with the growth of the stairs.

Hades kept his focus on her and her alone as he ascended the spiral staircase that formed beneath his feet, each step protruding from the wall just as his foot came down, carrying her ever upwards.

When they were high above the realm, a stone floor crept outwards around him and the walls continued upwards, punctured by windows and even a balcony, and then they closed over him, forming a jagged series of spikes that pierced the sky on the outside and a domed ceiling on the inside. From the middle of the ceiling grew a stone chandelier with three bowls. Blue fire burst to life in them and slowly shifted to gold as he focused, casting warm light over the goddess in his arms.

Light more suited to her.

Hades strode across the room, his black cloak flowing around his ankles, and a large stone bed formed beneath one of the narrow windows.

He eased her down onto it, pressed his left knee to the hard surface and leaned over her, the pointed tips of his talons digging into the stone on either side of her.

Lingering.

Unable to wrench himself away even when he had duties that required his presence and he knew it was better to leave now, while the darker side of his blood was subdued.

Her skin seemed to glow against the dark stone, her soft jade dress that flowed around her and the tumbling waves of her scarlet hair that fanned outwards a stark contrast to it. She was a splash of colour in his dark world, one that had his heart drumming hard and enthralled him. He lifted his right hand, keeping his left planted against the stone bed, and carefully teased a rogue crimson wave from her alabaster cheeks. He stared at the glossy strands that draped over his talons and then at her lovely face.

Feeling strangely lost.

He was sure she was a sorceress and had cast some kind of spell upon him to ravage his defences so easily, leaving him feeling vulnerable and exposed in a way he found he didn't like, yet couldn't prevent.

Hades stared at her, unsure of himself and everything for the first time ever. The longer he gazed at her, lingering so close to her, breathing in her delicate scent and drowning in her beauty, the stronger that feeling of being lost became. He couldn't name the source of it. Only that it was like a living, breathing thing within him now, occupying the space behind his breast that had been hollow for centuries.

It choked him. Seemed to steal the very breath from his lungs. Made his thoughts whirl.

Everything about this strikingly lovely female had him off balance.

Why?

He had waged war with titans without fear. He had fought countless battles in his own realm to ensure all in it dared not rise against him. He had controlled the darkness that ran within his veins to the best of his abilities, harnessing it to maintain his rule and keep his people subdued and obedient.

But this ethereal beauty had the darkness running wild in his veins, blackening his thoughts and turning them more violent than they had ever been, and whenever he gazed at her, he feared.

Bars of stone formed on the windows of the circular room, and wards followed them, powerful enchantments that would prevent her from escaping.

From leaving.

He stilled as he realised what he had done, dragging his gaze from her. He scanned the room, feeling the wards, ones more intricate than he had created in a very long time, all made while he hadn't even been aware of what he had been doing.

All done to keep her with him.

Hades swallowed and carefully brushed his hand through her scarlet waves. He lifted his hand, watching the strands slip through his fingers like tiny rivers of blood, warmth curling through him to combat the cold that had seeped fast and deep into his heart at the thought of her leaving.

Never.

She would never leave him.

She was his now.

His queen.

He bared his fangs as darkness swept through him, surging to overwhelm the warmth and the light.

No one would take her from him.

His gaze dropped to her lips, hunger rolling through him to have him leaning closer to her. He breathed in her heady scent, warmth sweeping through him again in response to it, as if it was ambrosia. It drugged him.

His gaze grew hooded again, fixed on her mouth.

He knew her scent. Her voice. Her beauty. How she felt in his arms. Now he wanted to know her taste.

"Wake, my queen," he murmured, lacing those words with his power so her little body obeyed his command.

Her eyelids fluttered, dark lashes dancing against her pale cheeks, and then they lifted, revealing luminous but sleepy emerald eyes that instantly locked with his, heating him right down to his bones and shattering his control.

Hades dipped his head.

And kissed her.

CHAPTER 5

Persephone's first thought upon waking was how blue his eyes were, shining like azure fire.

And then his lips descended upon hers.

All her thoughts fled, the ability stripped from her as feeling swept in to steal awareness of anything but the hard press of his mouth against hers. A startling yearning blasted through her in response to his fierce kiss and her body arched towards his, her blood turning molten as she ached for more.

And then her mind caught up with what was happening.

A male was *kissing* her.

The god-king of the Underworld was kissing her.

Panic lit her veins and stole her breath in response to that thought, and she flattened her palms against his hard breastplate and shoved. When he only kept kissing her, his mouth moving masterfully against hers, transforming panic into pleasure and threatening to shatter her resolve, she reacted on instinct.

She shoved with all her strength, this time pushing him off her, and slapped him.

Hard.

The fierce crack of her palm meeting his sculpted cheek echoed around her.

Shock filled his blue eyes as he stared at her, his cheek reddening where she had struck him, and then crimson ringed his irises as the dark slashes of his eyebrows knitted hard and his lips flattened. Beyond him, the golden fire that lit the room morphed into azure, matching the colour his eyes had been and casting cold light over the sharp glossy spikes of his crown and his pitch-black hair.

Persephone scooted out from beneath him and was across the room as quickly as her trembling legs could manage, placing as much distance as she could between them as his face darkened and her heart galloped. Her hands shook, her right one stinging from the slap.

She had struck Hades.

By the gods, what had she done?

When he pushed to his feet and turned on her, she backed into the curved black stone wall, fear gripping her as she readied herself for his wrath.

He lifted his gauntleted hand and touched his cheek, his eyes fully crimson now, and then his features shifted, something she couldn't name crossing them for a moment as his talons glided to his firm lips.

The way his claws brushed them made her deeply aware of her own lips.

Lips no male had ever touched before.

She hadn't expected her first kiss to be so… transformative.

Her entire body had come awake from the mere brush of his mouth over hers and the mingling of their breath, and echoes of pleasure continued to ripple through her even now, rousing a wicked need for more. Unwise. She tried to shut that need down as she caught her breath and fought to calm herself, struggling to regain control of her body.

She licked her lips, an action she regretted on two counts.

One: It made Hades's eyes darken and lower to her mouth, the hungry look that flared in them wreaking havoc on her body that she fought to hide from him.

Two: She could still taste him on her lips—all dark spice—and ended up recalling every moment of his brief bruising and savage kiss.

Her cheeks flamed.

Persephone turned her back on him to conceal the reaction and frowned as she found herself facing a small square doorway and a balcony barely big enough for one. But it was neither of those things that had dread pooling inside her, tangling with a stronger emotion that had her cheeks burning for another reason.

It was the forbidding black lands that stretched around her, illuminated by a scarlet sky.

The Underworld.

She pivoted to face Hades again, anger flaring within her as she glared at him. "Why am I here?"

"This is your home now, my little queen." His bass voice rolled over her to have heat curling through her veins before she could stop it, the fire of anger becoming that of desire again as she struggled to hold her withering look.

Had a male ever sounded so delicious? She certainly couldn't recall ever hearing a voice like his.

"I am not your queen." Her voice wavered as she fought the rising tide of her desire, attempting to quell it as she faced him. Her heart pounded faster, her limbs shaking as she looked back at the grim, dark world beyond the doorway. A lifeless world. One made of death. She couldn't sense any life in this realm. It was like a void to her. There was nothing. It was bleak and far too black, the only colour in it the unsettling sky and the ribbons of lava that streaked the faces of the towering mountains to heat the air and make it stifling. She turned her scowl on Hades again, fighting to appear strong and confident, even as she quaked and fear sank icy talons into her heart. "Take me home."

His profane lips peeled back off sharp white daggers as he took a hard step towards her, his crimson eyes flashing dangerously. "You are home."

Onyx invaded his irises like shadows seeping into blood and red fire ignited in his pupils.

Persephone backed off another step, tempted to use her powers to create a barrier between them, a move that would only anger him further. He glared at her bare feet, and then back into her eyes.

She had the feeling he didn't like it whenever she moved away from him as she just had—the action born of fear—but what had he expected from her? He had abducted her from her bright world and plunged her into darkness, and now he was talking madness.

She wasn't his queen.

"I want to go back to Olympus," she said, her voice trembling a little, hating how it did that and how she couldn't conceal her fears, even when she desperately wanted to hide them from him and appear as strong and commanding as he did.

He didn't respond this time. He lowered his gaze to her feet again, his eyes raking over her body in a way that made her all too aware of him and the fact they were alone, and he had kissed her.

Kissed her.

Her fingertips trembled with the desire to rise to her lips and touch them just as he had touched his with his black talons.

Had that kiss affected him as strongly as it had affected her?

It had been searing, startling, and it was now branded on her mind and her lips, his taste tattooed there forever. She wasn't sure she would ever forget it.

His dark eyebrows relaxed slightly, his features softening a little.

"Hades," she whispered, hoping that she wasn't imagining that lightening of his emotions. His eyes were shifting again, the black receding and the fire in his pupils guttering out. Could she reach him if she was gentle with her approach and convince him to let her go? It was worth a shot. She swallowed to wet her throat. "Take me back to Olympus. I want to go home."

His expression darkened in a heartbeat and shadows erupted from beneath his booted feet, sharp lances that stabbed at anything within their reach.

When one lunged for her, she staggered backwards and summoned vines to form a wall between her and the shadow. Only nothing happened. Her spine struck the wall as a gasp burst from her lips.

The shadow halted only inches from her waist.

Her gaze leaped to meet his.

Something flared in his eyes and then the shadow snapped around her wrist and she shrieked as it yanked her forwards, towards him. She flew into his arms, striking his hard metal breastplate with enough force that it knocked the breath from her lungs.

Persephone fought the shadow, her hand passing through it as she attempted to break free. Yet it could hold her as firmly as his hand did as it gripped her wrist, replacing his shadows, and he closed his other hand around her upper arm. She wriggled in his hold, refusing to be cowed by him and to let him have his way. When she tried to use her powers and nothing happened again, she denied the cold and the fear, refusing to surrender to it, and stomped on his foot instead.

He merely arched an eyebrow at that.

She did it again, and again, hammering the heel of her bare foot into his metal boot and getting nothing but a bruise to show for it. When she was sore and a little out of breath, and her situation hadn't changed one bit, she glared up at him.

And realised how close he was to her.

She stilled as she stared into his eyes, the foot difference in their height making her feel small. Weak. His masculine scent invaded her senses, as dark and spicy as his kiss had been, and seemed to work a kind of black magic on her, easing the tension from her muscles and sweeping the thoughts from her mind, and the fear with it, until she was simply standing there, gazing up at him.

What kind of spell had this dark god cast upon her to make her react to him this way?

She should be afraid of him. She was deeply aware of that. But as she lost herself in his eyes that were changing once again, the crimson giving way to that bewitching blue, she felt no fear.

And then he kissed her again.

It happened so quickly she didn't have time to evade him—or maybe she hadn't wanted to.

He bent his head and then his lips were on hers, the hard brush of them awakening something powerful and unsettling inside her that had her hands inching up to grip his arms and hold him in place.

Shock swept through her, a tidal wave that doused the desire that had flooded her with new, dangerous feelings, and fear followed it—fear of what he might do if she didn't stop him—fear that she might like it.

That she might *want* it.

When all he wanted was to own her just as many other gods did, to lay claim to her as if she was there to be taken, as if she wasn't an autonomous being with her own thoughts, feelings and desires.

Anger that he was like all the other males in her world—no, worse than the others since he had taken her captive and now called her his queen, as if she had no say in the matter—provoked a reaction she knew she would regret the instant her knee struck him between his thighs.

He grunted and his fangs grazed her lower lip, nicking it and flooding her mouth with the taste of her own blood as he jerked in response to the hard blow.

Persephone shoved him in the chest, pushing him off her and toppling him. He landed on the bed with a hard thump and clatter of armour, and she made a break for it.

Heading at speed for the steps that led downwards.

She gasped as Hades appeared before her, black tendrils of smoke caressing his shoulders and hands, and tangling in the sharp spikes of his crown. His eyes flared crimson again as she skidded to a halt and backpedalled, placing some distance between them so he couldn't seize hold of her again.

Only he remained where he was, a glowering wall of black that stood between her and her freedom.

"Do not attempt to leave this tower," he growled, his voice a dark snarl that would have conveyed his anger had his eyes not already told her of it. They were fierce crimson again, verging on black, and his fangs flashed between his lips as he spoke, continuing before she could even think to petition him to take her home or call him on the fact he was holding her captive, had somehow suppressed her powers, and the reason he didn't want her to leave was because he was intent on having her as his queen. He snarled, "There are beasts in this world that would make a meal of a delicate little female like you… or do far worse."

She swallowed hard as her pulse kicked up a notch, her senses sharpening as she strained to hear these beasts he spoke of and feared they were circling the tower, waiting for her to leave it so they could devour her.

Or was he lying to her, attempting to make her so frightened that she wouldn't dare leave and would obey him?

One glance over her shoulder at the forbidding black lands beyond the balcony doorway was enough to convince her that he was telling the truth.

She had heard tales of the fell creatures that roamed the Underworld, eating its occupants. Horned beasts. Gargantuan grey bipedal monsters. Winged wyverns.

Even things called Keres—ghostly white fiends who flew on bloodied wings over battlefields, waiting for warriors to bleed so they could descend upon them to sate their unending thirst.

She looked back at Hades.

But what beast in this world was more frightening than the one standing before her?

The tales whispered about him were legendary, stories spoken to scare children and adults alike.

The bloodthirsty and cruel god-king of the Underworld.

His features pinched in a scowl as she stared at him, as if he knew the path of her thoughts and didn't like it.

When he stepped towards her, she moved one back, and his scowl became a dark glare.

"You would deny your husband?" he growled.

"Husband?" Persephone spluttered, the shock his declaration had caused rapidly giving way to outrage as she realised she had been right about him. He did think he owned her. She bit out, "I do not remember marrying you. You are *not* my husband!"

He didn't miss a beat.

"You are mine now." His handsome features darkened with each word he hurled at her. "My queen. My wife. You would do well to obey me."

Persephone scoffed, her anger mounting so swiftly that she didn't feel in control of herself. It obliterated the side of her that screamed at her to not antagonise him.

"Obey you?" she barked, unable to believe her luck. She had gone from one controlling person to another, and she was damned if she would just lie down and accept her fate. "So, I am to be your slave? That does not sound much like a wife… or a *queen*. What you want is something I will *never* become."

This time when he moved, his stride was long enough that she couldn't keep the distance between them steady. He easily closed it, narrowing it down to nothing, and his power wrapped around her—immense and dark—and entrancing. She truly had never felt anything like it.

She had been in the presence of his brother, Zeus, more than once, and had felt his power as a passing breeze, subtle and gentle, warm almost. She had barely noticed it.

But Hades's power *embraced* her, becoming all that she knew.

It was cold, and strong, more like a gale than a mere breeze.

It was incredible.

She found herself staring up into his eyes again, transfixed and unable to move, and a little shocked by how her gaze boldly traversed the planes of his face, from the strong line of his jaw to the straight slash of his nose, to his fine cheekbones and the long black lashes that fanned against his ashen skin as he gazed down at her through heated, hungry crimson eyes. She had missed a spot. Her gaze lowered to the wicked perfection of his firm lips. How could she have forgotten them?

He inhaled. Ragged. Sharp. Those tempting lips parting with it.

That reaction to her gaze on his mouth startled her out of her reverie and had her eyes darting back to meet his.

Part of her expected him to kiss her again, as he had the last two times she had lost herself in the feelings he awakened in her, ones that were a little frightening. She didn't quite feel mistress of her own body whenever she found herself trapped in his gaze.

He remained perfectly still this time, lines bracketing his mouth that made her feel he was holding himself back. Rather than breaking away from him, she lingered, curious as to what he would do.

A dangerous game.

Persephone came to her senses as he growled low, flashing a hint of his fangs, and reached for her, gripping her waist to drag her against him. She twirled out of his hold and broke away from him, hurrying towards the other side of the room, foolishly attempting to throw another barrier up between them despite the fact she knew it wouldn't work.

Hades didn't let her get far.

He caught her arm and spun her around to face him, and her back met the stone wall as he hemmed her in, one hand pressing against the wall beside her head and the other catching her jaw. He tilted her head back, so their eyes locked again, and she couldn't breathe as he stared at her mouth and his hand dropped to her throat to grip it.

His irises were fully black now, his pupils shining like fire, and his ears…

They were pointed.

The transformation had happened swiftly. It had been instant and startling, and now she felt as if she was looking at a completely different person. The lines that framed his mouth deepened, his grin more like a grimace as he glared down at her, and every inch of him was tense. His hand trembled against her throat, his visage darkening as the seconds ticked past.

There was a war in his eyes.

An unmistakable battle.

Against what?

Persephone struggled to breathe and fought to keep as still as possible, unsure what he would do if she moved. Fear trickled through her as she swallowed and her Adam's apple rubbed the leather palm of his gauntlet. She awaited her fate as she watched that war playing out in his eyes, aware her future depended upon the outcome of the battle that had him locked up tight, frozen as he towered over her, breathing hard.

She stared at his dark visage, easily able to believe all the tales told of him in Olympus when he was like this. None of those stories had mentioned the intense battle she could read in his eyes though, and even sense in him as his hand twitched against her throat and his jaw flexed, clamping hard in response.

She wanted to know what was happening inside him, some crazy part of her wishing she could see into his mind to watch the war playing out. What was he fighting? This darker version of himself?

Was the Hades who had gazed at her softly through blue eyes, the one that didn't fit the image Olympus painted of him, waging war against this Hades who held her throat in a hard grip and was infinitely darker and more savage?

The barest flicker of blue danced like stars amidst the onyx of his irises.

His gaze slowly lowered to her lips.

A war erupted inside her too as they landed on her mouth, a battle between the side of her that wanted him to kiss her again—which made her feel wicked—and the side that screamed at her to push him away. Her breaths came faster, speeding in time with his as the air thickened and the silence stretched between them.

She couldn't take it anymore.

"Hades," she whispered.

Unsure whether it was a plea to let her go or an entreaty born of this dangerous desire to know his kiss again.

It shattered whatever spell he was under, reinforcing that feeling she'd had in the forest—she had power over him. She swore regret flickered in his eyes as he shoved away from her on a low, vicious growl, muttering things in a language she didn't know as he stalked to the stairs.

Persephone sagged into the wall, her breath leaking from her as she stared at his retreating back.

The sensation of power that swirled through her, stronger than it had been in the woods when she had spoken his name, bolstered her courage and something within her pressed her to take advantage of it. She trembled as she pushed away from the wall and uttered a demand.

"Let me go, Hades."

He stopped at the top of the steps and looked back at her, his eyes pure darkness as shadows danced across his shoulders and down his arms, and growled, "*Never.*"

With that, he stormed down the stairs, disappearing from view and moving beyond the reach of her senses, the brush of his power against hers fading.

The moment she realised she was alone, cold engulfed her and her strength flooded from her. Her legs gave out and she sank to her knees on the stone floor, gripping it with trembling fingers. She gave herself a moment, hating each second that she felt powerless and weak, afraid, letting it all flow over her and through her, purging it, and then she steeled her nerves and set her jaw and curled her fingers into fists.

Resolve swept through her, pushing out all her fear.

If Hades wouldn't take her home, she would find her own way there.

She wasn't sure how she was going to do it, but she was going to escape.

Before she did something both reckless and dangerous.

Like kissing him again.

CHAPTER 6

Hades stalked away from Tartarus, leaving the black stone columns of the entrance to the prison behind him. He flicked the blood from the talons of his gauntlets, an action so ingrained in him he barely noticed what he was doing as he focused his gaze on the distance.

In the direction of his temple.

The tower close to it taunted and tempted him, a beacon he couldn't escape no matter how far he strayed from it, attempting to maintain his distance from his queen.

His queen?

He scoffed at that and growled, "If she is my queen, why does she resist me so?"

Zeus had said he could take her, so the goddess was his now, but she refused to accept him, despite the desire that shone in her eyes at times. He had taken that flicker of heat as an invitation, as any male surely would have, but she had spurned him each time, denying him. He wasn't reading her wrong.

Or at least he didn't think he was.

It had been so long since he had been in the company of a female that he felt rusty—as witless as a young male with little to no experience. His past conquests had been centuries ago, too far back for him to recall any specific details.

Instinct had served him well in the past though—in battle and in ruling his kingdom—and he felt sure it was right this time too.

The awakening of her passion had been unmistakable. Her breaths had quickened. Her striking emerald eyes had darkened and her pupils had dilated.

And she had subtly arched her body towards his, beckoning him and making him overcome with a need to have her.

If they weren't signs of desire, then what were they?

That need she had stoked had continued to ravage him in their time apart, keeping him awake in his bed at night and distracting him throughout the day, making it difficult to focus on his duties.

When all he wanted to do was return to his queen and kiss her.

A foolish endeavour.

His *queen* would only turn on him again.

Striking him.

His talons flexed and he growled as fury spilled through his veins and filled him with an urge to strike back at her. He unleashed that black rage on the lands around him instead, refusing to harm his beauty. The sound of rock splitting filled the air as jagged fault lines branched out behind him.

"She would do well to obey me," he muttered in the language of the Underworld, a tongue he had spoken in front of her and had sensed her confusion in response to hearing it. He glared at his realm and at the soldiers who bowed their heads or lowered to one knee as he swept past them. "She would do well to be as deferential as these males."

But he had the feeling she would remain defiant, despite the fact he ruled this realm and was a king among gods.

It was infuriating.

And intriguing.

Hades set his sights back on the tower that reached high into the crimson sky, powerless to resist the pull that drew him towards it.

Towards her.

That pull was as fierce now as it had been the day he had met her, and again he foolishly wondered whether the Moirai had intervened to bring them together. For what purpose? To punish him in some manner? To taunt him with something he desired, but could not have? He doubted their actions had been magnanimous if they were behind his meeting with the goddess.

He huffed and muttered, "No god or goddess outside of this realm would do anything that might benefit me. They veil scorn with kindness, seeking to mock or belittle me."

And yet, as he gazed at the tower, that feeling in his chest sank deeper, fusing with his bones to tug him towards the goddess.

It had been days since he had left her, a tactic he often used on his prisoners in Tartarus, giving them time to become accustomed to their surroundings. Days that had been a torment to him, although he doubted they had caused her as much strife. His queen had no doubt been pleased that he hadn't come to see her and had left her alone.

She might have even attempted to escape despite his warnings.

Not that it would get her anywhere.

The only way out of the tower was to throw herself off the balcony, and he didn't think she was so desperate to escape him that she would break her bones to achieve it.

He had warded the door to keep it sealed shut to her and had made sure to keep her powers from her too, exerting much of his strength to create another ward that would inhibit them no matter where she went in his realm.

So, she could tire herself out all she wanted trying to break down the door or burst through the wall, and she would get nowhere.

Hades huffed again. "If she has attempted to escape, could I blame her?"

He had frightened her more than once, and she had revealed the depth of her fear to him when she had uttered his name, lacing it with desperation that had wrenched at him and severed the hold the darkness had had on him, freeing him of it and making him aware of what he had been on the verge of doing.

Forcing his kiss upon her twice had gotten him nowhere. A third attempt to make her compliant might have been his last, shattering the fragile flare of heat that shone in her eyes from time to time when she gazed at him. If he crossed that line with her, she would never be his queen.

He could see that now.

His brother had made it sound so easy.

The darkness that lurked within him had made it sound so easy.

Hades growled and a great crevasse opened up to his right, streaking across the land from him, and the two sides collided, crashing upwards into the spine of a new mountain range.

Both of them were wrong.

There was no simply *taking* his queen.

He had done it, spurred by his brother's words and the darkness, and she despised him for it and was intent on fighting him rather than accepting him as her king. The more Hades thought about it, the stronger a feeling inside him grew, gently whispered in his mind.

Zeus had tricked him.

His brother had manipulated him into abducting her, all to ruin his chance at securing the bewitching goddess as his bride, ensuring he remained alone.

Alone.

Hades drew to an abrupt halt and flashed his fangs as he scowled at the black ground.

He was not alone.

He resisted the urge to teleport to the tower that blasted through him, denying it because he didn't need company. He didn't crave it. Not at all.

Hades stared at the tower.

Canted his head.

Devised dark plans to make the goddess his forever as he fought the rising darkness, battling to hold it back, soul-deep aware he could not let it steal control of him again when he was in her presence. He would cross that line with her if it did. The darker side of his blood viewed her as his, wanted to bend her to his will and force her compliance. He couldn't allow that to happen.

He needed to master the darkness he had allowed to steal control from him for so long, letting it fester and grow within him. It would be difficult. He had given it too much free rein and now it wrenched command of his body from him too easily, and held him in its grasp too long.

Did he have the strength to tame it?

No.

Hades shunned that answer, because it came not from his heart but from the corruption that ran in his veins to taint them and twist him, distorting him into something he despised. The darkness pushed, raking claws over his mind, poisoning it with whispered words about his brother and that this was another betrayal. Zeus had planned it all, setting Hades up to fail so he would never have the goddess.

Not in the way he was beginning to realise he wanted her.

Hades rubbed his forehead and drew down a deep breath, and around him shadows gathered, forming jagged ribbons that snapped at the black earth. He dropped his hand and pressed the heel of it to his left eye, his teeth gritting hard enough that they creaked as he pushed back against the darkness.

His vile little secret.

How some would mock while others sought his head if they knew of this festering weakness inside him. His lips stretched in a tight grin. But none would ever know of it. This burden was his to bear alone. It was necessary. None could know of it. No one would understand. No one would care.

He lowered his hand and stared at the talons that tipped his fingers.

Shadows threaded between them, wisps of darkness that lovingly caressed his claws.

Everyone believed the darkness to be him, that the beast that rampaged and destroyed mountains and painted his lands with blood was simply him in a rage.

But it was so much more than that.

It was a slow, agonising death of the light.

A war he had waged for millennia, ever since he had been condemned to the Underworld by his own brother, and he was beginning to feel that he was losing his mind.

That one day, his humanity would be stripped from him by the darkness and he wouldn't return.

He would sink into the abyss.

Hades cast a glance around him at his realm, at the towering black mountains and the temples, and the people coming and going. He feared that when it happened, when he lost the fight for good, he would destroy this realm that was everything to him, would slay these souls that worshipped him, and damn them all.

His gaze drifted to the tower, a feeling beating within him as he stared at it. The goddess might be his only salvation. She had drawn him back from the darkness with just the sound of her voice, had given him the strength to defeat it by only speaking his name.

And by the gods, that revelation made him feel more vulnerable than ever.

The darkness stirred in response, rising as it had so many times when he felt like this, becoming a shield around his heart.

Because he feared.

He feared he might come to depend upon her and might believe she would save him, and rather than doing that, she might damn him by leaving him.

By despising him as deeply as he despised the darkness.

He had to secure her.

How?

He couldn't just take her, not as he had wanted, not as he believed he could. The darker side of his blood had been all too quick to attempt that, the thought that this bewitching female was his pounding in his veins and driving him to claim her—to conquer her. As he had slowly clawed his way back towards the light, or as towards the light as he could manage, he had realised what a grave mistake he had made.

And how he might have ruined everything.

In his haste to have her, he had worked against himself, revealing his darkest side to her and no doubt making himself appear as much a monster as all in Olympus believed him to be.

But he hadn't gone as far as to destroy all hope of securing her. He felt that deep in his black soul. There was still a chance. Albeit a small one. She might be his. He might not have ruined everything.

Not as his brother had clearly planned for him to when he had plotted his downfall and goaded him into taking her and forcing her to be his queen.

He would continue as he had planned instead, tamping down the dark whispers that urged him to claim his female, to touch and taste her and make her his, and focusing on teasing out that desire that had flashed in her eyes from time to time and drawing it to the surface. He had spent his every waking hour, and the ones where he should have been sleeping, going over every moment they had shared, studying them in minute detail and devising a strategy that would secure his victory.

This battle he fought with the goddess wasn't much different to every other war he had won. First, he would study his opponent, and then he would fine-tune his strategy as he learned more about her, focusing on any weakness she might present, and in the end, he would win and achieve what he had set out to do.

He would break down her walls.

The first part of his strategy was simple, but he hoped it would prove the most effective weapon in his arsenal.

He had decided to begin with his appearance.

His eyes had remained blue for the best part of the time they had been apart, and his fangs were in check, and beneath his gauntlets, his nails were rounded and normal. Even his ears were not as pointed.

She would find his appearance more pleasing now.

That would disarm her.

She would feel more at ease around him and in time she would grow used to him. As they conversed and he learned about her, she would begin to view him not as the monster the citizens of Olympus painted him as, but as a male just like any other she had encountered before.

He grinned slowly. Or perhaps a league above them.

A male who sparked her interest and fanned the flames of her desire.

From there she would come to want him, for longer than a brief kiss before she lashed out at him. He wasn't sure why she did that, but each time she had struck him, he had wanted to bare fangs and growl at her, had grown frustrated and had even come dangerously close to losing control.

He didn't want to lose control around her.

But the darkness that flowed in his veins was strong, a heady drug that easily controlled him, promising pleasure if he surrendered to it. It provoked and cajoled, and just the thought of bloodying his claws was enough to have it slowly stealing control of him, slipping it from his grasp little by little, so gently he didn't notice until it was too late.

Until his fangs were down and a hunger for violence consumed him and had him pivoting on his heel, filled with a need to return to Tartarus and drag another prisoner up from the spiralling depths for an hour in his interrogation room.

Hades welcomed the darkness.

Sank into it.

Clenched his fists and drew back on the reins, denying it. He breathed hard as he fought it, attempting to quell the hunger for bloodshed, to keep it in check so he didn't undo all his hard work. He wanted to see the goddess today.

He wanted her to look at him as if he was a man.

Not a monster.

He drew down slow, steadying breaths as he wrestled for control, slowly stealing it back from the darkness, and unsure how long he could maintain it. The moment he was back in control, he felt it slipping from his grasp again.

His thoughts turned to the goddess, his mind replaying how his name had sounded on her lips, and the world fell away, the darkness receding again.

Curious how it did that.

He angled his head and frowned at the ground, studying the shift in his mood and how the darkness had loosened its grip on him purely because she had filled his mind. His thoughts drifted back to a moment in the tower, when he had pinned her to the wall, her soft curves cushioning the hard planes of his body, inflaming him as she had gazed up at him with heat in her eyes.

He had wanted to kiss her, and by the gods, he felt sure she had wanted his lips on hers too. He had wanted so much more than a mere kiss. He had wanted all of her, had been on the verge of surrendering to his need to sink inside her and satisfy her desires—to claim her body and soul and make her belong to him—when she had whispered his name.

The sound of it breathed on her lips had shattered the hold his darker desires had on him, pulling him back towards the light before he had gone too far with her.

And had made him feel like the monster everyone portrayed him to be as he had realised what he had been about to do.

Fearing what he might do if he remained, he had taken his leave.

And hadn't returned.

Hades stared at the tower, a war erupting inside him, a battle between hope and despair—between light and darkness. If he went to her now, how would she react? Would she recoil in fear? Or welcome his presence?

Would she be pleased to see him?

He scoffed at that, the sound brittle and broken, reflecting how he felt inside. He felt on the verge of breaking, and he knew why. He looked down at his black talons, at the crusted blood on them. Fear. He feared her reaction.

He feared that despite his efforts to make his appearance more pleasing, she would continue to view him as a cruel, monstrous god.

One she wanted nothing to do with.

"I will win her," he growled and curled his left hand into a tight fist. "She will be mine."

If he had to mould himself into a softer male—a gentler male—then he would find a way to do that. If he had to vanquish the darkness to win her, he would try to do it. He would fight it with all his might, something he should have done long ago. She had given him a reason to defeat it. He would do anything to secure her as his queen.

Because in the scant few hours he had known her, he had come to realise he couldn't picture a future without her in it. He didn't want a future where she wasn't with him, by his side, as close to him as he could get her.

He chuckled mirthlessly.

Countless gods and beings had attempted to defeat him during the long course of his life. His own father had devoured him and kept him prisoner. His own brothers had turned their backs on him, condemning him to the darkness.

But none of them had broken him.

He uncurled his fist, his brow furrowing as he stared at his talons.

Hades feared she had that power.

He felt deep in the pit of his wretched soul that she could strike a blow that would break him, that it would only take a word or a look and he would be defeated.

A growl curled up his throat.

He squeezed his fingers into a fist again.

He would not be defeated by a mere slip of a female.

He took a hard step towards the tower and hesitated, and cursed himself for being weak. Fear was nothing but another weakness, and he had no room for them in his life. But he still couldn't convince himself to move. Doubts plagued him, a thousand needles that stabbed at his soul until it bled oily black blood that seeped into his veins, darkening his thoughts. If she would not submit to him, he would make her.

Hades snarled and shut down that thought.

He would not.

He needed to be gentle with her.

Only he wasn't sure how. He wasn't accustomed to being soft or tender. He wasn't sure he had ever been either of those things. Life had hardened him into a warrior from the moment he had been born. He blew out his breath as he gazed at the tower, attempting to expel the weakness that infested him. Could he be gentle?

Tender?

There was only one way to find out.

He swept his black cloak out behind him and stalked towards the tower.

CHAPTER 7

Hades's heart drummed an unsteady rhythm as he approached the black tower, each step closer he came to it quickening his pulse. He held back the darkness, ignoring the whispers that threaded through his mind, denying them. Things would go well. He would check on the goddess and do his best to appear gentle, and he would keep his hands to himself.

That last part might be easier said than done if she looked at him with any trace of heat in her gaze. Just a flicker of desire would be enough to torch his control.

He swallowed and flexed his fingers into fists and stretched them, determined to do things right this time. He could be as pleasing as the next male, as civilised as any she had encountered in Olympus. The darkness seemed to chuckle at that and he bared his emerging fangs at the tower, fighting the doubt that flashed through him.

"My god-king Hades." A male voice cut into his thoughts, the intrusion unwelcome.

The darker side of his blood snarled at him to cut the man down for delaying him, stopping him from being able to see his goddess, and Hades wrestled with it even as he wanted to obey it, wanted to remove this obstacle between him and the object of his desire.

Hades bared his fangs at the dark-haired male, a commander of one of his legions who wore black hoplite armour and carried his helmet beneath his right arm, the crimson crest of it brushing his bare biceps. His threadbare control threatened to snap as he stared the male down.

The commander wasn't alone.

A legion one hundred strong kneeled behind him in regimented lines, their heads bent.

Hades shored up his defences and clawed back control, unwilling to let the darkness rip it from him. These men were good. Loyal. They didn't deserve his wrath. They served him well and deserved his praise and his patience, not death.

Although, rewarding their service wasn't the only reason he somehow managed to hold back his dark urge to cut them all down.

He didn't want the goddess to see him eviscerating his own soldiers, painting his realm with their blood. So as much as the darkness purred at him to do it, Hades would not.

The darker part of him didn't like that.

"What is it?" Hades growled, shadows writhing around the pointed toes of his metal boots as he stared the male down, his blood quickening as he wrestled with himself. The urge to strike the male for disturbing him was strong, near overwhelming, and he had to fight his shadows, struggling to stop them from lashing out and slicing the commander to ribbons.

The male kept his head bowed, but his wary brown eyes drifted to the restless shadows that twined up Hades's legs.

Sweat beaded on the commander's brow as he struggled to give his report without his voice fading or breaking. "There has been unrest in the Elysian Fields. Several souls there struck out at others."

Hades's dark eyebrows knitted hard, his anger swift to rise. "I will see to it."

It wasn't like the occupants of the Fields to be restless. The place was a paradise, created for the kindest souls, for the heroes of this world. He had never had any trouble there before. It unsettled him and filled him with an urge to look at the tower, one he denied.

He kept his focus fixed on his commander instead.

"I will take the legion there." The male remained looking at Hades's boots, a tremble in his voice that betrayed his fear and had Hades glancing at his men.

Their emotions ran the same course as their commander's. They all feared him.

And Hades was fine with that.

He had taken great pains to ensure everyone in his realm feared him. Those who had dared to disobey him had ended up in Tartarus, tortured for all to hear, or their blood had nourished his black lands. Fear made for obedient subjects.

"Take the men from the barracks with you. I want this unrest subdued immediately. If it is not settled by the time I reach the Elysian Fields, it will be your head—" Hades cut off as a shiver tumbled down his spine and frowned at the curious feeling.

He studied it, his expression causing the commander to squirm, as if he was about to be devoured by Hades's shadows. Hades ignored him, seeking the source of the unsettling feeling, and his eyebrows pinched harder as he realised where it was coming from.

His head snapped up, his gaze locking on the scarlet-haired beauty standing on the balcony of the tower, her green eyes fixed on him.

Just the feel of her eyes on him was enough to stir the darkness, flooding him with an urge to lash out at his men, because if she was looking at him, then she was looking at them too. The thought of her looking at another male had his shadows lancing the ground, snapping dangerously close to the commander.

"Go," Hades barked.

Before his shadows devoured them all.

The commander was quick to push to his feet and signal his men, and as one they disappeared.

Hades continued to stare up at the goddess, darkness so thick it choked the light from him pouring through his veins as the blackest reaches of his soul murmured that she had been admiring the other males. No doubt comparing him to them.

He snarled and crushed that voice as he stalked towards the dark wooden door at the bottom of the tower.

She would want no other male.

He unlocked the tower door and pushed it open, stepping into the circular room at the base. His senses stretched upwards, attempting to pinpoint the goddess as he ran over his strategy and fought the darkness, trying to claw himself out of the mire so his plan would succeed.

He needed to appear more pleasing.

Gentler.

That ran on repeat in his mind as he mounted the spiral staircase, the clunk and scrape of his metal boots against the black stone drawing his awareness to his plate armour. He grimaced. It would be difficult to appear gentle given his current attire. Returning to his temple to change into a softer, less daunting outfit seemed the wisest course of action, but need overruled it and had him taking the steps two at a time.

Desperate to see her.

Hades tightly clutched the reins of his darkness, pulling back on it as he fought to keep it under control. The closer he came to seeing her again, the stronger and more defiant it grew, rousing dark needs within him and filling his mind with other thoughts—ones about possessing her.

By the time he had reached the top of the tower, he was near mad with a need to see her.

He stepped out onto the stone floor, sweeping around to face her, and came to an abrupt halt, some of the darkness abating as his gaze landed on her.

She stood at a distance, close to the balcony, and was facing him, her hands tucked behind her, one pressing against the curved wall.

Clearly ready for him.

No trace of fear touched the delicate planes of her exquisite face. Not a hint of it in her posture, other than the hand that had betrayed her to brace against the wall, as if she needed to steady herself. Her little fingertips dug into the black stone, clutching it as she stared at him, her luminous green eyes—no, not luminous. They were dull. And there were shadows beneath them.

And she was paler than when he had left her, her skin closer to white than cream.

Hades frowned at her, his blue gaze darting over her, and it struck him that the hand that clutched the wall wasn't steadying her because she feared him. It was steadying her because she didn't have the strength to stand unassisted.

"You did not sleep?" That question came out hard and demanding, pushed from his lips by his anger at the thought she might have spent the days they had been apart as untouched by the restful arms of sleep as he had been. "Have you not slept at all?"

Had it eluded her for the same reasons it had eluded him?

Had thoughts of their kisses kept her awake too?

He stared at her, willing her to answer those unspoken questions, surprised by how desperately he needed to know the answer to them. Hope built inside him. Hope that she might want him as fiercely as he wanted her.

She cut it down by throwing her hands up in the air, the sudden action making her wobble on her feet, and defiantly barking, "Could you sleep if you were in my situation? I am a prisoner. Held in a cell. Kept here against my will."

Hades's face slowly pinched in a scowl as she hit him with each word, wielding them as he would his bident, cutting at him with them. The part of him that wanted to warn her to take more care with how she spoke to him fell mute as she mumbled something under her breath, something he was sure she hadn't wanted him to hear as her cheeks pinkened and she cast her gaze away from him as he glared at her.

"My bed is also a stone slab."

He slid his gaze towards the bed he had provided for her and the anger he felt turned towards himself instead as he took stock of it.

He went to it, partly because he felt she was questioning his powers since he hadn't created some bedding for her, something soft to cushion her fragile frame, and partly because he didn't want her to suffer.

Which struck him hard and had him glancing her way.

His mood only darkened as he realised she was moving in time with him, shuffling away to keep the distance between them steady, and fear was building in her gaze now. A gaze that kept darting between him and the bed.

The corners of his lips turned downwards.

She thought he would force her onto it.

He had done his best to appear more like other males, and had been moving towards the bed to make it better for her, providing her with the comfort she needed, and she had presumed he had some nefarious agenda and would do something as dark and despicable as taking her against her will.

He glowered at her for that one.

The bitter anger that had been building within him, stoking the darkness and drawing it to the fore despite his attempts to calm it and remain in control—to remain gentle—reached a crescendo as her gaze shifted and she stared at his pointed ears.

Hades pivoted to face her and snarled, "What?"

She tensed and her hands leaped behind her back as she swiftly angled her face away from him, but those curious emerald eyes roamed back to him, and lingered.

And she surprised him all over again as she bravely found her voice rather than remaining meek as many would have in the face of his anger.

"Your eyes are different again today… and they change in strange ways… and your ears… I have never seen pointed ears on creatures other than beasts," she said, the barest hint of a wobble in her voice that told him she expected him to growl and snarl and snap at her in response to her observation.

Like the monster she had portrayed him to be.

"Never seen pointed ears on creatures other than beasts," he growled in the language of the Underworld, keeping his one-sided conversation secret from her. "The goddess thinks me a monster. A hideous one at that by her account."

The hope that had been foolishly building inside him shattered and he had to gather the pieces to claw it back together, unwilling to give up. A more sensible male might do that. Give up. Hades huffed. As sensible as he was, he would not give up. He should give up. He cast that whispered doubt from his mind. He would also not listen to the darkness. Not today.

He couldn't afford to let it take control.

The goddess was intent on provoking him though, rousing the darkness and feeding it.

She frowned at him, her fine dark red eyebrows knitting for a moment before they furrowed slightly and her voice softened. "You are not like the males of Olympus. They do not have such features. The sight of them—"

"Scared you," he snarled in their common tongue, feeling much like the beast she thought him to be as he stared her down, struggling against the darkness as it mocked him, as it dripped poison in his ear to fill his mind with a single thought—she would never choose a male like him.

And by the gods, that was a blade in his heart that twisted and stabbed, and severed pieces of it from him.

He tried to conceal his hurt from her, bringing up a wall of darkness like a shield, a barrier of impenetrable ice around his feelings that would stop her from wounding him again.

The great god-king of the Underworld.

Defeated by a mere goddess.

This endeavour was pointless.

Nothing he did would make her want him. His future didn't hold a loving queen. It held only hurt, a wound in his chest that would fester and destroy him, and his realm with him.

He had been one with the darkness for centuries, had embraced it, harnessed it and savoured it, and he was beginning to recall why he had surrendered to it so easily over the years.

Because when he was darkness incarnate, he had no weaknesses.

No soft emotions.

"What is the name of this goddess who seeks my head and attempts to cleave my heart from my breast?" he rumbled in the language of the Underworld, and then added in her tongue, "Tell me your name. You know who I am. I will know who you are."

Rather than shying away from the order or falling mute, she tipped her chin up.

"Persephone." Her green eyes hardened like blades, and he had the feeling they weren't meant to slash at him. They were to protect her. She expected him to say something cruel in response to discovering the identity of his queen.

No. It was more than that.

She expected him to mock her maybe. Discard her? As if she was unworthy of a place at his side, when he was the one unworthy of a place at hers.

He searched his mind, running through the gods of Olympus, and vaguely recalled mention of her. He was sure his brother had brought her up before, long ago. She was young, and he believed she had power over nature, which meant it was a good thing that he had stripped that power from her.

"You have heard of me. I can see it." She kept her chin up, but doubt clouded her eyes, laced with fear.

Not fear of him, but fear of his opinion of her.

Hades was no stranger to mental warfare, and he was beginning to suspect someone had been slowly attacking her for centuries, whittling away at her defences and stripping her strength from her. Rather than answering her, because he wasn't sure what kind of response would please her given her current inclination to see him as a monster rather than a man, he set his mind to rectifying one of the mistakes he had made with her.

Desiring to reforge the broken pieces of his hope by having her look at him with gratitude rather than scorn.

He held his hand out above the stone slab he had foolishly, cruelly believed would be adequate for her, treating her as he would a prisoner rather than a queen, and focused. Power slowly built within him, feeding off his strength and draining him as he murmured the words of a sort of ward in his mind. Rather than sealing or shielding something, this one created instead. As his strength waned, his mood darkened, turning irritable as her words churned in his head, mocking him.

By the time the soft bedding appeared, covering the stone slab, he wanted to growl and snap his fangs at her, or leave.

His gaze darted to her, the tethers holding his temper in check in danger of fraying and snapping as he gave in to his need to see her reaction, the part of him that expected her to turn on him or say something cold at war with the part that wanted to see that gratitude in her eyes.

Even when he knew he wouldn't.

Surprise and curiosity shone in her eyes, but they were short-lived. Whatever questions rose to the tip of her tongue, she denied them.

He could see it as her expression hardened and she folded her arms over her chest, her fingers digging into her biceps with enough force to leave white marks around them on her skin.

"I do not need a bed," she bit out. "I am not planning to stay. Let me go. My mother will be frantic by now, and Zeus will be aware I am missing. I do not know why you have really brought me here, but I want to leave."

"Why?" he snapped, rounding on her and expecting her to bring up her mother again or tell him it was because he had abducted her.

She said something far worse.

She looked over her slender shoulders at the world beyond the balcony and shook her head, causing her tangled waves of scarlet to sway against her skin. "This world is so dark… so stifling. It is so grim. As grim as those on Olympus paint it in the tales they share at the feasts. It is everything opposite to my home… It is not light nor beautiful. I cannot understand how anyone can live in this dreary, dead realm."

Hades's temper didn't just snap its tethers.

It obliterated them.

Anger boiled through him, a rage so dark he couldn't hold it back, her words ringing in his ears to mock and attack him, to stoke the fury that rolled over him like a black wave.

He was across the room in an instant, his gauntleted hands closing over her arms to rip a startled gasp from her, and had shoved her against the wall a heartbeat later. He towered over her, shadows pouring from beneath his boots as he quaked, as the world outside trembled in response to his rage, his hurt—a world that was part of him.

"This dreary… dead realm," he snarled in the language of his kingdom, the hurt welling like a black veil that smothered the light and dragged him down into the darkness at the same time. "This realm that is mine. This realm that is me. It is not light nor beautiful. It is not your precious Olympus… but it is real. That light and beauty you cherish so much, my little queen, is but a veil over an insidious darkness… covering all the vileness of Olympus. The lies. The betrayals. The philandering. All things your precious god-king allows to happen. All things he himself indulges in. And what of you, my beauty? Can you truly say you are happy in your pure, bright realm? Your scars may be invisible, but they are still there."

"What are you saying?" Her eyes darted between his as they darkened, the fear that had gripped her as surely as his hands were falling away as doubt and anger clouded her features. "Tell me what you are saying."

Hades glared down at her, fighting the darkness and losing the battle as she set her jaw and scowled right back at him, a challenge in her green gaze.

One that had him unsure what to do in response.

"Tell me what you are saying about me," she snapped, hurt flaring in her eyes now. "I demand to know!"

Her outburst deepened the feeling someone had been attacking her mind, cutting away her confidence and strength, but it was lost on him in that moment, overshadowed by her words about his realm and him.

His grip on her arms slowly tightened as the darkness continued to rise, stealing control from him piece by piece, with each harsh word she had cast at him. His lips stretched in a slow grin. A beast. Not a male. Not in her opinion. If she wanted him to be a beast, then he would be one. He would be everything she expected him to be. Cold. Cruel. Vicious. He would be the monstrous god-king of the Underworld she had heard stories about, titillating tales spoken by handsome young males no doubt, ones designed to thrill delicate maidens and excite them.

"How many handsome young males filled your head with wicked stories of me, my queen?" He pressed closer to her as he uttered those words in the language of his realm, angling his head towards hers, holding her gaze. He lifted his left hand and brushed his thumb over her lower lip, lightly grazing it with his sharp talon as he murmured, "How many of them conquered these lips as a prize for thrilling you with their lies?"

Lips he intended to conquer and kiss so thoroughly she would forget every male who had come before him.

He would erase them from her mind.

Her body.

Hades narrowed his gaze on her mouth, hunger sweeping through him to fog his mind and steal his focus. He tugged her closer, determined to take what was his and bend her to his will so she would want only him.

So she would know that she was his now.

Forever.

She flinched and hissed in a breath.

And the scent of her blood lacing the air froze him right down to his marrow.

Hades lowered his gaze to her arm, his eyes widening slightly as he watched the crimson droplet form where the black point of his thumb had pierced her tender flesh, stark against her pale skin.

Anger swept through him, directed at himself as he pivoted away from her, releasing her and distancing himself.

"You were not meant to harm her," he growled in the language of the Underworld, the flare of anger giving way to cold that engulfed him as he looked back at her, sure she would despise him even more now. "You were not to give in to the darkness."

He hadn't liked her viewing him as a monster, but now he had confirmed he was one, and he wasn't sure what to do or say to change her opinion of him.

One that seemed to be set in stone.

Emotions bombarded him as he wrestled with himself, as he fought to subdue the darkness again and wrench it back under his control. Impossible. It felt like an impossible task as her words rang in his ears, as her pained gasp tormented him. How this delicate goddess had thrown his world off kilter. He wanted to set it right again.

Hades's eyebrows pinched hard and the corners of his lips turned downwards as they flattened.

Or perhaps he just wanted to set it right.

He wanted to correct the course of his life, wanted to be the king his realm deserved, and wanted to win his war against the darkness and conquer it.

And he wanted her to help him.

He needed her to help him.

He needed to hear her tell him that he could do it and everything would be all right, and needed her to help him master his darkness, ridding him of it forever.

Hades's gaze slowly slid towards her.

But to ask that of her, he would have to tell her his deepest, darkest secret.

Never.

That fierce denial screamed in his mind and the barriers he wanted to lower around her came back up, shielding him from the potential hurt of her rejection.

He would not speak to anyone of the darkness.

But he would rectify his latest mistake.

He stalked back towards her and reached for her arm, compelled to fix what he had done and tend to her, but before he could take hold of her, she twisted away from him and ripped a section of her green dress off, using it to dab at the small cut that had spilled a scarlet trail down her arm.

Her glare was a knife in his chest as she distanced herself from him and he couldn't bear it, so he bared his fangs at her.

He had tried to be gentle, going against everything he was in order to please her, but it was far harder than he had anticipated, especially when she was so intent on provoking him.

When she turned away from him and drifted towards a window, her back to him and her hand pressing the scrap of green fabric to her wound, his anger deflated and his expression softened. He lifted his hand towards her and uttered words in his tongue that he feared telling her, because he was sure she wouldn't believe him if he said it in a language she could understand. He was sure she would turn on him and lash out at him again, inflicting another wound that would strengthen the darkness he wanted to vanquish.

For her.

"I did not mean to harm you," he murmured.

Rather than demanding to know what he had said this time, she remained with her back to him, her shoulders set in a rigid line and her spine rod straight. Telling him without words that she wasn't interested in him. That she wanted him gone.

His hand dropped to his side and he barely bit back the growl that rolled up his throat. Had he been one of her handsome Olympian males, no doubt she would have forgiven his error. She would have believed his words, ones he lacked the courage to tell her even now, when some foolish, soft part of him believed they might make her forgive him.

He only had to tell her.

Hades tried to get the words to leave the tip of his tongue, but the longer he struggled, the more the darkness rose to fill his mind with the things she had said and how she had compared him with the males of her world.

And had found him lacking.

The shadows beneath his boots grew restless as his mood blackened, a desire to travel to that white city and hunt down every male who had touched or even gazed upon his queen blasting through him. His talons flexed, eager to rip into flesh and spill blood, and he could feel it as his eyes transformed from blue, to crimson, and then to obsidian encircling fiery pupils.

Hades spun on his heel and stormed to the staircase, forcing himself to leave before he did something else he would regret. Something that would only cement her opinion that he was a monster.

When he wanted to be a man.

Not a king to be feared. But a man to be loved.

One worthy of his beautiful Persephone.

CHAPTER 8

Persephone flinched again as the door to the tower slammed below her with enough force that the entire structure seemed to sway, her fingers tightening over the wound and making it sting. The oppressive feeling of darkness that had been building in the room slowly cleared as the shadows that had become restless in time with Hades gradually settled and she felt she could breathe again.

She stoked her anger, clinging to it as fiercely as she clung to the piece of her dress she had pressed against the wound, denying his obvious desire to tend to it, and refused to regret anything as Hades moved beyond the sphere of her senses.

That cursed regret clouded her feelings despite her best attempts to deny it and had her drifting to the balcony to look for him, to foolishly try to reassure herself that the transformation from the male who had been almost kind to her to the one who had accidentally hurt her hadn't been her fault.

Even when she knew it had.

She hadn't meant to provoke him. She hadn't been able to stop herself. Whenever she felt he was judging her, she was overwhelmed by an urge to lash out at him, to deal the first blow in order to do what—protect herself?

By the gods, was his reason for turning on her the same?

She had known her words were hurting him, but had told herself she was imagining it, that the cold and cruel god-king of the Underworld wouldn't care about someone as lowly as herself saying such things to him.

Cold and cruel?

Persephone lowered her gaze to her bare feet.

She had been the cold and cruel one.

He had been different today. Not gentle. Not really. Lighter, perhaps? She looked at the bedding he had created for her, a task that had stolen some of that light from him. How taxing had it been to make her bed more comfortable? It seemed to have cost him a lot of energy. She had noticed how unsteady he had been seconds after he had completed his task.

And how he had hoped his gift would please her.

It had been right there in his blue eyes—an unmistakable need for her to like what he had done. And do what? Accept that she was to be his?

A troubling, small part of her she hadn't quite been able to silence during their time apart whispered that she *was* attracted to him, and that it had been kind of him to tend to her needs. She scoffed. Kind? He was holding her prisoner. He wanted to force her to be his queen—the Fates only knew why because he would gain nothing from making her his wife.

He was no better than every other male in her life.

She glared out of the window, struggling to ignore the voice that asked if she would have accepted his advances had he approached her differently?

If he had come to Olympus, to her home, and asked for her to be his queen rather than snatching her from the mortal world, would she have accepted his proposal?

The answer to that was startling, but simple.

Yes.

Despite the darkness that blazed within him, she was deeply attracted to him, felt drawn to him whenever he was near and couldn't banish him from her thoughts whenever they were apart. She had never felt anything like this before. No male in Olympus had ever caught her eye or captured the whole of her attention in the way Hades had, and no male before him had awakened such surprisingly strong emotions.

And desire.

The attraction she felt towards Hades wasn't just deep. It was fierce. It consumed. Made her crave. Made her bold.

It made her feel alive for the first time in her life.

And it also made her afraid.

If Hades could make her feel like this with only his presence and the memory of his kiss, how would she feel if she allowed his caress? If she surrendered to him completely?

She shut down that line of thought and refused to answer those questions, because they were as dangerous as the male who had evoked them. Although, that dangerous side of him was alluring. Not that she would let him see she felt that way. She wasn't going to reward his brutish behaviour, even when part of her secretly ached for his lips on hers again.

"Stop it," she muttered, her lips flattening. "Banish him from your mind."

No easy feat.

He took that moment to appear off to her left, striding towards the large black building that resembled a fort, with high walls and battlements, and a courtyard within the four straight sides. He cut an imposing figure as his black cloak flared behind him, and his shadows shifted restlessly beneath his feet, lashing out at things he passed. One unruly shadow even tossed a rock into a ravine that was new. She hadn't noticed it before at least. It branched outwards from the path worn into the black dirt, splitting into several crevasses as it stretched towards the mountains off to her right.

She studied him as she ran over everything that had happened, attempting to piece him together and understand him. The feeling that there were two sides to the god-king of the Underworld remained. When he had grown dark, she had seen that internal battle erupt again in his eyes, almost hidden from view by how cold and sharp they had become.

The curiosity that stirred in her grew stronger, and had her considering something that would be foolish at best and dangerous at worst.

Asking him about it wouldn't go over well.

Persephone moved to the small balcony that was barely wider than the door and refused to look down at the stomach-turning drop below her. She kept her gaze fixed on Hades, distracting herself from it, and leaned forwards to rest her elbows on the high stone balustrade.

"He had certainly known my name," she murmured as she propped her chin up on her palm, still keeping the strip of cloth against her wound with her other hand. "But I could not decipher his thoughts. Does he think me a minor, weak goddess as others do? Insignificant?"

That word made her flinch.

How many times had her mother—Demeter, goddess of the harvest—made her feel that way?

While Persephone had inherited some of her powers, including her ability to heal others to a degree, she was nothing compared to her mother. No one prayed to her to help with their harvest, or their unborn child. No one bowed to her when she passed them in Olympus. She had spent her entire life in the shadow of her mother, feeling as if she didn't exist at times.

"How many feasts have I attended where no one spoke a word to me?" She scoffed, and it came out sounding broken and not angry or bitter as she had intended. She tamped down the hurt that welled, denying it and refusing to let it get to her. She had no reason to be feeling down and to sink into the mire of depression. Or perhaps she did. She glared at Hades. "Will anyone even notice I am missing? I told him Mother would be frantic and implied Zeus would be trying to find me… but will Mother even care that I am gone?"

Persephone pulled down a breath, steadying herself before the answer to that question got the better of her and the weight of everything that had happened over the last few days became too much to bear.

"Perhaps I am better off here," she muttered, and there was the bitterness she had aimed for and completely missed before. It didn't last long before it morphed into a bone-deep sort of despair, one that had plagued her for years, steadily building inside her until it had become oppressive and part of her, like a festering organ that existed only to spread poison through her. Her mother only cared about being rid of her, and the other gods and goddesses barely even acknowledged her if they saw her in the city. "No one in all the realms would miss me if I just disappeared."

Hades looked over his shoulder in her direction, too far away for her to see if he was looking at her, but she felt it. His gaze was a warming caress, one that was strangely soothing, and he lingered, even coming to face her.

As if he had felt the depth of her misery and felt compelled to do something about it—even something as minor as making her feel she wasn't alone.

"Would you miss me?" she whispered. "I want to say that you would… but I do not know if you would miss me or your *queen*."

And he had stayed away for days.

A male who missed his female would not stay away for days. He would be eager to see her and would return as soon as possible. She had watched him pass between the large black temple to her left and the barracks to the right many times over the last few days, and he had never looked at the tower. She had even spied him at a vast distance, a speck of black exiting a columned building set into a mountain.

Screams frequently echoed from that building.

If she had to guess, she would say it was Tartarus, a prison that was home to the titans.

To Hades's father.

He kept his own father imprisoned, but she could hardly blame him. Zeus had often recounted the tale of his own heroism and how he had saved his siblings from their father, Cronus, and had led their side in the war against the titans, ensuring their victory.

"How different would that tale be if you told it?" she murmured to Hades and he turned his back on her, continuing towards the barracks. She sighed. "I imagine it would be quite different. I am starting to imagine all the tales told about you would be quite different if they came from your lips and not the whispers of others."

His lips.

Persephone's cheeks heated as the way he had kissed her flashed across her mind, how fierce his lips had been as they had claimed hers and how demanding too. And the way his tongue had brushed the seam of her mouth, enticing her into opening for him.

"Stop it," she muttered and gritted her teeth. "For all you know, all men kiss as he does."

She doubted that.

Men exited the square building and lined up before him, and she fell back into watching him, studying the dark king of the Underworld and seeking out more pieces of the puzzle that would help her understand him. A better use of her time would be finding a way out of the tower.

Persephone made the mistake of looking at the only method of escape she had found during her previous attempts.

The several-hundred-foot drop to the black ground had her heart lodging in her throat and she shook her head. Just the thought of falling was enough to make her push back from the balustrade and edge towards the door. She stopped when her spine met the doorframe, her heart thundering as she fought to calm it. She was not going to leap. While it wouldn't kill her, it would break bones. If she broke more than one leg, or her spine, escape would be impossible and Hades would catch her.

She could only imagine how furious he would be.

She pressed her hand to the black stone beside her and focused, feeling the power that flowed through her tower. She had studied wards as a child, and had learned to decipher many of them to pick them apart and undo them, but she had never encountered a ward like the one Hades had placed on her prison. It was intricate, and while she understood parts of it, many others were unknown to her.

Which meant she couldn't break it.

She sighed, studying the ward anyway, something she regularly did, devoting several hours a day to attempting to decipher it. It wasn't the containment ward that she focused on either. It was the other, subtler one she had gone searching for when the void inside her had begun to irritate her.

A void that was steadily growing colder the longer she was without her powers.

They were there. She was sure of it. But it was as if they were covered in layers of something, muted and, not numbed, but it felt close to it. She pressed her hand to her chest and studied the feeling. They felt just beyond her reach and no matter how hard she strained, how fiercely she tried to summon them, she couldn't draw them back to her.

Hades barked an order at the men in his strange language and moved along the rows, stopping from time to time to bite out hard-sounding words. He even hauled several of the soldiers from their positions. Another man who had to be a commander took them from him and marched them to one side of the regiment. By the time he was done, a group of a dozen men had formed there, and they moved away with their heads bent. Had they done something wrong?

Hades disappeared.

Persephone studied his lands a little longer, her thoughts slowly growing sluggish again, and when the crimson sky darkened towards black, and Hades hadn't reappeared, she went back inside.

And eyed the bed.

It beckoned her, far more tempting now than it had been, with its bedding that was plump and appeared soft. She trailed around the room, trying to resist it, and stopped near the steps that spiralled downwards. She looked from them to the bed. Either she could attempt to decipher the wards on the door again or she could snatch some sleep while Hades was gone.

Sleep won.

If she didn't rest, she wouldn't have the strength to keep fighting Hades, or the clarity of mind she needed in order to decipher his wards.

Persephone crawled onto the far-too-soft bed and sank into it, a sigh escaping her. It was like lying on a cloud. It cushioned her perfectly and seemed to wrap around her to embrace her, like a warm cocoon.

Sleep took her the moment she closed her eyes.

And she sensed the brush of his power against her as it claimed her.

CHAPTER 9

When Persephone woke, the sky was crimson again, and she was alone.

But someone had set a tray of fruit on a small table on the opposite side of the circular room.

She looked around, sure she would find Hades nearby, only he wasn't there. Rather than going to the food, she went to the balcony and watched the world and the coming and going of the people who visited the temple and the soldiers at the barracks.

It didn't take her long to realise she was watching for Hades.

She huffed, a little angry with herself.

Because she wasn't looking for him in order to protect herself or prepare herself for another fight with him. She was watching for him because that part of her that was drawn to him wanted to see him again, itching to seek out more puzzle pieces and perhaps risk asking him why he changed so abruptly at times, becoming another male.

When the number of temple visitors dwindled, she went back to studying the wards, occupying herself into the evening, and then slept again. This time when she woke, the food had been replaced.

Was Hades visiting her while she slumbered?

If he was, what did he do when he was near her?

Persephone touched her lips, a thrill skittering along her spine that she quickly shut down. If he had kissed her, she would wake. She was sure of that.

Maybe he wasn't the one who brought her food, or if he was, he didn't stay.

"Perhaps he is done with me and I will never see him again." She sounded bitter even to her own ears as she cast the black sheets aside and slid from the bed.

That regret that she kept denying bubbled back to the surface, twisting her stomach and making her feel wretched. If he was determined to stay away from her, she could hardly blame him. She had said terrible things to him, ones that had wounded him and angered him too. She drifted to the balcony, replaying his reaction and trying to remember the words he had growled in her face, wanting to study his language so she could somehow learn it and would know what he was saying when he spoke to her in that tongue.

A tongue he clearly knew she was unfamiliar with and that was the reason he resorted to using it, keeping the things he wanted to say secret from her. Why didn't he want her to know what he was saying? The only reason that came to her was one that had her mood shifting and the strength she had gathered wavering.

He was saying things about her.

Persephone shoved that out of her head before it could take root and drag her down into the mire that always awaited her whenever she let the opinions of others get to her, or thought about her life in general.

She focused on her work, keeping herself occupied by studying the sides of the tower. The stone was rough in places, forming possible hand and foot holds. Could she climb down? She couldn't see that many points where she could grip the walls from this angle. She moved to study the other side to see if there were any potential holds there.

And stilled.

Hades.

He walked the black lands a few hundred feet away, a shadow stalking across the grim terrain.

And he wasn't alone.

An enormous three-headed black wolf walked with him, standing twice his height, its glowing blue eyes fixed on Hades.

Persephone fell into studying him instead, leaning on the stone railing to catalogue everything about him as he walked with the beast, his lips moving soundlessly. Was he talking to it? When he petted the hound's shoulder and his body language changed, becoming more than merely relaxed, fascination gripped her. He was different with this creature. Not the hard, controlling male he had been with his soldiers. He was softer.

She could almost believe him capable of feeling as she watched him.

She wanted to laugh at that.

The cruel and vicious god-king of the Underworld capable of warm feelings?

It seemed impossible, but as she watched him interacting with the three-headed beast, talking to it and stroking it in a way that spoke of tenderness, it seemed possible after all.

Persephone ran over all the stories she had heard about Hades, recalling all she knew about him and had experienced for herself, and trying to apply it to the male below her, one she felt sure wasn't aware she was watching him. In fact, she felt certain that if he knew anyone was witnessing the gentle way he was with the hound that he would turn vicious and dark.

To protect himself.

Maybe this was just a trick, something he was staging to soften her towards him and make her more compliant.

She tried to convince herself of that and to be on her guard, but the more she watched him, the stronger a feeling grew inside her. One that struck a chord with her. He had proven himself dark and cold, but try as she might to be angry with him and to believe him a monster incapable of feeling, she couldn't.

Because he appeared lonely.

As lonely as she was.

And he brought up barriers just as she did whenever she felt she was about to be hurt.

She studied him more closely as he moved in a gentle arc towards the tower, still speaking with the hound, trying to see if she was right or whether she was imprinting her own feelings on him, attempting to find some common ground with him or simply seeing what she wanted to see.

Softening him because she was attracted to him.

She gave up pretending she wasn't.

This dark, imposing god roused more than anger and frustration, and fear in her.

He made her blood catch fire too.

Made it impossible to breathe when she was around him.

More impossible than the stifling heat that encompassed her all hours of the day, making her skin tacky and sleep uncomfortable at times. She fanned herself a little, longing for a cool breeze like the ones in her forest. She frowned. Strange that she longed for that and not the cool, sea breeze of Olympus. She should be wanting to return home, as she had told Hades, but she rarely thought about Olympus, and she was beginning to suspect she wouldn't care if she never saw the white city again.

He paused and moved to face the beast, no trace of savageness in his expression now. The handsome lines of his face were soft, laced with melancholy as he said something she couldn't hear, and then his shoulders heaved in a sigh and he moved on, his hand against the beast's furry flank.

When he was like this, he didn't fit the image she had of him at all, and she found it hard to believe it was Hades below her. A feeling grew in her chest as she watched him, as she saw another side of him, one he had revealed to her in this room at times too. Regret. Anger directed at herself. Guilt. She was no better than every other Olympian. She had judged Hades and feared him without even knowing him. She had listened to those tales of him and had believed them, never questioning them or seeking the truth for herself.

She took in the black, forbidding lands that stretched around her and the crimson sky, and how a passing pair of soldiers bowed their heads and went down on one knee as Hades approached them.

All the stories people told about him had a similar theme—he was always alone.

It was always Hades against someone else, or Hades committing some terrible act, and even when Zeus spoke of the Titanomachy, Hades always seemed to be alone.

She thought about how everyone perceived him—including her—and how even those he ruled behaved around him, and a feeling built inside her, birthing a question she wanted to ask him even when she knew it would be unwise and he would only lash out at her.

How lonely was he?

She often felt isolated, but not like this—not like him. The other gods—his family—stayed away from him, and he was even isolated from the light of the world. She took in his realm again.

All he knew was darkness and so he had become the embodiment of it.

It wasn't just this realm and his rulership of it that had made him that way either.

Others were responsible for his darkness.

No Greeks prayed to her, but she knew how they prayed to him, and if they prayed to her in the same way, she would prefer to remain beyond the sphere of their supplication and attention. When the Greeks prayed to him, they turned their faces away and struck the ground to ensure he heard their pleas, and their offerings were grim and dark things. The slaughter of black sheep. The spilling of blood.

And none dared speak his name.

They called him other things.

They feared him.

And before today she had never really thought about how differently they worshipped his brothers.

When the mortals prayed to Zeus, they raised their hands and faces to the sky.

They spoke his name with pride.

They offered love and not fear.

And for some reason, that made her feel sad.

And angry.

Persephone curled her fingers into trembling fists and stared at him, trying to understand how it all made him feel and failing, because she couldn't imagine how deeply the behaviour of the mortals and his own family had scarred him.

Or how lonely it made him feel.

Whatever pain she had felt during her life, it was insignificant compared with the pain he must carry in his heart.

Hades stilled and glanced her way, and she averted her gaze, pretending she wasn't watching him by checking on her wound. She peeled the strip of fabric she had bound around it away. It was only a scar now, healed by the sleep she had snatched. She brushed her fingers over the small silvery line. He hadn't meant to hurt her. She knew that in her heart.

She looked back at him.

He was gone.

Where had he gone?

"You have not touched your food again."

She gasped and whirled so quickly her head spun, coming to face him as his deep voice swept around her. Her eyes widened as they landed on him, her heart beating faster as she tried to think of something to say, but her voice failed her. She hadn't noticed it before, but he wasn't wearing his armour. In its place was a fine black tunic that reached his thighs, and tight black trousers with knee-high boots. The outfit hugged his lithe figure, revealing a hint of the body hidden beneath.

Rather than looking at her, he kept his profile to her, his gaze on the untouched fruit platter.

"Be ready to dine with me in eight hours from now," he said, the words spoken softly but clearly an order.

She straightened her spine and found her voice. "I do not exactly have anything to change into or even water to wash with to make myself presentable, my god-king Hades."

His eyes narrowed, crimson flaring around his irises as he slanted a look at her. She couldn't tell whether it was anger or the heat of desire that put that scarlet in his gaze, but her body reacted as if it was the latter, warming and making her painfully aware of him as he came to face her.

He stared at her, the crimson spreading. Was he thinking about her bathing? Or was this flare of heat because she had called him *her* god-king Hades? She hadn't meant it like that. She hadn't intended for it to sound as if he belonged to her. She had been trying to mock him or irritate him or something. Frustration rolled through her. She wasn't sure what she had been trying to do. It had just come out, bursting from her lips because she was angry.

That was it.

She was angry.

And it wasn't anger that he had been treated poorly in his life. It was anger that he was treating her poorly.

Outside, a great mournful howl went up, and Hades glared beyond her at the balcony, his eyebrows knitting hard and the corners of his lips turning downwards. A series of growls followed it, together with male voices speaking in hushed, calming tones. Persephone didn't need to look to know Hades's hound was acting up, evidently upset by his sudden disappearance.

"Perhaps you should see to your pet?" she said, her tone somewhere between scathing and haughty, even when that irritating voice at the back of her mind hissed that he was taking care of his pet—of her.

"I will see to those things," he rumbled, his voice far too wicked and sexy. "You will have the finest water to bathe in and a gown to match your beauty."

She held her ground and resisted the fire that licked through her veins, and the heat that scalded her cheeks at his compliment, unwilling to let him see how easily he affected her. "My gown will be the same colour as this one you spoiled with my blood."

She waved her hand down her body, bringing his attention to the dull brown spots on the green fabric.

He scowled at her, black eyebrows meeting hard above eyes that held more scarlet, and almost moved a step towards her but then he curled his fingers into fists and rocked back onto his heels.

And nodded.

What else could she get from him?

He seemed to be in a compliant mood.

Persephone decided to do a little prodding and test the limits of what he would do for her to discover how far she could go before he denied her and grew snappish. How badly did Hades want his queen?

Her.

It was time to find out.

CHAPTER 10

"If I am to remain here until you come to your senses or someone comes for me, then I want a bath brought to me each day, and I want fresh covers for my bed—silk covers—and I want these wards gone. I want to be able to come and go." Persephone feared that last order might be a step too far.

Sure enough, Hades's expression darkened and he flashed fangs, but it wasn't her demand to be given some freedom that had apparently angered him.

"Who will come for you?" he boomed at her. "Your mother? Another male? I will know."

A sensible female might have backed down and even apologised in the face of his fury, but it stoked something inside her, setting fire to her courage and bringing it to the fore, together with a wicked need to tease and challenge him.

She might be his captive, but she wasn't going to be some spineless, compliant prisoner. She was a goddess, and if he hadn't stolen her powers, she could easily have escaped him.

She couldn't do that, but she could push him a little to see what he might reveal—to see if he truly did desire her and not just any female as his queen. He had called her beautiful, but she struggled to believe his compliment had been anything other than shallow words devised to seduce her into doing his bidding and giving up her fight. During her captivity, she had mulled over all the possible reasons he could have for taking her captive, and had settled on the most logical one.

He had taken her because she was an Olympian and he had stumbled across her, finding her alone and vulnerable, easy to capture. This was no doubt a ploy to anger his brother, Zeus. She knew they didn't like each other. She was a pawn in a game devised to strike out at Olympus by taking something that belonged to it. That was all.

Maybe if she revealed the truth—that he didn't want her because he thought her beautiful and desired her—she would finally get something through her own thick skull.

No one could want someone as powerless and worthless as her.

Persephone flinched at that mental barb, one that dug a hook into her and refused to be shaken, even as she tilted her chin up and pushed ahead with her plan. "I am betrothed."

Shadows suddenly swept around her and his eyes went pitch black, the fire that blazed in his pupils and his sudden transformation stealing her breath together with the way the floor trembled. She staggered for balance as it bucked and shook, the entire realm quaking, and reached for the wall to steady herself. Her heart raced as a great cracking sound echoed around the mountains and her head swung towards the balcony.

She rushed towards it, adrenaline making her blood thunder and pulse spike, needing to see what was happening and fearing it was the tower that had split in two and was about to drop from beneath her feet. She stopped short of the balcony, her gaze darting to the flimsy stone platform that was all that stood between her and a terrifying fall.

That same gaze leaped to the walls as the shaking continued and she braced her hands against both sides of the doorframe and squeezed her eyes shut, silently willing it to stop and sure the entire tower would crumble under the onslaught.

She had never felt such a powerful quake before and was shocked to discover they happened here, in a realm ruled by a god.

Hades's hands closed over her shoulders, his bare skin warming hers, and she had the feeling he was holding her back and stopping her from stepping onto the perilous balcony.

He lowered his head and she tensed as his breath fanned across her neck, making her nape tingle.

He murmured, "It is best not to provoke me."

Shock swept through her as he skimmed his hands up her bare arms and over her shoulders, and ran his thumbs up her nape, teasing it and making her shiver. The tremors subsided as he gently caressed her, his hands draped around her throat and gaze searing her, sparking a thought that made her turn towards him.

It was him.

The earthquake hadn't been a natural occurrence—it had been a response to his shift in mood.

The realm had responded to his rage.

His palms glided down from her throat to her shoulders, the warmth of his touch and the sparks that skittered through her almost distracting her.

To test her theory, she said, "I only state the truth. My mother intends to marry me off."

She held back her flinch as she uttered those words so glibly when they pained her and made her want to indulge in a rage of her own, one she felt sure might have had sharp vines bursting from beneath her feet had she had access to her powers.

Hades darkened, the sculpted angles of his face seeming to grow sharper as shadows filled the air around him, and the warm amber flames in the chandelier turned cold blue. His eyes slowly narrowed on hers. She gasped as something brushed her leg, and her head snapped downwards, her eyes widening. Shadows. Panic blasted through her as they snaked around her leg.

Persephone tried to bend to brush them away, but Hades refused to let her move.

He seized her arms in a bruising grip and his shadows tightened their hold on her too.

"You must forget this male," he growled, his voice blacker than his realm.

"Why?" Her eyes searched his, seeking the answer in them as she tried to lean to one side to swat at the shadow that was now passing her knee, a little distracted by it. If it kept heading upwards, it would near the apex of her thighs.

His voice was all raw sexuality and wickedness as he rumbled, "You are mine now."

Talking as if he owned her again? If he had worded his declaration more carefully, she might have been warmed by it. Her heart might have been swayed and that vicious little voice in the back of her mind that mocked her might have been silenced. But instead of complimenting her or saying how deeply he needed her, he had spoken of her as a possession.

Fear morphed into potent anger that scorched her veins.

No one wanted her because they desired her.

No one cared about her.

Everyone just wanted to move her around like a pawn, using her as a piece to win in a game she didn't understand, treating her as if her only worth was securing them some kind of stupid victory over someone else. Her mother had done it when she had agreed to marry her off to a god of low standing, securing her position above Persephone in the pantheon and claiming a victory over Ares too, denying him what he desired. Aristaeus had done it when he had agreed to marry her, securing himself a higher position in the pantheon and strengthening his connection with her mother, ensuring he would be invited to attend feasts that had been denied him before and that more mortals would know of him and might even pray to him more often.

Now, Hades was using her, and she might not understand why yet, but she was damned if she was going to sit back and let him do as he pleased, treating her as too many had before him, as if she was inferior and should merely do as she was told, obeying her superiors.

She was done being treated as if she was worthless.

She was done being made to feel as if she had no value. No power. No use in this world.

It hurt too much. The thought that Hades didn't really want her, that the male she desired above all others only wanted to use her, hurt too much—far worse than anyone or anything had hurt her before.

Her barriers came up hard, slamming shut around her aching heart, too late to shield it.

"I will never be yours," she spat, the words bursting from her lips as her heart stung, a reaction she couldn't contain as all the pain, all the harsh words and snide ones her mother and others had thrown at her, rolled into one agonising, sharp feeling inside her.

It was a push too far.

Rage blazed in his eyes and then he was gone.

Persephone gasped and sank to her knees, holding on to the doorframe for dear life as the entire tower shook and swayed, and outside one of the mountains erupted, throwing a great plume of ash and ribbons of lava into the air as crimson lightning crashed down with thunderous booms.

"Idiot," she muttered as she clung to the tower, chastising herself for inciting his anger when she was so high above the ground.

No. She was a fool for inciting it regardless.

Persephone swallowed to wet her dry throat as the trembling finally subsided again and she sank to her backside, her spine meeting the wall near the doorframe. Her mind raced, a thousand moments colliding inside it as she tried to figure out what was wrong with her. Angering the god-king of the Underworld, a male with a legendary temper, was nothing short of suicidal.

And speaking to anyone in the way she had spoken to him wasn't like her at all.

She had never sought to provoke anyone before.

She had always done what others wanted, seeking to please them, as if that was her lot in life. But for some reason, she couldn't do that with him.

Whenever he issued an order or a demand, she felt compelled to do the opposite.

Just to provoke him.

And whenever he wounded her, or she felt in danger of being hurt by him, she felt compelled to lash out at him, to push him away.

To protect herself.

"What is wrong with me?" she murmured as she folded her arms over her knees and rested her chin on them. "I have lost my mind. There is no other explanation."

It would explain why she kept talking to herself.

She huffed.

Felt certain of one thing.

She was playing a dangerous game with the god-king of the Underworld.

One that might get her killed.

Actually, she was sure of two things. That and the fact he wouldn't want her company at dinner and she wouldn't see him for a few days.

She had barely finished that thought when a dark-haired woman dressed in a black diaphanous gown cinched with crimson bands beneath her breasts and around her waist, appeared from the staircase.

Crossed the room.

And laid a similar black dress with embroidered bands of gold on the bed.

Persephone huffed at the sight of it, her mood souring for a heartbeat as she shoved to her feet. She stormed across the room, seized the gown and held it out to the servant.

"Take it away. I do not want it." She pushed it at the female, who backed away and scowled at her, as if she was insane.

She felt as if she was. Hades had her spinning out of control. Something about him had unlocked something inside her, gates that had held back a torrent of pain and suffering, and now she couldn't close them again, even when she was desperate to seal them shut and return to how she had felt before. She didn't want to feel like this. She didn't want to feel worthless. No. That wasn't quite right. She didn't want to feel worthless to Hades. She didn't want him to treat her as everyone else did. She wasn't sure she could bear it.

Persephone kept pace with the servant, her pulse rocketing as her anger spiked and her heart screamed that she wouldn't let him. "If he thinks he can dress me in black, he has another thing coming. Take it away and remind your master that I asked for a green dress."

The woman took the dress and Persephone tipped her chin up, a glimmer of pride running through her veins from the small victory.

Only the servant laid the gown back on the bed, smoothing the wrinkled material with steady fingers.

Persephone huffed, debated making another attempt to force the woman to take it away, and decided against it. She could hardly blame the servant for not wanting to take it back to Hades. He would be furious and would probably take his anger out on her.

She couldn't get this woman into trouble with her master, not when she could understand her fear so well. Not fear of Hades, but fear of the head of the household. Fear of her mother. How many times had she disappointed or angered her mother and paid the price for it? How many times had she witnessed her mother punishing servants for something they had done?

Her heart clenched, her thoughts turning to Mira and her maidens. The Fates only knew how Demeter had reacted to them returning without Persephone. She squeezed her fingers into a tight fist above her heart, hoping they hadn't been beaten, but aware her mother would have flogged them for failing to protect her.

She didn't want this servant to suffer such a fate, but that didn't mean she would wear the dress.

Or let the woman go so easily.

"I was… ah… curious about something." Persephone softened her tone and smiled at the servant, trying to set her at ease as she set her own plan in motion. Two could play at games and Hades was about to find out she could be a worthy opponent, and wouldn't go down without a fight. "Whereabouts in the Underworld are we? Is it far from the gate to Olympus?"

The female had been relaxing and maybe even softening towards her, but she locked up tight as the questions left Persephone's lips. Perhaps she wasn't as worthy an adversary as she had thought. She was new to games, but she was a fast learner.

Persephone quickly raised her hands, not wanting her to leave. "I am only curious. It is not as if I can leave this tower to reach the gate."

Her attempt to reassure the servant failed dismally.

The woman's features hardened and she bit out harsh-sounding words—in the same language Hades had spoken.

Persephone didn't need to understand it to know that the servant was angry, and was no doubt going to tell Hades what she had asked, but she refused to be deterred as another opportunity presented itself.

"That word you just said. What does it mean? I believe it was… ah… *riesal?*" It had sounded like that to her ears anyway and it was something Hades had said. When the servant glared at her with suspicion darkening her eyes, Persephone was quick to smile softly and add, "I only want to understand the language. It would not do for a queen to be unable to speak with her people."

For a moment, Persephone was sure the servant wouldn't tell her.

But then the woman muttered, "Realm."

"Realm," Persephone echoed. Hades had been speaking of his realm? She tried to recall anything else he had said and only one word stood out. "And what does… *asha*… mean?"

The servant glanced off to her right, towards the staircase, and then back at her, her voice low. "Me… or mine."

Hades had been talking about his realm and himself? He hadn't been saying things about her?

A wave of relief surged through her, chasing away the pain and loosening the hold her gloomy thoughts had on her, allowing her to claw her way back out of the mire. Almost. She skirted it, thoughts of the things Hades had said and her theory about him only wanting her so he could strike a blow at his brother attempting to pull her back down.

Persephone huffed and mentally swept her hand through the air, the decisive action intended to put an end to her miserable thoughts. Unfortunately, they persisted, whispering moments from her past at her, comments other Olympians had made about her and things her mother had said to her.

Ripping apart what little self-confidence she had.

She tried to find a way to distract herself from her dark thoughts, hating how she always let them get the better of her. Another two words Hades had said came to her and she turned to ask the servant for more translations, but footsteps echoed up the staircase and the woman was quick to back away and move to one side as more females appeared. The front pair wrestled with a beaten gold bath and the rest carried steaming pitchers of water.

Persephone kept her distance, warily watching them as they set the bath down opposite the foot of the bed and filled it, each woman leaving once her pitcher was empty. When the bath was full, the dark-haired woman took a large square of black fabric from the final servant and laid it over the sweeping edge of the tub, and then followed the others out.

Leaving Persephone alone.

To stop her gloomy mood from pulling her down into the mire, she focused on what she had learned, putting it to memory and formulating a plan, attempting to be positive instead of letting her past push her down a spiral of negativity.

"Riesal is realm. Asha is me or mine. What other words could I learn if the same female brings my bath tomorrow and the next day? Enough to understand Hades?" She stared at the bath, doubting she could learn the language that quickly and sure that Hades was manipulating her, giving her something she wanted in order to make her do as he bid.

She glared at the black dress and then looked at the water. She wanted to be angry with him and refuse this luxury he had given her, but she would only be spiting herself. And it might be nice to relax a little. It might even improve her mood.

She drifted to the golden bath and skimmed her hand through the milky blue water that looked as if it had come from a mineral-rich pool like the ones she had seen in Olympus. She had never bathed in one herself, but her mother swore by the restorative powers of the waters, while denying Persephone's desire to go to one to discover their power for herself.

Apparently, the bathhouses were no place for a young goddess.

She wasn't that young, and she knew younger goddesses than she had gone to the baths. She stared at the water as her fingers cut through it. It might not be the public baths of Olympus, but it was a chance to try the water, one she couldn't resist. She stripped off her green dress, letting it pool on the floor around her feet, stepped out of it and into the bath.

Sank to her shoulders.

Sighed as the water warmed every inch of her and made her tingle. She could feel herself relaxing as it seeped into her pores and the steam bathed her face and she breathed it in. Bliss. Was this what she had been missing her entire life?

She frowned at the water and toyed with it. She had been missing so many things, and while he could be infuriating at times, and she still wasn't sure what he was up to, Hades was showing them to her, allowing her to experience them.

This mineral-rich water that soothed her to her core and felt as if it was restoring her strength and easing her troubles away.

The feel of a man's lips on hers.

She touched them, painting them with the water, and felt a ghost of his bare hands on her arms and shoulders.

And his breath on her nape.

She shivered and sank deeper into the water.

Her mind on Hades.

And wicked thoughts heating her blood.

CHAPTER 11

Persephone's eyes slipped closed as she finished draping her washed dress over the edge of the bath and savoured the heat of the water. She tried to push Hades out of her head. He refused to go, her mind tormenting her with replays of his breath and his thumbs on her nape, sending a chill tumbling down her spine and spreading through her.

She shouldn't want him.

Some part of her felt that.

But was it just that part of her that constantly wanted to please her mother and be a good little goddess of Olympus?

She opened her eyes and frowned at the rippling surface of the water and her knees as they breached it, studying that feeling and chasing the threads of it, trying to find the answer to that question. She had spent the centuries of her life doing what others wanted or expected of her. And then her mother had announced her betrothal and finally something within her had rebelled, but not really. She had simply spent more and more time at her haven, hiding away in it rather than confronting her mother or standing up for herself.

Instead of putting her foot down, and putting an end to her mother's controlling ways, she had made feeble attempts to change her mother's mind.

And when that hadn't worked, she had run away rather than staying to fight.

She skimmed her fingers over the water, watching the ripples that followed their wake, and shook her head. She had been weak. She had been weak her entire life. She looked around her at the cold black walls of her tower and sighed.

And then she had met Hades.

He ignited something within her, a strength she hadn't known she possessed. Rather than fearing him as she felt she should, she had found her courage. Her fire. For the first time in her life, she was standing up for herself, and it was with someone who should have been far more terrifying than her mother, or scared her more than anything.

But he didn't.

He snapped and snarled, and grew tremendously dark at times, as if he was the embodiment of it, and in response to his outbursts and his anger, and that wicked light that entered his eyes, she felt emboldened. More courageous. And when he grew too dark and she felt he might go too far, and might even regret his actions as he had when he had cut her, and she whispered his name…

She felt empowered.

Stronger than she had ever felt.

She felt that for the first time in her dreary life, someone heard her. Someone noticed her. Someone *wanted* her.

That gave her pause and she frowned at the surface of the water. Hadn't she decided that Hades only wanted her because he was using her to get to his brother or strike a blow at Olympus? The more she studied the feeling blooming inside her, the more she pushed back down the negativity that had flooded her and coloured her view, and the more she replayed how Hades behaved around her—how he responded to her—the stronger she felt she was wrong about him. *Again.* She let out a frustrated sound as she completed the circle he had her constantly treading, finding herself back at the start where she felt sure he truly wanted her.

Someone in this world wanted her.

Not just to possess her or elevate themselves in Olympian society. Not to strike a blow at Olympus. Try as she might to convince herself to believe that was his plan, it wouldn't stick. She would have to be blind not to see the way he had looked at her at times, revealing something to her, something she felt sure he didn't want her to see.

He wanted her because he needed her. He desired her. He had looked as if his very happiness hinged upon the things she said or did, and when she had been too harsh in some foolish attempt to protect her heart, he had looked wounded.

It was thrilling.

Life-altering.

Her view of the world was no longer the same. If Hades took her back to Olympus tonight, she wouldn't be able to return to who she had been. Her home there would feel more like a prison than this tower.

She sighed.

And she might foolishly miss the god-king of the Underworld.

"Would he miss me?" she whispered, a sorrow welling inside her despite the fact she knew he would never let her go. She shook her head. "I am too swept up in him."

It was dangerous.

"Mother would think me mad." She chuckled and toyed with the water. "Wanting such a male… Do I truly desire him? Is he truly so wicked and evil?"

She didn't think he was. She looked at the room again, seeing beyond the walls to the forbidding black lands where there was no light. No life. Only death. Zeus had all but banished him here. She knew that much about his life. He had been given the Underworld and the duties that came with it, responsible for the souls of the dead and guiding them to their afterlife. He had been here since long before she had been born. She could only imagine what being in the Underworld for millennia had done to him.

He had a strong bond with this grim realm.

"If he is evil, then it is this place that made him so." She leaned her head back against the wall of the beaten gold tub and her brow furrowed. "But I have seen light in him. Flickers of it. He loves that terrifying beast as if it is… his pet. It is his pet. I was right about that."

She'd had a cat once, when she had been young, and she had loved it with all her heart, but one day her mother had ordered it gone from the house and her heart had broken. She had screamed, and begged, and sobbed. Her mother had taken her only companion away despite her protests and how upset she was.

Persephone smiled. "I have the feeling that if someone tried to take Hades's pet away, he might destroy them."

Her smile faltered.

"And what would he do if someone tried to take me?"

His reaction to what she had said to him had been fierce and terrible, shaking the entire realm.

She sank deeper into the water, so it came close to her lips.

"Does he want me that badly? Desire me that much?" She already knew the answers to those questions. His reaction had left no room in her head for doubt. Hades wanted her. But why? She frowned at her knees, her certainty wavering again, the doubts creeping back in to darken her mind and her heart, and then chuckled. "He does not want me in order to elevate his place in society, that is for certain. Making me his queen would only lower it. Am I truly just a pawn in his game… or something more?"

She silently chastised herself for being so gloomy, allowing those barbs that had hooked her to pull her back towards the mire. She hated how easily her past tore her down, how she constantly felt worthless, and found it difficult to believe someone could believe her beautiful or want her.

Hades had implied he found her beautiful.

She warmed at that, recalling the look that had been in his eyes. A look that had made her *feel* beautiful. Seen. Desired.

Persephone focused on that instead of the cold voices at the back of her mind, shutting them out and denying them. Those voices from her past were the reason she found it so hard to accept that someone like Hades might actually want her and she might be more than just a pawn to him. Her mother's voice. The constant criticism. The decisions made for her. All of it had ripped apart whatever confidence and self-worth she had from a young age, and she was tired of it. She was tired of feeling useless. Worthless.

No more.

Everything changed right now.

Right here.

From this point forwards, she wouldn't let her mother influence her and she would stand tall and be bold, and be confident.

Persephone tipped her chin up, that confidence already wavering as doubt crept in.

To shut it out, she focused on Hades instead of herself, intending to continue piecing together the puzzle to find the answer to that question.

The first thing that came to her was the feel of his breath on her nape. His strong hands on her shoulders and throat. The scent and heat of him as he pressed close to her back.

His whispered warning not to provoke him.

She shivered.

"But I like to provoke him."

Those words left her lips unbidden and her eyes widened as she felt the truth of them. She sat up in the bath.

"I do like to provoke him. No, not provoke. Tease, perhaps. I like the way he reacts to me. It makes me feel… seen." Her mood faltered and she held her knees, resting her chin on them.

She huffed a moment later and shoved her sorrow aside, refusing to wallow in self-pity. She sat up again and then sank back into the bath, not caring that some of the water splashed over the sides of it. It rocked around her, tiny waves that made it look like a stormy ocean. She felt that storm inside her, a tempest of emotions that held her in its grasp, shaking her to her core and refusing to calm. His fault. He had done this to her. From the very moment she had set eyes on him, she had felt as if something fundamental had changed within her.

Or something had awoken.

Was this how other females felt when they encountered males they found attractive?

She had overheard her servants and even other goddesses talk of desire and wanting, and their sexual experiences, but she had never experienced any of that for herself before Hades. There was something darkly alluring about him and whenever he was near—whenever he was looking at her—an ache built in her body, one that slowly stole her focus and made her feel hazy.

And lustful.

She desired Hades.

She wanted him.

Not just want. A chill swept through her as she realised something. She *needed* him.

What would she do if someone took Hades from her? Her fingers curled into fists. She would fight. She would rage. She would harness every drop of her power and use it to take him back.

Her eyes slowly widened. She wasn't merely on dangerous ground. She was deep in the quicksand, rapidly sinking beyond her depth. Hades was no mere man. He was no minor god. He was legendary. A king. A ruler of an entire realm. She had no place believing she could be his wife.

His queen.

She shook her head, dislodging those thoughts. She was just caught up in her captor, and maybe she wanted to rebel a little. It seemed like a reasonable excuse for the way her body was heating and that wicked ache was building inside her, making her breasts feel heavy and the apex of her thighs tingle. She wanted to rebel against her mother and what better way was there than to seduce the dark god-king of the Underworld?

"Seduce?" She swallowed and gave another hard shake of her head, but that word remained lodged in it, the wicked images it conjured turning the heat in her veins into an inferno.

One that had her fingers tracing down from her neck to the valley between her aching breasts.

Could she seduce Hades?

Not surrender to him, but seduce him?

He would steal control and take all of her. It would be too dangerous. He was too dark, turned too easily, and thought he could take what he wanted without any regard for what she wanted. He was too used to being a king—a ruler—issuing orders and having people obey.

He would do the same with her.

She didn't want that.

She didn't want to be another possession to him, or another subordinate. She wanted to be more. Did Hades even know what he wanted when he said she was his queen? Did he simply desire one because his brothers had theirs, because he thought taking her from Olympus would strike a blow at his brother, or did he want one because he recognised that he was lonely? In either case, did he want her to be his queen because he felt she could serve him well, or because he felt something for her?

She rubbed her head, trying to stave off a headache. If he just wanted a queen, then he could find another for the position. If he wanted her—truly wanted her—then he was going to have to work for her heart and she wasn't going to make it easy.

He would need to change and learn to control his darkness.

She wasn't sure that would be easy for him. This world of darkness had seeped into his soul to blacken it, transforming him into a male everyone feared, one who was quick to rage and thought everyone should obey him. His soldiers respected him, but it was done out of fear. People prayed to him, but it wasn't done with love—but fear.

Everyone feared Hades.

Except her.

She had seen past the veil, through his mask to the other side. She had glimpsed his pain. His loneliness. It echoed the one inside her. She would draw that pain up, would ease that loneliness, and show him that he wasn't alone and he wasn't unloved, and that there was someone in this world who understood him and didn't fear him. There was someone in this world who could see past the stories told about him to the male he really was.

She had never felt useful before, had never felt anyone would want her help, or that she could even really help someone. Everyone always ended up looking to her mother instead of her.

But she felt she could help Hades.

And she wanted to help him.

She *would* help him.

It wasn't going to be easy. It would be dangerous and a battle she might lose, but for the first time in her life, she was going to fight.

Because her heart whispered Hades might be worth it.

What would he be like tonight at dinner? The almost-gentle male or the darkly demanding one?

Her finger drifted lower as the ache built and she couldn't stop herself from imagining his breath against her nape, his mouth close to her ear, and his hands caressing her flesh. She tried to curb her desire, but he wouldn't leave her mind, and a mischievous part of her whispered that it would be better to face Hades with her lusts sated so he couldn't see the heat of them in her eyes and act upon them.

Her cheeks flamed at the thought of touching herself—flaring hotter than the sun as she thought about touching herself while thinking of him—but curiosity had her finger skimming lower and lower.

She had never felt pleasure before, even by her own hand. She had never felt the heat of desire, so she had never really thought about exploring her own body. But now she was curious and aroused, and very alone. She glanced around, poking her head over the sides of the tub to make sure that was still the case, and her thoughts turned even more wicked.

What if Hades returned and caught her pleasuring herself?

What would he do?

Her eyes slipped shut and she imagined him striding towards her, a stricken and hungry look on his face, his blue eyes wide as he watched her hands. She cupped her breasts, feeling the weight of them, and stifled the cry that wanted to leave her lips as she brushed her hard nipples. Sparks shot through her body, like tiny bolts of lightning, and she did it again, a gasp leaving her as they grew more intense. By the gods! She arched her spine and her hands became Hades's hands, the side of the tub behind her becoming the hard planes of his chest. She moaned as he cupped her breasts, as he thumbed the peaks and dropped his lips to her throat, sending shivers dancing down her spine.

His fangs scraped her delicate skin and she shivered at the feel of them and the threat of them piercing her flesh, and arousal pulsed through her, powerful and shocking, at the thought of him biting her. She wanted it. It was wrong of her on so many levels, but she wanted his fangs in her throat, holding her in place as he explored her.

Persephone let her mind run wild, refusing to hold it back in this fantasy. Here she could do anything.

She took over from his hands, some bold part of her wanting to tease him, to torment him with the sight of her touching her own body when he couldn't. She trembled as she pinched her nipples, the apex of her thighs throbbing in response, and tiny sparks skittered through her. Her breaths quickened and she denied the fear and the feeling she shouldn't be doing this, surrendering to the desire instead and chasing her pleasure.

She skimmed her hand over the flat plane of her stomach and shunned the embarrassment that tried to scald her cheeks as she plunged it between her thighs. At the first brush of her fingers between her petals, she gasped and her spine arched, her breasts cresting the surface of the water. The cool air hardened her nipples, teasing them as if it was breath, and she clutched the edge of the bath with her free hand, gripping it as she stroked between her thighs.

Good gods.

Her breaths shortened, her mind growing hazy as she teased herself, fondling the tight bead. Waves of pleasure swept through her, rushing outwards to her hands and feet before rolling back towards her feminine core to gather there and feed the ache. It became a wild need as she pictured Hades looming over her, his blue gaze tracking her hands, his bare chest straining with each hard breath he pulled down as he watched her. She imagined locking eyes with him as she touched herself, stroking her slick heat and running her gaze down the honed perfection of his body to the hard length that jutted from between his thighs.

She wanted that.

She cried out as she pressed a finger into her sheath, pleasure rocking and shocking her as she imagined it to be his erection. Her head tipped back as need stole control, as she lost herself in her pursuit of release and thrust her fingers into her slick core. Her other hand slipped from the edge of the bath, her fingers grazing her nipples before a wicked need bloomed inside her, a desperate and wild one that had her hand dropping to join her other one.

Persephone flicked her fingers over her aroused nub as she plunged her fingers inside her.

And barely stifled the scream of pleasure that tore from her lips as her entire body shook and shuddered and her sheath spasmed, warmth and bliss spilling through her as she climaxed.

"Oh gods," she muttered, swept up in her release, each wave that hit her stronger than the last, unsure it would ever cease.

Imagined-Hades reached for her hands as she pulled her finger free, lifted it to his lips and sucked on the digit, tasting her, his eyes dark with arousal.

Persephone shuddered and sighed as she sank into the water, every inch of her sated and her mind foggy. She slowly smiled and savoured the ripples of bliss that continued to flow through her. Why hadn't she ever done that before?

No trace of embarrassment touched her cheeks as she thought about what she had just done. She revelled in it instead, feeling alive and warmed from head to toe, and incredibly eager to do it again. She had a lot of lost time to make up for. If the water hadn't been growing cold, she might have waited a while and done it again.

Although she didn't want to risk Hades walking in on her while she was in the bath.

Or did she?

Her cheeks did flame now. She would be dining with him later. This realm was tied to him somehow. What if he knew what she had done? Her eyes widened and she prayed to the Moirai that he wasn't aware of the things people did while in his realm. What if he didn't know but spotted it in her eyes when he saw her again?

What if she couldn't stop herself from being awkward around him and he asked what was wrong?

She grimaced.

What if by fantasising about him and touching herself to relieve the ache in the hope it would give her more control around him, she had only made things worse?

She had the terrible feeling she might find it harder rather than easier to control herself around him now.

Because a bold part of her wanted to know how it would feel if he was the one giving her pleasure.

CHAPTER 12

Hades had managed to stay away from the tower and Persephone for the entire day, a feat that had felt akin to torture. But it was a torture he deserved.

Again, he had come close to harming her. Only this time, he had managed to regain control in time and had left her rather than lashing out at her. It was progress, he supposed, and he would take that small victory over the darkness and use it to strengthen his hope that he could be near Persephone without hurting her.

He didn't want to hurt her.

Hades glanced down at his boots, sorrow washing through him, the surging wave of it so powerful that he couldn't hold it back. He hurt so many when the darkness had him in its grip. His heart ached and he idly rubbed the centre of his chest. His regrets were as deep and fathomless as that dark abyss that lived within him, and well deserved.

But if he hurt Persephone—truly hurt her—he wouldn't be able to live with the weight of regret and guilt it would cause, or the self-loathing.

Could he be near her without mention of other males or thoughts she could never want him clouding his mind and giving the darkness an opportunity to seize him?

Hades wasn't sure.

He lifted his head and gazed at the tower, doubt swirling together with hope. There was only one way to find out the answer to that question. He would go to her as planned and face his fears, and if the darkness grew to strong for him to control, he would somehow find the strength to leave again.

And would stay away from her until he was certain he could control it when he was near her.

A voice at the back of his mind warned that overcoming the darkness alone would take too much time. Could he live without seeing Persephone for that long?

Hades wasn't sure.

Today had been torturous and he had only needed to occupy himself for the better part of a day.

He had busied himself with dealing with the disquiet in the Elysian Fields, and reading the reports from the legions, burying himself in work and avoiding any summons to go to Tartarus, entrusting the commander there could handle the situation. If he had gone to Tartarus, the malevolence and anger rooted in that place would have roused the darkness, undoing all his hard work to keep it in check.

When he had returned to his chambers, he had been accosted by his head servant, the female he had sent to deal with Persephone. She had meekly informed him of the things his queen had asked about, admitting she had taught her the meaning of two words of the language of the Underworld, and repeating several times that she hadn't answered her questions about the location of the gate to Olympus.

His little queen was curious, and rather than angering him, it pleased him in a way. She wanted to know more about his realm, and was wise enough to know learning the language of it would be to her advantage.

When his servant had asked whether she should remain mute around Persephone, Hades had given her leave to answer his queen's questions—within reason. She was not to tell Persephone of the gate. Hades couldn't risk her knowing its location if she escaped.

He had also told her to only reveal the meaning of every other word she asked about, keeping her in the dark to a degree.

Some foolish part of him hoping Persephone would turn to him for instruction instead.

In the last hour of his day, his ability to focus had utterly failed him and he had ended up standing on the paved area that surrounded all sides of his black temple, positioned between two of the immense fluted columns that supported the overhanging roof, staring at the tower.

Wondering if he really could vanquish the darkness.

Wondering what Persephone was doing.

Was she waiting for him?

He felt he was waiting for her.

He felt he had been waiting for her his entire life.

"My god-king." A blonde female stopped near him and he didn't take his eyes off the tower.

"You are to deliver my usual dinner to the tower but with enough for two. I will be dining there tonight." His voice was steady despite the nerves that trickled through him, or was that excitement?

When had he last dined with someone?

He felt the servant's surprise and glowered at her, and she bowed her head and hurried away from him. It was unusual that he would have a guest for dinner, and that he wouldn't be taking it in his grand dining hall, but it wasn't the servant's place to silently comment upon it. He needed to have words with her superior, ensuring it wouldn't happen again.

Hades pivoted on his heel, his heavy cloak whirling outwards with the sharp action, and strode into his chambers, slamming the wooden doors behind him. He didn't stop until he was at the large bed positioned against the opposite wall and gazing down at the outfit he had carefully selected.

He hadn't failed to notice that Persephone had been more at ease around him when she had seen him without his armour, or that flicker of heat that had darkened her eyes as she had taken him in, her leisurely once over making him feel she had been stripping him in her mind.

So, he had chosen another of his tunics, one that was even more form-fitting, and a pair of buttery soft black leather trousers, hoping the former would entice her into gazing upon his body and the latter would make her want to touch it.

Hades stripped down to nothing, casting his clothes aside, and pulled on the trousers, lacing them over his crotch. He tugged on the tunic and buttoned it, and then stepped back into his boots and fastened them.

He looked himself over and then crossed the room to the full-length mirror near a side table and inspected his appearance. The outfit suited him, and revealed his physique. He tugged the hem of the tunic down over his thighs, his fingers shaking. He brought one hand up before him and glared at them. Flicked them. He had no reason to be nervous.

Telling himself that didn't stop him from feeling it.

It felt as if a lot rested on tonight, and the closer he came to seeing Persephone again, the worse his nerves became.

He reached for the purple glass bottle on the side table, uncorking it and swigging the ambrosia it contained. A warm haze rolled through him as it slid down his throat and heated his stomach.

Drinking might not be wise, but each sip of ambrosia he'd had since returning to his chambers had taken the edge off his mood and chased away his nerves, and was even helping to mellow him out. He took another swig, savouring its effects and how the darkness he could feel lurking within him grew quieter, and then tipped the bottle away from him and stared at it.

He wouldn't drink too much. Just a sip now and then.

He needed to keep the darkness subdued and his nerves at bay if he was going to make it through this evening without messing up. He wanted to be relaxed around Persephone, not constantly on edge, waiting to make a mistake or grow dark and frighten her.

He wanted to spend one visit with her without scaring her, if only so he could prove to himself that it could be done.

He needed to know he could be with her and remain in control.

Needed that so badly he lifted the bottle to his lips and took another draught.

Proving he could be a gentleman to both himself and Persephone was important. Vital.

He studied his appearance again. Preened the wild strands of his short black hair and neatened it so the sharp spikes of his crown stood out. He frowned at it and debated whether to take it off or leave it on.

Hades lifted the semi-circular crown off his head. He did look less daunting without it. It had been many centuries since he had been around others without is crown, but if it would make him appear less frightening, he would go without it.

Tonight was all about showing Persephone that he could be as handsome and charming as any Olympian male.

Hades set his crown down on the side table, blew out his breath and stalked out of the temple, heading for the tower. The closer he came to it, the more his cursed nerves rose, and he began to regret leaving his crown behind. And his armour. He felt oddly bare without them. Vulnerable.

Which irritated him.

He tipped his chin up and walked with more pride, and courage, because no slip of a female was going to make him feel weak and vulnerable, or nervous. He was none of those things.

He was all of them.

He huffed, shoved the door of the tower open, and slammed it behind him. A faint note of lilies greeted him, and he looked back at the door and pressed his hand to the wood. There were subtle scratches on it. Nail marks. His fingertips tightened against the wood. His queen had tried to escape him again. Each time he found marks on the door, he repaired them, using his connection to his realm at great cost to his strength. It was necessary though. He was keeping track of her efforts, that same foolish part of him that wanted her to turn to him for instruction in learning the language of the Underworld wanting her to stop trying to leave him, showing him that she wanted to be his.

It wasn't going to happen.

Hades healed the wood and pivoted away from the door, and stormed up the stairs, crushing the weakness that infested him and purging it. He was strong. The strongest and most powerful god there was. He had no reason to fear a goddess who had her powers bound.

Shadows snaked around his boots and the ones cast by the flickering blue torches mounted on the walls gathered to him.

He clenched his fists and paused on the curving staircase, sucking down a breath to steady himself and purge the darkness, and his anger. He needed to appear gentle—to *be* gentle. If he approached her like this, she would grow defensive again and would view him as a monster. He pulled down another breath, seeking calm amidst the riotous storm of his emotions.

When he felt sure he was back in control and his darkness was subdued, he continued to the top of the tower and stepped into the room.

His anger flared back up again as his gaze landed on Persephone where she leaned in the doorway of the balcony.

Wearing her green dress.

"I gave you a gown to wear," he growled as he stalked towards her.

She merely glanced over her shoulder at the black-and-gold dress where it was spread out on the bed, untouched, and then sighed. "Black is for mourning. Since the only thing I am mourning is my freedom, I do not feel inclined to wear it. Besides… I asked for a *green* dress to replace the one you ruined."

This was not a good start. She was already on the defensive, and he could hardly blame her when he had barked at her the moment he had stepped into the room.

Hades curled his fingers into tight fists and clenched them as he fought to remain calm. Gentle. When all he wanted to do was strip her and make her wear the dress he had fashioned for her, one that would reveal her tempting curves. Instead of forcing her to wear it, he strode to the bed and eased onto it, feigning calm and pretending he was relaxed when he was far from those two things.

When she glared at him, her green eyes ablaze with irritation he had no doubt caused by treating her bed as if it was his own and doing as he pleased, he stroked the area beside him.

"Come, my queen," he purred, liking the idea of her sitting with him far too much—so much he let it addle his mind and loosen his tongue.

Another mistake.

Her jaw set in a hard line and she scoffed. "No. I am more than happy where I am, my god-king Hades."

The anger that had been rising inside him, stoked by her refusal, fell away as his mind latched onto what she had called him, just as it had the last time she had spoken of him in such a manner.

As *her* Hades.

As if he belonged to her.

It was a curious feeling that flowed through him whenever she spoke like that, making him feel that he was hers. It wasn't quite pleasure. Not the kind he had sought long ago anyway. It didn't satisfy his body. He frowned as it struck him.

It satisfied his heart.

It pleased that part of him.

And it made something else dawn on him too. He wanted to be hers. He wanted her to say what she had just uttered and mean it with all her heart. He wanted her to stake a claim on him and to make him belong to her and her alone.

He needed that so fiercely that it made him restless, had his mind whirling with ways he could make her desire and need him in the way he desired and needed her.

"Sit." He patted the bed again, half lost in his thoughts still.

She folded her arms across her chest, her emerald eyes narrowing on his in a challenge as her delectable lips flattened in a mulish line. "No."

Her refusal irked him, tainting his pleasing thoughts of making her wild for him, and he glowered at her.

"Many females in this world would be overjoyed to sit with me." He tasted the lie in those words, and cursed the doubt that pierced his heart like an icy needle to chill the warmth she had stoked in it by calling him hers.

She arched a fine dark red eyebrow at him.

"Then summon one of them if you desire company," she bit out.

"I desire your company," he growled and before he could slam a lid on it, the darkness growled at him to make her sit with him, as restless with a need to make that happen as he was, and his shadows had ripped from the stone floor and snapped around her wrist.

She shrieked as they pulled her to him, onto the bed right beside him, so close her sweet scent of lilies teased his senses and the feel of her near him addled his mind more than the ambrosia. When he realised what he had done, he was quick to release her from his shadows. She scooted backwards, away from him, and he reacted on instinct, lunging for her wrist and locking his hand around it to stop her from leaving.

He needed her to stay.

He wanted her close to him.

Wide emerald eyes leaped from his hand to meet his.

The feel of her trembling beneath his touch was a dagger in his chest, punching so deep it pierced the darkness and scattered the shadows. He lowered his gaze to her delicate arm and his hand that tightly gripped it. Another mistake. His biggest one yet.

He struggled to convince himself to release her, had to wage war against his own body and that powerful need to keep her near him. The fierce way she shook gave him the strength to defeat that need, to loosen his grip and release her. She was quick to snatch her arm away and clutch her wrist to her chest. She rubbed it as she shuffled away from him, her eyes never leaving him.

Wary. Frightened.

Her fear was a potent drug, but not in the way fear was when he sensed it in others. When Hades felt it in her, he was overcome with a powerful need to calm her and ease her fears.

To protect her.

He almost chuckled at that, the irony of it all shredding his hope again. He could hardly ease her fears and calm her when he was the cause of them. He could protect her, but he would have to protect her from himself.

Hades looked at her, watching as she rubbed at her reddened wrist, her head bent and eyes lowered as she came to her feet on the other side of the bed.

"I am sorry," he murmured, not hiding his regret from her, or his apology by speaking a language she didn't understand. She deserved to hear how deeply he regretted his actions, and he hoped she might also hear that he hadn't meant to hurt and frighten her. It had been a momentary loss of control.

Her green gaze lifted to him, soft and without a trace of fear in it now. Or hardness. If she lashed out at him, if she wanted to strike at him out of anger, he wouldn't fight back. He would take whatever punishment she gave him.

But rather than striking him verbally or physically as he expected, she heaved a long sigh and drifted away from him. Turning her back on him.

And that punishment was far too harsh.

He couldn't bear it.

Hades stared at her back, yearning for her to turn so he could see her face, so he could bathe in her beauty and her warmth, and so he would know he hadn't messed everything up.

He sat up more on the bed, leaning towards her slightly, unsure what to do. Which was a strange predicament to be in. He always knew what to do.

But not this time.

He wanted Persephone to look at him, to grace him with her company, and he wasn't sure how to make that happen. He looked at the dress she had discarded, deeply aware now that it had been another mistake. His queen was light and life. She was brightness and colour. She was right. A black dress wasn't suitable for her.

"I should have given you a green dress as you requested," he murmured, unaware he had said it aloud until she turned a surprised look on him.

Her eyes slowly narrowed on him as she canted her head. "You are awfully talkative tonight."

Her gaze was both inquisitive and suspicious, as if she believed he was up to something, which he was, but that wasn't the reason he was feeling rather congenial. An idea struck him like a thunderbolt—a way of making her relax.

And it might help him too.

Hades held his left hand out and focused, concealing the effort it took to summon the violet hexagonal bottle he had left in his chambers.

When it appeared in his hand, she frowned again.

"Is that ambrosia?" She sounded shocked, and even more suspicious now.

Hades made himself comfortable on her pillows, stacking them up behind his back and fighting the effect her scent had on his body, how it ravaged his control and had him aching to touch her again, to kiss her. He pulled the stopper out of the bottle and offered it to her.

"Take a sip and find out," he husked.

CHAPTER 13

Persephone's cheeks pinkened for a heartbeat before she covered her blush by pulling a face and waving him away as she turned to face the balcony again.

No matter. Hades wouldn't be discouraged. She could snap and snarl at him all she wanted tonight, but he was cataloguing her cues, observing her closely enough to spot the tells that gave her feelings away. She had been tempted to taste the ambrosia.

And pleased he was being talkative rather than going straight for baring his fangs and ordering her around.

She had the ambrosia to thank for that.

He sipped from the bottle, savouring the sweet burn of the liquor that kept the edge off his mood and stopped the darkness in its tracks, freeing him to be *gentle* with her. He was coming to hate that word. He held back a sigh. Needs must though. Zeus had tricked him into abducting her and now Hades needed to repair the damage his brother had done, and he couldn't do that without tempering his darker side. He also couldn't do it without setting aside the king in him and embracing the man.

He had gleaned a few things from their time together.

Persephone didn't want a king who would rule her. She wanted a male who would love her. Cherish her. Do anything for her. He needed to make her see that he could be that man. He wasn't as incapable of feeling as people made him out to be, and he wasn't a monster who thrived on bloodshed and death.

Hades stared at her.

Not anymore at least.

He had been attempting to change himself for the better, so he would please her, and she had already changed him. He hadn't woken in a rage since he had taken her. He hadn't lashed out at his citizens for no reason. In fact, looking back on the things he had done to those in his care filled him with immeasurable guilt.

Worse so than usual.

Because of her.

He stared at her, feeling to the very pit of his dark soul that she was responsible—that she was a light that was bathing that soul to chase the shadows out of it and free him from their grip.

"What are you thinking while you stare at me?" she whispered with a fearful glance over her shoulder.

Not fear of him. Again, she feared what he might say and already her barriers were coming up. Why did she do that?

"I am wondering who hurt my beautiful queen so much that she cannot bear to hear what others think of her." He sat up, the ambrosia forgotten as he frowned at her and seethed with a need to find whoever had hurt her and cut them down, to make them pay for the invisible wounds they had inflicted upon her.

She was quick to look away again, her shoulders going rigid, making him feel he had pushed too far and ruined everything. He had wanted her to be more talkative and speak about herself, and now she would fall mute and distant again.

"Persephone," he murmured and her shoulders managed to tighten further, her fingertips suddenly pressing hard into her arm. Because he had spoken her name, and she didn't like it? A sense of hopelessness tried to claim ground within him and he let what he had wanted to say fall away, growing mute in her place.

But then she shyly glanced over her shoulder at him, a need in her eyes that he could name.

She wanted him to continue and distract her from whatever sombre thoughts were weighing her down.

He cleared his throat and tried to think of something to say that would please her and draw her out from behind her barriers, and almost smiled when he settled upon a topic he knew would do the trick.

"The forest where we met was enchanting. Was it your creation?" He kept his gaze on her face as he asked that, studying it for signs he was reaching her and she was pleased by his choice of subject, and the praise he had laced into his words.

She nodded and stroked her arm, her air growing awkward, and he felt sure she wouldn't speak and would continue to torment him by not letting him hear her sweet voice, but then her lips parted.

"Do not tell anyone about it." Her words were more of a plea than an order, slipping from her laced with fear, something he gathered didn't please her because her expression hardened and she glowered at him. "I mean it."

"Ordering me around again? My queen is most certainly bossy." Hades ran his fingers through his hair and leaned into the pillows, weathering the withering look she cast him.

Or was it another suspicious one?

He was beginning to believe she found this side of him more unsettling than when the darkness had him in its grip. Because he was easier for her to deal with then? She could draw a line between them and deny that spark of attraction that flared in her eyes from time to time, keeping him at arm's length because a sweet, gentle goddess of Olympus shouldn't want a monster for a husband.

But he wasn't a monster right now.

And he found it unsettling too, but also kind of *nice*.

His entire day hadn't been consumed with bloodshed and violence, and a seething endless hunger for both. He had walked the grounds and talked with Cerberus. He had gone over the rosters and reports without slipping into a rage over any unrest in his realm. He had even filled a few hours reading a book.

When was the last time he had done that?

He looked down at himself. When was the last time he had worn anything other than his armour?

Too long ago. So long ago that his mood soured as he thought about it and he shoved his mind back on track, diverting it away from himself and back to her.

He didn't mean it to, but his response to her order came out gruff. "I would not tell anyone. Who would listen to me if I did?"

She went rigid again.

"Some of the goddesses and gods in Olympus are my friends," she snapped, tugging a frown from him because he wasn't sure what had caused such an outburst. Was it an attempt to make him jealous? He was about to ask her when her face slackened and her eyes widened again, and she averted her gaze, refusing to look at him. She muttered beneath her breath, "He did not mean it like that."

He caught it and frowned as he filed it away and resisted the temptation to bring up the fact she believed no one would listen to him if he told them of her secret forest because no one was interested in hearing about her.

She was right, and he hadn't meant it like that. He had meant no one would listen to him. No one in Olympus ever did. Everyone there drew a line between them, but in a different way to his Persephone. The line between him and the Olympians divided them entirely and without condition, and what was on their side was their business alone, and what was on his was his business alone.

And Hades was fine with that.

He pushed it to one side as he grew agitated, black thoughts of the Olympians and the things they had done or said to him in the past clouding his mind, rousing the darkness and bringing it back to the fore. He tamped it down with another sip of ambrosia, clinging to his almost-good mood, and focused back on Persephone and his desire to know more about her.

Because he wasn't the only one feeling talkative tonight.

He would send some of his finest men to visit Olympus and ask more about her, uncovering the reason she felt so alone. He shook his head slightly. No, he would tease it out of her. It would be far more pleasing to find out about her from herself and might bring them closer, scuffing that line she wanted to keep between them and making her see that he did have a heart and he could care about someone.

He was starting to suspect he already cared a great deal about her.

That he was falling for her.

His black eyebrows knitted. Or had he already fallen?

He hadn't felt the same from the second he had set eyes on her, and that unsteady feeling was only growing worse, filling him with needs only she could satisfy. Not physical needs, but emotional ones.

The silence stretching between them became oppressive, and he wanted to take her mind off her slip, so he said, "How long did it take you to create the forest?"

She looked back at him again. "Years."

"How large is it?" He sipped the ambrosia. "It seemed vast."

She shrugged. "I am not sure. I found a dreary spot of desolate land and wanted to bring it to life and make it my own, and each time I visit, I add another tree."

He didn't miss the glance she gave out of the door as she said 'desolate land' or how her expression pinched.

Thanks to the ambrosia, he was feeling kind enough to let her slight tumble from his shoulders rather than hit its mark. If he tried to look at his realm from her perspective, he might even admit it was desolate.

But he wouldn't.

This realm was his and it was part of him, and he loved it as it was. Hades pulled a face at the ambrosia. Perhaps he was drinking too much. He was beginning to sound like a sentimental fool.

"Then you must have been visiting it frequently and for decades, because even if I allow for the trees spreading naturally, there had to be close to ten thousand in that forest." He eyed her closely as she frowned over her shoulder at him.

What had made her want to build a place of her own, so far away from Olympus? Most gods and goddesses he knew were happy in that city, lounging around in their temples. Doing nothing.

"I added many at first," she bit out, as if that accounted for the number of trees he had sensed in her woods. "A thousand at least."

He angled his head and continued studying her. "You have that much power?"

She pivoted to face him and hit him with a hard look. "Yes, I have that much power! Release the hold you have on it and I will show you how much power I have."

He had hit a nerve again. He filed it away. His little goddess didn't like people judging her power. Which made him feel others had belittled it in the past. Which made him angry. Shadows curled around his arms, snaking towards the bottle of ambrosia, but rather than taking a swig to calm the darkness, he set the bottle aside on the stone floor and sat up, the whole of his focus on his queen.

"Persephone," he husked and held his left hand out to her, willing her to cross the line she had placed between them and take it and show him that this wasn't a futile endeavour and she could come to want him.

Maybe even love him.

When she remained where she was, denying his need to soothe her hurt, he curled his fingers into a fist and withdrew it. The shadows closed over it, their tender caress a comfort to him, and he glared at his hand as he gathered the words, aware he needed to keep them soft and the sort her Olympian males would employ in a moment like this.

But he couldn't.

Because he couldn't stand by and allow others to belittle her, to make her feel she was weak and of little consequence. Zeus had done that to him once, and it had moulded him into a dark male, one who sought to show his might at every opportunity, who refused to allow others to see any trace of softness or warmth. He had spent millennia striving to be the strongest, the most powerful.

The most feared.

"What are you thinking?" she whispered and he lifted his gaze to her, aching to know if she truly desired an answer to that question or whether she had asked it because she felt it was the polite thing to do.

Her green eyes held his, genuine curiosity in them, together with a trace of softness that tugged him into speaking and saying what was on his mind, although he held back the worst of it and focused on her instead.

"I am thinking you should not let others mould you with their words, transforming you into something you are not. I saw your creation, Persephone. I saw your power, and it was... beautiful."

She looked away from him, turning her cheek to him, and he swore tears lined her lashes before she blinked them away.

Did his words mean that much to her?

Would she have reacted this way if any other male had said them?

"What are you thinking?" he murmured, a need to know her thoughts filling him, a desire to know if they were about him. He frowned at what he was doing. The last time he had cared about someone's opinion of him, it had ended with him hurt and caged in this dark world, all of the light stolen away from him.

Hades stared at Persephone.

She was light.

She was life.

And he found himself leaning towards her as a flower would, thirsty for her light, craving more of it, as if she was a source of life for him.

"I am thinking you have had too much ambrosia." Those teasing words leaving her lips, spoken in a light tone, one that was warm and familiar, had him casting a black look at the violet bottle.

"I was thinking the same." He huffed at it and how deeply it had affected him, chastising himself for taking too much and allowing it to addle his mind. Right now, he didn't feel like a god-king, much less a god-king of the Underworld.

Persephone smiled, her soft lips curling into a faint one that lasted only a moment before she caught herself, but the damage was done.

It hit him in the chest like a spear, lancing his heart.

"By the gods, you are beautiful," he uttered in the language of the Underworld, an attempt to keep his feelings concealed from her that he feared had failed as the words came out soft and almost breathless.

A crinkle formed between her scarlet eyebrows and her green gaze grew shrewd again. She was trying to understand the language, picking out the words and probably filing them away to ask his servants about later.

"What does that mean?" She drifted a few steps towards him, leaving the balcony behind, and that handful of steps and her desire to learn from him instead felt like a victory to him. He had tried to draw her towards him all night, and she had resisted. If he had known he only had to pique her curiosity by speaking the tongue of his realm, he would have been speaking it from the moment he set foot in the room. She glowered at him. "You spoke like that before. It is not a language I know."

"Ask me to teach it to you and I might just be foolish enough to do it, little queen," he murmured in the tongue of his realm as his gaze drifted over her, taking in how strikingly lovely she was when she was facing him without fear, staring him down and looking ready to plant her hands on her hips and put him in his place. Odd that he almost liked the thought of her ordering him around. He nearly smiled too. "I tell you that you are beautiful in this tongue and you cannot rebuff me, for you do not understand these words that pour from some deep place within me, one that had been buried in darkness before your sweet voice caressed my ears and your beauty enchanted my soul."

Some part of him expected her to pick him up on the words he had used that she had learned from his servant, but instead she attempted a ruse, as if his servant wouldn't have immediately informed him of her questions and what had transpired between them. His little queen was devious, or at least thought she was. She hoped to fool him into telling her more about his language, when all she had to do was ask him to teach her it.

Her lips flattened. "It is not fair that you speak in a tongue I cannot understand. If you want to be cruel to me, then you can leave."

She turned her back on him again and tipped her chin up.

He growled as she snatched her beauty from him, her punishment cutting him deeply, but not as deeply as her order to leave. He vaulted from the bed and was across the room in an instant, his hands closing over her shoulders as her heat enveloped him and her scent of lilies calmed him.

Warmed him.

Hades stilled and pulled down a breath to steady himself as he realised how close he was to her now, and felt the softness of her skin beneath his callused palms. She was trembling. Fear. She feared him again. Or she feared something perhaps.

He gazed at her exposed nape and frowned as he lifted his hand to her crimson hair. It was damp, fashioned into a plait that circled her head like a crown. Her fair skin was clean and almost as alluring as the thought she had bathed before he had arrived. He wanted to ask her about that, if only to see the blush that would stain her cheeks.

Hades almost scoffed aloud at that.

If her cheeks reddened, it would be with anger before she ruthlessly compared him to males far more worthy of her attention.

He didn't want that, but some reckless, desperate part of him desired to see if she would indeed blush over something he said, overruling the sensible one that said to remain silent on the subject.

Hades dropped his head and murmured against her skin, "Did you bathe nude?"

She tensed and whirled out of his grasp, coming to face him, her luminous green eyes enormous.

And filled with banked heat.

Her mouth flapped open and then closed, and her brow furrowed, and her heartbeat ticked a fast rhythm in the tempting column of her throat, making his lips itch with a desire to trace the line of it and feel that fluttering pulse against them.

A reaction he had caused.

But not quite the one he wanted.

He thought for a moment she would remain in control and deny his dark desires to see the effect he had on her, and then a hint of rose climbed her cheeks and she didn't know where to look. Her gaze left him, darting everywhere as it avoided him.

After a few seconds of struggling, she finally found her footing and snapped, "It is none of your business."

She had bathed nude.

"By the gods," he uttered in their common tongue this time as he turned towards the beaten gold bath and scrubbed a hand down his face as his shaft swelled at the image of her in it, the milky blue water barely concealing her naked curves. "You shall be the death of me."

He looked back at her. A mistake. His gaze instantly dropped to her body, hungrily raking over those curves, his mind running amok and taunting him with fantasies of stepping up to her and seizing her waist in his hands to pin her to the wall so he could take his fill of her and sate this need that was only growing more and more agonising each day. The way her small hands balled into fists had him pulling back on the reins of his desire, driving awareness through him. If he attempted to kiss her, he would frighten her and would undo all his hard work. He had to be patient.

He had to make her want him so fiercely that she would readily submit to him.

The darkening stain on her cheeks and the flare of heat in her eyes said the reward for his patience would be sweeter than ambrosia. It would be bliss. He needed to remain strong and deny the darkness that goaded him into seizing what he wanted and taking it right now. He was a god-king. She should admire and want to please him, as everyone in his realm did. She should be on her knees, begging for his aching cock.

Hades growled and slammed a lid on that dark desire, denying it.

Because he didn't want her subservient. He didn't want her to be like every other female in his kingdom. He didn't want anything they did to be born of a sense of duty, something she did because it was the way of things and those lower than a god-king were merely there to serve him in any way he wanted. He wanted more than her body.

He turned away from her.

He wanted her heart.

Hades strode away from her before he did something he would regret, each step he placed between them tearing at him. He reached the bed and eased back onto it, and was uncorking the bottle of ambrosia to take the edge off again and dull his needs when the servants arrived with the food.

Four females set the wide trays of roasted meats, vegetables, cheese and fruits down onto the table. The fifth placed a carafe of wine down together with two cups. They each bowed as they left, and when he heard the tower door close far below him, he gestured to the food.

"Eat," he growled and then sipped the ambrosia. "You must be hungry."

Persephone eyed the food as suspiciously as she had eyed him during their time together, looking between the trays and him. He had to be imagining that flare of heat in her gaze whenever it brushed over him. He put it down to the ambrosia as he waited to see what she would do.

Willing her to taste the food.

Take the bait.

If she ate food of his realm, she would never be able to leave.

She would be forever tied to him.

CHAPTER 14

Hades knew.

Persephone had feared he would, but he had all but confirmed it when he had asked about her bath and whether she had been nude. Her cheeks flushed all over again, every inch of her heating and a wicked ache forming between her thighs as she thought about what she had done in the bath.

A bath that was still in the room with them.

Hades's calculating blue gaze landed on her again, searing her, and she diligently kept hers off him, afraid of what he might see if their eyes locked. She was just being foolish. There was no way for him to know what she had done and if he did know, she was sure he would have mentioned it rather than just asking whether she had bathed nude.

By the gods, she hadn't missed his reaction to her betraying blush though.

The way his lips had parted and his gaze had grown dark with desire, his pupils expanding to devour the blue of his irises, had roused her own needs, but it had been the flush of colour that had graced his sculpted cheeks that had made her tremble.

Again.

Had his thoughts been as wicked as hers had been when she had been in the bath?

As they had been when he had pulled her onto the bed next to him?

Being that close to him, breathing in his dark, spicy scent and feeling his heat, had almost wrecked her control and she'd had to tense and fist the sheets to stop herself from reaching out and taking hold of him.

Even now that ache to kiss him remained.

Burned through her.

Attempting to torch her fragile control.

She fought to stifle another wave of heat that rolled through her as she thought about what she had done while she had been thinking of him. Her fingers twitched and she balled them into fists, and Hades frowned down at them.

He moved away from her, allowing air to rush into her lungs again as the distance between them grew and his heat and scent no longer enveloped her. She remained where she was as he lounged on her bed again, battling for calm and control. She couldn't let her unruly desires get the better of her.

But she also couldn't help but wonder what it would feel like to be with a man.

With Hades.

Before he had walked into the room, she had resolved to learn more about him and to keep her distance while she did it. But the delectable sight of him had wreaked havoc on that resolve, flooding her with a need to be close to him, to trace her hands over his chest and discover whether it felt as hard as it looked in the fine fabric that hugged it. Her nerves had shot into overdrive, the realisation that she was alone with a man, something she had never experienced in Olympus, rattling her. She had been alone with Hades before, but this whole affair felt far more intimate, and she was finding it hard to trust herself around him.

She wanted to pounce on him.

Ached to kiss him.

If she did, he would take all of her. That hunger that had been in his eyes when he had pulled her onto the bed and when he had loomed before her just moments ago warned that he wouldn't stop at just a kiss.

Not this time.

Would he be a rough and forceful lover?

Or a gentle one?

Maybe he would flicker between the two, being rough and then gentle as his mood shifted.

Her entire body seemed to ignite at that thought, or maybe it was the fact her gaze landed on Hades's legs and his tunic had ridden up when he had sat down, revealing something startling.

And enticing.

She had never seen one before, but there was no mistaking the outline of his erection beneath the soft black leather of his trousers. She swallowed hard, her face flaming and blood thundering as she tried to drag her gaze away before he caught her staring. Had she done that?

Had the thought of her nude and bathing made him hard for her?

"Eat," Hades snarled, sounding more irritated than aroused, and then sipped the ambrosia. "You must be hungry."

She glanced between the food she hadn't even noticed arriving and him, her gaze lingering the longest on him, as if he was magnetic and she couldn't resist his pull. Heat blazed through her veins whenever her eyes landed on him, awareness of the fact he was primed for making love rousing images in her mind that were hard to deny and ignore.

Good gods, she was hungry.

Startlingly so.

But it wasn't the food she wanted to pounce on and devour.

It was Hades.

He was temptation incarnate as he lounged on her bed, his form-fitting tunic and trousers concealing nothing and revealing everything, and his black hair tousled and wild. She struggled to keep her eyes on his face as she looked at him, and noticed something.

He was waiting.

She looked back at the food, a suspicion whispering through her mind. His powers were vast and mostly unknown to her, but she had been pulling together the scraps of her knowledge of him since her bath, looking for clues that might stop her from falling into a trap. His wards were powerful and they prevented her from leaving the tower and inhibited her powers, but they could be broken.

She feared he might have other ways to keep her here permanently, without the need to cage her.

The fact he was watching her so intently as he waited to see if she would eat was a red flag waving wildly in her face. She eyed the food and the wine. If she ate it, would something happen to her?

Was it drugged?

Would it make her compliant, loosening her inhibitions until she couldn't hold back her desire?

She shook her head and turned her back on him, drifting to the balcony again. She had noticed more things about his realm in his absence. Including the dark orchard in the distance, just beyond the edge of her vision so she hadn't been able to make it out before. The trees were fuzzy, blending with the black lands, but she had spotted them when one of the volcanoes had thrown up great ribbons of lava on a thunderous boom that had shaken the tower and startled her.

Fruit.

Grown in this realm.

Persephone couldn't believe anything would grow in this black soil, in this darkness, but there it was. It had held her attention for close to two hours, fascinating her as she had mulled over what kind of fruit would grow in this place without light. She wanted to see it more closely, a deep yearning to touch those trees and feel the presence of nature and life around her again flooding her every time she so much as glanced at it.

Hades would never allow it.

The orchard was far beyond his temple, between it and a steep cliff that dropped off to the rear of the tower. She thought there might be a river of lava down there, because a constant glow emanated from within the canyon, casting amber light into the air and illuminating the cragged faces of the mountain range on the other side.

"What has your attention?" Hades's deep voice rolled over her, an edge of agitation in it.

He was displeased she wasn't paying attention to him and was content to stand here looking out at the view rather than admiring him. She wasn't going to apologise for being bad company. If he wanted a female to fawn over him and attend to his needs, he should have looked elsewhere. She was sure many of his servants would service their god-king's every desire.

A hot wave of anger surged through her, unwanted and sudden, as powerful as it had been when he had mentioned females before. It struck her out of nowhere, hitting her hard and fast and making her feel as if she was spinning and liable to topple as she realised something.

She didn't like the thought of Hades with another woman.

Persephone glared at him as his gaze scalded her back, keeping up appearances so he didn't see how shaken she was by her fierce reaction to that revelation. She had never been jealous before and she wasn't jealous now. This whole situation had her in a spin and she was out of her depth.

She glanced back at him again.

She had been feeling out of her depth from the moment she had set eyes on him.

And it was only getting worse.

He wasn't helping matters either. He was so different tonight, and while she wanted to blame the ambrosia, she was feeling honest with herself enough to admit that he had been different this morning too. He was changing.

Because he wanted her to accept him as her husband and this shift in his behaviour was just a way to ensure that happened, and that she succumbed to him?

Or was it because of her influence?

She almost laughed at her ridiculous thought that she had any influence on someone, especially him.

This change in him wasn't because of her. It was because he wanted her and rather than taking her by force, he had settled on breaking through her defences instead, an obvious attempt to make her more compliant so she would accept his advances and the new life he had laid out for her. He was trying to make his own life easier for himself. If she was compliant, then she wouldn't fight him. She would be a good and meek queen who would do his bidding rather than refuse him.

Hades stalked to the table, plucked a bunch of dark grapes and laid them on a silver platter, and took them with him to her bed, where he lounged on it again in a far too sexy and alluring manner, as if he belonged in it.

He set the platter on the covers beside him and crossed his feet at his ankles, his long legs stretched out before him. His fingers brushed through the wild strands of his onyx hair, something he had done more than once and had drawn her attention to it. Mostly because her fingers had itched to do that and know the feel of his hair beneath them, but partly because he wasn't wearing his crown tonight. Another attempt to soften her towards him and make himself appear more like any other man?

Another trick?

He sipped ambrosia from the violet bottle and then fed himself a grape, and then another. His searing blue gaze landed on her and then back on the grapes, and then her again.

"If you even think about suggesting I feed those to you, you will find the flat of my palm against your face again." She tipped her chin up and stared him down.

But moving to strike him would place her dangerously within his reach.

His profane lips curled into a hint of a breathtaking smile that had her pulse fluttering in her throat and heated her blood to an unbearable level.

By the gods, Hades shouldn't be allowed to smile.

It was devastating, tearing down her defences as quickly as she could shore them up to stop him from seeing the effect he had on her with only a ghost of a smile. If a real one graced his lips, she would be done for. It would be game over.

The fact that the god-king of the Underworld, a male her family and all of Olympus portrayed as soulless and pure evil, could smile felt wrong, but at the same time, as it wobbled with his frown and the comprehension dawning in his eyes, it felt right.

Hades could smile.

He had just forgotten how.

And remembering looked as if it had spooked him.

His throat worked on a hard swallow and his expression darkened, the air around him seeming to grow dim as he glared at his legs.

Persephone had shifted a step towards him before she had realised what she was doing. She caught herself before he noticed, holding herself back even when she wanted to go to him. She wanted to comfort him. She ached to tell him that it was all right and that it wasn't a crime if he smiled. Smiling was a good thing. It lightened the heart. It chased sombreness away. She had often smiled when she was feeling down, forcing herself to do it until it had stuck and she had started to feel better.

If she told him that, would he look upon her with pity or with gratitude?

Or maybe he would rediscover his laugh and do so in her face.

She cursed the fear that held her back from saying or doing things she wanted. It was an affliction she couldn't shake though. Too many times in her past she had tried to join in with conversations or offer some kind of insight or help, only to be mocked or scorned. Not always aloud. Sometimes the god or goddess in question could mock or scorn her with just a look.

Would Hades do such a thing?

The thought he might cut her deeply, far deeper than anyone else ever had and it was only the thought of him doing it. If she spoke up and he cut her down, laughed in her face or mocked her, or told her it wasn't her place to speak in such a manner, she might never recover.

No amount of smiling would make her feel better.

"You are troubled again." Hades sat up, drawing her focus to him and away from herself, and she blinked as she looked at him, unable to believe her eyes. The black slashes of his eyebrows furrowed above glittering blue eyes that held a wealth of concern and the red corona of banked rage. "I swear, Persephone, should you ever tell me of your dark thoughts… of the source of your hurt… I will see to it they suffer as you do."

Something within her whispered that if he ever told her of his dark thoughts, if he revealed the source of his hurt, she might do the same. What dark beast had Hades awoken in her to make her think like that? Was it the influence of his realm? She wanted to glance at it, but couldn't tear her eyes away from his.

Or was it her growing feelings for him?

She felt… fiercely protective of him, and she didn't understand why. The thought of him hurting made her want to lash out at the world. It wasn't like her. But then, she had never had anything she had wanted to protect before.

No, that wasn't true.

She had wanted to protect her pet cat, and when her mother had taken it from her, she had been filled with rage and hurt, and had lashed out at the temple garden, filling it with black vines and making the plants wither. How had she forgotten that? She frowned as the memory crystalised, experiencing the distress and anger she had felt all over again. She had been in a black mood for days afterwards. She should have remembered.

Unless her mother had made her forget.

She looked at Hades, sure he hadn't had anything to do with her missing memories, but aware that the power to suppress them came from his realm. The waters of the Lethe made people forget. Her mother must have taken some and given them to her, and Persephone was sure she hadn't done it to ease her pain, but rather she had done it to stop Persephone from destroying her garden over and over again.

"Speak to me of your pain, Persephone. I will see to it that the one who caused it will suffer for eternity," Hades snarled and shadows darkened the corners of the room, gathering there to blot out the light.

That crimson began to spread, devouring the blue of his irises, and his ears grew more pointed again. The stark ferocity of his expression, half-worry half-fury, bewitched her and almost had her speaking and telling him all the names of those who had plunged daggers into her heart, but she held back and pushed her pain back down inside her, deeply aware his words weren't just words. They weren't something he said to make her feel better as she had heard many people do in the past when listening in on private conversations.

They were no idle threat to appease the other party.

Hades meant every word he said.

If she gave him the names of those who had wounded her in the past, chipping away at her confidence and strength, he would hunt them down and drag them into the Underworld.

And slaughter them.

Even her mother.

"I do not want blood on my hands. You speak so easily of killing, as if it is nothing… when taking a life is a terrible thing to do," she whispered and he flinched, his head rearing back as if she had struck him.

She realised she had in a way.

Guilt and regret swept through her and she ventured another step towards him, fighting for the right words, the ones that would make him see she hadn't meant to wound him by insinuating he was a terrible person because of his duty. She kept forgetting his role in this world was death, the overseer of severing souls from their corporeal forms and ushering them into the afterlife.

Hades turned his noble profile to her and drank from the bottle again, a deeper draught this time.

"Hades—" she started, not wanting him to be angry with her, or to feel the need to drink himself to death over something she had said. It had been callous of her to say such a thing to him and to tar him with a brush that painted a black picture of him, when he hadn't chosen his role in life.

Zeus had forced it upon him.

He slid a look at her, lowering the bottle from his lips, and she choked, the things she had wanted to say getting stuck in her throat as their eyes locked.

When a full minute had passed and she still hadn't found her voice, he heaved a sigh and went back to drinking and feeding himself grapes, while she wrestled with herself, hating how weak she was.

Why couldn't she speak openly to him?

Because he would mock her.

He wouldn't.

Whenever her guard had dropped and she had revealed a glimpse of herself, he hadn't mocked her or said a single cruel word. He had gentled and had looked pained, earnest, and had wanted to know more. He had wanted to share her pain.

She wanted to share his pain too, but they were far too alike, and she knew how it would go if she found the courage to ask him about it. If she asked him of his pain—his suffering—he would react as she had and clam up, refusing to speak of it.

But there had to be a way to convince him to share the burden of it with her.

She just wasn't sure how yet.

"Sit," he murmured and stroked the covers beside him, his voice black magic that coaxed her into doing as he wished—as she wished.

The rebellious, wicked part of her wanted to sit with him. She wanted to be close to him. As close as she could get. The annoyingly sensible part of her reminded her that it wouldn't be wise.

Why wouldn't it be?

Was it so wrong of her to be attracted to him?

To want him?

If she went and sat with him, would it shock him? Please him?

Her mind betrayed her again, imagination running wild and leaping forwards to picture him capturing her wrist and tugging her beneath him.

Persephone averted her gaze, looking anywhere but at him as her pulse rocketed and that heat bloomed inside her again, revealing how deeply she would like that. Her gaze landed on the bath and she couldn't tear it away. She pictured him as she had in her fantasies, standing over her in the nude, hard and ready for her. And now he was here, on her bed, inviting her to sit with him. She could live out those wicked fantasies.

Nerves flickered through her and her palms dampened, and she was tempted to go back on her refusal and ask for that sip of ambrosia he had offered earlier, because she wanted to steady herself.

But that sip would be a double-edged sword. It would calm her, but it would weaken her defences too, loosening her inhibitions. She had witnessed plenty of inebriated males and females at the festivals on Olympus. People who hadn't liked each other at the start of the evening had been all over each other once the right amount of ambrosia had been imbibed.

Hades offered the violet bottle again, as if he knew her thoughts, tipping the neck towards her and saying nothing as he tempted her.

Persephone resisted.

Barely.

He shrugged slightly, set the bottle down on the platter with the grapes, and pushed to his feet. He crossed the circular room in a handful of strides and plucked a pomegranate from the colourful display of fruit.

Hades opened it with a hard twist of his hands and offered one half to her.

His eyes locked with hers, holding her in place as he extended his hand to her, the look that glittered in them sending a cold sort of chill skating down her spine. He was waiting again. She could sense it. See it. He wanted her to eat the seeds.

Persephone shook her head.

His handsome face darkened and the air around him dimmed as shadows gathered, and she felt she had been right to be suspicious of the food. He was up to something. What would happen if she ate the pomegranate seeds? Would she lose her inhibitions?

Or would their effect be something worse?

Her eyes widened as it hit her and she looked out of the window at the distant orchard and then back at him, the thought he would go to such a length to keep her here in his realm stoking her anger and snapping something inside her.

"I will not eat something that might bind me to this dead realm—to you," she bit out, hurt that this whole evening had been a lie, an act by him to lure her into eating something that would keep her here by force when she had thought he genuinely wanted to get to know her and had even been courting her in his own fashion.

Shadows burst from beneath his feet and he snarled, flashing his fangs as he swept everything off the table, sending it tumbling to the black stone floor, and then he advanced on her.

Only as he stalked towards her, all darkness, fangs and crimson eyes, she was hit by a feeling that was far from fear.

Desire.

Persephone held her trembling hands up, afraid of what she might do if he came any closer, her heart racing and blood thundering, and that ache blooming inside her—one only he could satisfy.

Hades pulled up just short of her and stared at her, his chest straining against the soft material of his black tunic with each hard breath he sucked down, revealing honed muscles. A chest she wanted to explore with her hands. Would it feel as hard as it looked? She had seen males bare-chested before, but she had never touched one. Curiosity held her in its tight grip, making her yearn to slowly undo his tunic and expose his body to her hungry gaze.

Dangerous.

She tipped her head back, meeting his gaze. He was so much taller than she was, and so much darker, and the need that shone in his fierce gaze should have been startling and shocking, only it echoed within her too, had her blood thrumming in her veins as awareness of how close he was drummed inside her.

She only needed to reach out and lay her hands on his chest and he would know she wanted him too. She needed him too. The part of her that clung to everything she had been taught and told to be screamed at her that it wasn't right. She shouldn't want him. Hades was everything an Olympian like her shouldn't desire in a male.

But by the gods, he was.

Hades lifted his hands towards her, as if her stifled need to reach for him was controlling him and making him reach for her instead.

And then he stopped with his hands just inches from making contact.

His eyes blazed crimson fire as he looked at his hands and suddenly lowered them, luring her gaze to them as she ached to scream at him to do it—touch her. She was too afraid to make the first move. Couldn't he see that? She wanted him as fiercely as he wanted her.

Her eyes widened as she saw the short dark claws that tipped his fingers and a gasp escaped her, one she failed to hold back despite the fact she knew it would shatter their moment and wound him.

Hades curled his hands into tight fists that had blood squeezing from between his clenched fingers and pivoted on his heel, stalking away from her again. He didn't stop at the food he had scattered across the floor or at her bed this time. He strode to the staircase and descended it without even looking at her.

When the last of his shadows had trailed from sight, she released the breath she had been holding.

And disappointment swamped her, together with a need to speak to him and apologise.

Persephone raced to the staircase and hurried down it, driven by a need to make him stay.

Only he was gone.

She stared at the door on the lowest level of the tower and sank to her backside on the steps, regret swift to fill her as she cursed herself.

And cursed Hades a little too.

Because she knew he would avoid her again, remaining away from her and not giving her a chance to apologise. His hurt would fester and darken him again, and that man he could be with her would be gone the next time she saw him.

Persephone had half a mind to put the black dress on.

Because she mourned losing the gentle, attentive Hades.

The one he only showed to her.

The one who made her feel special for the first time in her life.

CHAPTER 15

Darkness blazed a path through his veins and shadows wrapped around his soul as Hades stalked across the black lands, heading away from his temple. His fingers flexed, the onyx talons of his plate armour slicing through the air in the way he wanted to cut through flesh and bone. A cold grin stretched his lips as he thought about the list of prisoners he was to visit today.

It faltered as his treacherous mind latched onto the one he hadn't visited in seven long days, and he seized the chance to draw back on the reins, pulling the darkness back under his control again. He would need to see her soon, if only to use her light to cast the shadows from his mind and his heart, but he wasn't sure he could trust himself around her.

Not yet.

How much longer could he go without seeing her?

It had already been seven agonisingly dreadful days.

He couldn't remember much about some of them.

The darkness had been too strong.

It had used Persephone's reaction to him to fuel his fears and weaken him, and then it had poured shadows through his mind, blackening it to strip his humanity from him. He had left her the moment it had seized him, clinging to the last threads of his control long enough to shut her in the tower and cast a ward to protect her. One he had known he wouldn't be able to undo while lost to the darkness.

It had taken him then.

Torn him down and rebuilt him as a monster.

He remembered nothing of the first day. On the second, he had found himself deep in an area of the realm far from the temple, his hands bathed in blood and carnage surrounding him, a sea of broken bodies so distorted that he had come close to retching.

For the entirety of the third day, Hades had locked himself in his chambers in the temple and had fought the darkness, slowly clawing back control. An ache to see Persephone had grown inside him, a desire to speak to her of the darkness. He wanted her to know of it and how it took him, if only so she knew how to defend herself and maybe not provoke him.

That part of him also hoped that if he spoke to her of his pain, that she would speak to him of hers.

The thought of sharing his pain with her had only given the darkness something to use against him to weaken him again. Fear had settled in his heart, tormenting him with the thought that she would mock him, that she would laugh at him, and it had merged with other fears. Fear that he might not have come back this time. Fear of what might have happened to Persephone without him there to keep her safe. Fear that he might be the one to harm her.

Aware that he was losing control, Hades had cast new wards on his chambers, keeping himself contained, and had fought the darkness. He had battled it with memories of the times Persephone had gazed at him with heat in her eyes, the softness of her voice, and the sweet scent of her, and it had worked.

Just memories of her were enough to drive the darkness back.

That had strengthened his hope, and by the fourth day, he had quelled the darkness enough that he had felt close to normal again and had returned to his duties. But he was tired, exhausted from the constant fight against the darkness, and from the fear and doubts he had drowned in.

Hades didn't feel much better today.

He glowered at the ground, feeling as if invisible arms were pulling him down into a dark mire, troubled by how fierce the darkness had been, and that Persephone had been the one to provoke it and had given it the strength to hold him under its spell for a whole day, or possibly two, before he had surfaced and begun to claw back control.

She could tame the darkness in him, but she could also make it wild. He needed to be more careful around her. What he needed to do was speak to her about the darkness, but while part of him wanted to do that, ached to let someone in at last, the rest of him snarled at him to keep it secret. It growled and snapped fangs, and barked that he couldn't trust her, that she was an Olympian and she would mock him, would use knowledge of it against him somehow.

Or believe him a monster.

Telling her about the darker side of his blood would drive her away.

"Never," Hades growled, crushing the thought of telling her. He wouldn't do anything that would jeopardise his future with her. He couldn't lose her.

She was his now.

Wasn't she?

He silenced that fear and his thoughts of her, focusing back on his duty and refusing to succumb to them as he did whenever he was alone, whether that was in his bedchamber or when he was moving between places as he was now. He even thought about her when he was walking with Cerberus.

He had even talked to his pet about her.

Cerberus hadn't been pleased by that. The great three-headed beast had snapped and growled, gnashing fangs that were each as long as Hades's forearms. Apparently, Cerberus didn't like Persephone.

Hades's gaze betrayed him and strayed to the jagged tower that punched high into the crimson sky, its backdrop a volcano that had become restless in the last few days, causing several more to erupt around it as it spilled streams of lava down the harsh planes of its face. The heat thickened the air and dampened his nape, irritating him. He wiped the sweat away with the leather palm of his gauntlets and bared fangs at it, and it cracked in response to his anger, a wide fissure splitting one side of it open. That fissure belched bright orange waves of molten rock.

Making the temperature soar.

The river of lava swept downwards into the canyon and he held his hand out, scowling at the mountain and drawing on his power and his connection to the Underworld. The black rock of the mountain knitted back together, healing before his eyes, and once it had been restored to how it had been before his mood slipped its leash, he lowered his hand and drew in a fortifying breath as his fingers trembled and a wave of fatigue rolled through him.

He needed to conserve his strength, something he wouldn't have to do if he had been able to sleep at all the last few days rather than fighting the darkness Persephone had provoked or lounging on his bed restless from thoughts of her.

Still, he also needed his throne temple, and the flow of lava into the canyon would have been too much for the river. It would have broken its banks and consumed his smaller temple there at the base of the canyon and his throne with it. Extracting the building from the cooled lava and restoring order to that area would have cost him more in strength than healing the mountain.

Hades rubbed his tired, gritty eyes and growled. Maybe if he went to see Persephone and saw she was all right he would be able to sleep.

And maybe she would recoil in disgust as she had the last time he had seen her and he would be plunged into a mood so dark the entire Underworld would erupt in flames.

Or the darkness would take him and he wouldn't come back this time.

Hades glared at the tower, his mind turning over everything that had happened during their evening together. He had thought it had been going well. He had learned things about her and had been gentle bar a few slip ups, and he had held himself back more than once. She had spoken to him and had been civil, for the most part.

And then, just when he had begun to believe there was hope for him and that his desires—his wants—might not go unfulfilled, just when he had begun to decipher his feelings for her and realise the depth of them, she had gone out of her way to anger him.

But he swore it hadn't been fear or fury that had flashed in her green eyes as he had stalked towards her. It had been desire. Need that had swept him up in it and made him a slave to her, flooding him with a consuming hunger to satisfy her and please her.

When he had reached for her, aching to touch her, she had cast a shocked look at his hands. Anger had brought his claws out, had pulled the darkness to the fore so quickly he hadn't been able to hold it back and he hadn't realised his nails had transformed until he had been reaching for her.

He had felt something other than an urgent need to satisfy her and a desire to possess her in that moment.

He had felt… *hurt.*

Still felt hurt.

It was the only word that fitted the raw, bitter and agonising feeling that had hit him the moment she had lowered her wide eyes to his hands and continued to hollow out his chest even now.

Hades's brow furrowed, the darkness loosening its hold on him as he gazed at the tower, aware he should check on her. Leaving her alone wasn't the answer. He reached out with his senses, as he always did whenever he passed, checking on her and reassuring himself that she was still there. His gaze drifted to the empty balcony. More than once he had caught her standing there, and she had pivoted away from him and disappeared inside, stealing the pleasure of her beauty from him.

He continued to send her food, and she continued to refuse to eat it. He half-smiled at that. His little goddess was wise. She knew what eating food of his world would do, but she wasn't sure which had come from it and which he had brought in from the mortal world, so she avoided all of it.

She didn't refuse to bathe though.

Whenever his servants had returned from emptying her bath, they had rapped knuckles on his door and reported that she had used the water he had provided. His queen liked to bathe. Perhaps he could use that to his advantage somehow. He wasn't sure how.

He scoffed.

Asking her to bathe with him would only see her pulling away from him again.

Hades heaved a long, weary sigh. Nothing was going right for him at the moment. Since their evening together, a slew of new problems had rolled in for him to deal with, and he was beginning to feel she was the source of them. Somehow, she was influencing his realm to strike out at him and make him pay for abducting her and refusing to take her back to Olympus.

Or perhaps the darkness was to blame.

Darkness she had provoked.

He stalked forwards, his glare rooted on the point beyond the barracks, where Tartarus stood, and he clenched his fists so hard his arms shook as muscle clamped down onto bone. He wouldn't give her up though. She could destroy this realm and he wouldn't surrender her. He needed her too much.

His mood blackened again, every small thing that had happened over the last few days clawing at him to drag him down deeper into the darkness.

First, several people in a far district of the Underworld had attempted to set themselves up as rulers of that area, and the legion posted there had reported it to him. Hades had been forced to leave his chambers to crush them. It had only taken a matter of minutes, but it had soured his mood and he had been even more exhausted when he had returned. He frowned. Something was very wrong in the Underworld, and he wasn't sure he could blame Persephone and some kind of power she was exerting to strike out at him. He couldn't even blame the darkness.

It wasn't like his subjects to act in such a manner, as if they didn't fear him.

His wrath had ensured that those in the district feared him now more than ever, and he had left the legion there to watch over them, constructing a permanent residence for the soldiers from the black rock and earth. Which had cost him greatly, but he had concealed it from all present. It wouldn't do for his men to see he was weakened.

Then, the prisoners in Tartarus had grown restless, and he had spent several hours there, quelling them so they no longer battered the bars of their cells and attacked each other, tearing the weaker apart to bathe the spiral staircase that drove deep into the earth with a river of blood.

Finally, Cerberus had slipped his leash during a patrol around the grounds with the temple guards and had taken himself off for a walk, something which wasn't like his beloved pet.

Hades was beginning to suspect Cerberus was acting out, attempting to get his attention, and that Persephone was the reason he was misbehaving.

He had found Cerberus over forty leagues east from the temple after an entire day of searching for him. The beast had been bounding around with one of the gargantuan grey bipedal creatures that roamed the mountains in that area of the Underworld and were often violent towards any who strayed through their territory.

When Hades had eventually gotten Cerberus back into his stable, he had received word that Nyx, goddess of night and one of his most powerful allies, required an audience, and had accepted her request only to be told it would be inconvenient for her to attend that evening and she would visit the next day.

Hades had the feeling he hadn't been keeping himself busy the last few days to avoid seeing Persephone because he couldn't shake the way she had looked at him. Everything in his realm had conspired against him to keep him away from her.

He glanced up at the tower again, and stilled.

Persephone stood on the balcony.

He turned towards her, no longer able to resist the craving to be in her company and attempt to court her again. If he could call it courting. He stared up at her, deeply aware it had been a mistake to take her and place her in that tower, and hold her captive, as if she was a possession and belonged to him now. She was far from belonging to him, and his rash actions had only made his work to make her want him as her husband even harder.

As he gazed at her, the darkness that had been constant company during their time apart slowly loosened its grip on him, and that feeling she had bewitched him grew stronger. She must have cast a spell upon him in those woods. His mind had been clearer than it had been in a long time and part of him felt as if he had woken from a nightmare and fallen into a dream. He had even smiled. Truly smiled. Not a vicious cold grin born of his darkness, but a smile born of warmth and light.

Hades couldn't quite put his finger on what was different about him, but he knew she was the cause of the transformation.

He couldn't remember ever feeling so much like a man.

He glanced down at the black talons of his gauntlets.

But still a monster.

Persephone's gaze remained trained on him, and he tipped his head back to look at her again, needing to see she was still there and was no longer shying away from him. How did she see him? Was he different in her eyes too?

Just as she was different.

Or perhaps he had simply been wrong about her.

When he had stolen her from her world filled with light and colour and plunged her into one filled with darkness, he had expected her to wither and fade more each day he held her here, keeping her as his queen.

He had expected her to wilt as any other delicate goddess of Olympus would have.

But not his Persephone.

She had *bloomed.*

Becoming a ray of light and a streak of colour he had come to crave, had grown addicted to and now couldn't live without.

Hades took a step towards the tower, driven to go to her and talk with her, and try again to make her love him.

Movement off to his left snared his attention though and he glared in that direction.

CHAPTER 16

Nyx strode towards Hades, her midnight blue gown flowing behind her and the arcs of silver-blue metal that swirled from her chest to her waist to form her breastplate catching the light of the nearby volcano, flashing gold. It warmed her alabaster skin too and turned the silver threads in her long onyx hair gold.

He had once thought her beauty unrivalled, with her flawless skin and high cheekbones, and striking inky-to-ice blue eyes, and might have taken her as his consort if not for her husband, Erebus.

But no longer.

She didn't even come close to Persephone.

His love was light and warmth, and colour he craved more than anything in this world. She was soft and gentle, but fiery too, and far from meek. She stood up to him and refused to let him have his way, even going as far as provoking him on purpose at times. Teasing him, he thought might be the better term for it. Sometimes, she teased him, with a mischievous light in her eyes that told him she was enjoying herself. She didn't fear him, and that was a rare quality. With her, he didn't want to crush her rebellious behaviour. He wanted to nurture it. He wanted to draw out that side of her and make her so comfortable with him that she would fall for him.

As he had fallen for her.

"You are not listening." Nyx didn't sound pleased about that, so he shifted his focus to her, shunning the revelation that he had fallen for Persephone.

He had never been in love before.

It was new, and unsettling, and made him wild with a need to see her and search her eyes for a sign she might come to love him in return.

"What is the matter?" Hades kept his voice steady and even despite the turmoil that erupted inside him. What if Persephone never came to love him in return? Could he endure such a hollow existence? He pushed that fear aside and devoted the whole of his attention to Nyx, who was now eyeing him closely. He glowered at her. "I was informed you requested a meeting. I do not have time for silence. I have matters that require my attention."

Nyx slid a look at the tower off to her left. "So I have heard."

Hades ignored that remark. "I do not have time for this, Nyx."

He went to stride past her, but she shifted into his path.

"My apologies, my god-king." She demurely dipped her head, but he could tell she wasn't done. It was right there in her eyes as they lifted to lock with his again. "I heard reports of the unrest that has afflicted one of the regions most distant from your temple. It is close to my territory and I only wished to offer my assistance in ensuring the citizens there remain under your control."

He narrowed his eyes on her. "Something which is expected of you, as you well know, so what is the real reason you have come all this way from your temple to mine?"

Nyx cast another look at the tower, wariness rolling off her now as she dragged her gaze from it to settle it back on him. Hades could sense the undercurrent of fear that rippled through her, an unease that had his eyebrows drawing down.

"I give you leave to speak your mind, Nyx." Hades held her gaze, close to demanding she tell him the true reason she had come all this way to see him, his impatience and ire growing the longer she kept him from his destination.

Persephone.

"I do not think it wise to keep a goddess of Olympus in the Underworld," Nyx said as if she knew his thoughts, "Nor devote so much time to her. I think she is a dangerous distraction that might cost you dearly, my god-king."

Hades might have laughed at her insinuation that another god had the power to cause him harm had his mood not darkened at the thought of someone coming to take Persephone from him. "No Olympian will be coming to take her back. I spoke with Zeus and told him I had found a female I wanted to be my queen, and that she was an Olympian. Zeus told me to take her and make her mine, which is exactly what I am doing."

He omitted the fact he felt Zeus had tricked him, and that every hour of every day he felt more and more certain that eventually his brother would demand he return Persephone.

Nyx stared at the tower, her head angled back and her blue gaze rooted on the top. Her voice was distant and laced with a troubled edge as she murmured, "Still… are you sure this is wise?"

Hades didn't mean to, but he glanced at Persephone, and the second his eyes landed on her, he didn't have the power to drag them away. She looked angrier than usual today, but he wasn't the subject of the black look on her face. Her glare was directed at Nyx. Curious.

"It is none of your business." Hades managed to find the strength to tear his gaze away from Persephone, mostly because he hoped that if he didn't appear that interested in her that Nyx would stop probing into his personal life.

Nyx never had been good at recognising the boundaries of their relationship. This wasn't the first time she had overstepped the mark, crossing the line between subordinate and friend. She had done it countless times in the past, and he had bonded a little with her over their mutual dislike of his brothers and the Olympians.

He wasn't in the mood for it today though.

Nyx smiled wickedly, her eyes never leaving Persephone. "How does your courtship go?"

Hades wasn't going to answer that. "I need you to look into something for me. I desire to know if anyone has noticed that Persephone is missing."

Nyx finally dragged her gaze away from his goddess.

She gracefully inclined her head. "Consider it done, my god-king."

"If there is any other business you wish to discuss, do so, otherwise you may take your leave." He almost waved her away, eagerness to enter the tower and speak with Persephone pushing him to be rid of Nyx as soon as possible.

"I wish to discuss your courtship of an Olympian goddess." Nyx's rosy lips curled into a mischievous smile.

"Leave," Hades barked and did wave her away as he scowled at her, because he didn't want to talk about his failings.

He was meant to be a strong and feared ruler, but he didn't feel strong whenever he thought about Persephone. He felt weak, and afraid that nothing he did could make her want him in the way he needed her. He felt doomed to fail and lose her.

Nyx offered him a soft, somewhat understanding look as her smile faded, the teasing note leaving her voice as her hand lifted, as if she wanted to touch him to comfort him.

Her words were comfort enough, softening his hardening heart and pouring hope into it.

"Things were difficult between myself and Erebus at first too." She grunted as something struck her on the side of her head with enough force to make her stagger to her right.

Hades frowned at the pomegranate that tumbled across the black earth. An apple followed it, hitting Nyx on her breastplate and smashing against it, showering her with pieces of pulp. Hades wrapped her in his shadows, drawing them up from the earth to shield both of them as Nyx turned incredulous eyes on him.

"Did your pet just hurl rotting fruit at me?" Her eyes brightened with diamond stars as those words lashed from her lips and her fine eyebrows knitted hard.

"Let it go," Hades ordered as the bombardment finally ceased.

The goddess of night didn't look as if she would as starlight pricked her skin, making it glitter, but then she demurely dipped her head, the action stiff.

"I take my leave then." She teleported, but disappeared from his senses for only a heartbeat.

Hades growled as his gaze swung up to the balcony of the tower.

Where Nyx had reappeared in front of Persephone.

CHAPTER 17

Persephone stomped around her room, bored out of her mind. She shot daggers at the black stone floor and the walls that formed her prison, her mind on the one who had constructed it and swept her away into this dark world.

His dark world.

Hades was definitely avoiding her again, just as she had feared he would, and it was all her fault. The sight of long black claws where his nails had been had completed the picture of a monster many had in their head when it came to him, complementing his crimson eyes, fangs and pointed ears, and his savage behaviour.

Only it had dawned on her that her reaction to them hadn't been born of fear or terror, but from curiosity. Over the days they had been apart, she had returned to studying him and poring over everything that had happened while they were together, the course of her thoughts fixated on why those claws had appeared.

He had reacted on a physical level to his emotions.

Just as the realm reacted to them.

It fascinated her.

She drifted to the window that faced the direction of the temple, a place she had spent many hours over the time they had been apart. She had spent every minute of them pondering all the little things she had learned about him during her captivity, piecing together a better picture of Hades. Each piece that had clicked into place had revealed a different image of him, one that fitted the male he had been at their dinner, before she had angered him.

Wounded him might be the better words for it.

Persephone willed him to return to her. Not because she ached to see him again. Not because she needed to see that her thoughtless, cruel words hadn't shattered whatever fragile emotions he felt for her. Not at all. She just wanted to apologise. It had nothing to do with this violent, desperate need to see she hadn't ruined everything.

Her stomach growled.

Persephone rubbed it as she glanced over her shoulder at the trays of food that tormented her. Trays she had covered with the black dress Hades had given her, trying to make them less tempting. Out of sight, not out of mind. Her mouth watered at the thought of biting into one of the ripe pieces of fruit and she almost moaned as she imagined how the sweet juice would quench her thirst as the tender flesh sated her hunger. What she wouldn't give for something she could eat. If he would let her go to her forest to pluck some of the cherries and apples from the trees there, she would probably swear to stay with him forever.

He would never allow it. He wanted her to eat the fruit he provided daily, tempting her as she grew weaker and weaker. He wanted to bind her to this realm—to him. He didn't want to give her a choice and trust she might choose to remain with him.

How much longer could she hold out?

As a goddess, she only needed to eat to keep her strength up and could go without food for weeks or months before hunger dragged her down to a mortal's strength. Even then, she could continue without food, ticking along for years. She might even grow used to the level of strength and energy she had when she was only as strong as a human, and then she could probably go decades between eating.

Was Hades willing to keep her captive for that long?

The thought of remaining shut in the tower for decades had her anger flaring hot in her veins and made her want to go to the balcony and scream and yell until Hades grew so sick and tired of her that he let her go.

But the thought that he might do just that had her remaining where she was, keeping still and silent as something in the region of her chest ached.

Persephone sighed and swept her gaze over the mountains as she realised it was too late for her. She was no longer a prisoner, because she wanted to be here. She wanted to be near Hades—the only man to have ever made her feel alive—the only person who had ever made her feel seen.

The longer they were apart, the stronger her need to see him again grew, and other things were slowly changing too. The realm was appearing less frightening and less dark by the day, which unnerved her, because it left her feeling she was starting to view this place as her home and was trying to come to love it as Hades did, seeking out the things that weren't so different from her world or the signs that it could be a better, brighter place if she set her mind to it. The orchard drew her gaze, rousing that hope that she might be able to grow things here, plants that would soften the harsh appearance of this realm.

She had also spent far too many baths thinking about the ruler of this realm.

And sometimes when she retired to bed when she was tired too.

And also sometimes when she woke alone.

She couldn't hold back the flush of heat that swept through her as flashes of her fantasies filled her mind, awakening that wicked ache between her thighs that increased her need to see Hades.

Damn him.

Movement to her right caught her eye and she looked there. Hades. By the gods, he was glorious as he strode across the black land, dressed in his full onyx armour and his spiked crown back in place, nestled among the thick unruly tangle of his black hair. He moved with purpose, long legs chewing up the distance between him and his destination, a male on a mission, and her heart fluttered as she thought he might be coming to see her.

She moved to the balcony when she lost view of him, overcome by a powerful need to keep her eyes on him, the tension that built inside her falling away again as her gaze landed on him. He had never looked so fierce. So angry.

So alluring.

Shadows streamed behind him, fluttering around his long black cloak, and his gauntleted hands flexed as he walked, fingers curling and uncurling constantly.

A sensible, good goddess of Olympus would fear him.

But even with his pointed ears and crimson eyes, and his black armour and crown in place, she couldn't bring herself to feel that emotion. The sight of him pleased her, warmed the reaches of her heart that had grown cold in their time apart, and brightened them, chasing the shadows from them, as if he drew them to him.

He paused and turned to look up at her, and she felt sure he would come to her today—that he would finally stop punishing her for the things she had said. Perhaps she could reason with him. Between mulling over what she knew about him, studying him and fantasising about him, she had been practising things to say to him, hoping to word things in a way that wouldn't anger him, because she… liked his presence. She liked being around him, close to him.

He wouldn't like what she wanted to ask him though.

She was worried that her mother would be upset about her disappearance and would be causing all manner of trouble in Olympus. If he agreed to set her mother's mind at ease, she would agree to remain here for a time as his guest rather than his captive.

Her desire to bargain with Hades went out of the window when a black-haired female approached him. The goddess was stunning, her tall and lean frame clad in a striking blue gown with a breastplate fashioned from swirls of silver metal, and even at this distance Persephone could tell she didn't compare to this female's beauty.

Hades's words whirled in her mind, his taunt that many females in his realm would fall at his feet and beg for a chance to be with him darkening her mood.

Was this female one of them?

This newcomer didn't appear to be a servant, and she made the meek females who brought Persephone's bath water and food look bland and ugly, and unfit for Hades. If he had to choose a female to sate his needs, he would pick someone as beautiful as this one. She was sure of it. She clenched her fists and shut down that line of thought, and the dark feelings it stirred, denying them and focusing instead on studying the female and Hades, cataloguing how he acted around her in an attempt to discern his feelings towards the goddess.

Persephone wished she could hear what they were saying as Hades glared at the woman, seeming aggravated by her. Satisfaction rolled through Persephone at the dark looks he gave the goddess, and how his rigid posture and the sharp angles of his face reeked of irritation and anger. She wasn't a female he wanted to bed then.

But then anger burned up her blood to scorch her heart when Hades's hard look softened and the goddess offered him a sweet smile and tender look, and lifted her hand to touch him.

Before she knew what she was doing, Persephone had stormed into the room, whipped the cover off the fruit and had bundled it up in her arms. She halted on the balcony and hurled the first pomegranate at the goddess, launching the missile with such force and anger that it startled her when she realised what she had done.

It hit the female square on the side of her head and Persephone couldn't hold back, even when she knew continuing her attack would only get her into worse trouble. Anger overshadowed the sensible side of her that screamed at her to stop, and she gave herself over to it, satisfaction sweeping through her to make her want to grin as an apple she launched hit the woman's breastplate and exploded, covering her in bits of pulp.

And then her mood veered towards a black rage.

Because Hades swept his shadows upwards, forming a wall between Persephone and the goddess that the next piece of fruit she hurled struck instead of the female.

Protecting her from Persephone's wrath.

When she had emptied her arms, the rage remained, veiling the world in red. She seethed with a need to strike both Hades and the goddess now, and pivoted to look for something else to throw.

Something heavier.

Her gaze snagged on and darted back to the ambrosia Hades had left.

Persephone stormed to it and seized it, unsure whether she wanted to down the whole bottle or hurl it at Hades as she strode back to the balcony.

The goddess appeared only inches from her.

A gasp burst from Persephone's lips, her heart shooting up into her throat to hammer a sickeningly fast rhythm there.

Before she could catch up with what was happening, the goddess backhanded her, striking her hard across her left cheek.

Persephone crumpled, pain zinging through her skull to make her vision wobble, and gripped the stone floor as she hit it. The coppery tang of blood flooded her mouth and her shock gave way to anger so fierce her head snapped up and she glared at the beautiful woman who towered over her.

Persephone stared at her, nerves rising through the dark emotions that clouded her heart to make her unsure of what to do. Her cheek throbbed, her eye on that side aching. If she had her powers, she would bind the goddess in sharp vines and make them constrict.

That gave her pause and had some of her rage leaking from her. This wasn't like her. She had never been violent towards anyone, but she wanted to be violent towards this female, and it rattled her. It didn't matter that she couldn't do it because her powers were bound. She wanted to do it, and it was wrong of her. She had no real reason to attack this female.

The goddess apparently didn't have the same problem Persephone had when it came to being violent and harming others. She exuded a darkness so thick and cloying that it pressed down on Persephone.

Persephone stared at her, her lungs constricting and heart labouring as she faced the goddess. Stars pricked the female's blue eyes and shimmered over her porcelain skin, but they didn't emanate a warm kind of light like the stars that shone above Olympus. Their light was cold and dark almost, a malevolent kind that had Persephone shrinking away from her.

The goddess looked her over, slow and leisurely, her eyes flooding with darkness that had Persephone inching backwards, her rage falling away as fear swamped her. This female meant her harm and looked as if she would do it, regardless of what her god-king wanted.

Was this goddess also jealous that Hades had another female?

The woman advanced a step towards her.

And then Hades was there.

He looked down at Persephone where she sat on the floor and then at the goddess, no trace of emotion on his handsome face, and the foolish part of her that felt safe now he was near faded away, leaving her as cold as his gaze. Her brow furrowed as she lifted her right hand and gingerly touched her lip, and she hissed in a breath when it stung.

Hades's eyes narrowed on her mouth.

Crimson fire erupted in them, devouring the cool azure, and then they went black.

Scarlet lightning ravaged the realm outside the tower.

Shadows tore from the floor.

They slammed into the goddess and hurled her across the room with such force that the tower shook as she smashed into the curved stone wall. Blood burst from the goddess's lips and a grunt left her as the shadows seized hold of her and threw her to the floor, and then dragged her towards Hades. He bared fangs in her face, shadows streaming from his shoulders, and then threw her away from him again. This time when the goddess hit the wall, the shadows didn't grab her. She hit the floor with another pained grunt.

It all happened so fast Persephone could barely make sense of it, and then his shadows were wrapping around her and sweeping her up into his arms, twisting her so her back was to his front. His left arm banded across her chest, draped over her shoulder as his hand clutched her ribs near her breast and he pulled her back against him. His other hand closed over the front of her throat, forcing her to tip her head back into his shoulder, and shadows embraced her.

But it wasn't done to harm or cage her.

He was protecting her.

The metal plates of the vambrace that protected his forearm shielded her heart and the plates on his gauntlet shielded her throat. He had chosen this position so he could protect those vital areas from this goddess's wrath, and had no doubt kept her in front of him so he could keep an eye on her.

She shivered as his talons grazed the skin of her throat.

He lowered his mouth to Persephone's ear and whispered, "That was not very nice."

She wasn't sure whether he was talking to her, or to the goddess who had picked herself up off the floor and now faced them.

The shock of it all dissipated in an instant as Persephone caught up and found her balance again. She stoked her anger, refusing to let him or this goddess scare her, and denying the softer feelings that continued to shake her. She wasn't comforted by his embrace. She didn't feel safe.

She definitely didn't feel aroused as he held her and his front pressed against her back, leaving not even a molecule of air between them.

The goddess before her narrowed calculating starlit eyes on her and Persephone felt as if she was peeling back her layers and would see her true feelings for Hades, and would tell him.

So she panicked, because she wasn't ready for him to know. She was bone-deep afraid that a powerful male like him wouldn't feel the same way about her and that he only wanted her as his queen because he was taking something from Olympus, and that any goddess from her realm would have satisfied him.

She feared he would only break her heart.

"Get off me." She shirked his grip and turned to push him away from her, but he captured her wrists and held her firmly, keeping her pressed close to him.

His gaze seared her, so intense that the foolish part of her whispered she was wrong and that he wanted her, not any other goddess. It was her that he desired. Only her. That feeling was there and gone in a flash as his gaze lifted to land on the goddess behind her. Persephone wrestled with him, fighting to break free of him, and he tightened his grip on her, refusing to let her go.

The goddess chuckled, clearly amused that Persephone wasn't strong enough to break his hold, and the fire ignited inside her again, an inferno that had her trying to turn towards the goddess.

But Hades still held her fast, making that impossible.

The fire became fury, a rage so deep it burned away all reason and all softness, and hardened her heart to stone as she kicked at Hades's shins, unwilling to be mocked by him too.

"Let me go! You clearly have a female. You do not need me!" The words came out far more bitter than she had anticipated, laced with hurt that she couldn't quite hide beneath her anger.

Hades instantly stopped fighting her, his now-crimson eyes widening and a trace of blue encircling his irises.

Persephone slammed her mouth shut. She had said too much.

The goddess murmured, "The little Olympian desires you."

"I do not," Persephone snapped, panic pushing the words from her lips. "I would never want a monster like him!"

The words were out of her mouth before she could stop them and she immediately regretted them, that terrible feeling only growing as Hades stared at her in silence. She kept her gaze away from him, not sure she could bear the hurt or the anger that would be in his eyes.

Pain she had caused again.

Her shoulders deflated, her fight leaving her as despair swept in to cool her rage. She hadn't meant what she had said, but it didn't change a thing. She had been cruel to him again. She shifted her gaze to his chest, the closest she could bring herself to looking at him. She was despicable.

She was the monster.

Would he ever forgive her?

She wasn't sure why she said such terrible things to him. No, she was. It was a foolish need to protect herself that made her lash out at him to drive a wedge between them, and it didn't only hurt him. It hurt her too. She didn't want any distance between them.

She just wanted him.

And it scared her.

Hades set her away from him, his fingers trailing off her wrists and sparking a desperate need to make him take hold of her again as cold welled inside her, whispers that he didn't want her tormenting her.

"Nyx. Carry out your orders." His deep voice rolled over her, lacking emotion, and Persephone's gaze leaped up to meet his, but his crimson gaze was fixed on the goddess behind her.

What orders had he given the one called Nyx? Fear jolted her and she looked at the goddess, afraid it involved taking her or hurting her.

"Are you sure?" Nyx said.

Hades nodded, his air sombre and tone cold. "I am."

Nyx gave him a look as she bowed her head, one that was all sympathy, and then she was gone.

Persephone turned to look at Hades, an apology leaping to the tip of her tongue, forged by the fear he was going to leave her or worse, take her home.

It died as his gaze lowered to her, the intensity of it robbing her of breath as it clashed with hers, and he husked, "Why did you throw the fruit at Nyx?"

Fire flared inside her again and she squared up to him, determined to speak her mind on this subject even if it angered or hurt him, but her nerve failed her and other words came out instead, a lie to cover her true feelings.

"Because I am sick of seeing it in this room," she snapped. "I wanted it gone."

His head slowly tilted to his left as he studied her. "Why not throw it out sooner? Why throw it at Nyx?"

His gaze drilled into her and panic bolted through her again, dampening her anger as she floundered, afraid of admitting the reason she had attacked Nyx with a hail of pomegranates, apples and oranges.

Persephone turned to walk away from him, no longer willing to say something that would only make her vulnerable and easy to wound, but she didn't get far. He seized her right arm and forcefully pulled her back around to face him, and loomed over her.

His voice dropped to a far too sexy rumble.

"Was it because you believe Nyx to be my lover?"

Persephone clammed up.

He towered over her. Dark. Menacing. Radiating fury as shadows danced at his feet. But she didn't see a monster. She saw a man, one desperate to know the reason behind her outburst, to divine the feelings behind it, as if his very life depended upon the answer.

And she felt drawn to him.

Ached to ease the pain he hid so well behind his stern mask.

"Were you jealous?" he whispered, crimson eyes searching hers, seeking the answer.

She wanted to deny it, but she couldn't find her voice when he was looking at her like that, as if she could be a source of joy and happiness for him, and not just pain and frustration.

Hades released her wrist and brought both of his hands up, cupping her face with them and holding her gently as he gazed down at her.

His voice was rough and raw as he growled.

"Do you want to know how jealous I would be if I saw you with another male?" He brought his head down towards hers as his left hand dropped to her shoulder and their cheeks touched, sending sparks of electricity arcing through her to make her body come alive, together with the snarl in his words that made her believe he meant every last one. "My jealousy would be so vast and dark that this entire realm would feel it. I would shake this planet to its core with my rage if another male so much as looked at you… because you are *mine*, Persephone."

She gasped as she trembled, as his words shook her to her core, their dark promise rousing her feelings and making her burn for him. She couldn't stop herself from leaning into him, bringing their cheeks into firmer contact, swept up in the moment and the heat of his body close to hers. The ache he always made her feel grew stronger, magnified by his scent and his power as it wrapped around her, and the feel of his hands on her and his breath on her neck.

Need blazed through her, burning up her blood.

A need that felt as desperate and wild as Hades looked as he drew back.

He gazed down at her, hunger lighting his now-blue eyes, that possessive look in them sending a hot shiver rolling down her spine and making her bold and reckless, because no male in this world had ever looked at her like that.

As if they loved her.

All she needed to do was tiptoe and he would kiss her.

He would take the invitation she offered.

Persephone rocked forwards on her toes.

And snapped back onto her heels as he spoke.

"I have seen you looking at the orchard." His tone was soft, laced with hope that echoed in his eyes as he awkwardly cleared his throat. "Perhaps you would like to see it? Would it make you feel better?"

The moment slipped through her fingers, and in the wake of it shock that she had been on the verge of taking matters into her own hands and kissing him instead of waiting for him to kiss her coursed through her, and she was sure he had seen it as her cheeks flushed and he blinked at her, surprise flashing in his eyes.

"I would like that." She struggled to hold his gaze, willing him not to say anything or call her on the fact she had wanted to kiss him. She tried to smile but it wobbled and died, and she shrugged stiffly. "I am surprised you are allowing it. I thought this room was my home now and I was not allowed outside it."

She meant to tease him, but his handsome face turned deadly serious again.

"This entire realm is your home if you wish it, but only once you say you are mine." He held his hand out to her, his sharp talons not scaring her, and held her gaze. "Until that day, I am afraid you will have to make do with me as your escort… and even then, I am not sure I would be able to let you stray beyond my sight."

She stared at his hand, his words ringing in her mind, fuelling her hope and her courage. He had touched her many times, and she had touched him, but taking his hand seemed so intimate, even when his skin was covered by his gauntlets.

She raised her hand and hesitated, drawing it back to her an inch before curiosity won against all her doubts and fears, the thought of seeing more of his realm, and of him, driving it to its victory.

Persephone placed her hand into his.

And gasped as darkness engulfed her.

CHAPTER 18

Hades reluctantly set Persephone away from him, forcing himself to release her as they landed close to the orchard. It was hard to convince himself to do that. The possessive side of his blood snarled at him to keep hold of her and keep her pressed close to him, and find an excuse to not let her go. It wasn't only the protectiveness that had ignited in him that had him desperate to remain close to her. Rage simmered in his veins still, a replay of how he had found Nyx looming over her and the crimson that had painted Persephone's lower lip stoking it and keeping it at a constant burn. The darkness swirled at the edges of his mind, stalking and waiting to pounce. He wanted to keep it at bay, and being near Persephone would help him battle it and hold it back.

"I apologise for Nyx's behaviour," Hades growled, and Persephone turned to look at him. She glided back to him, her nearness quietening the darkness. It purred at him though, murmuring tempting words about finding Nyx and hurting her more, ensuring she would never dare strike his queen again. "I apologise for not reaching you in time to stop her."

A small frown creased Persephone's brow. "There is no need to apologise."

"There is every need." He frowned right back at her, unable to understand how she could be so calm and could forgive him so easily. "Nyx will be punished."

Persephone shook her head now, her expression shifting towards surprise laced with a sort of anxiousness. "Do not. It is not necessary… and besides… I was the one who started it."

True. But Nyx had been the one to end it, and incite his rage. His gaze lowered to Persephone's mouth and his brow furrowed. He reached for her and surprise claimed him too when she didn't move away. She didn't even withdraw when he gently stroked his thumb over her lower lip, inspecting the cut on it. It was shallow. He pressed his knuckles to the side of her jaw and tilted her head, raising her cheek towards his gaze. The bruise was hardly noticeable.

Nyx had held back.

The goddess of night must have been aware that Persephone was weak from refusing to eat and had tempered her strength when she had lashed out at his little queen.

"She would have done well to hold herself back entirely and not strike my goddess," Hades snarled in the language of the Underworld, his mood taking a darker turn as he stared at the bruise on Persephone's fair skin.

"There you go again." Persephone sighed, her voice far too light given the graveness of the situation. She should have been angry that Nyx had hit her, not quick to forgive her and let it go. Instead of slipping into a rage as he had, she had accepted it and moved on, refusing to punish Nyx. Persephone inched closer to him, her emerald eyes bright as she tilted her head upright again, causing his hand to slip to her throat. "Tell me what you are saying and I will not mind that you speak that language around me knowing full well I do not understand it."

"And if I tell you and you discover I speak of killing Nyx, what would you do?" He canted his head, holding her soft and steady gaze.

She rolled her shoulders in a small shrug. "Ask you not to do that? I meant it, Hades. I do not want blood on my hands."

Hades didn't catch what she said after she uttered his name. It was a blur, lost in the warm haze that swept through him and bathed his soul in light that chased the darkness from it. She wielded such power with his name, and the glimmer in her eyes said she knew it. She knew how deeply the sound of his name on her lips affected him.

"I do not want to talk about it anymore. Come. I want to explore." She pirouetted away from him, the layers of her soft green dress swirling outwards with the sudden action.

His gaze tracked her as she moved away from him, her bright green eyes darting over the uniform lines of the dark trees that covered a large area between his temple and the stable block.

He glanced at their surroundings, making sure no other male was in the vicinity, close to his precious Persephone, and breathed a little easier when he discovered they were alone, the dark possessiveness she provoked in him settling and freeing him of its grip.

As it fell away, his mind locked onto something else. He struggled to believe she had been—*was*—jealous of Nyx.

But even just the thought she might be was a balm for his weary soul, giving him hope that he could change the course of things between them and win her heart. He wanted her as his queen—a loving queen and not one who despised him and merely put up with him. He wanted all of her. Body. Heart. Soul.

He wouldn't settle for anything less than her love.

And that meant he needed to win her heart, and to do that he intended to seduce her and draw those feelings he saw in her eyes from time to time to the surface, making her accept them.

And him.

Which meant he needed to be charming and not frightening, and that felt like a monumental task, one he might have said was impossible before their moment mere minutes ago. She had liked his possessive, growled words. She had liked how he had come to her rescue. She had liked his hands on her. It had been there in her eyes.

Followed by fear.

Not fear.

Nerves.

He was no stranger to them himself. They gripped him as he watched her approaching the orchard and fought to find his balance, seeking things to say that would please her. What if he only aggravated her again? Or provoked a defensive response? She was quick to shield herself with harsh words whenever she felt vulnerable.

He needed to be careful with her.

Gentle.

Hades pulled down a fortifying breath and set his mind to work, forming a strategy that would ensure he was the victor in this battle of hearts. His first play? He removed his gauntlets and tucked them into the leather belt that encircled his waist just below the hard plate of his chest piece. Going to his chambers to change into something less formidable wasn't an option, but he could still soften his appearance.

Persephone glided through the trees, her luminous emerald gaze drifting over their canopies that reached together to tangle into one dark green roof spotted with bright red fruit. She was as graceful as she had been in her forest, her bare feet unerringly avoiding the pebbles to land on the smooth ground even though her eyes remained away from it, and her scarlet hair matched the colour of the pomegranates she inspected. Her gaze landed on him, bright with the excitement she failed to conceal, and her rosy lips curled into a faint smile.

A dazzling ray of sunshine in his dark world.

One that drew him to her.

"They are incredible. I am surprised you can grow such fertile trees in this black soil." Her voice tapered off at the end and her smile faltered.

Hades tried to let that remark bounce off him without hitting its mark. The way she clammed up and her shoulders stiffened spoke to him, telling him that she hadn't meant her observation to come out sounding as if she believed his realm was dead and devoid of life. The same way she had reacted back in the tower, when she had lashed at him and called him a monster. He hoped the similar reaction meant she hadn't meant that either.

"Pomegranates." There was a hint of accusation in her tone that matched her expression as she looked from the fruit to him.

Hades reached up, plucked one from a branch, and closed the distance between them as he opened the ripe round fruit and offered half to her. She pulled a face and pushed his hand away, her fingers brushing his, and a thrill chased through him, stealing the breath from his lungs and making his gaze leap to meet hers. Her wide eyes locked with his, her startled look telling him she had felt that too.

She was quick to snatch her hands away and tuck them behind her back, and as she turned away from him, he was struck by an urge to take hold of her arm and make her face him again, to make her let him brush his fingers against hers to steal another taste of that thrill that had gone through them both. He tamped it down rather than acting on it, maintaining his distance and his calm, and unsure how he managed either when need was a rampaging beast inside him.

Be charming.

Gentle.

He told himself that on repeat as he discarded one half of the pomegranate, and then plucked one of the jewel-like crimson seeds from the half he had kept and popped it in his mouth, savouring the explosion of flavour as he broke the skin. He looked down at the fruit and then at Persephone as she glided deeper into the trees, replaying her reaction to his offer of half of it.

She was wise to him.

She knew that eating this fruit, in particular, would bind her to his realm.

To him.

No matter. He would find another way to keep her with him and buy himself the time to make her fall in love with him.

He trailed after her, drinking his fill of her as she explored the orchard, watching as she relaxed by degrees and even began humming to herself. He had done that. He had drawn her out of the darkness and all it had taken was bringing her close to this small patch of nature.

He ate another seed. Had Nyx gone to Olympus as he had requested? By the gods, he hoped she didn't take it upon herself to reveal where Persephone was. He hadn't missed the looks Nyx had given him, ones that had backed up her words and made it clear she felt it wasn't wise to keep Persephone.

He knew that, but he couldn't give her up.

Hades gazed at his little goddess, an urge to sigh sweeping through him as she meandered through the trees, looking as if she belonged among them, here in his dark realm. She almost looked happy as she reached her arm up and feathered fingers over a glossy red pomegranate.

But then her hand dropped to the trunk of the tree and that happiness became disappointment.

And he knew why.

It was his fault.

He had bound her powers so she couldn't use them in his realm, and she had hoped the ward he had cast to seal them had been placed on the tower. She slid him a look, one that cut his soul to ribbons, and he discovered he couldn't bear seeing her so disappointed, but he also couldn't bring himself to allow her access to her powers.

She might escape him.

Leave him.

"Did you make these?" She took in the trees again, shaking off her disappointment, but it lingered, there in the depths of her green gaze as she stroked the bark.

How did the absence of her power feel to her?

He had been without his for the first centuries of his life, when he had been trapped within his father, devoured by him and held within another realm. That had been so long ago that he couldn't recall what it had been like to be powerless and he suspected what he had felt then wouldn't come close to how Persephone felt now. He hadn't known his powers or formed a sort of bond with them. She had. She'd had them all her life and he had taken them from her, locking them away.

Did it make her feel empty?

Hades regretted that it might, and part of him wanted to apologise for the precaution he had taken, but rather than revealing that he had a weakness she could exploit—a power she had over him that made him want to do whatever she bid in order to please her—he focused on answering her question.

He nodded. "In a fashion. I had them transported here."

"So, they were not grown here?" She eyed them suspiciously, her gaze calculating, and he had the feeling she was trying to figure out whether that meant she could eat the fruit, since they were not of this realm.

He could have lied to her, enticing her into eating their fruit, but he didn't want their relationship to be built on a foundation of lies, so he said, "They were saplings when I planted them and this earth has nourished them, with help from my horses, so for all intents and purposes, they were grown here… and the fruit is born of this soil."

"How long have they been here?" She explored one of the trunks with both hands, coming to face the tree, and placing her side to him. She had a beautiful profile, and a face filled with wonder as her gaze tracked the branches that fanned outwards above her. She was enjoying herself, and it warmed his heart to see it, soothing some of his fear and relaxing him. "They look as if they must be at least fifty years old."

"Nine hundred years." He liked the shocked look she turned on him. "They have been here nine hundred years."

She gaped at him. "They are older than I am."

He slid a surprised look at her, one he couldn't quite conceal before she saw it.

She frowned at him now, a little pout to her lips. "I am not so young. It is not my fault you are so *old*."

She swept away from him, her steps light, and glanced over her shoulder when she rounded another tree. Their gazes locked for a heartbeat before she disappeared from view. She was teasing him.

No one had ever dared to tease him before.

Hades found he liked it.

Although he was sure he wouldn't enjoy it if it was anyone but Persephone teasing him.

When she swept around another tree, her left hand grazing the trunk as she circled it and her green gaze on the fruit it bore, he eased towards her, closing the distance down to only a few feet.

"If your powers were not bound, do you think you could grow things here?" Curiosity tugged that question from his lips and tension crept into his muscles as he awaited her reply.

She pulled a thoughtful face, her bright gaze falling from the dark leaves above her to the black earth beneath her bare feet. That look became one of longing that had a feeling ringing inside him—she wanted to try. She wanted to transform his dark realm into something more colourful and alive.

"Perhaps." Her soft voice teased his ears, a breathless little sound that drew him closer still. She didn't seem to mind his proximity as she studied the earth and then lifted her head and took in the orchard. "I managed to make the forest grow and plants take root in that dusty stretch of land at the end of the world. I imagine I could do it here too. Is all the realm like this?"

"Why do you ask?" He circled her, plucking another seed from the pomegranate and popping it into his mouth.

"It would be a good indicator of whether this soil could sustain a more diverse array of plants than just these trees." She swept her hand down the trunk of one, her scarlet eyebrows knitting.

Hades debated whether to tell her or keep quiet on the subject. When she glanced at him, a striking look of curiosity mingled with hope in her eyes, he found he couldn't remain mute and deny her.

"The Elysian Fields are a paradise." He drank his fill of how her face lit up, her entire visage brightening before his eyes as she planted both palms against the tree and leaned into it, peering around it to him, her scarlet waves falling away from her slender shoulders. When she looked at him like that, so open and unafraid, he found it impossible to hold his tongue. He wanted to please her and sate her curiosity, if only to keep her looking at him in that way. "They are lush and green, and filled with drifts of crimson poppies. The sky is bright there, blue and dazzling, and verdant mountains enclose the Fields on all sides. There is even water there. Crystal clear lakes and rivers that snake across the vast plain."

Her fine eyebrows knitted. "If there is such life and light there, why is it not everywhere?"

He frowned right back at her and then took in the orchard and the glimpses of black mountains beyond them. "Because it is reserved for heroic souls, and much of the Underworld is reserved for the good and the bad."

"The good must live in darkness?" She pulled another face. "That does not seem very fair. What kind of reward is it for the way they lived their mortal lives if they are made to live in the same conditions as the bad during their afterlife?"

Hades glowered at her now. "Your view of this realm is coloured by what you have known your entire life. You do not know how this realm works or what life here is like for the good souls."

It wasn't very good, she was right about that, but he wasn't going to admit it. He lowered his gaze to the floor, trying to see it from her perspective and then those of the good souls who called vast stretches of the Underworld their home. He held back a grimace. The lives of the good souls could be infinitely better. He had placed their villages in groups so they would be together, but had failed to separate them from the souls of people who had done terrible things in their lives. There were often skirmishes between the two factions, with regular violence and other terrible acts being committed by the bad souls.

Those souls even attacked the breeds born in the Underworld from time to time, causing tension across the realm and anger towards Hades.

From now on, he would make sure the wretched souls who were sent to him were held at a distance from the rest of the population of the Underworld, in a walled environment they couldn't escape, and would keep legions posted there to maintain order.

He glanced at Persephone as she drifted away from him, his feet moving of their own accord to keep the distance between them steady, as if she had a rope tied around his waist and it had pulled tight and now tugged him along with her.

She was changing him.

He hadn't really cared about the welfare of the souls in his care before she had come into his life. Now, his head was filled with plans to improve the lives of the good and those born in his realm. Rather than ruling through fear and demanding their respect and adoration, part of him wanted to earn it. He wanted them to respect him because he was a good king—to adore him because he provided for them.

He didn't want them to fear him.

He gazed after Persephone. What power this slight, delicate female had over him. With only a look, she could wrap him around her finger and make him ache to do whatever she commanded. With only a glance, she could strip him of his armour and leave him feeling vulnerable and exposed.

With only a smile, she could slay him.

That smile graced her lips as she rounded a tree and peered at him.

Persephone nodded at his shadows where they danced around his boots, a flicker of interest in her eyes as they lifted from the black ribbons to meet his.

"What about your powers?"

CHAPTER 19

A pleasing sort of feeling rolled through Hades in response to the knowledge that Persephone wanted to know more about him too.

"They will not harm you." Hades held her gaze, needing to see she knew that and wanting to reassure her that he meant it. He would never harm her. Or at least, he would try not to, but sometimes when she provoked him, the darkness was strong and it was hard to hold it back and retain control of himself.

She drifted deeper into the trees and quietly murmured, "I did not think they would."

Warmth spread through him.

Hades followed her, unwilling to let her leave his sight for even a second. That urge became overpowering when a beast called in the distance and her shoulders went rigid, her head snapping in the direction of the harrowing roar. He closed the gap between them in a handful of strides and barely leashed the desire to take hold of her arm to draw her against him and into the shielding cocoon of his arms.

Her green gaze sought his.

"I was not lying when I said there were beasts in this realm who would mean you harm if you crossed paths with them." His fingers flexed at his sides as he fought the need to sweep her into his arms and his senses stretched outwards, his shadows probing at the land to pinpoint the beast. It was beyond the mountains, far away enough that she wasn't in any danger.

She threw a black look at the orchard. "I do not know how you can live here. There are no beasts on Olympus that seek to devour those who wander the realm."

Rage lanced Hades's heart, her words driving the spike home to pierce it, and darkness flooded him, so swift and fierce he couldn't hold back the surging tide or the hurt that followed in its wake.

The ground beneath his boots quaked in response to the sudden, violent swelling of emotion within him.

Persephone gripped the nearest tree to steady herself and threw a curious look at him. "Was that you?"

Hades refused to answer that question. He strode through the trees away from her, needing some space and air. He tugged at the collar of the leather tunic he wore beneath his armour, struggling to breathe as the air seemed to lodge in his throat and the darkness pressed in on him. Much to his pleasure, Persephone hurried to keep up with him, remaining close to him.

Although he wasn't sure whether it was because she wanted to be near him or because she feared the beast would swoop down and snatch her if he wasn't with her.

"Did you cause that quake, Hades?" Her question came out softer this time, an imploring note lacing his name that had him halting to look over his shoulder at her. Her gaze darted around her, fear dancing in it. Fear that fell away as it lifted and collided with his. She murmured, "Did you?"

Hades wrenched his gaze away from her, unsure he wanted to see her reaction when he admitted, "The realm shifts with my mood."

He drew down a steadying breath and let it flow out of him, seeking calm amongst the turbulent sea of his feelings as he battled with the words he wanted to say—words he had told her before but in a tongue she didn't understand.

"You share a deep bond." She slowly moved around him, her steps cautious and measured, coming into view and stopping before him. She angled her head and gazed up at his face.

Hades lifted his head and straightened his shoulders, purging the fear and the sliver of shame he felt, because he was god-king of this realm, and he shouldn't care what a slip of a female from Olympus said about it.

But he did.

He cared a great deal about what she thought of his realm.

Of him.

He muttered, "I am the Underworld, and the Underworld is me. When things are out of balance in my realm, I am out of balance… and vice versa."

He waited with bated breath to hear her reaction to that admission.

"That sounds troublesome." She idly plucked a leaf from one of the trees and twirled it in her fingers, studying it as she quietly asked, "What are your family like?"

Hades shrugged, relief flowing through him to ease the tightness of his muscles and have him relaxing again as he realised his bond with the Underworld didn't disgust her or make him frightening. He savoured the sensation of peace that swept around him and how she wasn't shying away from him or trying to escape, relaxing enough that he didn't even care that she had asked about his family, a topic that normally enraged him. He wasn't sure this peace could last, even when he wanted it to go on forever.

In an attempt to make that happen, he thought about his family and what he could tell her that would please her.

But it was his brothers she was talking about.

"I do not see my brothers often. Neither of them stray into this realm unless it is to be of trouble to me, and I am not welcome in their realms. But this, you already know." One glance at her was all it took to confirm she did indeed know that he wasn't welcome in Olympus. What tales had she heard about him? He wanted to know, but didn't dare ask. He sighed and looked beyond the orchard to the cragged black mountains. "My duty keeps me busy and keeps me here, and I am fine with that. I have no need of my brothers."

His mood darkened again, even Persephone's light unable to keep the shadows from his mind as he thought about his brothers and how they treated him. Poseidon had looked up at him once. He had been the centre of his younger brother's universe, and the one Poseidon had always turned to when troubled or when he had gotten himself into trouble. Poseidon had relied upon him.

How quickly his brother had betrayed him when Zeus had come along, turning his back on him and shifting his loyalties to another.

Persephone cast him a look he could only call pity and then stepped towards him. When she was close to him—so near he could feel her warmth and her scent invaded his lungs, calming him a little—she lifted her hands. He frowned at her, unsure what she intended to do, but it didn't stop her.

She gently smoothed the furrow between his eyebrows and then lowered her hands, pressed her index fingers into the corners of his mouth, and pushed upwards.

Forcing him to smile.

"I always feel better when I smile," she murmured, her voice black magic that had the urge to knock her hands from his face falling away.

The sombre edge to her eyes said it didn't make her feel better. That was just the lie she told herself to cover her sorrow and pain.

Hades couldn't stand it.

He swept her into his arms, tucking her close to his chest and ripping a surprised gasp from her, and held her.

He bent his head to press his cheek to hers, and fiercely whispered, "Tell me who hurt you."

She tensed and he knew she wouldn't tell him.

Hades growled. "How am I to mend you and defeat your darkness when you will not tell me of it?"

"My darkness?" she murmured and he feared he had said too much.

Knew he had when she pulled back, pressing her hands to his chest and resisting him when he tried to tug her back to him.

Her emerald eyes searched his, searing and sharp, but soft too as her eyebrows furrowed.

"How am I meant to defeat your darkness if you will not speak of it?" Her voice was soft, beseeching, and by the gods, he wanted to talk to her about it, but he couldn't. Not now. Not yet. Maybe not ever. He wasn't sure he would ever be ready to speak of it to someone. She sighed and shook her head slightly, barely moving it. There was no trace of pity in her expression or her voice as she said, "I have seen how you change, Hades. I have seen the war within you and how hard you fight it, and I want to know of your darkness. Will you tell me about it?"

Perceptive little female. No other had noticed how the darkness affected him. All who had seen it had believed it to merely be his rage. But not Persephone. She had seen right through him.

His heart whispered at him to tell her. Now was the perfect opportunity.

But what if he told her and it ruined whatever was happening between them?

Fear of that happening had him growling, "That is not something I am willing to speak about."

And he instantly regretted it when she pulled free of his hold and moved away from him, her shoulders lowering as the distance between them grew.

Her voice was small as she said, "If that is the case, then I am not willing to speak of my darkness."

He walked behind her for a spell, battling with himself again. Only this time it was a war between fulfilling her wish and speaking to her about the darkness, and keeping silent on the subject.

Would she understand if he talked to her about it?

Would she agree to remain with him if he told her how just her presence soothed it and gave him better control over it?

When the silence stretching between them became too oppressive, he thought about what they had been discussing before she had tried to make him smile, attempting to return to how they had been then. He wanted her to speak to him again. He wanted to see her smiles. He wanted her to tease him some more.

He just wanted to know he hadn't messed things up again.

They had been speaking about his brothers. Did she have siblings? He wanted to know.

"What of your family?" he said.

Her shoulders tensed and her fingers stiffened against the leaf she toyed with, and then she looked in the direction of the tower. "You seem close to that three-headed hound."

She was evading his question. His dark eyebrows knitted and he studied her, trying to divine the reason why. Didn't she like her family?

Were they the source of her darkness? The ones who had hurt her mentally and emotionally?

Rather than pressing her for answers to assuage his need to know why she didn't want to talk about them, he focused on drawing her closer to him and making her more comfortable around him again. Pushing her would only drive her away from him. In time, he would find a way to convince her to speak to him about her darkness.

And he would find the courage to speak to her of his.

"Cerberus." He almost smiled as he thought of his pet and realised she must have seen him with the beast more than he had known.

That near-smile caught him off guard and threw him off balance to have him staring at the ground as he pondered something.

When was the last time he had really smiled?

Hades looked at her, aware she was the reason he kept coming close to doing something he couldn't remember ever doing before. She was the cause of this growing feeling of lightness inside him.

She twirled the leaf in her fingers, her gaze creeping back to him, and her question caught him off guard this time.

"Did you really mean what you said?" She circled a tree as he frowned at her, gracefully gliding back into view on the other side of the trunk and casting him a shy glance as rose climbed her cheeks. "Would you shake this planet to its core if another male looked at me?"

"I would," he growled, his mood taking a sharp, dark turn at just the thought of another male gazing upon her.

Hades wasn't sure whether it pleased her or not as she turned her cheek to him and kept walking, her luminous emerald eyes on the leaf. He wanted to ask her, but the thought she might laugh at him or reject him had the question sticking in his throat, and once again he felt vulnerable, as if this bewitching female had stripped all his armour from him.

They reached the edge of the orchard and she looked back towards the tower, sheer longing on her face as she turned her gaze from it to the black lands that stretched before her in the opposite direction to the tower.

She pointed with the leaf. "What is that?"

Hades glanced at the long building constructed of columns of onyx stone and dark wood. "A stable."

"For horses?" Her eyebrows rose and she looked pleased at the thought it might be.

"For Cerberus."

For a moment, she had looked interested, her eyes bright with something akin to excitement, but the moment he mentioned his beloved pet's name, she was backing away into the cover of the trees. He tracked her with his gaze, not liking that fearful edge her eyes held as she kept them locked on the stable. She feared Cerberus, when she had no cause to because the hound would never harm her.

When she caught him watching her, she was quick to say, "I am just a little tired."

Covering her fear and perhaps shame too. Because she had judged Cerberus on his appearance and believed him to be a monster that would savage her?

In the same way she had judged Hades.

She wouldn't look at him. She cast her gaze at the leaf and remained staring at it with her head bent for almost a full minute, hiding in her study of it. When she nibbled her lower lip and repeated herself, he took the hint.

Hades held his hand out to her.

She didn't hesitate to place hers into it.

He closed his fingers over hers, savouring the feel of them and the trust she had shown by taking hold of his hand, as if it was the most natural thing in the world for her to do, and teleported with her. When her circular room materialised around them, she didn't snatch her hand away.

She lingered.

Her gaze drifted to meet his.

Hades wanted to draw her into his arms and kiss her, but pushed back against the desire, maintaining control and fearing that if he let his desire get the better of him, he would only destroy the progress he had made with her. She hadn't protested about being taken back to the tower, and she seemed to have genuinely enjoyed his company.

Both of those things left him feeling that this day with her had gone well, and that it was best to leave before he overstepped the mark.

He lifted the hand he held and pressed a kiss to the back of it, breathing in her delicate scent of lilies, and murmured against it, "Goodnight."

He teleported away from her, but in the moment before he disappeared, as his hand slipped from hers, he heard her whisper.

"Goodnight, Hades."

And his heart swelled with warmth and hope that drove out the darkness.

CHAPTER 20

Persephone had come to a decision in the two days Hades had remained away from her, leaving her to gaze from the balcony at the orchard where they had walked. She was going to ask him for more freedom so she could explore this small part of his realm.

In exchange, she would give her word that she wouldn't try to leave.

Not that she really could leave since she couldn't teleport like other gods and she didn't know the way to a gate that would take her back to Olympus. Leaving meant hurling herself into more danger than she felt she was in now, placing herself at the mercy of the wilderness she could see from her tower.

At the mercy of that beast she had heard.

She shuddered at the memory of its bellowing roar, an echo of the adrenaline that had flooded her in that moment running into her veins again to have her rising from her bed. She paused at the edge of the mattress and looked back at the pillows.

"Another night of refreshing sleep." She frowned at how deeply she had slumbered since her walk with Hades. "Anyone would think he has set me at ease."

Anyone would be right about that.

Since their stroll around the orchard, she had felt more relaxed, and far less afraid of this realm. Fear had given way to curiosity, and the more she pondered what she knew of the Underworld, the more she wanted to know about it. She had hundreds of questions she wanted to ask Hades about the Elysian Fields, and how the souls lived here—did they have homes? Villages? Friends?

She also wanted to know what kind of beasts roamed the realm, and what sorts of breeds called it home too. Was it only the gods and goddesses of the

Underworld and the souls of the dead, or were there other breeds living here too? Olympus had many breeds, such as centaurs and cyclopes. Poseidon's realm had the nereids.

If Hades would only visit her, she could ask him all the questions burning on the tip of her tongue, driving her mad with a need to know the answers to them.

If he visited her, she could try again to ask him about what he had called the *darkness*. And maybe this time, he might speak to her about it.

Persephone flopped back onto the bed on a sigh, her arms outstretched at her sides. "If Hades would only visit."

He seemed determined to remain away from her though. She had watched him coming and going from his temple, and even walking the beast he called Cerberus, and only four times had he looked her way. One time he had stopped and stared, and she had felt sure he would teleport to her, only he had finally kept walking towards the barracks.

A hot shiver rolled through her as his growled promise rang in her mind for what felt like the millionth time. That snarled vow that he would shake this world if another male so much as looked at her had starred in every fantasy she'd had since he had returned her to her room, only she had changed it so she had kissed him.

She wasn't sure why she had felt compelled to ask him if he really would, but his answer had pleased her. No, it had more than pleased her. There wasn't a word strong enough to convey how satisfied she had been to know he wanted no other male to look at her, to know how violently he would react if it happened. It shouldn't please her. She knew that.

But every hour she was here, and every minute she spent in his company, things were changing, and, in a way, it was frightening.

Before, she couldn't wait to escape.

Now, she was lazing on her bed wondering if she would see him today.

Persephone toyed with her hair, her arms draped on the soft bedding above her head and her legs dangling over the edge of the mattress. Would Hades visit today? Maybe she could convince him to spend some time with her, luring him up to her. He might not have left his home for the barracks yet.

She could catch him on his way there.

She sat up and her stomach growled loudly at the sight of the platter of fruit on the table, and she rubbed it through the layers of her green dress. She couldn't eat. The pomegranates Hades continued to send her were definitely of this realm, and she wasn't sure what other things he was growing here, beyond her sight. For all she knew, all of it could come from the Underworld. Eating something belonging to this realm might tie her to it forever.

"Would that be such a bad thing?" she murmured.

And froze.

"It would be a bad thing," she said, mentally chastising herself, and then swinging back the other way as she frowned at the stone floor. "Why? Because he is Hades? He is not as frightening as others make him out to be, or so heartless."

In fact, she was beginning to suspect that beneath his hard, sometimes scary exterior, beat a tender heart capable of the deepest sort of love.

That smile that had almost graced his lips when he had spoken of Cerberus had been affectionate, and bewitching. Now, she wanted to tease another one out of him to bathe in how gorgeous he was when he smiled with warmth, when his guard lowered and he relaxed around her.

She wanted to be the cause of that smile.

Her stomach growled again.

To take her mind off her hunger, and to maybe catch Hades as he moved between the buildings, she wandered to the balcony and stepped onto it.

Things looked different again today. Every morning she came to this spot, something had changed. The volcanoes in the distance were now dormant, the glowing rivers of lava that had streaked their faces now glossy black veins. She looked for more changes, curious about the power Hades wielded in this realm and how it responded to his mercurial mood.

Was it similar to her power in a way?

She didn't think he could create living things as she could, but she had the feeling he could mould this realm into whatever he wanted it to be, shaping buildings from the black earth and rock—like her tower.

Persephone added another dozen questions to the list in her head and frowned as she spied a glow in the sky far off to her right. She squinted, even though she would never be able to make out anything at such a vast distance, feeling a little foolish for even attempting to see what was happening. It looked as if something was on fire just beyond the next mountain range.

Something large.

Cold power pressed against her spine and she twisted to face the room, her hands coming up in front of her, something which startled her almost as much as the black-haired goddess standing before her. She had been ready to strike at Nyx to protect herself. She had never punched someone before, had never even considered it, but every instinct she possessed had her on the verge of lashing out at the goddess of night.

Before Nyx could strike at her.

Nyx's blue eyes narrowed on Persephone's raised fists and then slowly lifted to lock with hers. "I received quite the tongue lashing from Hades about my behaviour. I have learned my lesson. I will not touch his pet again."

Pet.

Persephone wanted to growl as Hades could at that term. She had thought of herself as his pet before, but to have another call her it was insufferable.

"What do you want?" Persephone bit out, keeping her fists up and her distance from Nyx.

Nyx's delicate black eyebrows rose slightly. "You, gone from this realm."

Persephone's eyes widened and then she frowned at the goddess. "Why? Because you want Hades for yourself?"

The thought she might set fire to Persephone's blood and had her fingers curling into tighter fists.

"By the gods, no. I have my own husband to satisfy my carnal needs, daughter of Demeter." The way Nyx's lips curled into a hint of a smile had Persephone faltering, that knowing look she levelled on Persephone wrecking her confidence. Nyx knew about her, and she doubted she had learned of her from Hades. No. The wicked light that glittered in Nyx's eyes said she had uncovered details about her, things she believed would be a disadvantage to Persephone, which meant Nyx had been seeking information on her.

Suddenly, what Hades had told Nyx made a dreadful sort of sense.

He had sent his subordinate to Olympus.

Was that the reason he had stayed away?

Surely Nyx had told him the things she had learned upon her return, and now Hades knew what a poor match Persephone was for him, how everyone in Olympus looked down on her and no mortal worshipped her. By the gods, he probably wanted rid of her, and that was why Nyx wanted her gone from the realm.

She was here to carry out her god-king's orders and remove her from the Underworld, freeing Hades to find a more suitable queen. Her heart took a direct hit at that thought, her hands dropping as a strange kind of hopelessness washed through her to numb her.

Nyx's eyes narrowed further, her fine eyebrows knitting, and she canted her head to her right. "Such a weak little thing. I can see your false confidence falling away, revealing the goddess everyone painted you to be, one without spine and strength. You truly are unfit for him."

Persephone glowered at her, covering the sharp jab of pain in her heart with the scowl, and the way Nyx scoffed shattered what confidence and strength she had mustered.

"Spare me the act. It might fool Hades, but it does not fool me." Nyx's gaze moved beyond her, settling on the dormant volcanoes, and disappointment laced her voice, mingling with a hint of disgust and anger. "You are no good for my god-king. Look at how the Underworld has changed since your arrival. I thought it unusual at first, but nothing to be concerned about… but then I learned of you… and I know this is not just something that will die down and the realm will settle again."

Nyx lifted her right arm and Persephone flinched, the automatic, fearful reaction tugging a cold and knowing smile from the goddess as she casually swung her arm to point towards the glow Persephone had been studying.

"Entire districts are burning," Nyx's voice lowered to a fierce growl, "and you are responsible."

Persephone shook her head, not quite following the goddess. "How am I responsible? I have done nothing—"

"Nothing?" Nyx spat, cutting her off, and the delicate beauty of her face darkened into a scowl, the pale blue that ringed her pupils brightening. "You are changing Hades, and there are gods and goddesses of this world who see it as an opportunity to seize power. Hades is blind to it… blinded by his infatuation… his obsession with you. If this is allowed to continue, then Hades *will* fall."

A gasp escaped Persephone as her head whipped towards the distant glow and her heart constricted, her right fist coming to rest between her breasts against it. Nyx wasn't here to remove her on Hades's order, which meant he either didn't know the information Nyx had gathered on her, or he did and he didn't care that she was inferior to him in every way. A weak bud of hope sprouted in her heart and struggled to blossom, faltering as she stared at the blaze beyond the black mountains, Nyx's words ringing in her ears.

She didn't want to be Hades's downfall. She didn't want him to lose his realm. She hadn't been able to understand his attachment to this dark world at first, but over the time they had spent together, she had come to realise it meant everything to him. It wasn't just duty that had him dealing with the souls of the dead—it was a strange sort of passion. He was passionate about his realm, and protective of it too. He shared a deep and powerful bond with it that was unlike anything she had seen in another god, even his brothers. That bond he had was born of love.

He loved this realm.

She couldn't allow him to lose it, not because of her.

"What can I do?" Her brow furrowed as her gaze sought Nyx, a wild kind of desperation flooding her to have her almost taking a step towards the goddess. "I can help him. If I had my powers—"

"Leave."

Persephone shook her head at that stern word and the hard look in Nyx's eyes that made it a demand, unsure whether she was refusing because she didn't want to leave the Underworld or because she didn't know how.

"I cannot," she said as she struggled to decide which it was. "I do not have my powers. Hades has sealed them. I do not know the way to a gate either. If I leave, I will be vulnerable."

And part of her felt that vulnerability might stem from her heart and the fact she had left Hades.

Or perhaps it might be that she would be leaving that heart behind, with him.

He wouldn't understand if he returned to find her gone. He wouldn't know why she had left him. He would think she had escaped because she didn't want to be his queen, when her desire to leave was born of feelings that were quite the opposite.

Feelings that hit her hard and had shock rolling through her.

She was falling for him and she wanted to protect him.

She wanted to show him, and maybe Nyx, that she was strong and could be brave, that she was worthy of a place at his side, as his queen. She wanted to show herself that too. She had never fought before, but she would fight to protect Hades and his realm.

"I will help." Nyx sidled closer, the chilling brush of her power enough to have Persephone edging back until her bottom pressed against the railing that enclosed the balcony.

Persephone warily eyed her, unwilling to trust the goddess, but aware she had little choice. If she wanted to help Hades, then she needed to do something, even when she feared it might hurt him and he might not understand why she had done it.

"Take me to Hades," Persephone said.

Nyx gave a hard shake of her head. "No. That would not be wise. He is deep in the midst of battle. A place far too dangerous for you to venture. I know the location of the gate to Olympus. I can get you to it."

Olympus.

Her heart buoyed and then dropped at that word. She had wanted to go home. She glanced around the room and at the realm. Now, she wasn't so sure.

"If you remain, Hades will fall. He will lose everything." Nyx's words chilled her heart, crushing her desire to remain, because she couldn't be so cruel as to place her own needs above his.

Nyx was right, and this realm was everything to him. She couldn't let him lose it. She would go, but she was also coming back—with aid for Hades. As soon as she reached Olympus, she would seek an audience with Zeus and tell him what was happening, and Zeus would come to his aid to help him restore order.

Not that she dared to tell Nyx that. The goddess of night was still glaring at her, looking ready to personally throw her through the gate to be rid of her and restore order to the Underworld for her god-king. Persephone wasn't sure her leaving would help. The realm responded to Hades's mood, and he would be furious when he discovered she was gone.

So she resolved to be quick.

If she was fast enough, Hades might not even know she was gone. Still, she wavered.

Nyx noticed it and lunged for her arm, and swept her into a teleport that landed them in the middle of a valley that had a forest of gnarled black trees sweeping across the centre of it. The goddess shoved her towards them and released her.

"Go. The gate is in that direction. Keep travelling east along the road." Nyx backed away from her.

Before Persephone could turn to ask her how far the gate was, or argue that Nyx had said she would take her to the gate, or even mention that east was the direction she had been heading with Hades when that beast had roared, the goddess was gone.

Leaving Persephone alone.

Had she just been tricked?

CHAPTER 21

Persephone looked around her, trying to spot the blaze so she could figure out which way to head in order to get back to the tower, only she couldn't see the glow from her position. The mountains around her were too tall, their sharp peaks blocking out the sky. They hemmed her in and she couldn't spy a path that would take her over them or even around them. There was only the faint track that led east.

Towards the black forest.

For all she knew, she could be leagues from the tower and Hades's temple. Nyx wanted her gone so it stood to reason the goddess might have dropped her off near the gate to Olympus, keeping her word in a way. Not that Persephone trusted the goddess to keep her word. She was beginning to believe Nyx had been lying to her the entire time.

But what if she hadn't been and Hades was in danger of losing his realm?

Persephone shored up her courage and strode forwards—heading east.

Moving away from the mountains would give her a clearer view of the sky and she might be able to spot the glow again so she could calculate how far she was from the tower. If nothing else, it was moving her closer to the gate. She could reach Zeus and he could bring her back to Hades. She was sure he would want to help his brother.

Every step that carried her further from Hades, her heart grew heavier. She cast a look over her shoulder from time to time, an ache to turn around and go back to him forming behind her breast, but she steeled herself and kept moving forwards. The glow in the sky was faint, at a great distance from her, or perhaps the fires were dying out. She wasn't sure which it was, but returning to Olympus for help seemed the more sensible course of action than climbing a mountain in the hope it would get her back to Hades.

Persephone's steps slowed as she reached the swath of gnarled black trees, her desire to return to the tower growing stronger as she looked at the path that wound through their sharp branches. She wrapped her arms around herself, a chill skating down her spine. A forest had never looked so forbidding.

Frightening.

She had a bad feeling about this place that eclipsed the one she had about Nyx.

The goddess of night was up to something, and Persephone was beginning to fear she might be the one making a play for Hades's throne, weakening him by removing Persephone from his reach so she could take him down. She looked over her shoulder in the direction she had come, the need to find Hades increasing. She had to warn him. She set her jaw and shook her head, ridding herself of the temptation to turn around. It was quicker to get to Olympus and convince Zeus to bring her to his brother.

If Nyx had really dropped her near the gate.

Persephone forged onwards, but not along the path.

She avoided it, making her own route through the dead trees. Their blackened trunks and branches glittered in the fading light, and she frowned as she skimmed her fingers over cracks in their surfaces. They looked as if they had been scorched and turned to charcoal. She inspected her fingers and the black soot on them.

Had someone set fire to this forest?

She looked around her, taking in how vast it was as it stretched in all directions as far as her eyes could see.

What kind of blaze could have devoured this entire forest before someone could put it out?

That bad feeling in the pit of her stomach grew worse and she quickened her pace, hurrying to get through the forest as fast as she could, a need to reach the other side drumming inside her in time with the galloping of her heart. She flinched as one of the branches snagged her hair and she grasped the tangled red lengths to tug them free. She made it only a few steps before a lower branch snared her dress. She twisted and pulled herself free and gathered her skirts, bunching them up so they no longer hindered her. No matter what she did, branches caught her hair and her dress, forcing her to stop and free herself, as if they were trying to slow her down.

She lifted her head and turned slowly as a feeling sank through her. Was she heading the right way? Panic flooded her veins as she turned in a slow circle, trying to get her bearings, her heart labouring as her breaths shortened and fear she had been turned about when fighting the branches chilled her blood to icy sludge.

Persephone stilled as a sound cut through the thick, eerie silence that had been her only company for what felt like hours.

A howl.

She stretched her senses outwards, cursing the wards Hades had used on her and how they dampened them, placing her at an even greater disadvantage. Her fingers flexed as she tried to locate the beast and she instinctively reached for her powers. That void inside her where they should have been had never felt so cold and dreadful as another howl went up. This one louder.

Closer.

Persephone twisted on her heel, her gaze darting around the forest. Where was the creature? How large was it? If it was moving through these charred trees without making a sound to alert her to its location, then it had to be small, not much larger than she was. Could she fend off and possibly even defeat such a beast?

There was only one way of finding out.

She took stock of all the trees, hurrying from one to the next, and stopped as she found what she was looking for.

Persephone gripped the long, lance-like branch in both hands, pressed the sole of her right bare foot against the trunk and heaved backwards, putting her weight and all her strength into breaking it free. She gritted her teeth and grunted as she wrestled with it, sweat beading her brow as the stifling heat and fatigue worked against her. She had thought the trees would be weakened by the blaze that had destroyed them, but they were stronger for it. That both worked against her and in her favour. Her spear would also be stronger, if she could get it off the tree.

Another howl went up and she stilled again as snuffling and twigs snapping followed it.

And she sensed it closing in on her.

Her pulse rocketed and her limbs shook, but she steeled her heart and sharpened her mind, refusing to let fear get the better of her. Hades's words about the creatures of his realm rang in her mind, laced with the mocking barbs Nyx had cast at her. The goddess of night was right, and she wasn't strong or a warrior, but she could be. She would prove to Nyx and to herself that she could be both of those things.

She had never fought before, but what better motivator was there than her life being on the line?

Persephone shoved her foot harder against the tree trunk and unleashed a rather not-at-all feminine growl of effort as she heaved backwards, gripping the branch so hard that her fingers ached. She shrieked as it suddenly gave way and she landed on her back with a harsh grunt, the heavy branch falling on top of her.

The beast charged into the small clearing.

Persephone grabbed the branch and scrambled to her feet, running around a tree to gain some space and buy herself time to plan an attack.

Time the scaly, horned black creature didn't give her. It continued its charge, lowering its large head, shifting it into a position where the two horns that protruded forwards from its bony brow and the one that jutted from above its nostrils were pointed right at her.

She hit a hard right that had her bouncing off a tree and pirouetted around it and kicked off again, another shriek bursting from her when the creature slammed into the tree behind her, smashing it to pieces.

A swift prayer to the Moirai left her lips as she ran, struggling to keep hold of the heavy branch she had foolishly thought to use as a weapon. The pointed tip of it had looked like a perfect spear for stabbing the beast, until she had seen it possessed seven spears of its own. Two more protruded from its head on each side, the lowest pair jutting backwards over its broad shoulders and the middle pair sticking upwards. If she tried to stab it from the front, it would catch her with one of its own weapons. Not only that, but a thick bony plate covered its forehead and travelled down its long muzzle.

Her spear would break on it.

Her only chance was getting behind the beast, which was easier said than done given its speed. It matched hers despite the fact it was twice her size and had to weigh several hundred pounds.

She clenched her hands around her weapon, refusing to give up. She would just have to slow it down. It was larger than she was, and she doubted it could smash its way through every tree in the forest without the impacts taking a toll on it. Eventually, it would tire and an opening would present itself.

Persephone hit another hard right and then an immediate left, placing another tree between her and the beast and weaving deeper into the heart of the forest. Her breath sawed from her lips. Of course, she would also tire if she kept running like this.

She cursed Hades. If he had given her food she could trust, she wouldn't be in this position. She would be stronger.

If he hadn't sealed her powers, she would have been even better off, able to use them to protect herself and maybe even fight.

She cursed Nyx too, sure now that the goddess had dropped her in this valley on purpose and had been aware of the hungry creatures that called it home. Nyx didn't just want her gone from the Underworld.

She wanted her dead.

Persephone grunted as the beast barged through another tree and a chunk of it caught her in the back, knocking the breath from her. It also knocked the creature off course, so it missed her with its horns.

And shot past her.

She unleashed a war cry as she thrust her spear at it, not wasting a second, part of her stunned by how quickly she had reacted to take advantage of the opening. The point of her weapon struck home, lancing the black beast's flank, and a pained bellow burst from it.

It kicked off, escaping her, and her heart lodged in her throat as it turned towards her and halted a short distance away.

Blood spilled over its rough skin as it stared her down, its midnight eyes giving nothing away.

Persephone readied her weapon again, steeling and steadying herself, preparing for their next clash.

Seconds ticked past, each one fraying her courage.

And then the beast turned tail and ran.

Her shoulders sagged, the tip of her spear falling to strike the ground as her strength and the tension flooded from her, followed by an incredible sensation that made her feel invincible. Was this what victory felt like?

She could certainly see why many gods and some goddesses enjoyed a good battle. It had been frightening, but exhilarating, and now she was buzzing.

If only Nyx or Hades could have seen her. Neither of them would have doubted her courage and strength anymore. Still, she sighed, she had shown the most important person that she could fight and could be brave, and face whatever life threw at her.

She had shown it to herself.

She frowned and angled her head to her left.

The strange sound she had heard during her fight against the beast was louder now.

Clearer.

Like thumping.

Whooshing?

She frowned and turned this way and that, seeking the source of the noise as it grew louder still, the heavy beat becoming the only thing she knew. Her stomach clenched as something hit her.

It was coming from above.

Her head snapped up in time for her to see a great black-winged shadow pass overhead.

The beast angled its long body, its pointed tail slicing through the air as it beat its wings, and a glowing red eye scanned the forest. She ducked down and pressed against a tree, never more aware of her bright scarlet hair and green dress, and how black everything was in comparison to her. Her heart lodged in her throat as she stilled, terror gripping her as she stared at the sky, trying to spot where it had gone.

She looked at the branch she still gripped, a weapon that would be useless against such a beast, and then in the direction the other creature had run, a cold feeling sliding through her.

It hadn't run because she had chased it off.

It hadn't run from her.

It had sensed this larger creature closing in on their location and had fled from it.

Her gaze slowly drifted to the weapon in her sooty hands as her breaths shallowed.

Charcoal.

She swallowed hard.

The trees had been scorched by an inferno.

By wyvern fire.

Everything went still and silent, and then a roar rolled across the land, raising the fine hairs on her nape and arms and sending a chill shooting down her spine—the same roar she had heard when walking with Hades.

Persephone kicked off into a stumbling run through the trees.

Just as intense heat blazed across her back and golden light threw her shadow out before her.

CHAPTER 22

Unease slid down Hades's spine as he removed his gauntlets to tuck them into the waist of his black armour as he approached the tower.

Nyx stood at the base of it, speaking with several of his temple guards. His gaze leaped to the top of the tower and then back to Nyx, and the urge to teleport to her and discover what had happened was strong, but not as strong as his need to reassure himself that Persephone was still in her room.

He stepped into the darkness and out the other side, coming to a dead stop in the centre of the circular room at the top of the tower. He swung around, gaze darting over the bed and the bath, and the scant furniture.

The room was empty.

His heart hammered a hard beat against his ribs, so fierce it felt as if they might crack under the duress.

He might crack.

Hades teleported again, landing close to Nyx this time, startling her. She spun to face him, her right hand coming up to flutter close to the silver-blue arcs of metal that formed her breastplate and her dark-to-light-blue eyes widening.

"My god-king," she murmured throatily, her voice hitching as if with sorrow.

He narrowed his eyes on her and barked, "Where is she?"

"Gone. Your little pet escaped and now she is gone." She reached her other hand out to him and that sorrow in her voice painted itself across her fine features.

But Hades was not fooled.

"What did you do?" he snarled as darkness swept through him to swallow the light, plunging his soul back into the abyss Persephone had been slowly drawing it up from. His nails transformed into claws as his teeth lengthened into fangs and his vision sharpened as shadows swathed his mind and something within him purred at him to force Nyx to answer him.

Shock swept over Nyx's face, fooling the guards judging by the looks they cast at her, but not him.

Her little act wasn't convincing in the slightest.

Hades shot his hand out, grasped her throat and yanked her to him, until her face was mere inches from his. He flashed his fangs in her face as he closed his fingers, pressing the tips of his claws into her flesh.

"Where did you take her?" he boomed and the land beneath his feet fractured, tiny fissures streaking outwards in all directions and causing the guards to move back.

Or that might have been his rage that made them swiftly distance themselves from him.

Shadows whipped around his feet as he glared into Nyx's brightening eyes.

"Answer me!" He turned with her, kicked off and slammed her with such force into the side of the tower that blood burst from her lips, splattering his left cheek. He drew her towards him and shoved her back again, smashing her back into the wall. "I said, answer me!"

Her face crumpled, her fine eyebrows furrowing as desperation flooded her eyes, and she wheezed, "It is better she is gone. I did what I thought was right. I did what I had to for this realm and for you. She is not worthy of you—"

Hades scowled at her as he tightened his grip on her throat to choke her, anger raking his insides, clawing and dragging him down into the deep dark, away from the light. "You dare believe you have the right to decide what is best for this realm and for me?"

"Uprisings… mutinies… the lands changing…" She squeezed each word out as he closed his fingers more tightly around her throat and bore down on her, her eyes wild now. "She… will… be… your downfall."

"This realm has been shadow and blood for too long," he growled close to her face and bared his fangs again as he thought about what she had said. There was unrest in many regions, with several factions attempting to gain power, which he easily crushed and restored order wherever it happened, and the lands were changing, but he felt the changes were for the better. The realm was growing more stable, and life had improved for many of his subjects because of it. "I have neglected it… and it has taken Persephone to make me see that. I have been blind. I have not been a good king to my people."

"Lies," she hissed and glared at him now. "You are… good… king."

Hades loosened his hold on her, but didn't release her as he shook his head and studied the feelings growing within him, ones that had been quiet before but roared at him now, opening his eyes just as Persephone had to make him see how wrong Nyx was.

"No. I have not." His brow relaxed, the tension easing from his muscles. "I have terrorised those under my care and have allowed dark and violent souls to run amok in my realm for too long. I have not been a good king, Nyx, and while I have long appreciated your unwavering support, I cannot condone what you have done. I cannot forgive you."

Her eyes widened again and she rapidly shook her head. "She will be your downfall."

"If she is to be my downfall… then I readily accept my fate. I would do anything to have but another day with her. Another hour. I would sacrifice everything for it. I would go to war with my own flesh and blood for it." Hades smiled slightly, and Nyx looked stunned to see it. His anger abated, trickling from him as he stared at Nyx and saw in her eyes the reason she had done what she had.

She cared about his welfare, and had been trying to protect him in her own way, but she had been serving her own needs too, and that had his anger spiking again.

"You are wrong about her, Nyx," Hades said, his gaze drifting up the height of the tower and heart aching to see his little goddess standing on the balcony there, waiting for him. "Persephone is not the one unworthy of me. I am the one unworthy of her."

The need to see her and tell her the things that were in his heart, casting away the barriers and revealing his true feelings to her in the hope she would accept him as her husband had him releasing Nyx and turning away, his focus shifting to the gate to Olympus.

"I will bring her back. Zeus will not stop me from bringing her back to the Underworld." He went to step away from Nyx.

Only her words stopped him.

"She is not in Olympus."

Hades pivoted to face her, the darkness sweeping through him again, his rage spiking as he caught the fear that flashed across her eyes as his shadows writhed around his feet and he glared at her. "What do you mean, she is not in Olympus?"

Nyx swallowed hard and inched back against the wall of the tower. "I did what I thought was right for your sake and the sake of this realm. She was a danger to you both. I thought that if she was gone—"

Hades seized her by her throat again as cold shot down his spine and the unease he had been feeling morphed into despair and fear. When Nyx had said Persephone was gone, he had presumed Nyx meant she had run away, had left him and returned to Olympus.

But Nyx meant she was dead.

Not dead.

He clung to that fragile thread of light and hope within him that told him she wasn't dead and he wasn't too late to save her. If she had died, he would know. Her soul would be on its way to him, ushered to him by Thanatos so he could judge her and find her place in the Underworld.

"Where did you take her?" he snarled in her face and had to fight to stop himself from strangling her so she could speak.

"East," she wheezed. "The scorched lands."

"The wyvern nest?" His eyes widened as chills swept over his skin, numbing his rage and his mind as he imagined Persephone there, exposed to the dangers of that valley and the ravenous hunger of those beasts. He had bound her powers. She had no way to defend herself against them. Fury at himself joined his anger with Nyx and he pivoted and cast her away from him, hurling her towards the guards. Without looking at them, he barked, "Lock her in Tartarus and let her think on what she has done."

"My god-king—" Nyx started.

Hades didn't wait to hear her protests and pleas.

He launched into a teleport and out the other side. The ground split beneath his boots as they touched down, shadows bursting from beneath them as he sprinted forwards, his wild gaze scanning the desolate valley as his heart thundered, pouring darkness through his veins that clouded his mind and made it impossible for him to use his connection to the realm to locate Persephone. His claws grew longer, his fangs sharper, as it stole control of him and flooded him with a hunger for violence. He seethed with it as it mingled with his rage to propel him forwards at speed, into the heart of the valley.

Where was Persephone?

Fear threaded through his anger and hunger, lacing them together into a feeling that clawed at his heart, shredding his soul as he searched for her and couldn't find her. The warm air carried the faint scent of blood, jacking up the despair that sank talons into him to squeeze the remains of his heart.

Among the coppery tang of blood was a more delicate scent, one that wrenched at him and pulled him firmly into the abyss.

Lilies.

Hades sprinted through the trees, leashing his need to teleport, aware that if he surrendered to it, he might miss her. The sharp branches cut at his face as he blasted through them and his shadows swept around him, severing them before he could reach them in order to protect him. The scent of his own blood joined that of Persephone's as warmth trickled down his right cheek.

He broke out into a clearing on the other side of the forest.

And the air exploded from his lungs.

Persephone.

She stood in the middle of the plain, her tangled mass of scarlet hair and the soft jade of her dress making her stand out amongst the black landscape and despite the looming night.

The sharp, hot rage that had gripped him fell away at the sight of her, relief sweeping it away as she pivoted to face him and her wide green eyes locked with his. His gaze catalogued the blood that streaked her face and drenched the front right side of her dress from her thigh downwards, where the delicate fabric had been shredded.

By talons.

He took a step towards her, a slave to his need to take care of her, to tend to her wounds and ensure she was all right. He ached with a need to sweep her into his arms. Pleasure rolled through him as she began moving towards him rather than running away, no trace of fear in her eyes as she gazed at him, despite his fangs and his claws, and the darkness that reigned in his eyes.

He had to appear every bit the monster those in her realm made him out to be, and yet she was running to him now, a flicker of desperation crossing her features, as if she couldn't wait to be back in his arms.

"Run!" she screamed. "Run, Hades!"

Hades's mood instantly blackened again, the rage pouring through his veins like hot acid as he realised she wasn't running to be back in his arms—or at least it wasn't the only reason she was now moving at speed in his direction.

A great black wyvern dropped out of the dark sky like a shadow, swooping at her.

She shrieked and ducked, and then swung wildly with a branch, spinning on her heel and smashing it against the dragon's paw to knock it off course as it came dangerously close to snatching her. Her grip on her makeshift weapon failed as she followed through with the blow and it fell from her hands, leaving her wide open.

On a vicious growl, Hades teleported to her and swept her into his arms and into another teleport. She gasped as the darkness swallowed them, the way her hands came up to grip his arm and his shoulder pouring bliss through him that had no chance of dampening his fury. He stepped out of the teleport with her at the fringes of the forest and set her down, unable to obey the side of himself that roared to take her back to the tower.

He needed to deal with the wyvern right now, refused to delay even a moment longer than necessary.

It would pay for what it had done to his Persephone.

Hades stepped away from her, her attempts to grasp his leg and stop him lost on him as he strode onto the plain and glared up at the wyvern where it circled overhead, crimson eyes seeking its prey.

It spotted him.

Rather than retreating, it let out a fierce roar followed by a stream of fire that streaked across the black ground where he had been standing, the intense heat of it melting the rock.

It was too slow.

Hades appeared on its back and gripped its right wing, and ducked backwards as it swung its great head, the long horns that protruded from it coming close to clipping him. He wrenched hard on the wyvern's wing and it shrieked as it pitched left and went down. Darkness devoured Hades, seizing control to have him barely aware of what he was doing as he tore into the beast, as he ripped it apart with his bare hands, fuelled by the image in his head of Persephone bleeding and her stark fear as she had run to him.

Warmth splattered him, drenching his face and his hands as he ripped flesh and broke bone. As the agonised howls died and the frantic struggles of the wyvern beneath him ceased, awareness rolled back over him.

Hades stared down at the mangled mess beneath him, at crimson flesh and blood, white bone and black scales. It didn't even resemble the wyvern it had been. He staggered off the remains, breathing hard, each one he sucked down reeking of blood. His muscles shook as he scrubbed a hand over his face, trying to clear the blood away, aware he would scare Persephone if he went to her as he was now. He trudged back across the plain towards the forest, each step a labour as his tired body ached and he felt as if he had fought a war against an army, not just a battle with a dragon.

He stared at his bloodstained hands.

Fear.

Fear he had lost Persephone, and then fear she was dead, and then fear from seeing her almost plucked from his reach by the wyvern, was responsible for the fatigue sweeping through him. That fear continued to beat inside him, chipping away at his remaining strength, but the moment he reached the forest and saw Persephone standing at the fringes of it, another branch held in a white-knuckle grip before her, it melted away.

Hades couldn't help himself.

He strode right up to her and swept her into his arms as she dropped her weapon, clutching her to him as he banded one arm around her back and palmed the back of her head with his other hand.

Clinging to her.

He bent his head and breathed her in, and shivered when she brought her hands up and planted them against his back.

Holding him.

By the gods, her reaction made him greedy, made him want to keep hold of her and never let her go. He ached to savour this moment, to drink his fill of it before she realised what she had done and released him or pushed him away. The fear returned, only this time he feared her letting him go and stealing the pleasure of her touch from him.

He just needed to hold her a little longer.

He had almost lost her.

"Nyx," he growled, unable to hold back the spike of anger that speared him as he thought about what might have happened if he hadn't returned to the tower, no longer able to resist his need to see Persephone.

If he had been only minutes later, he might have lost his little goddess.

His love.

"I will kill her," he snarled, his mind darkening, the abyss beckoning again as pleasing images of adding Nyx's blood to the wyvern's that covered him tempted him into teleporting to Tartarus. "As she tried to kill you."

Persephone emerged from his embrace and gave a soft shake of her head as her green eyes sought his, but the anger and hurt in them were unmistakable. She could mask it all she wanted, but Nyx's actions had wounded her.

His sweet, wonderfully diplomatic queen held her nerve as she gazed up at him and spoke words he could see had taken her a lot of effort to keep calm and even.

"She worries you will lose this realm and that all of these troubles… they are caused by me. Nyx only wanted me gone so you would not be dethroned. I do not want that to happen either." She placed one hand on his chest and her gaze fell to it, and her scarlet eyebrows slowly lowered as she murmured, "She did try to kill me, didn't she?"

And then her eyes leaped up to meet his.

"But that is no reason to kill her." Persephone pressed her fingertips into his chest. "I am not dead, and Nyx is a valuable ally to you, and perhaps she is right about some things—"

The way she cut herself off and averted her gaze made him want to demand to know what things Nyx had been right about. He frowned as he recalled what the goddess had said to him about Persephone being unworthy of him, and had to clench his teeth to hold back a growl as he realised Nyx had said those things to her too, filling her head with doubts and clawing away her confidence, stripping it from her just as others had before her.

"I understand you must punish her. It was wrong of Nyx to act as she has and it is tantamount to treason," her gaze sought his again, "but do not kill her. I do not want her death on my hands, or you to lose a powerful ally you might need in the future. I worry that she might attempt to overthrow you if you are not firm with her. When she teleported me here, I feared she might seek your head to take your throne. Perhaps you could just teach her the error of her ways and remind her that you are king in this realm?"

His gentle little goddess. He basked in her tenderness and her light, unsure he had ever found a soul that was more good and beautiful than she was, but he also had to fight to hold back the tide of anger that swelled within him as he ran over her words and felt she was doubting his strength.

He barked out a laugh at that.

Framed her face with his palms and made sure her eyes remained on his as he gazed down at her and kept his voice soft, despite the darkness that raged within him and demanded he show her that he was strong, that she was wrong about him. She hadn't meant to belittle him, but he couldn't let her slight go uncorrected either.

"No god, goddess, or titan in this realm can overthrow me, my little goddess," he husked as he held her gaze. "They are but irritating flies, buzzing around me, and easily crushed. My power here is absolute. You have no need to fear I will lose this handsome head of mine."

She glanced beyond him to the remains of the wyvern, the look that graced her sublime features speaking to him and telling him she believed him because she had just witnessed it for herself.

He ran over everything she had said to him, picking out all the things that had shown the depth of her concern for him, and had strengthened his hope. Her unguarded words seared themselves on his soul, a balm that deepened the feelings he had for her, drawing them to the surface. He could almost believe she loved him.

And he might have lost her before ever hearing her speak to him as she had just now.

He might never have known she had feelings for him.

Whatever they were.

"I meant to return," she whispered, snaring his attention and drawing the whole of his focus back to her just as his mind began to wander dark paths filled with pleasing thoughts of what he was going to do to Nyx as punishment. He stared down at Persephone, not sure he had heard her correctly. She shyly met his gaze. "I thought to bring an army with me to help you."

Hades scoffed. "You thought to ask my brother for aid?"

He couldn't believe it. Not the fact she had openly declared she had been leaving with the intention of returning, something which was incredible enough, nor the fact she had meant to bring an army of Olympians back with her. To his realm.

He wanted to bathe in how good she was, and the fact she had wanted to aid him, and hadn't been leaving him forever, but he got stuck on the fact her plan included his brother and bringing Olympians into his realm.

Hades's expression darkened and hers slackened, a spark of fear igniting in her eyes as they leaped between his, that look telling him she knew she had said something wrong.

"Never seek to involve my brother and Olympus in matters of the Underworld," he growled, putting force behind each word so she would never make the same mistake again. "The business of my realm is mine to handle, not Zeus's or Poseidon's. No Olympian will set foot on my soil. On this I will not be moved."

She had started to shrink back, but then she got that fire in her eyes and her spine straightened and her shoulders went rigid, and she glared right back at him. "I meant only to help. I did not realise your need to control everything and be in command at all times ran so deep, but for the record, I am an Olympian… in your realm… brought here by you… therefore you have broken your own rules. Perhaps I should return to Olympus as planned so I no longer taint your wonderful realm."

She wrenched free of his grip, tipped her chin up and swept past him, the anger that clouded the air around her making it hard to breathe as he desperately thought of something to say while reeling from her verbal blows.

Her indignant air was somewhat ruined when she placed her right foot down, hissed in a pained breath and bent forwards to clutch at her thigh.

His anger was ruined with it.

"Persephone," he breathed and rounded her, the concern that had arrowed through him growing as he saw the unmistakable stain of fresh blood coating her hands and her green dress.

He frowned and cursed himself for forgetting she had been injured. It should have been at the front of his mind, tending to her the first thing he had done the moment he had returned to her, but instead he had let his anger get the better of him and had come dangerously close to driving a wedge between them again. He bent and swept her into his arms, cradling her under her knees and around her back, and teleported with her before she could loose the angry protest he could see rising to the tip of her tongue as she pushed at his shoulders.

Hades landed in his bedchamber with her and she stilled, her enormous green eyes sweeping around the room and an echo of her shock rolling through him too. He had intended to return her to her room, and somehow he had ended up in his.

Her gaze landed on him, incredulous and demanding.

He refused to voice the reason he had brought her to his room, unwilling to make himself vulnerable. He needed her safe. She was hurt and he needed to tend to her, and ached to make her feel she was safe and nothing could harm her now she was with him again. If he told her that, she would withdraw again, or might shift the blame for her injuries onto him.

Nyx would suffer for what she had done.

But for Persephone's sake, and the sake of his realm, he would not kill her.

His mood darkened again as he strode to the large bed.

"What are you doing?" Her voice trembled, betraying the nerves he could already sense in her.

He growled.

"Tending to you."

CHAPTER 23

Persephone's small hands pressed against the pauldrons of Hades's black armour as he carried her across his black-walled chambers, heading for his large bed.

"Really, there is no need. It is only a small cut. It will heal. Take me back to my room." She sounded flustered.

"No," Hades bit out, the thought of leaving her alone and unprotected rousing his darker side again, pulling it back to the fore and making him seethe with a need to snarl and lash out at anyone who strayed close to his room.

His senses stretched outwards to pinpoint everyone nearby and track them, pleasing images of them foolishly nearing his queen and him cutting them down filling his mind to distract him. Persephone continued to protest, but he refused to hear them. When she tried to push free of his arms, he tightened his grip on her and she gasped, the pained sound cutting at him and dragging him back to her.

Hades loosened his hold and gently set her down on his bed, and with a glare at her he hoped was commanding, growled, "Do not move from that spot."

He turned and crossed the room to a side table. He grabbed one of the cloths that had been folded beside a golden bowl of water, wetted it and washed his face and hands to make himself more presentable, and then removed his gauntlets from his belt to set them down on the table. He gathered the bowl and two clean cloths, pivoted and frowned at Persephone.

She hobbled across the room, heading for the closed wooden doors to his right. When she noticed he had caught her, she moved quicker, wincing whenever she placed weight on her right leg.

Hades teleported to the small table beside his bed, set the water and cloths down, and then teleported to her. She gasped as he swept her back into his arms and scowled up at him as she beat her fist against his chest, only hurting herself as she tried to pummel it through his breastplate.

He set her back down on the bed as gently as he could manage given the fact she was intent on infuriating him.

She immediately wriggled away from him, shimmying to the other side of the bed. Hades growled and seized her arm, and tugged her back to his side.

"Stay," he bit out as she wrestled against him, refusing to obey him.

"I can tend to myself," she snapped in return and slapped at his hand on her arm.

When he didn't release her, she twisted and reached for the cloths, and ended up almost knocking the water all over the floor. Hades quickly grabbed the bowl, so only a little spilled, and shot her a black look. She scowled right back at him.

He grabbed the top cloth and the bowl and sat on the bed, and again she tried to escape him. He placed his hand on the other side of her legs, hemming her in, and she looked as if she was going to give him hell, or perhaps he was frightening her. He reined in his frustration and drew down a breath to calm himself.

"I wish to tend to your wounds." He let the words tumble from his lips, sure they would only make her want to bolt even more.

They had the opposite effect. Rather than continuing to fight him, she stilled and studied him, her green gaze seeking his. He felt as if she was searching for something in his eyes—the reason he needed to take care of her? Hades let her see it. He let her see that he needed to assuage his guilt about what had happened to her, and he needed to be the one to take care of her, so he could see with his own eyes that she would be well again.

She loosed a little huff, folded her arms over her chest and sank back against the headboard of his bed.

Hades took it as an invitation to take care of her and set about ripping one cloth into long strips and the other into four pieces. He placed those four pieces in the water and set the strips aside on the bed. He parted the torn layers of her dress, wrung out one of the pieces of cloth, and cleaned the blood from her skin, working methodically and avoiding the puncture wound. It was deep and she had lost a lot of blood. He was surprised she could walk at all. The injury cut into her muscle on the outside of her thigh. She was lucky the wyvern hadn't caught her on the inside of her thigh. She might have bled out before he could reach her.

Anger at Nyx spiked his blood again and he purged it, focusing on tending to Persephone. He would punish his subordinate later. Right now, taking care of his love took priority and nothing was more important than reassuring himself she would be fine, and ensuring she would heal swiftly.

When her leg was clean, he focused on the wound, dabbing at the angry red edges and telling himself on repeat that she would be fine as a heavy sensation built inside him, thoughts of losing her tormenting him. She was a goddess. With some rest and sleep, she would be healed in no time. A few hours sleep would turn this wound into nothing more than a sore scar.

Hades took up the strips of material, gently raised her leg so her knee was bent, and began binding the wound, passing the material under her thigh and then over it, making tight passes with it.

Persephone began squirming.

"Keep still," he murmured, not wanting her to loosen the bandages. He needed them tight.

She didn't.

She wriggled harder as he made another pass with the bandage, threading it beneath her leg, and he glanced up at her.

And then back at her.

Her cheeks were bright pink and she refused to meet his gaze.

She kept staring at her leg.

Not her leg, he realised as he lowered his gaze there. She was staring at his hands, and he was suddenly very aware of where they were as he looked at them too. The wound was high up, close to her hips, and he had been passing his hands between her bare thighs, dangerously near to the juncture of them.

He was thankful for his armour as his cock shot steel-hard, the codpiece of it concealing the evidence of his sudden arousal from her. The blush that threatened to climb his cheeks as they both stared at his hands was in danger of giving him away though. He forced himself to keep working, slowly tamping down the surge of desire that had his hands close to shaking as his skin brushed hers. She was all softness and warmth, and he found himself grazing his thumbs across her thigh with each pass of the bandage, slowing down as he savoured touching her.

By the time he had run out of bandage and was forced to tuck the end in to secure it, he was painfully aroused, his heart racing and blood thundering as he fought to tear his gaze away from her thigh.

Her hands trembled as she smoothed her dress down over the apex of her thighs, covering herself, and then brushed her fingers over the bandage. He lifted his gaze to her face and she shyly met it, the blush of colour on her cheeks deepening.

The urge to lean towards her, capture her blazing cheek and pull her to him as he claimed her lips pounded inside him, battering his iron will. He stared at her lips, aching to take them and taste her again, to feel them beneath his and know that she was with him again, safely back in his arms. The tip of her tongue poked out, sweeping across her lower lip to dampen it and torment him, as if she was readying herself for his kiss and ached for it as fiercely as he did.

His gaze darted up to collide with hers. Banked heat darkened her green irises, beckoning him and making him teeter on the verge of surrendering to his need to kiss her, but the flicker of fear stopped him.

Hades pulled back on the reins of his need, clawing back control, and somehow found the strength to resist. He gathered the soiled cloths and placed them in the bowl, and set it on the small table beside the bed as he stood. His gaze drifted to her again as she angled her head back to look up at him, a soft expression on her face that was part fear, part need that called to him. Kissing her now would be a mistake. She had been through a lot and he could see it was catching up with her, her mind beginning to fill with all the things that could have happened. He had been in her position enough times, fresh from a battle for his life, to know that soon she would crave a physical outpouring of her relief.

He wanted her, but not like that. He didn't want her to use him to satisfy the hungers that were about to hit her, that bewitching blend of relief and a desperate need to feel alive, to bathe in the fact she had survived. She would resent him for it once her mind had cleared and she was thinking straight again.

And he might resent himself a little for it too.

Hades forced himself to back away from her as he husked, "You may have my chambers if you swear to remain here and rest."

She nodded and then frowned at him, a flicker of disappointment tugging at her fine eyebrows. "Where are you going?"

He reached the twin wooden doors and paused for a moment to drink his fill of her beauty and savour the relief that she had survived, stealing enough of her to see him through the night so he could resist returning to her and taking advantage of her.

"Back to help my men." He frowned at his bare hands, walked to the side table, and grabbed his gauntlets. "And then to Tartarus."

The flicker of darkness that crossed Persephone's eyes said she knew what he intended to do there, and only made him want to hurt Nyx even more, because he hated seeing those dark thoughts in Persephone's gaze. He hated the thought of her being tainted by them as he was. He wanted her to remain in the light, to always shine with warmth and tenderness.

Or perhaps he merely wanted to protect her from all the darkness of this world, and he had failed in that task.

He tugged his gauntlets on as he strode back to the door, waiting for her to speak, some part of him wanting her to stop him or show him that she wanted him to stay with her, or reveal that she was glad to be back with him. He needed something to go on. Another sign that she wanted to be with him.

He was fooling himself.

For all he knew, her words about wanting to bring an army from Olympus to aid him had been a lie designed to dampen his anger and keep it in check so he didn't lash out at her for attempting to leave him. She had probably said whatever she had thought he wanted to hear in order to protect herself from his wrath.

Even the way she had held him had probably been an act.

He looked back at her, hoping it hadn't been and trying to convince himself her behaviour and her desire to bring an army for him so he could retain his throne had been real.

Persephone remained still on his bed, her gaze on her knees, and he thought she would let him go without another word, without the sound of her voice to comfort him through the coming hours or a sign that his hope wasn't unfounded.

How wrong he was.

When he opened the door and went to leave, she unravelled his world with two simple, softly spoken words that stole his heart and claimed it as hers forever.

"Be careful."

CHAPTER 24

Hades couldn't think about the events of yesterday without flushing with both rage and desire. He gripped his left shoulder and rolled it, grimacing as it grated in its socket and his muscles throbbed and twinged. His entire body seemed to ache, sore right down to his bones from his fight to protect Persephone and his battle to restore order to the Underworld. He should have rested after his battle with the wyvern, but his men had needed him in the western regions. Together they had managed to quell the rebellion and capture the people behind it. They were now in Tartarus.

With Nyx.

The goddess of night knelt before him under the single shaft of light in the darkened room. She grunted and stiffened as the large bare-chested male behind her struck her with the whip, the worn leather lashing at her spine.

"Again," Hades muttered. "Harder."

The male obeyed, striking her again, the whir of the whip slicing through the air and the harsh crack of it on her back sending pleasure rolling through Hades that fed the darkness within him. His shadows writhed around his feet, snapping at the ground in time with the whip.

He moved a step closer, coming to tower over her, and she weakly lifted her head, her bloodshot eyes seeking his.

He eased into a crouch before her, his left forearm resting on his bent knee, and her head drooped. She struggled to lift it again as her harsh breaths filled the tense silence. Behind her, the male shifted from foot to foot, his restlessness matching that of Hades's shadows as they crept towards the goddess, agitated and hungry to lash at Nyx as the male's whip had close to a thousand times.

"Why did you seek to destroy what is mine?" he murmured, his voice low and even, tightly controlled, just like his shadows.

Nyx's bloodstained throat worked on a hard swallow and she croaked, "She is inferior. Weak. A female too delicate and unfit to be your queen. I did only what I thought right for this realm… for you."

Hades bared fangs at her and his shadows shot towards her and seized her, wrapping around her arms and throat and slowly tightening as he glared at her.

"Inferior? Weak? Persephone is powerful in her own way, and that way is beautiful. She brings light and life and joy into this world. She is everything opposite to me." Hades tightened his shadows until they squeezed her flesh, making it bulge between the ribbons of black that held her. "You interfered in my business, despite what I told you. For that, Nyx, you deserve death… but that *inferior*, *weak* goddess you despise so much has granted you mercy."

Her blue eyes were wild as they sought his, filled with disbelief and a hint of relief, but also wariness, as if she couldn't quite bring herself to believe what she was hearing and trust that his queen had spared her. He wasn't sure whether it was because she knew under normal circumstances he would kill her for her betrayal, or because her view of the world was so dark, coloured by her life in his realm, that she couldn't believe Persephone wouldn't want her head in exchange for what she had done to her.

As if his gentle, beautiful queen would seek to harm another. If he had learned anything about her, it was that she abhorred death.

Hades tried not to take that personally, silently telling himself that she didn't despise him for his role in this world. She had run to him. She had tried to protect him. After he had rescued her and teleported her to the shelter of the trees, she hadn't found another branch to use as a weapon so she could defend herself against the wyvern.

She had found it so she could continue fighting—so she could aid and protect him.

That instinct to protect him, and the things she had said, reinforced his belief that she was coming to feel something for him.

That she cared about him.

"You owe your life to the goddess whose one you tried to so callously take," he growled from between clenched teeth. "You would be dead already if I had my way."

His shadows tightened further, turning her face red and then purple, and then he shoved to his feet and released her. Nyx gasped, choking as she pulled down great gulps of air and bent forwards to clutch at the blood-slicked stone floor beneath her. Her dark hair fell in matted ribbons to cover her face as she struggled to recover.

She whispered something he didn't quite catch.

"Repeat yourself," he demanded.

Her arms shook as she pushed herself up and her voice was still faint. "I know of her mother… of her."

Hades shot a dark look at the male. "Leave us."

He waited for the door to close and the male to move to a distance before he crouched before Nyx again.

"Speak," he growled, impatient to learn of his goddess.

"She is… daughter of Demeter," Nyx wheezed and struggled to sit up. Her head tipped back when she managed it, lolling before she found the strength to keep it upright.

"Demeter," he murmured with a frown. "Her power over nature makes sense now."

Nyx gingerly touched her throat. "Compared with her mother, she is nothing. The mortals pray to Demeter, not her. She is a mere shadow of her dame."

Hades refused to believe that. He brushed his thumb across his lower lip as he mulled it over, and muttered, "Or she is being held within the shadow of her."

He had met Demeter once, many centuries ago at a feast in Olympus, back when Hades had been invited to them on occasion. She was a cold sort of female, a haughty one with too much pride, and she had looked upon him with obvious disdain. He couldn't imagine such a warm, caring female like Persephone coming from her loins. There was nothing warm about Demeter. Or caring. In fact, Hades felt sure the only person Demeter cared about was herself.

Which had something else making sense to him.

Something which made the ground beneath his boots crack as he balled his hands into fists.

Demeter was the reason Persephone lacked confidence. She had inflicted those invisible scars on her own daughter, and he had no doubt she had done it to hold her daughter back, fearing Persephone would surpass her and take her place.

"Olympians," he snarled, his mood taking a sharp, dark turn as he compared Demeter's behaviour to that of Zeus's towards him. His brother had sought to keep him in the shadows too, and had sown doubt in his mind many times over their centuries together, keeping him down so he wouldn't rise up and take his place. He glared at Nyx. "What else did you discover?"

"Very little. Your future queen is difficult to learn about. As far as I can tell, she does not have any close companions among the gods and goddesses of Olympus." Nyx relaxed a little, which would have been the perfect time for Hades to strike her down had Persephone not spared her. "I learned only that she apparently does not socialise much and is often not at the feasts with her mother. She is overlooked, it seems. I am sure she attends many feasts where she goes unnoticed among the louder, more audacious Olympians, who presume she did not attend."

So his little queen was overlooked by all. How did that make her feel? Did she feel like an outcast? He frowned at his knees. Did she feel as he did?

Demeter wasn't solely responsible for her scars then. Everyone in Olympus had ignored and shunned Persephone, stripping away her confidence and making her feel inferior to them. He flexed his fingers and gripped his knees, digging his talons into the top of his boots. He would need to show her that she wasn't inferior, that she was strong and courageous.

He needed to make her see herself as he did. She was beautiful, and warm, and brave, and powerful. She was a ray of light that drove back the darkness of this world. A gift that brought it to life.

Nyx's gaze boring into him had him scowling at her, but it didn't wipe the knowing look from her face, the one that said she had seen the path of his thoughts and she knew.

She knew he was a sentimental fool where Persephone was concerned.

That he was madly in love with her.

"What else?" he growled, keeping his scowl in place.

"She governs the earth, and has a kind temperament, which the Olympians mistake for weakness." Nyx gave him a regretful look. Because she had mistaken it for weakness too. "Not many in the city talk about her, but they talk about Demeter. She is seeking her daughter. It is only a matter of time before someone discovers she is here, Hades."

"Let them come." He pushed to his feet, the shadows gathering around them as he willed Demeter to be the one to come for her daughter. He would show her the error of her ways too. "Olympus cannot take Persephone from me. She is mine."

"I will speak with Thanatos and Hypnos about increasing security around—"

"You will speak to no one," Hades interjected. "Your time in Tartarus is not done. You will remain here and receive a thousand lashes a day until you convince me you believe Persephone is fit to be my queen."

She glared at him, as if that would take her centuries.

It probably would.

"I will return tomorrow." Hades pivoted on his heel and swept from the room before Persephone's influence on him had him changing his mind and releasing Nyx. He couldn't. Persephone was right and Nyx had committed treason of the highest order by attempting to kill his queen. He would stand firm and keep her imprisoned.

He strode along the columned corridor of the entrance hall of Tartarus and out into his realm.

He scowled at the black ground as it crunched beneath his boots, his eyebrows knitting hard and the corners of his lips turning downwards. Anger rolled through him again as his thoughts turned to Demeter and how she treated her daughter.

Hades pulled down a deep breath and expelled it, seeking calm and trying to let his anger go. Not only his anger towards Demeter. Nyx had meddled, and it had placed Persephone in grave danger, but he felt it had also broken a barrier between him and his little goddess, one that he might not have overcome if not for Nyx's intervention.

He stilled and stared at the lands around him, a flat plain that rose into jagged peaks on all sides and stretched in a long curve from Tartarus to his temple. His gaze drifted to the tower he had built from the black earth, his thoughts swift to latch onto Persephone and warmth blooming inside him. Her words rang in his ears, not the softly spoken ones she had left him with after he had tended to her but the ones she had lashed at him with in the valley after he had saved her.

And ones before that too.

That warmth grew stronger, even as his blood chilled. His mind and body switched between the polar feelings as he thought about Persephone, going in circles. No one had ever made him see his failings in the way she had, or awakened feelings in him that were powerful and easily overwhelmed and seized control of him. He couldn't remember ever feeling so out of sorts. Not out of sorts, he reasoned as he gazed at the tower. She was bringing a softer version of himself to the fore, one he hadn't realised existed, and that was the reason he felt off balance at times around her.

He wasn't used to feeling the things he did when he was near her, and when he was miles from her. She lived in his thoughts, a permanent resident he couldn't evict, even in the midst of battle when his mind needed to be sharp and focused. She was there. Filling him with a need to survive so he could return to her.

So he could see her again.

Hades swept his gaze over the mountains that reached high into the sky, their sharp forbidding peaks like the fangs of a beast. His kingdom. His home. While he had grown to love it, he had despised it at first, and now Persephone had opened his eyes, he could see how it had shaped him and how his dark feelings in turn had shaped it.

He could see all his failings.

His gaze lowered to the ground, his mood shifting towards sombre as he felt something else deep in his soul.

He was alone.

And he had never felt it as much as he did now, with Persephone's tender words echoing in his mind and that soft look she had given him imprinted on his heart.

He couldn't recall the last time someone had shown real concern for his wellbeing.

He smiled wryly. Nyx only cared about the state of the realm. Without him ruling the Underworld, her own position would be in jeopardy. He wasn't sure she had acted out of care for his wellbeing when she had tried to send Persephone away.

But Persephone's concern had been genuine.

And while it pleased him, it had also unleashed a plague of thoughts in his mind that refused to be wiped out.

Hades glanced up at the tower again and frowned as shock swept through him.

Persephone stood on the balcony. She had left his chambers, breaking her vow, but had returned to the tower, sacrificing her freedom. Why?

He half expected her to go inside as he stared at her, but she remained where she was, her gaze searing him and making him yearn for her. Every soft gasp and shy glance she had given him when he had been tending to her filled his mind, stealing his focus away from his surroundings and narrowing it down to her. He rubbed the pads of his fingers together, still able to feel the satin of her skin and the warmth of the valley of her thighs.

By the gods, he had never craved a female as fiercely as he craved her.

He felt sure she would know the depth of his need and his desire as he gazed at her, yearning to be close to her, to trace his hands over her bare skin and savour her shocked and pleased little gasps and how her green eyes would grow dark with need.

He felt sure she would go inside, breaking this moment.

Her reaction to his nearness had been enough to tell him that she wasn't used to being that close to a male, and the knowledge that she might be untouched provoked a dangerous need in him, one that had pounded inside him throughout their time apart and continued to drum in his mind now.

He wanted to be her one and only.

The darkly possessive part of him that wanted to claim her and then guard her from the world, ensuring no other male laid a hand on her, awakened as he gazed at her, as his heart galloped and his blood heated. She would be his and his alone.

His queen.

His love.

Rather than leaving and shattering the moment, she leaned on the balcony, her fall of scarlet hair tumbling over her shoulders to hang before her arms.

The temptation to teleport to her and speak with her, to coax her into accepting another kiss was near overwhelming. Hades resisted it, slowly crushing the need, but it was strong. Consuming. He glanced at the ground and then back at her, not daring to believe she might burn with the same tormenting need that he felt. Her blushes last night were more likely to be born of shame rather than desire.

She had run from him after all.

When given the chance, she had fled.

His thoughts trod that dark path, taking him deeper into it until cold swept through him, the warmth of Persephone lost on him as doubts clouded his mind. Those doubts blotted out the affection Persephone had shown him, pulling him away from the truth and bending reality towards a colder, darker place, easily defeating him. Was he doomed to be alone for all eternity? Surrounded by many, but feeling as if he was the only one in this vast, dark realm?

Hades lowered his gaze to the black earth and stared at it, feeling as if his own shadows were swirling through him, slowly blotting out the light to plunge his soul into darkness.

And then a delicate green bud broke the surface of the dirt and blossomed into a bright red rose.

And by the gods, he should be furious that she had somehow found a connection to her power, but instead he stared at the flower, deeply aware that she had made it for him. It wasn't an attempt to escape, just as her foolish failed run towards the gate to Olympus yesterday hadn't been one.

That had been an attempt to protect him, something which was as foreign and strange to him as what she was doing now, with this flower.

The rose was an attempt to show him that he wasn't alone, even when he felt he was, and it touched him.

Hades looked up at her and the ache to be close to her, to feel her soft curves pressing against his again, was too strong. He didn't want to be alone. Not anymore. She had made him see just how lonely he had been, and he couldn't go back to that life. He couldn't live without her.

He needed her.

He teleported to her, ripping a gasp from her as he appeared behind her and she whirled to face him. He swept her into his arms, hauling her against him, and backed her into the stone frame of the door, his heart racing and fire surging through his veins. He ached to kiss her as she gazed up at him through bewitching green eyes, to know the taste of her again, but fought it.

She didn't.

She punched her fingers into his black hair, pulled him down to her and claimed his lips.

His eyes widened as she slanted her mouth over his, her kiss bold and electrifying, shaking him to his foundations. A desperate little gasp escaped her as she tugged him closer, her kiss growing fevered and wild.

And then when he began to kiss her back, she planted her hands to his chest and shoved him back to arm's length.

And shook her head.

Hades growled at her, rage burning up his blood to replace the desire she had roused, fury that she had reined in her passion just as his had claimed hold of him, stirring his body into a frenzy of need. He wouldn't have it. He bent his head and tried to kiss her again, but she locked her elbows and braced her hands against his chest, stopping his attempt. He didn't miss how her eyes darkened as she palmed his pectorals, or how his body burned to know the feel of her hands on his bare skin rather than his black leather shirt.

When he had ditched his armour during his visit to Tartarus, he had thought it a mistake to obey his need to remove the restrictive metal pieces and render himself vulnerable in order to feel he could breathe again.

Now, he was glad he had removed them.

Her eyes tried to fall to his chest as her small hands remained planted against it and a blush climbed her cheeks.

She liked the feel of his body.

If she asked it of him, he would let her explore it at her leisure. She could do as she wished with him.

Hades barely leashed the urge to say those things aloud, the side of him that wasn't addled by her touch and her kiss holding his tongue. Courting her required a more delicate approach. If he tried to goad her into admitting she wanted him as fiercely as he wanted her, she would clam up again and bolt, and he would lose all the progress he had made towards winning her heart.

So rather than kissing her or convincing her to unlace his shirt, he murmured, "How did you produce a bloom in this realm?"

Her face pinched. "Because you sealed my powers?"

He shrugged, refusing to apologise for taking precautions.

Her features relaxed and then turned pensive. "I do not know. I saw you there… and you… and well, I… and then it just happened."

Was the realm responding to her?

Or perhaps it was him.

He felt bad about the things he had done to her and that feeling was growing stronger each day. Now, she had enough power to manifest the bloom, and some foolish part of him didn't want to seal it and steal it from her again.

Hades shut that line of thought down, killing it.

He needed to be more careful.

He gazed at Persephone, taking in that glint in her eyes as she looked at the world outside her tower, one that said she was already thinking about how she could use her returning powers, and cold stole through him.

If he wasn't, then he might lose her.

CHAPTER 25

Persephone broke away from Hades, ducking under his left arm to distance herself from him as her heart pounded and her lips tingled from their kiss. Her kiss. She had kissed him. She wanted to palm her face and groan, but wanted to smile at the same time. She hadn't planned to do it. It had just happened.

Much like the flower she had made for him.

She moved towards the bed, needing the air as Hades's power and the weight of his gaze curled around her. He wanted another kiss. No, not just another kiss. He wanted more from her, and for a heartbeat, she had been tempted to give it to him. Her palms hummed with the feel of his hard chest and how frantically his heart had drummed against them, relaying his desire to her.

Persephone reached the end of the bed, turned and kept walking, unable to keep still as she flexed her fingers. His hair had been soft beneath them, silky against her skin, and his lips had been hard and unyielding as he had caught up with her and begun to kiss her back.

She blew out her breath, seeking calm and control and finding none.

At least he was keeping his distance rather than pressing her, lingering near the balcony as he tracked her with his gaze.

"How is your leg?" His deep voice rolled over her, doing wicked things to her body.

So wicked in fact that it took her a moment and a glance at him to take in what he had said. He levelled a pointed look at her right leg, and she looked down at it. Her eyebrows rose and lips parted.

"Oh. It is fine. Healing, I think." She toyed with her skirts, fidgeting with them as his gaze drilled into her thigh, making her far too aware of her body and the heat he always roused in her. She tugged at the green layers of material. "I washed my dress again, but I do not think it made much difference. The soot from the forest is difficult to wash out."

She mentally grimaced at her rambling and cursed her nerves. They were his fault. His asking about her leg had her mind filling with the way his hands had passed between her thighs and his skin had brushed hers, and how that fierce heat had gathered low in her belly. The flood of arousal he had caused had been shocking, and try as she might to keep still, she hadn't been able to in the end. She had squirmed and fought a losing battle against the desire to seize his hand and force it higher, so it brushed the apex of her thighs and gave her some relief.

Fire consumed her, the thought of him touching her setting her aflame, and she had to fight to stop herself from blushing and giving away her wicked thoughts.

He slid a look at the gown that was still draped over a chair one of the servants had brought for her—a black gown that would have concealed the dirt from the charred branches she had used as weapons. That look worked wonders to dampen her desire. As effective as a bucket of icy water tipped over her head might have been.

She gave him a look in return, one that said she wouldn't be wearing it. She had asked for a green dress. If he provided one for her, she might change into it, but she wasn't wearing black. Her skin was too pale for that colour. Black clothing made her look as if she was dead.

She glanced at Hades. His skin was paler than hers, but for some reason, the colour suited him. It accentuated his fine figure, and added to his dark air. She couldn't imagine him in any colour other than black, and perhaps a splash of crimson that would match his eyes when they changed.

His expression darkened as it shifted to her, that corona of scarlet emerging in his blue irises, and a thrill bolted through her as he growled, "I would resurrect that beast to slay it ten times over every day for the rest of eternity if I could."

She swallowed and stared at him, sure she shouldn't find such threats of dark violence arousing, but she did. Her heart fluttered. Heat climbed her cheeks. She quickly looked away before he noticed it.

The silence felt stifling, so she said the first thing that came to her.

"The wyvern or the other beast?"

Hades growled, "*Other* beast?"

Persephone looked over her shoulder at him, her eyebrows rising as confusion swept through her, but then she remembered he had only seen the dragon. "There was a smaller black beast. It possessed a thick hide, seven horns and was around this high at the shoulders."

She tiptoed and reached her right arm up.

"It attacked me, and—"

"It did *what*?" he boomed, cutting her off, his face darker than she had ever seen it.

His shadows burst from beneath his boots, and she gasped as they wrapped around her, embracing her as if they were his arms—as if they wanted to protect her too.

"I will slay this beast," he snarled, anger flashing in his now-crimson eyes, and his fangs gleamed as he grinned coldly. "It will pay for what it did."

"If you would let me finish." Persephone swatted the shadows away, planted her hands on her hips and glowered at him, an echo of the thrill she had felt after chasing the beast off rushing through her veins.

Or perhaps that tingling buzz was because of how fierce and dark Hades looked as he plotted the demise of the creature. She tamped down the flare of desire his dark appearance caused and focused on relaying what had happened, because she wanted him to know that he wasn't the only one who had changed in their time together.

"It was terrifying—oddly exciting—but I found this long, pointed branch, and I snapped it off and—and I wielded it like a spear… or perhaps a sword. I used all my wits and evaded the creature, and when I saw an opening… by the gods, it was like some kind of warrior instinct had hold of me. I stabbed it, plunging my spear deep into its flank to draw blood," she thrust her right arm forwards, as if the beast was right in front of her, caught up in the excitement of her tale—the first tale of adventure she had ever told anyone—because it was the first real adventure she'd ever had, "and then it ran. Well, and then the wyvern showed up and I think perhaps it might have scared the beast off rather than me, but I like to think it was my victory—what? What is that look for?"

His gaze had warmed and turned blue, and his handsome face had softened as she had rambled.

She could easily fool herself into believing he was proud of her when he looked at her like that.

No one had ever been proud of her before.

She wasn't sure how to react.

But then the warmth in his eyes turned to regret, and his dark eyebrows lowered, his features hardening a little again.

"I am sorry you had to fight the beast. I am sorry you were ever in danger." His blue gaze darted between hers, and seeing him like this, so different from the snarling, dark male he had been when they had first met, softened her heart towards him even more. He sighed. "I am sorry I failed you."

She blinked.

Her heart warmed.

The heart he had stolen from her.

She shook her head and took a step towards him, not wanting him to feel responsible for what had happened to her. "I am fine, Hades. I am well. In fact, I have never felt better."

He ventured a step in her direction, and then halted, a pained look flitting across his face before he eased back again. He wanted to come to her. She wanted it too. She wanted him as close to her as he could get. Not so she would feel better, but so he would. She wanted to assuage his guilt and make him see that her experience yesterday had changed her for the better, had shown her that she could be strong and brave, and could fight her own battles.

And as frightening as it had been, it had been worth it to see that look on Hades's face—the one that had revealed the depth of his feelings.

And that he was proud of her.

He casually leaned against the doorframe, far too sexy and alluring in all-black leather that hugged his figure and his hair tousled by her fingers.

And his tempting lips reddened by her kiss.

He cleared his throat, his face pinched, and then he muttered, "You returned to the tower."

She smiled at how stiff he was, and how he had struggled to find something to say. His striking blue gaze drifted around the room and then settled back on her.

She rolled her shoulders. "I do not mind it here."

And it had felt safer than remaining in his chambers, occupying his bed. Had she stayed there, her will to resist him might have shattered.

As it almost had just now.

She padded across the room to the window that overlooked his temple and stared beyond it. "Can we walk the orchard again?"

She glanced back at him, catching the surprise that flashed across his handsome features.

"Your leg does not hurt too much?" His gaze lowered to her thigh again to sear it and make her blood run far too hot.

She was tempted to fan herself as she turned to face him and shook her head. "Not at all."

Even if it had hurt, she still would have wanted to go to the orchard. Excitement chased through her again as she thought about the flower she had produced. She wanted to see if she could do more. Like adding a splash of vibrant green to the dark leaves of the pomegranate trees. She wanted to test the limits of her powers in this realm now that whatever Hades had done to her was losing its effect.

His eyes narrowed.

"You will not be able to use your powers." Those words leaving his lips both infuriated her and surprised her. How easily he could read her. He pushed away from the doorframe, straightening to his full height, his expression cold, but not cold enough to conceal that flicker of regret that crossed his eyes as he said, "I have sealed them again."

Her lips flattened and her fists clenched, but one glance over her shoulder at the orchard was enough to have her anger with him fading again. "I would still like to go."

Whatever he had done might not stop her powers now, and even if they did, she wanted to walk the orchard and maybe talk with him more about his powers and this realm.

His expression remained hard and devoid of emotion, and she was sure he would deny her, but then he held his hand out to her.

Persephone crossed the room to him and slipped hers into it, secretly savouring the way his eyes darkened as her palm slid across his and a thousand tiny bolts of lightning struck in a line up her arm. His thumb closed over the back of her hand and his fingers brushed her wrist, eliciting another thrill that had her breath hitching as he held her immobile with his heated gaze.

And then darkness enveloped her.

When it receded, she was standing at the fringes of the orchard. She went to step forwards, but Hades kept hold of her hand, stopping her, and she looked back at him. He stared at their joined hands, a look she couldn't quite read on his face as the crimson in his eyes faded to leave them a striking shade of pale blue.

"Hades?" she murmured, tempted to ask him what he was thinking as he gazed at their hands like that.

Did he like holding her hand?

She liked it.

Despite his ferocity and everything people of Olympus would have her believe about him, his grip was gentle, as if he was afraid of hurting her. She wasn't made of glass. Hadn't she proved that? He could hold her as tightly as he had when he had saved her from the wyvern and she wouldn't shatter.

It struck her that she hadn't thanked him for what he had done.

She turned back to face him, closing the distance between them again, until his warmth embraced her and his power hummed over her skin. "Thank you."

His blue gaze leaped up to lock with hers, his eyebrows rising high on his forehead. She smiled at his surprise. Had no one ever thanked him for something before? Or maybe he wasn't sure why she was showing gratitude towards him. She had to admit it was probably confusing given the fact he was still technically holding her captive.

Not that she felt like his prisoner anymore.

"For saving me from the wyvern. I never thanked you." She glanced at their linked hands as his fingertips brushed her skin, a sharp thrill chasing up her arm in response to the caress, and then met his gaze again.

"You do not need to thank me. My intervention was selfish in nature." He inched closer to her, until he was all she knew as she tipped her head back to hold his gaze. That gaze scorched her as he breathed, "The wyvern sought to take something of mine."

A shiver traipsed down her spine and her breath lodged in her throat, her heart pounding a wild, unsteady rhythm as those words seared themselves on her mind together with his possessive look.

She knew she should tell him that she wasn't his, but the words refused to come.

They would be a lie.

She couldn't breathe as she stared at him, as awareness of him seeped deep into her bones and she fought the commanding desire to lower her gaze to his lips and kiss him again. She wasn't sure how long they remained locked in their silent battle, but the longer it went on, the stronger a feeling inside her grew—he was fighting the urge to kiss her too. She willed him to be the one to break, to give her an excuse for kissing him, one that would silence the side of her that still warned her to keep her distance from him.

She cursed that side of her. The good little Olympian. The one who had been raised to be far too prim and proper, to follow the rules and obey her mother without question.

His dark eyebrows slowly drew down, his features hardening as the moment slipped through her fingers, wrenched from her by thoughts of home and how horrified her mother would be—how shocked the whole of Olympus would be—if they knew she was standing here in the Underworld, falling for its dark ruler.

Hades lifted his free hand and cupped her cheek, his palm cool against her overheating cheeks as anger rose within her, born of frustration and a feeling that she couldn't shake.

She had always been a prisoner.

Her entire life, she had been a captive of convention, and her mother had been her jailer.

And the longer she spent in this world, the more she began to feel that Hades had freed her of that life. He had opened her eyes to how her life had been, how oppressive she had found it, and had awakened her rebellious side—the one that wanted to kiss him again and make him fall in love with her.

The one who wanted to be his queen.

"Your thoughts are dark, my love. Speak to me of them," he husked and then something akin to shyness crossed his eyes before he narrowed them, hardening them again and driving out the emotion.

Because he had called her *his love.*

He had revealed his feelings to her, and maybe to himself too, and by the gods, she wanted to reach up and frame his face and tell him that it was all right because he was her love too.

The side of her she couldn't quite shake yet made her hold her tongue instead, and she didn't push the words out, because she wanted him madly in love with her, unable to live without her and willing to do anything to have her as his queen—his equal—before she told him what he wanted to hear.

How things had changed.

Her demanding dark god had stolen her from her world and brought her to his one, declaring she was his queen now, whether she liked it or not, and now he hesitated and often grew uneasy around her, and soft admissions of his feelings were enough to fell him and make him falter.

He wasn't alone.

These feelings were new and a little frightening to her too.

But they would face them together.

"I am fine," she murmured softly, wanting to reassure him that her mood wasn't anything to do with him. "I was thinking about Olympus."

He growled low, as if just the thought of her thinking of that place was enough to put him in a dark mood of his own.

Because he thought she wanted to return there.

How wrong he was.

She lifted her hand to his chest and sighed as she tore her gaze away from him to settle it on the trees as his heart thundered against her palm, the hard rhythm betraying his feelings together with the flare of heat in his eyes. He liked it when she laid her hands on him.

"Tell me about your family." Each word that left his lips was carefully weighed, and she smiled at the fact he knew it was a sore subject for her and one she wasn't likely to want to talk about. "I have met your mother, Demeter, a long time ago."

Her *darkness*, as he had called it, stemmed from her family, and while just the thought of talking about her life in Olympus hurt her, dredging up memories and opening wounds she constantly tried to seal, she resolved to do it in the hope that it would prompt Hades into speaking of his darkness.

"Then you probably know my mother is oppressive," she muttered and slipped free of his grasp, part of her feeling bad for how she had spoken of her mother, and the rest of her growing angry as she recalled everything her mother had ever said and done to her. If she was going to talk about her family rather than change the subject this time, she needed to be moving to unleash some of her pent-up frustration. "She is the reason I created the forest."

She touched the trunk of the first tree and frowned as she felt nothing. Hades *had* shut her power down again, placing it beyond her reach, and disappointment was swift to sweep through her as she gazed at her hand on the dark bark.

She loosed another long sigh and let the words tumble from her heart. "The whole of Olympus is oppressive."

He snorted. "You are not wrong about that."

The corners of her lips curled into a faint smile as he moved past her and leaned against a tree, his expression dark.

"So many gods and goddesses my age have the freedom to move around the city, doing as they please, their positions quite different from my own." She pressed her palms to a tree and leaned forwards, so her chest rested against it as she gazed around the trunk at Hades. She pulled a face. "I often wonder if my life might have been better if I had been born into one of the servant classes. At least then I would have my freedom for part of the day. My only family treats me as if I am someone who should do her bidding without question, even if what she wants me to do is abhorrent to me."

His face slowly darkened, his eyebrows meeting hard and his lips turning downwards, and the dark power he emanated grew stronger as the shadows cast by the trees wavered and flowed towards him.

She pushed away from the tree, fighting to hold her tongue and failing. "I am a prisoner in my own home."

Guilt swept through her the moment those words left her lips and she cast her gaze down at her bare feet, battling the urge to take them back.

They were the truth.

One she hadn't wanted to admit to herself.

"For centuries, I have obeyed my mother, attempting to please her... fearing upsetting her. I have walked in her shadow, have borne the cold words meant to carve my strength from me to keep me in my place, and have followed convention to the letter, but my mother... she stole my last freedom from me and something within me just... snapped." Or shattered. She felt it might have been her heart. She loved her mother, but her decision to marry her off to an idiot of a male who thought he could own her and she would simply move from obeying her mother to obeying him instead, had been too much. It had broken her heart, and that heart still ached even now, when she was miles from Olympus.

Because she feared she would one day have to return there and this freedom she had found with Hades would become but a fading memory.

She started as Hades's hands came down on her shoulders and his heat met her spine.

He skimmed his hands down her biceps and pressed closer, his mouth lowering to her ear and his words tempting her as he whispered, "You do not need to return to that life, Persephone. You do not need to be near someone who would question your strength or wound you in such ways. You do not need to return to a world where people do not see your value or your beauty."

She turned in his embrace and sought his eyes, needing to see that he meant that. She saw something else in them. Something she knew he wouldn't voice. Regret. Now that he knew her sad little tale of woe, he felt bad about what he had done. It was there for her to read in his gaze as it left her to drift in the direction of the tower.

She blew out her breath, pushing her anger and hurt back down inside her, not wanting to feel either of those emotions or think about her mother and what awaited her back in Olympus. She wanted to seize this moment, to live her life for once, the way she wanted to live it.

Hades's gaze dropped back to her, his expression deadly serious. "I know of a way to release your pent-up anger."

He was talking about sex.

She arched an eyebrow at him, trying to appear unsurprised and unflustered by his blatant offer to bed her, but heat flared across her cheeks. She silently cursed the fact she hadn't been able to conceal her reaction to his words, and willed him not to mention how she blushed whenever she thought about sex.

His eyes widened slightly, and he was quick to say, "I was speaking of riding my chariot. Whenever I am angry—"

"Something that happens often," she interjected, trying to lighten the mood and distract him from the fact her thoughts had immediately turned to sex when he had mentioned finding release.

He arched an eyebrow at her now. "Not as often as you might think. As I was saying. When I am angry, I go for a ride. It is thrilling and takes my mind off things for a time. The thunder of hooves, the wind against my face, the excitement of racing across the realm and the challenge of controlling the horses and the chariot… I always feel better afterwards."

It did sound tempting.

"I have never been on a chariot before, although I have seen others riding on them through Olympus." She canted her head to her right as she tried to imagine his chariot and pictured them on the back of it in the way she had seen those people in her city, but the image didn't fit.

He wasn't talking about a gentle ride. He was talking about pushing the horses to their limit and courting danger. And gods, it was thrilling. That little Olympian that was growing fainter and fainter inside her whispered not to do it, attempting to hold her back. Persephone ignored it and embraced the daring side Hades had awoken in her.

She held her hand out to him and smiled.

"What are we waiting for?"

CHAPTER 26

The four enormous black horses kicked at the ground, scuffing the dirt as they shifted restlessly in their harness. The front left one snorted and tossed its head, the whinny it unleashed echoing around the stables. Hades cast it a look and went back to fastening the leather straps that attached the beast to the black-and-gold chariot. It was beautiful. The onyx lacquered wood was polished and reflected her body as she waited, and the elegant gold edging and filigree was a sublime contrast to it.

"Step up." Hades flicked her a glance as he finished tightening the last strap and then gathered the reins. "But do not jostle the chariot too much. On second thought, remain where you are."

"Why?" Persephone froze halfway through stepping onto the back of the chariot, fear flashing through her. She backed away from the vehicle.

"The horses tend to set off as soon as I am mounted." He bunched the reins in his right fist and swept his left arm around her waist and she gasped as he lifted her and walked with her pinned to his side.

Heat swept through her, turning her mind hazy and pulling her gaze to his noble profile as he stepped onto the chariot and set her down. She drifted in thoughts of kissing him, and then shrieked as the horses took off just as he had said they might and she fell backwards.

Her heart shot into her throat as she flailed and tried to find her balance.

Hades's arm banded around her waist, tugging her to him and righting her, and her hands landed on his chest and shoulder as he gazed down at her.

He husked, "I have you."

Truer words had never been spoken.

She reached for the curved edge of the front of the chariot, gripping it tightly as she convinced herself to release Hades and make the most of this chance to see more of his realm. Hades didn't release her though. He kept his arm around her waist, holding her tucked against his side with her back to him, slightly in front of him.

She hadn't realised how fast they were moving.

The black landscape that had appeared forbidding at first whizzed past her as the horses thundered onwards, their huffs and grunts as they galloped as one filling the silence.

She focused on it to tame the rising fear that swelled inside her as the chariot rounded a narrow bend at breakneck speed, Hades's mastery of the vehicle not lost on her, but definitely pushed to the back of her mind as she tightly held on, afraid she would fall off as the whole conveyance leaned to the left. The route ahead of them, up a pass between two mountains, was narrow too, and winding, and she was sure Hades would slow at least a little so they didn't strike the sheer rock walls or the boulders that had tumbled into the road in places where it was wider.

He cracked the reins and urged the horses onwards instead.

Their speed increased and she tensed, her entire body locking up as fear fully took the helm. She turned to ask Hades to slow, hating the idea of admitting she was afraid and maybe this had been a mistake.

But they crested the highest point on the pass and her breath left her in a rush.

The whole of the Underworld stretched before her.

She could see miles into the distance, across a plain where jagged mountain ranges jutted into it to divide the flat land and villages and what looked like another barracks. Her gaze darted over everything, her fear forgotten as they turned and headed downwards, the narrow road leading them towards one of those villages. Wind whipped against her, making her dress flutter around her legs and her hair slap her in her face to obscure her vision. She released the chariot and gathered the scarlet lengths, twisting them together and holding them at her shoulder.

And only realised what she had done when Hades's hold on her tightened.

She leaned into him, warmth rushing through her as she trusted him to keep her safely on the chariot and savoured the feel of him against her.

They passed at speed through the nearest village, a collection of black stone buildings with dark tiled roofs, and she didn't miss how the souls in it stopped to watch Hades pass, moving to one side of the road. Not Hades, she realised. They stared at her, their gazes curious.

She locked eyes with one woman, turning in Hades's arms to track her as they passed her and she drifted into the distance.

Unmistakable hope shone in her eyes.

There had been fear on the faces of many of the villagers as they had approached, but that fear had disappeared when they had seen her. Why? It dawned on her. Hades ruled this realm and the impression he had given her was that he wasn't a kind king, that he ruled with an iron fist, and hadn't even separated the good souls from the wretched, evil ones.

But Nyx had said he was changing.

She looked at him, wanting to confirm her suspicions about the reason the villagers had looked at her with hope, and maybe even a little gratitude. "Were any of those people bad souls?"

Hades didn't take his eyes off the route ahead as he shook his head, his deep baritone holding a hard note. "No."

She stared at his profile. "Have bad souls lived there in the past?"

She had wanted to ask if they had lived there before he had met her, before he had started to change, to shed the darkness and step towards the light—because of her.

He slid a look at her, a brief glance that sent a thrill down her spine together with his words. "Once. I have since separated them. The souls of the wicked now reside in another area of the realm."

"All the wicked have been moved?" She frowned at him now as she struggled to tame her hair again and pin it to her shoulder. "Not just from this village, but from all the others too?"

"From many of them now. I am still working on moving them." He urged the horses onwards with a snap of the reins and flicked a brief glance at her before his eyes darted back to the animals.

He felt awkward again, and it wasn't because she was staring at him. It was because he had done something kind—something to improve the lives of his people—and he feared she might pick him up on it.

She wanted to say it sounded as if it was a lot of work, and now she understood his long absences, but instead pointed towards a glow in the distance. "Is that a fire?"

He shook his head again. "A lava lake. It lies beyond the next range."

"Can we go there?" She slid him a hopeful glance. A lake that emanated such a glow sounded intriguing.

He met her gaze, caught it and nodded, and then pulled on the reins, guiding the horses around to the right and picking up a faint track that cut across the black earth in that direction.

They passed through another village where the same thing happened. People stopped what they were doing and stared at her, several of the men even drifting forwards to the edge of the road.

Hades loosed a vicious growl and pinned her closer to his side, the dark power he emanated growing stronger, and she gasped as shadows fluttered around her. They danced in front of her face at first, but when a large male packed with muscle and wearing only thick leather trousers moved out from the shelter of what looked like a blacksmith, his body streaked with soot, the shadows grew sharp.

Like swords.

Persephone gasped when Hades drew the horses to a sudden stop and momentum threw her forwards. Her stomach slammed into the curved front of the chariot, knocking the wind from her lungs and ripping a grunt from her lips. She clutched the edge of the chariot and pushed herself upright.

One look at Hades was all it took to know something was wrong.

Very wrong.

He stood beside her on the chariot, his features rapidly darkening, as if a storm cloud was rolling across them. She stared at him, transfixed by the changes that came over him as he glared at the blacksmith, but shocked by them too. As crimson flooded his irises and then seeped into his pupils to transform them into fire, and onyx invaded his irises in its wake, she could almost see his humanity being stripped from him.

The light severed from his soul to leave him drenched in darkness.

All shred of emotion left his eyes as they grew sharp, and dark, and cold, and it was like looking at another person.

How did it feel to him?

That battle she had witnessed more than once in his eyes ignited again as his lips pulled taut and flattened into almost a grimace, and his fingers flexed and curled into tight fists. His gaze remained locked on the blacksmith as his fists trembled at his sides and his shadows remained pointed at the male. She had never seen him so dark. The male before her was the one Olympus whispered about. With his pointed ears, sharp fangs that flashed between his lips as he sneered at the blacksmith, and unearthly eyes.

The monster.

But Persephone could see beyond that monster to the man. A man who was fighting to hold himself back, as if he wasn't quite master of his own body. As if this darkness he emanated was an affliction. Something crushing. Something controlling. Something that had to be hard for him to deal with.

Hard on him.

But he didn't have to bear it alone.

Persephone lifted her hand to place it on his chest and bring him back to her, hoping her touch would give him strength and help him shatter the hold this darkness had on him.

Only she touched nothing but black smoke.

Hades was gone.

She spun on her heel, her heart lodging in her throat as she whirled to face the blacksmith.

The male staggered backwards as Hades appeared right in front of him and lunged with his right hand, attempting to snare the male in his talons. On a rumbling growl, Hades swiped at the blacksmith again and the male twisted away from him and slammed into a bench that stood against the wall of the building he had exited. The man fell, his arm scattering metal tools across the floor. The other villagers gasped and ran, the sounds of doors slamming filling the tense silence and jarring Persephone, shaking her out of her stupor.

Hades's shadows took aim at the male as he tried to get to his feet to escape.

And rushed towards him.

They would kill him.

Persephone leaped from the chariot and ran around Hades, placing herself between him and the blacksmith, and shoved her palms against Hades's chest.

"Hades," she bit out, half angry, half afraid, but determined to stop him.

His shadows halted and his gaze dropped to her. Fire shone in his pupils, his black irises an abyss around them, and he bared his fangs at her and then at the male he intended to cut down.

Because that male had looked at her.

"Hades," she whispered again, and meant to tell him not to harm the male, only his name leaving her lips seemed to work black magic on him again and his gaze darted to her.

And remained locked on her this time.

She felt his shadows wrap around her again. Soft now. A gentle embrace that tugged her against Hades. He banded his arms around her too, bent his head and inhaled a shuddering breath. His grip on her was surprisingly gentle as he held her, each exhale stirring her hair and tickling her shoulder.

And then he abruptly broke away from her, gripped her arm and pulled her with him. When they reached the chariot, he caught her by her waist and lifted her onto it, and stepped up behind her. His left arm banded around her waist, holding her pinned to his side.

Together with his shadows.

They were as possessive as Hades as they wrapped around her.

Hades cracked the reins and the horses whinnied and broke into a gallop.

As they charged out of the village, she heard the blacksmith mutter a faint prayer of thanks to her, and didn't miss what he called her in lieu of her name.

God-queen of the Underworld.

She stared into Hades's eyes as they galloped onwards, lost in them and the heat that poured through her veins in response to his tight grip on her, the feel of his body against hers, and the thrill born of the fact he had been telling the truth to her that day.

He really would cut down any male who gazed upon her.

That shouldn't thrill her. She knew it. But it did. It lit a fire in her veins that only grew hotter as Hades returned to driving the chariot, turning his profile to her. He was all darkness. His ears were pointed, the tips flaring through his mussed black hair. His irises were onyx embracing fire. The spikes of his crown rose like daggers from his hair. His fangs flashed between his profane lips as he sneered and snapped the reins. And his claws were out.

She shouldn't find him so alluring when he was like this, all darkness and danger, but by the gods, she wanted him now more than ever.

When his gaze slid towards her, she didn't look away. She locked eyes with him, the fire he roused in her fading a little as she watched the war that continued to play out in his gaze. He was still fighting his darkness. That had her focus shifting from the need that thrummed inside her, to a desire to know more about this side of him.

"Speak to me of your darkness, Hades," she murmured, keeping her tone soft and light in an effort not to anger him or provoke him in any way. She didn't want to make this fight harder on him. She just wanted to know why it happened and how it felt so she could help him with it.

The black slashes of his eyebrows dipped low and knitted hard, a crease forming between them as his eyes narrowed on her and his lips flattened.

That look was all it took for her to know he wouldn't tell her about it.

Not today at least.

Persephone sighed, but didn't press him.

Which seemed to surprise him because his features softened and something akin to relief flickered in his eyes before he turned his profile to her and guided the chariot around a cluster of large boulders.

Persephone placed her hand over his right one where it gripped the reins, her gaze on it for a heartbeat before she lifted it to his noble profile and softly said, "I know you have secrets… and that you will tell me in your own time."

He slanted another look at her, his eyebrows pitching low again, and his features darkened.

His voice was little more than a rumbling growl as he said, "Never stand between me and another when my eyes go black."

Persephone studied those eyes, watching as crimson slowly seeped from his pupils into his irises, driving out the obsidian. His hand trembled beneath hers and she palmed it, wanting to comfort him and chase away the fear she could see building in his eyes.

Hades tugged her closer to him, pinning her against his side so she had to angle her head back to keep her eyes locked with his.

"Swear to me that you will run, my love. If I ever change around you like that again, vow that you will run. Swear it to me." His grim expression and the hard, demanding edge to his voice didn't conceal the fear that built in his eyes as they darted between hers.

He was truly afraid that he would hurt her, and she didn't want him to suffer like that, allowing doubts and fears to tear at his strength. Doubts and fears that might shred this fragile thing between them to ribbons and destroy it by making him distance himself from her in some foolish effort to protect her from himself.

"I will run," she said, and relief washed across his features until she added, "If I feel I cannot help you."

Hades shook his head. Hard. His expression was as dark as his realm as he glowered at her.

"No. You will run regardless. You will not try to help me. You will run," he snarled.

Persephone might have meekly given in to him once, but he had been the one to awaken the fierce, unyielding side of her that would do all in her power to protect him and to help him.

"No. I will never run from you again. Not unless I feel you are beyond my help," she countered. She needed to show him she believed he wouldn't hurt her, because he had no shred of faith in himself. He believed he would hurt her.

So she had to believe that he wouldn't.

When he bared fangs at her and looked as if he might snap them and growl, she lifted her hand to his chest and smoothed her palm across it.

That simple touch was enough to soothe the savage beast and calm him. His gaze fell to her hand, softening and turning almost hazy as she stroked his chest. Did he like the feel of her hand on him? Did he like it as much as she liked touching him and feeling all that hard, honed strength beneath her fingertips?

That fire he had started in her burst back to life, fanned by the feel of his body beneath her questing fingers. She lifted her gaze to his face and his eyes collided with hers, the banked heat in them scorching her.

She pressed closer to him, aching for his lips on hers.

CHAPTER 27

They rounded a bend in a pass at breakneck speed that jostled Persephone out of her fantasy about kissing Hades. His arm tightened against her back, his shadows holding her in place so she only swayed with him. She tore her gaze from him and looked ahead of them, a shiver cascading over her arms as the walls of the pass opened up into a small valley nestled among high peaks.

A waterfall of lava ran down the face of one of those black mountains and fell into the lake of molten rock that occupied most of the valley floor.

Incredible.

The heat was intense, and had moisture beading on her skin as Hades guided the chariot around the edge of it. She swiped at the droplets that gathered on her chest, and Hades growled. Her fingers stilled, her pulse picking up as she slowly lifted her eyes to his face. His gaze remained fixed on her hand.

On her chest.

The flames in her veins became a wildfire that threatened to torch her control.

She swallowed and couldn't deny the urge to brush her fingers over her damp flesh, to tease him and make him crave her as fiercely as she craved him. She stroked the swells of her breasts.

Gasped as darkness suddenly enveloped her and cool air rushed around her.

It wasn't a teleport.

Her eyes widened as she stared back at the opening onto the valley, catching a glimpse of the lake, and then tilted her head back and looked at the huge cavern that now surrounded her.

Her breath rushed from her.

"By the gods," she muttered, another shiver dancing over her skin.

Crystals clustered at the edges of the cavern and protruded from the ceiling, each three times as wide as she was, and in their hearts, violet light glittered, casting a soft glow over her.

And Hades.

She looked at him, bathed in muted light, into eyes that glowed crimson with hunger.

That searing look was fire.

And it torched her control.

Persephone seized the reins near his hand and pulled on them, bringing the horses to an abrupt stop as she grabbed Hades with her other hand and tugged him down to her. He swooped on her lips on a wicked growl, swallowing her gasp in a hard kiss that poured frantic need through her.

That same wild feeling seemed to consume him too.

He hemmed her in against the edge of the chariot, bending her slightly over it as his body met hers, the full contact between them tearing a moan from her and flooding her with a need to feel him naked against her. Her entire body trembled and hummed with need—desire that swiftly stole control from her. She was a slave to it, all reason forgotten, all fears falling to the back of her mind.

There was only Hades and this burning need to have him.

She clawed at his leather shirt, snapping the laces and pulling it off him. He eased back an inch to help her, his lips leaving hers only as long as it took for him to pull it over his head. The second it was gone, he claimed her lips again, and she claimed his chest.

Oh gods. He was steel covered in silk beneath her questing fingers, the way his muscles flexed as he moved bewitching her and cranking her temperature up, until she moved past frantic into something more, something wilder. Before she was aware of what she was doing, her hands had glided downwards, stroking the ropes of his stomach, and were tugging at the fastenings of his trousers.

Hades growled again and his hands joined hers, making faster work of the lacing than she could have, and then he gripped her hand and brought it against his bare cock.

Her entire body seemed to pulse as her palm met his hard shaft, moisture swift to pool at the apex of her thighs as realisation slowly dawned on her. She was touching a male. Touching Hades. Nerves tried to get the better of her. Hades vanquished them by lowering his mouth to her throat and growling against it as he kissed her, and for a heartbeat, she thought he liked kissing her throat.

And then she realised she had started wantonly stroking him.

And apparently couldn't stop.

Even as her cheeks flamed at what she was doing and her mind tried to scream that they were moving too fast, her hand continued of its own volition, wrapping around his cock to grip and stroke him from the base of his shaft to the blunt crown.

Hades yanked her dress down to expose her breasts, and she gasped as he palmed one and pulled the hard bud of the other into his mouth. Thrills skittered through her, shooting like arcs of electricity from her nipples to her feminine core. She leaned back and glanced down, past Hades's dark head as he laved and sucked her nipple, sending more whips of lightning down through her body, to her hand where it gripped his long cock, working up and down it.

A pulse of arousal shot through her, a single thought screaming in her mind.

She wanted that inside her.

Hades's thoughts must have been travelling a similar path to hers, because he grabbed the skirts of her dress and pulled them upwards, the sensual glide of the soft material over her bare thighs sensitising her skin and making her ache to feel his hands on them. He didn't make her wait. He released her skirts and palmed her thighs instead, inching her dress up as his hands roamed upwards and the material caught on his wrists.

"Persephone," he murmured as he drew back, his crimson eyes meeting hers, searing her and drawing a moan from her as she realised he wasn't just breathing her name.

He was asking her a silent question.

She nodded and pushed down her nerves, not wanting him to see them as her body came alive at the thought they were doing this. Soon, she would know what it was like to be with a man, to have him inside her, joined with her. She trembled and stroked him harder, unable to hold herself back as her arousal soared, as a fierce need to make him hurry consumed her.

Hades growled and looked down at her hand, his lips parting as she quickened her pace. He breathed harder, one hand leaving her to brace on the edge of the chariot, and she gazed at him, mesmerised by the sight of him and feeling more powerful by the second. His chest strained with each panted breath, his eyes growing darker as he began to rock his hips into her touch, as his gaze grew hooded and his lips parted further. His arm tensed as he gripped the edge of the chariot, his breaths washing her breasts.

He looked on the verge of growling again as his face twisted.

She was doing this.

Affecting him like this.

Giving him pleasure.

Pleasure she felt too as she watched him, as the sense that she had power over him grew. Would he spill from just her hand if she continued?

He didn't give her a chance to find out.

On a wicked snarl, he claimed her mouth and ripped her undergarments away. His kiss was frantic, hot, and demanding, but it was the brush of his fingers over her exposed mound as he cupped her that had her going up onto her tiptoes and gasping into his mouth. He stroked through her folds, a low growl leaving him and a moan leaving her as his fingers reached her slick nub and he fondled it.

"Hades," she breathed and clutched his shoulders, stroking him forgotten as she fought for balance, feeling as if she might fall as he mercilessly teased her, driving her towards a climax she could definitely find from just his hand.

He pushed her thighs apart with his other hand and wedged himself between them, and her heart thundered, the need to feel him filling her growing wild within her, almost painful. She pulled him closer, driving him on as she stole command of the kiss, nipping at his lower lip with her blunt teeth.

On a blood-heating growl, his cock breached her and he filled her in one delicious, incredibly painful thrust.

She cried into his mouth, unable to hold it back as fire shot through her.

Hades stilled and drew back to stare at her, shock painted across his features and his eyes going from red to pale blue. She shook her head, willing him not to mention that she was untouched and not wanting it to stop him. She needed him too much. He couldn't stop now. She gripped his nape and pulled him back to her, seizing his lips in a kiss she hoped would silence him and convince him to continue.

He groaned, the sound pure male and sending a thrill down her spine to make her temperature soar, and then he was holding her tightly as he drove into her. Each frantic plunge of his shaft stole her breath and ripped a moan from her, the fast pace of his thrusts telling her that she wasn't alone. He needed her as badly as she needed him.

He pinned her to him as he took her, as he filled her with every inch of his cock and made her mourn the loss of it with each withdraw. She couldn't stop herself from lowering her hands to his backside and slipping them beneath his leathers. She moaned as she gripped his bottom, feeling it flex with each powerful thrust of his hips, and tilted her head back as she soared higher.

Hades kissed and nipped at her neck, and then her throat, and when his lips wrapped around her nipple again, and he sucked it hard enough that pain mingled with the hit of pleasure, she cried out at the ceiling of the cavern.

Her high moans echoed around her, the sound of them making her feel wicked and adding to the pleasure building within her as Hades's grunts joined them together with the sound of their bodies meeting as he took her harder.

Faster.

His thrusts shortened and deepened as he gripped her waist and held her in place, the force of them rocking the chariot. She clawed his hair as he pounded into her, keeping his head pressed to her breasts as need took over, as she flexed her body around his, the hunger to find release becoming unbearable.

It hit her like a storm, a thousand lightning bolts that struck her all at once and had her screaming at the cavern ceiling as her body jerked and thighs shook, and heat and bliss pulsed through her.

Hades moaned as her body clenched and unclenched him, still thrusting into her, riding her release. He lowered one hand to between their bodies and she gasped as he stroked her pert bead, as he flicked and fondled it, reigniting her passion and startling her as it built again, swiftly rising towards a second crescendo.

She hadn't thought that possible.

Hades proved it was as he squeezed her nub and drove into her, and his shaft throbbed with each grunt that left his lips as he wedged himself deep inside her and spilled hot jets of seed.

And stars winked across her vision as release hit her too, the feel of his climax driving her to find another of her own.

She could barely breathe as it hit her and consumed her, as she clung to Hades and lost herself to sensation, to the feel of him pulsing inside her. He kissed a path up her chest and neck, and claimed her lips in a soft, slow kiss, his breaths mingling with hers. She savoured the feel of him inside her and his kiss—a kiss that spoke volumes to her. He was sorry he had hurt her, and he was pleased he had been her first, and that this was only the beginning for them.

She couldn't wait to see what came next, was already thinking of the next time they could make love, and maybe live out some of the fantasies she'd had while alone in her bath.

He lifted his head and gazed at her, his look as soft as his kiss had been. His guard was down, and hers was too. She framed his face with her palms, keeping his gaze on hers and bathing in the love she could see in his eyes, drinking her fill of it before he hid it from her again. He didn't need to hide it. They were both falling, although she felt sure that wasn't the right word.

They had both *fallen*.

His gaze took on an awkward edge and he tried to look away from her, and she didn't want him to apologise for what he had done, or feel he had done something wrong by taking her in the way he had.

She loved his passion and his ferocity.

It matched her own.

She had always thought herself timid, but Hades had shown her that she wasn't. He had awakened a passion in her that was wild and fierce, and demanding. A passion that already wanted him again, and wanted him to be just as rough as he had been their first time.

He didn't look ready to hear that, so she settled on teasing him to lighten the mood instead.

"You were right," she said, still a little out of breath.

He frowned and met her gaze again. "About what?"

She smiled naughtily.

"I do feel better for my ride."

Hades grinned, stealing her heart with how gorgeous he was when he unleashed a smile, and claimed her lips in another toe-curling, searing kiss.

One that said they were far from done.

CHAPTER 28

Hades rested on his side on his bed, his head propped up on his right hand and his gaze fixed on Persephone where she slept facing him, her naked curves tucked beneath the black sheets. Despite how exhausted he was, his mind churned too quickly for him to find sleep as she had, his thoughts locked on his love as fiercely as his gaze was.

She was all he was aware of, the world narrowed down to her.

He lifted his left hand and ghosted it over her bare arm, the temptation to touch her great but not as strong as his desire to let her sleep and recover. The darkness that had awoken within him the moment he had realised she was untouched, and that she had given him something precious, continued to hold him in its grip, and he wasn't sure it would ever release him. The knowledge that he was the only male her body had ever known had a deep possessiveness flowing in his veins, a powerful and consuming desire to hide her from the world and keep her to himself.

She was his.

Only his.

And the Fates help anyone who tried to take her from him.

His gaze drifted over her, an ache to be inside her swelling within him again. He wanted to sink into her wet heat and pleasure her for hours, ruining her to all other males so she would only ever want him.

As he only ever wanted her.

No other female would be enough for him now. No other female would rouse his desire. Only her. He might have claimed her, but she had claimed him too. She had branded her name on his heart, his body and his soul, securing it as hers.

Only hers.

He drank his fill of her, unable to stop thinking about how tightly she had gloved him, or how she had come alive in his arms, and how much pleasure he had felt when she had broken apart, her climax shaking his world and altering something fundamental inside him. He had craved her before, but not like this.

He would go to war for just a taste of her lips.

The urge to wake her so he could have her again was strong, but fear held it in check.

Fear that she would have closed herself off again and view what she had done as a mistake and deny him.

Or say that she didn't want him.

Hades frowned as he studied her soft features, troubled by the incredible thing that had happened when she had found her first release, something he had concealed from her by keeping her shrouded in his shadows while he had dressed and tucked her against his side as he had turned the chariot around and driven them out of the cavern.

Hundreds of glowing blue flowers had erupted from the black earth around them.

No matter what he did, her powers kept rising to the surface, to within her reach.

His power over her was growing weaker.

Or she was growing stronger.

He wasn't sure which it was, but he didn't like it.

He had tried sealing them again, but had hesitated to finish the ward, even when he feared that if he left her powers intact, she might leave. By her account, she had been kept in an invisible cage her entire life, and knowing how she had suffered, he couldn't place her back in the tower or strip her powers from her. He couldn't hurt her like that.

But what if she left him?

Hades wasn't sure he would survive that. Not now. He was too deeply in love with her. Done for. Hers. Whether she wanted him or not.

He frowned and risked stroking his fingers down her bare arm. A little smile curling her lips was his reward for his courage, one that warmed the cold reaches of his heart and soothed his fears. She was growing warmer towards him, and rather than running away again when he had left her in his chambers, she had chosen to return to the tower. She had chosen to kiss him, and had instigated their moment on his chariot. And now she was sleeping in his bed.

With him.

He liked to think she might remain here with him if he asked her again. She might agree to be his queen.

His wife.

Hades gazed at her, envying her. She slept so soundly, while sleep eluded him, refusing to come even when he closed his eyes and rested his head on the pillows. He had tried sleeping several times, had even tucked Persephone in his arms to hold her against him and breathe her in, but his thoughts were too frantic.

He dropped a soft kiss on her brow, eased out of the bed, and looked back at her. He wanted to hold her again and feel her curves pressed against him, but he wouldn't find any rest or peace if he did. He needed to walk and think, to mull over everything and find a way to make her agree to be his, because living without her was no longer an option.

Hades tugged his black leathers on, jammed his feet into his boots, and pulled a loose black linen shirt over his head. He didn't bother to tuck it in. He strode to the wooden doors and paused there to glance back at Persephone, the urge to return to her strong. Lazing beside her wouldn't help him clear his head so he could think straight and find a way to win her heart. She addled his mind whenever he gazed at her, desire stealing control of him whenever he was close to her. It was better he went for a walk.

Still, it took monumental effort to convince himself to step out of the door and leave. The war between staying and going lasted so long he was sure dawn would come and she would wake before it was decided. When he finally found the strength to leave her sleeping, he eased the doors closed behind him, checked the area to make sure no male was near his beloved, and then strode away from the temple, heading for the stable block.

Cerberus perked up when he neared, his three great heads lifting from the dirt and glowing blue eyes seeking Hades. The black hound's long tail thumped against the ground, causing tremors Hades could feel as he closed the distance between them. Before he had reached the gate, Cerberus was on his feet, his heads easily hanging over the low wall to nuzzle and lick him. He frowned at his pet's behaviour. Cerberus was often attentive, but never this attentive.

The hound barely waited for him to open the gate to let him out, lifting a paw as if to step over the wall to gain his freedom, which wasn't like him. Despite how low the wall around his enclosure was, Cerberus always waited inside it for Hades to open the gate and never left his paddock without Hades's permission.

"What has gotten into you today?" Hades eyed the three-headed hound as he swung the gate open and Cerberus trotted out and around him, and nudged him in the back, pushing him forwards.

Hades frowned over his shoulder at his pet when Cerberus kept pushing, making him stumble towards the open plain where they often walked.

And away from the temple.

"Stop that now," Hades grumbled and Cerberus obeyed, running circles around him instead and herding him towards the middle of the plain without nudging him. Maybe he had kept Cerberus cooped up for too many days, neglecting his needs. He looked back over his shoulder at the distant temple, something tugging his gaze in that direction. "We should not stray too far from Persephone."

Cerberus growled.

Hades arched an eyebrow at him.

All three heads bared fangs at the temple.

Hades sighed as he realised why Cerberus had been pushing him and why he had been so eager to go out for a walk.

"Jealousy does not suit you." He lifted a hand to stroke the muzzle of Cerberus's middle head, but Cerberus snapped fangs at him. Hades glared at him and Cerberus lowered his heads and averted his gaze. He sighed again and petted him. "I am sorry I have been preoccupied, old friend. Come, let us walk. I have much energy to burn."

Cerberus perked up again and raced away from him, only to stop and then run back. The beast repeated this as Hades strolled across the plain, heading for the distant volcano that tossed great plumes of billowing smoke and ash into the air and belched lava. Hades shook his head, marvelling at how much energy Cerberus had and sure he would wear himself out before they made it far into their walk. It didn't stop Cerberus from running to him and away, and then checking on him and bounding back to him.

Another weary sigh escaped Hades as he glanced over his shoulder towards the temple. "I fear she will leave me."

Those words leaked from him, and putting them out there made him feel vulnerable, but also a little better for admitting his fear.

His gaze sought Cerberus as his pet stopped close to him, towering over him and panting hard.

"If Persephone leaves, I do not know what I will do. I love her, Cerberus. Without her, I will be a shell of myself… A hollow, dead thing."

Cerberus snarled and flashed fangs again.

"Are you going to growl whenever I mention Persephone?" He tipped his head back and met Cerberus's bright blue gaze.

His hound growled.

"Very well." Hades started walking again. "But it will not stop me from talking about her."

Cerberus trailed beside him and then began nudging him in the back again, loosing low, quiet growls from time to time as he worked to drive Hades further from Persephone. Hades chuckled, turned and planted his palms against the muzzle of Cerberus's middle head.

"I have room in my heart for both of you." He stroked Cerberus's muzzle, hoping to soothe the beast. "Persephone has not replaced you, nor will she ever. You are my oldest, wisest, and most beloved companion. If anything were to happen to you, I would tear this world apart to take you back."

If anything happened to Persephone, Hades would do the same, but he kept that to himself.

Cerberus perked up again, licked him with a tongue that was as wide as Hades's body, and then bounded away from him. Hades grimaced and wiped his hands down himself, clearing the slobber away and not enjoying this new, jealous side of Cerberus. Cerberus hadn't licked him since he had been a pup, when he had quickly learned that Hades didn't enjoy being bathed by his tongue.

His hound snarled and Hades frowned at him, and his brows rose as he watched Cerberus wrestling with the tree trunk Hades had brought back for him from the Elysian Fields a long time ago. The bark was gone, and the wood had been chewed, and the ends were rounded from Cerberus gnawing at them, but it was still in one piece, something which always surprised him given how much Cerberus enjoyed playing with it.

As expected, Cerberus dropped the long, gnarled piece of wood near Hades. Hades made him wait, amusing himself with the anticipation that built in Cerberus's eyes and how his big body tensed whenever Hades made the slightest move. When Cerberus sat and stared at him, a puzzled look on his faces, Hades used his shadows to hurl the piece of wood, catching him off guard.

Cerberus barked, the sound deafening and making Hades's ears ring, and then thundered after it.

Hades turned back towards the temple, pausing to throw the toy for Cerberus whenever his faithful hound brought it back to him, enjoying the calm and the air, and how his thoughts began to settle.

He would win Persephone's heart. He no longer doubted that. He had seen the looks she had given him from time to time today, ones filled with longing and tenderness. She was falling for him too. Might have already fallen. He only needed to continue to let her in as he had been, lowering his guard around her to show her the side of himself he usually kept hidden from others, and victory would be his.

She would be his.

Cerberus lost interest in the toy and walked slowly towards him, panting hard, all three tongues lolling out of his mouths. Hades walked with him to the stable but rather than placing the hound back into the paddock, he continued past it and Cerberus followed him. He stopped when he had a good view of the orchard, the temple and the tower, and patted the ground. Cerberus came to him and laid down, and Hades sat and rested his back against his pet's side, using him as a pillow.

He sighed out his breath and closed his eyes as he relaxed into Cerberus, listening to the beast's breathing as it finally slowed, the sound of it lulling him towards sleep too.

Hades sank into it.

Hoping he would dream of Persephone.

CHAPTER 29

Persephone had half expected to wake in the tower, but instead she woke in Hades's bed where she had fallen asleep in his arms. Only she was alone. She sat up and looked for him, but the large black-walled chamber was empty. Where had he gone?

She scooted to the edge of the bed and frowned as her gaze snagged on something.

A dress draped over a chair that had been positioned facing her, so she would see it as soon as she rose.

She stood and brushed her fingers over the fine, soft fabric.

The green fabric.

She smiled as she lifted it and held it before her. It was beautiful. The layers were sheer, the way they draped over each other turning them from transparent to opaque, and there was a gold band around the waist and under the bust. The embroidery was delicate, subtly depicting flowers and leaves.

A dress made for her.

It seemed Hades was finally coming to learn the ways to her heart.

Persephone pulled it on and tightened the fastenings of the bands so the dress fit snug to her frame, buzzing a little as she looked down at herself. She lifted her head and looked for a mirror, and found one across the room. She hurried to it and stared at her reflection. It truly was a beautiful dress. Far more beautiful than any she had owned before. All her dresses in Olympus paled in comparison to this one.

She wished Hades was here to see her in it.

She finger-combed her unruly scarlet waves, determination sweeping through her to bring her courage to the fore. If he wasn't here to see her in it, then she would just have to find him so he could. Once her appearance was as good as she could get it without wasting time bathing, she hurried to the doors, hesitated for only a second, and opened them. If Hades was mad at her for leaving, she doubted it would last long.

A kiss was probably all it would take to make him forgive her.

She felt a little giddy at the thought of kissing him again, and her body warmed, her blood heating and desire rising. She wanted to do more than just kiss him. She ached for him again, had been having delicious dreams of him that she wanted to turn into a reality.

Persephone stopped at the edge of the paved area and pulled a face. How was she meant to find Hades?

She looked off to her left, towards the main temple where she could see people coming and going, debated asking a guard and then discounted the idea. Hades would probably kill any guard he saw her talking to, the sight of her close to another man rousing that dangerously possessive side of his blood, and she didn't want death on her hands.

Rather than heading towards the temple, she walked in the opposite direction and went around the back of the building. Her feet carried her swiftly towards the orchard, her heart supplying he was probably there, picking more pomegranates to tempt her into eating their seeds.

As if she needed them to bind her to this realm.

Her heart was already bound to it because Hades was here.

He wasn't in the orchard either.

She pouted and went to turn towards the temple to try it after all, and then she realised something.

She could feel the life in the trees.

Her eyes slowly widened and she pressed her left hand to the rough bark of the one closest to her, sure she was mistaken. Sensation flooded her, flowing into the void Hades had created by sealing her powers. They were back again. She turned and placed her right hand on the tree too, closed her eyes and pulled down a slow breath to steady her racing heart. She focused, warmth spreading through her, together with shock.

She had been so wrong.

This realm wasn't dead.

As she reached through the earth, her power flowing through the roots of the tree to meet those of the one beside it and then the next, she could feel the depth of the life that called the Underworld home. The roots spread far, reaching beneath the temple where she sensed the guards and the souls who had come to it, and out to the mountains. She felt the life in them, and in the valley beyond, hundreds of creatures that moved at different speeds, some even chasing the others. She sensed the village she had passed through with Hades, and felt the warmth of the souls there. They were happy as they went about their lives. There was so much life here. It was incredible.

Before she got caught up in seeing how far her returning powers could reach, she drew them back to her and narrowed her focus down to the area around the temple.

And smiled slowly as she found what she was looking for.

She pushed away from the tree, severing her connection to the realm, and hurried through the orchard.

Froze as her gaze caught on Hades.

He rested propped up against the side of Cerberus, his hands folded over his bare stomach and his eyes closed, and a pillow of black folded cloth behind his head. The beast dwarfed him even when it was lying down. She shook her head at the sight of him. He didn't look like a ferocious king as he dozed against his pet's side. He looked like a man. One who didn't have a care in the world.

Cerberus lifted his heads as she approached and she smiled shakily at the beast.

Who bared fangs in return.

Hades frowned and yawned, and stretched, his muscles shifting in a glorious symphony beneath his alabaster skin with the action and distracting her, but not enough for her to miss the way Cerberus looked ready to snap at her as he snarled.

Hades opened his eyes and frowned at her, and then his pale blue gaze shifted to Cerberus and he said something in his strange tongue. He pushed onto his feet, grabbed the folded piece of cloth and opened it to reveal it was a shirt. He tugged it on and then petted the hound's flank, continuing to speak to him, and Cerberus whined and looked thoroughly berated.

Was Hades telling him off for being aggressive towards her?

"Do not," she said, feeling for the great beast as it cast a sorrowful look at its master. "He is only protecting you."

Hades looked at her, his black eyebrows pinned high on his forehead, and then he smiled as if he was pleased she cared about his pet. Cerberus meant a great deal to Hades, and therefore he meant a great deal to her, even if he was insisting on showing her only aggression in return for her kindness.

When Hades beckoned her to come to him, and she tried, Cerberus bared his fangs and barked at her.

Hades cast him an unimpressed look.

"Perhaps it is best I take him back to his paddock." That look turned apologetic as Hades shifted his gaze from Cerberus to her. "Wait here."

She nodded and his gaze lowered to her dress, and darkened with hunger. Heat flared in her veins and she fidgeted with the layers as his gaze seared her, rousing wicked thoughts about him stripping the dress off her.

He rubbed a hand over his mouth and muttered something in his strange tongue, and then idly reached behind him to shove Cerberus towards the stable. He backed away with the beast, his eyes locked on her as if he didn't have the power to wrench them away, and she covered her smile with her hand when he tripped and almost fell, stumbling into Cerberus.

"I do not look that good in this dress." She gripped the skirts and fanned them outwards.

Hades growled, "You look beautiful."

She blushed, unable to stop the heat from climbing her cheeks.

"Do not move. I will be right back." He turned and shoved Cerberus forwards, casting a pained look over his shoulder at her from time to time as he hurried the beast towards his paddock. The moment the hound was inside and the gate was closed, Hades disappeared, leaving swirls of black smoke behind him.

And reappeared behind her.

She gasped as he banded his arms around her waist and kissed her throat, each one cranking her temperature up and melting her, making her sink into him so her back pressed against his front.

And rousing wicked thoughts about his fangs.

"I take it the dress suits me?" She giggled.

He gripped her and spun her in his arms, his look pure hunger as his gaze collided with hers, and his voice tight. "Even more than I imagined it would. Do you like it?"

He looked as if the small talk was paining him. She glanced down at the hard outline of his shaft in his leathers and realised it probably was. He didn't want to talk. He wanted to devour her. She wanted to devour him too.

Talking was overrated.

She stepped into him, pressing her body against his, and gazed up at him. "I love it."

His eyes darkened and lowered to her lips, and she tiptoed, silently urging him to take what he wanted, and give her what she needed. He groaned and dipped his head, claiming her lips in a searing kiss that heated her blood to boiling point and shredded her control.

Persephone tunnelled her fingers into his hair and moaned as she opened for him and their tongues tangled, his dark taste flooding her and making her crave more. Darkness swept around her and when it receded, they were inside a building. Hades backed her into a black column as she tried to take in her surroundings without breaking their kiss.

The stable.

She thrilled at the thought of him taking her here, where anyone could come across them, that wicked part of her he had awakened finding it exciting. That excitement only grew as shadows snaked up her body and twined around her wrists, raising them above her head as he lowered his mouth to her neck and gripped her skirts. He yanked them up, cool air washing across her thighs and then her buttocks, and she groaned in time with him as he palmed their bare globes.

He drew back, his searing crimson eyes filled with a possessive light that enthralled her, and his fangs flashed between his lips as he uttered low words that had heat flaring on her cheeks.

"You were untouched," he murmured, his eyes remaining locked with hers. "I should be gentle with you this time… but I find I cannot. I need you too much, Persephone."

"Good," she breathed.

His eyebrows pinched. "Good?"

Her heart thundered, her face flaming hotter as she admitted, "I do not want you to be gentle with me. I want you as wild as you were after our chariot ride."

He groaned, the sound strained and agonised, as if she had pained him, and pressed his forehead against hers. "Persephone."

Her name was a plea, and maybe praise too, giving her the impression that he liked that she could match his wickedness and that he didn't need to be gentle with her. There would be a time for gentle later. Right now, she just needed him inside her.

She went up on her toes, a moan bursting from her lips as he cupped her mound and stroked his fingers through her damp petals. A guttural groan left his lips too as he caressed her, that wicked moan rolling into another as she spread her thighs, opening to him. He swept his fingers down the length of her and pressed two inside her, filling her with them and startling her.

"Oh gods," she uttered, her heart galloping and blood blazing as he moved them inside her, taking her with them as his gaze remained fixed on her face.

Her cheeks flamed again as he stared at her, watching what he was doing to her. The momentary embarrassment faded as she met his gaze and saw the heat in it, the need she was rousing with only letting him touch her as he pleased and showing him the pleasure he gave her. The tethers on something within her snapped, and it roared to the fore, vanquishing her fear and her nerves, and unleashing her. She moaned as he plunged into her, as his thumb teased her bead with each thrust of his fingers, and began rocking on his hand, desperately seeking more from him.

She held his gaze the whole time she worked her body on his fingers, wantonly riding them, using them to pleasure herself. His gaze grew darker, sparks of fire igniting in his irises as his shadows tightened around her wrists and he plunged deeper, faster.

"This is mine," he growled as he took her with his fingers, his dark gaze possessive and commanding. "I will ruin you to all other males and you will want only me. *Need* only me."

He already had.

And she already did.

A cry flew from her lips as release hit her, so loud she felt sure the entire compound would hear her.

Hades's gaze grew darker still as he watched her climaxing, as her body milked his fingers and she struggled to catch her breath. That look in his eyes told her everything he was feeling. He liked to watch her breaking apart because of him.

She wanted to watch him break apart because of her.

Before she knew what was happening, dark vines had burst from between the flagstones of the stable and had twined around Hades's wrists and pulled him down onto his back. He growled and wrestled with the vines, anger flashing across his face as he fought to get free.

Persephone raked her gaze over him, heart racing and heat blooming as an idea formed, igniting a need she couldn't deny. One that would have made her blush once, but now only made her burn. She sauntered towards him, gathering her courage with each step.

Hades snarled, baring his fangs as his shadows attacked the vines and more sprouted to bind his wrists and keep him pinned.

"Release me," he barked.

"No." Persephone shook her head, unwilling to let him go.

He had no reason to fear her vines, not like she could see he did as his eyes flashed onyx and his struggles increased, a desperate look crossing his face. She hadn't bound him so she could run away as he feared. She had done it so she could get a taste of what it was like to be in control for once.

He flashed fangs again as his shadows grew more restless and he wrestled against her vines, his gaze darting between his wrists and his legs. Darkness invaded his irises, together with fear and mounting panic that had her stopping dead.

Persephone shook her head and reached a hand out to him, aching to soothe his fears.

"Hades," she murmured, her tone soft and calm.

His gaze darted to her.

And he stilled.

Persephone slowly lifted her skirts and stepped over him, so her feet were on either side of his calves. His gaze tracked her as she eased to her knees, moving to sit astride his legs, that fear that had coloured them beginning to turn to interest. That interest grew as she leaned over him and framed his face with her palms, keeping her gaze on his, hoping he could see in it that she wasn't intending to harm him, and she believed he wouldn't harm her.

She lowered her head and brushed her lips across his, keeping the kiss soft and teasing, and light. His struggles slowed, his body going lax beneath her as he craned his neck towards her.

Eager for more.

Persephone gave it to him, savouring the kiss and the feel of him beneath her almost as much as she savoured the flare of heat and the flicker of azure blue in his eyes when she drew back.

She ran a look over him, trying to decide where to start now that he was at her mercy.

"Release me," he murmured, no longer sounding so commanding, or as if he really wanted her to do it.

She shook her head and settled for starting with his legs. She skimmed her hands over his leather-clad thighs and up to his hips, and Hades gave up fighting as she narrowed the gap between them so they came to rest on the outline of his erection. He rolled his hips instead, pain flashing across his face as he tipped his head back into the flagstones and rubbed against her palm. He wanted her.

Persephone moved her hands away.

Hades growled, an admonishing one that demanded she touch him again.

She refused to do as he wanted, something that put a wicked glint in his eyes that told her he wasn't angry that she wasn't obeying him—he was thrilled by it. He liked being at her mercy. She stroked her hands over his thighs, feeling his tensed, honed muscles beneath her palms, and then back up to his hips. She leaned over him, brushing her hands under his loose black linen shirt, following the intriguing ridge of muscle that arched over his hips. She ventured forwards, her hands gliding higher, pushing his shirt up to reveal his stomach and navel, and the trail of dark hair that led her gaze back down to his crotch.

This time, she couldn't resist unlacing him, the need to see him in all his glory too powerful to deny. He fought the vines as she slowly teased at the lacing over his groin, his torso flexing and attempting to distract her from her task. When he managed to wriggle one vine loose, she chastised him with a glare and tightened it again, and pleasure rippled through her. She had never thought to use her powers for something so naughty, and he only had himself to blame for his current predicament. Using his shadows to restrain her had made her think of using her powers to do the same to him.

And here they were.

She finished unlacing his trousers and bit her lip as she parted them to reveal him. His hard length sprang free and he stilled again, his breaths ceasing as he stared down his body to her. Waiting to see what she would do.

Persephone clung to her courage and stroked her fingertips up his shaft, and jumped when it kicked, jerking towards her. Curious. She stroked it again, and again it moved, so this time she palmed it and curled her fingers around it. She eased her hand down, exposing the head, and stroked her thumb over it.

"Persephone," Hades gritted with a pained look on his face.

A war erupted inside her. Stroke him to a climax, or ride him to one?

She debated it as she feathered her fingers along his cock and explored his body with her other hand, slowly easing forwards until her knees were near his ribs and his shirt was pushed up around his shoulders. Glorious. She released him and palmed his chest, grazing his pebbled nipples with her fingertips, and then stroked them down his abdomen, over rock-hard muscles that had arousal pooling between her thighs.

Such strength.

His hungry gaze followed her hands, his breaths coming faster as she explored him, putting his body to memory, her fingers roaming across the chiselled planes of it at a slow pace. One that was excruciating judging by the look on his face. She refused to be rushed. His cock kicked again, snaring her attention. Not wanting it to feel left out, and aching to touch it again, she stroked him with her left hand as she leaned over him.

He moaned and arched towards her as she brushed her lips across his chest, kissing and licking a path across it and then downwards. That moan made her bold, boosting her courage, and she flicked her tongue over his left nipple. His groan deepened and he rocked his hips, thrusting into her hand.

Filling her head with how good it had felt to have him inside her.

Exploring him fell to the back of her mind as a need to feel him inside her again surged to the fore, and she crawled up his body.

His gaze grew hooded, bright with interest and hunger as he looked from her face to his hips. She pulled her skirts up with her free hand and settled herself above him, poising him at her entrance. He groaned, the guttural sound driving her on together with the desperate, wild look on his face. He wanted to be inside her too.

Persephone eased back, taking the blunt crown inside her, and bit her lip as he stretched her, only it didn't hurt this time. She felt only pleasure as she slid her body onto his, as he filled her and completed her, and that pleasure increased a hundredfold as she looked at him where he lay beneath her, vines securing his wrists, at her mercy.

His hands closed around the thick green vines, gripping them tightly, his entire body tensing as she moved on him. His breaths hitched, his head tipping back as she rode him, as she rocked on him and pressed her hands against his chest to brace herself. With every press and withdraw of his shaft, her need grew fiercer, her control fraying. More vines shot from the ground, snaking around his legs and holding him in place. He groaned as she took him harder, as she pressed her nails into his chest to leave red marks on his pale skin and bounced faster. Faster.

Her breasts bobbed with each frantic thrust of her body against his, her breaths growing shorter and quicker as she pressed her hands harder against his chest, as she held his gaze and desperately reached for release. He groaned and tried to thrust into her, but her vines held him down, stopping him from moving. Something he liked judging by how his groan became a wicked growl that had pleasure rippling through her and his expression darkened, growing even more hungry.

"Persephone," he gritted, sounding as desperate as she felt.

She moved position, leaning over him and gripping his shoulders. He craned his neck and she captured his lips, moaning as his kiss seared her and his chest abraded her nipples, sending sparks skittering through her. She rocked faster, frantic now, reaching for the release that was just beyond her reach.

It slammed into her as shadows swept between her thighs, going from intangible to solid as they stroked over her pert bead.

She cried out, her entire body convulsing and quaking, her spine arching as heat and light engulfed her. Hades followed her over the edge, grunting as he throbbed and spilled, the feel of his climax adding to hers. She breathed hard in time with him as she struggled to come down from it, as she remained frozen above him, lost in bliss and feeling as if she was floating.

At some point, her vines must have loosened, because Hades's arms curled around her and he drew her down to his chest. His heart thundered against her ear as he continued to throb within her, hammering a discordant melody with her own. She didn't have the strength to move. Every inch of her felt heavy and sated, and trembled.

Hades stroked a line down her spine and up again, his caress heating her, rousing her and restoring her strength as desire swelled, a need to have him again. She wasn't sure she would ever get enough of him.

"That was…" he murmured, his voice gone low and gravelly, "Enjoyable."

She chuckled. "You more than enjoyed it."

She stroked his chest, waiting for him to deny it. When he had climaxed on the chariot, it had been intense, but nothing like the release he had just found. He still pulsed inside her, his shaft yet to settle. When he had come, each kick of his cock had been fierce, close to pushing her to another release.

"No denial?" She lifted her head to look at him.

He shook his head, and she smiled at how glazed his eyes were, their now-blue depths a little hazy and distant.

Persephone pushed up and he tightened his arms against her back, stopping her.

"Where are you going?" he rumbled.

"I want to bathe." A thought crossed her mind as she looked at him, one that was tempting and made her want to go through with it.

"We shall share a bath." He stroked her back again, his look growing heated, telling her that he was already planning to make another of her fantasies into a reality.

She lifted both her hands towards his face, but didn't cup his cheeks. They continued upwards.

"What are you doing?" He frowned at her again.

"You ask too many questions. Where are you going? What are you doing? I am doing this." She took hold of his crown and eased it from his head, releasing it from his tousled black hair.

The spikes were angled backwards, smallest at the front and largest at the back. It seemed to be made of some kind of stone rather than metal, and it was cool to the touch.

He tried to take it from her. She pushed to her feet and was six feet from him before he could grab it. She smiled teasingly at him as he growled and lifted the crown above her and placed it on her head.

His growl tapered off.

A dark, bewitching look filled his eyes.

"Does it suit me?" She pulled a thoughtful face.

Hades teleported to her, appearing in a swirl of black smoke, and his arms were around her before she could move. Rather than stealing his crown back, he gazed down at her, his expression fierce, but holding a hint of tenderness.

"If you want a crown, my love, you only need to ask," he husked, the pleased growl in his lush baritone sending a shiver down her spine as he drew her closer still. He feathered his fingers down her cheek, and brushed his thumb over her lower lip, teasing her mouth open as his gaze lowered to it, growing hooded. "You only need to accept me as your husband."

Her husband.

She shivered a little, finding she liked the idea of that.

Hades as her husband.

Not a male who sought to rule or own her, but an equal who would stand by her side, who looked as if his very future hinged upon her accepting him. She would make him happy if she did. It was right there in his eyes as they filled with love and a dash of hope.

He brought his mouth close to hers and whispered the most tempting words she had ever heard against her lips.

"Say the word, Persephone, and you will be my queen."

CHAPTER 30

The darkness was a creeping rot inside Hades, slowly poisoning his mind.

He kept pace beside Persephone, remaining close to her, within the sphere of her beautiful light as they strolled around his temple. Ten days had passed since their chariot ride, and Hades had never felt happier.

He was also sure he had never felt so possessive, or protective of someone.

Persephone's emerald eyes were bright as she admired the exterior of his temple, her gaze running over the towering onyx columns and the golden braziers of azure fire. There was a bounce in her step that would have told him of her happiness, and excitement, if her wide smile hadn't shouted it at him. That smile—that excitement—was the sole reason he had agreed to take her to his temple today.

He had avoided bringing her here, despite her frequent requests to see it, for good reason. That reason was building inside him now, slowly devouring pieces of the light she had restored inside him these past few weeks. With each masculine voice that reached his ears, the rot spread faster—devoured faster.

Her gaze landed on him.

And lingered.

"Hades?" Her voice was as soft as the kiss of summer sun as she studied his face, a hint of concern in it and the look she gave him.

"I am fine," he muttered.

The same response he had given her several times already.

He was not fine.

Since their moment on the chariot, unease had been building inside him, and he grew dark whenever a male so much as walked near Persephone, even when she was tucked safely within his chambers and the male in question was beyond the walls. He couldn't bear another man being near her. He wanted her all to himself.

The darkness wanted her all to himself.

Both sides of him were in agreement on something at last.

No male would look upon his queen and live.

Persephone stepped in front of him, a crinkle forming between her fine scarlet eyebrows as she formed a beautiful blockade that forced him to stop too. She gently shook her head, lifted her hand and brushed her fingers across his cheek in a maddening caress.

"We could walk the orchard instead." While her tone was light and sincere, he could see in her eyes she didn't want to walk the orchard.

She wanted to see his temple.

What his love wanted, his love got.

Hades shook his head and raised his hand. He mirrored her, sweeping his knuckles across her fair cheek, and then threaded his fingers through her fall of crimson hair, savouring how soft the silken threads were against it.

And the wicked urge to fist and hold her in place for a bruising kiss.

He had tightened his hand in her hair and had pulled her against him before he was aware of what he had done, but she didn't gasp or protest. No. His little queen arched against him, pressing her breasts to his chest, and licked her lips as her gaze fell to his mouth.

Hades dropped his head and claimed her lips in a fierce kiss, bending her to his will as he gripped her hair. She moaned, the wanton sound fanning the flames of his passion, until he was on the verge of teleporting her back to their chambers so he could take her again.

He set her away from him instead when he sensed two females passing them. He scowled at the servants where they crossed the open stretch of land beside the temple, and they ducked their heads and hurried in the other direction. Satisfied that he was alone with his love again, he turned back to pull her into his arms for another kiss.

And growled when he found her halfway along the temple, her gaze dancing over the carvings on the walls of it.

Hades strode towards her, his long legs making fast work of closing the distance between them, allowing him to reach her before she dared to peek into the open doorway in the side of the temple. Rather than looking inside, she turned her steady emerald gaze on him.

"Remain close," he growled as he battled a sudden surge of darkness.

Just the thought of her being near so many males ravaged his defences and had him slipping, had the darkness rising to tighten its grip on him. It whispered through his mind, stroking black talons over it as it murmured of other males and keeping her close, and fed his fears, preying on them.

Hades fought it as he placed his hand against her lower back and kept his gaze on her, attempting to shut out the other people. Awareness trickled like ice down his spine beneath his armour. If he let it take him, the darkness would have him painting the walls with the blood of every pilgrim and guard in the temple.

Persephone would be horrified.

She would reject him.

Turn her back on him.

Her words rang in his mind—her disdain for bloodshed and killing—pushing him firmly to the edge as they entered the temple side by side. He tried to focus on quelling the darkness and keeping it at bay, using Persephone's presence to give him strength together with how she would react if the darkness took control. He glanced at those in the temple as she moved deeper into it, heading for the colossal black stone statue of him in full regalia at one end of it.

Male and female pilgrims dressed in little more than rags shuffled in a line towards that statue, looking weary and worn, as if they barely had the strength to remain standing. In their hands, they clutched dusty bottles and food wrapped in cloth—meagre offerings meant to appease him and show their gratitude.

The sight of them was like a punch in his chest.

The people of his realm should not look so tired and thin.

Guilt slammed into him when one female with straggly grey hair cast a bleak, but longing look at the chunk of bread she clasped to her chest.

Hades growled and stepped forwards, reaching for Persephone's arm to pull her out of the temple before she could notice how poorly he had been treating his citizens. She would despise him if she saw how filthy and hungry they were. How desperate. How had he not noticed it before?

He flicked a glance at Persephone, sure it was her doing. She had opened his eyes. She had made him look at his realm with clear ones and see his faults, and his wrongdoings. His failings.

Persephone frowned at his hand as he came close to snagging her wrist with it and then turned her bewitching gaze on the pilgrims. Her dazzling emerald eyes shifted from the line of people to him, no trace of anger in them, and then drifted around the room. She was looking for something.

He knew what she sought.

Rather than taking hold of her, Hades strode to the statue and grabbed a golden bowl of fruit someone had placed between his feet. It had probably been an offering made by one from the breeds born in his realm, ones who called it home in a different way to the souls sent to him. Those breeds had wealth and large estates where several families lived, and could come and go between the Underworld and the mortal one, and even Olympus.

He summoned a guard with a wave of his hand. The male nearest him dipped his head, causing the crest on his black helmet to sway, and approached him.

Hades held the large bowl filled with grapes, oranges and pomegranates out to the male. "See to it this is distributed among the needy and gather the names of their villages."

So he could look into them and ensure the souls there were nourished and could take better care of themselves.

The male worked his way down the line, and each soul he served looked beyond him to Hades and bowed their head as they accepted the offering of food. All except the elderly female. When the guard offered her fruit, she took an orange, and as the male moved on, she broke away from the line and approached Hades.

Two guards stepped into her path, crossing their spears to stop her.

"Let her through," Hades said, aware how closely Persephone was watching him.

The guards eased back, but didn't leave, as if this female was a threat to him and he needed their protection.

The woman hobbled towards him and when she was close to him, she held her scrap of bread out to him. Hades stared at the meagre offering and then at her, and shook his head. Which didn't please her.

She offered it again, thrusting it towards him.

Persephone stepped up beside him, placed her hand over the woman's, and gently pushed the bread back towards her. "Your presence is gift enough for Hades. You need this food more than he does."

She meant her words to be kind, he was sure, but they were a knife in his chest.

It stabbed so deep he flinched.

Persephone noticed it, and how the darkness surged in response to the vile words spinning through his mind. It coaxed and cajoled, hissing at him. These pilgrims looked down upon him, believing he needed their food. Persephone looked down upon him, disgusted by how he allowed his subjects to suffer. She despised him. She would find any other male in this room more pleasing company than him. Wanted any other male in this room more than she wanted him.

The guards looked back to check on him.

But all he saw were them looking at his Persephone.

His love.

Intending to steal her from him.

"Return home now." Persephone ushered the woman away, her actions hurried.

She knew the woman was in danger.

Hades fought the darkness, struggling to hold it back as it continued to taunt him with images of Persephone and other males, with visions of her looking upon him with scorn and lashing out at him for his failings. He curled his hands into fists that had his emerging claws digging into his palms to draw blood.

One of the guards made the mistake of turning towards Persephone as she urged the elderly woman away from Hades.

The moment the male's dark eyes landed on her, Hades was lost.

Darkness blasted through him and erupted out of him, shadows swift to wrap around the male and seize hold of him. Hades growled as he dragged the male towards him, the guard's terrified scream ringing in his ears and making him shiver as pleasure rolled through him, pushing him deeper into the abyss.

Pandemonium erupted in the temple, several guards rushing towards him as the pilgrims scattered. Hades bared his fangs and hurled the male he held at the guards. The male struck two of them and they landed in a heap on the floor. His shadows tore from the black stone floor, and the temple shook as they gathered and devoured the light.

Hades narrowed his black gaze on the guards as they tried to scramble onto their feet, their fear flowing around him—through him—turning his head hazy and flooding him with a seething need to rip them apart.

And then green vines shot from the floor, weaving together to form a wall between him and the men. He growled as that wall rapidly expanded outwards, rising up to the ceiling and stretching from wall to wall.

Cutting him off from the guards and the pilgrims.

But it wasn't only the wall of vines that was stopping him.

Persephone stood before it, her arms outstretched and her steady green gaze fixed on him as she shielded everyone from his shadows and wrath.

There was no judgement in her eyes, not as he had expected—not as the darkness had hissed there would be, feeding his fears.

There was only tenderness, and understanding, and a wealth of concern.

Her tone was even and calm as she said, "My apologies all. Your god-king is grateful for your tribute, and is pleased to see you, but tensions have been high across the realm and he is in need of rest. I humbly request that you exit the temple as I require a moment with your god-king."

Hades bared fangs at her, the darkness goading him into attacking her instead, just as he had feared it might. He willed her to do as she had promised and run from him, even when some part of him was aware that if she ran, he would chase her. He would hunt her down.

Rather than fleeing with the others, she did something that stole his breath and shocked him so thoroughly that the darkness lost its grip on him.

She came to him, bravely facing him at his worst, uncaring of the shadows that lashed at the floor near her and unafraid of him as he snarled and flashed fangs at her, warning her away.

By the gods, she was incredible. So brave. So strong.

She didn't stop until she was toe to toe with him, her gentle gaze holding his and her soft voice curling around him like a warm breeze to ease the tension from his muscles and calm him.

"All will be well," she murmured and lifted her hands, framing his face with her palms. "Come back to me, Hades."

She was a balm to his soul, a light that illuminated the darkest reaches of his heart and slowly began to drive the shadows back as she continued to gaze up at him through soft, tender eyes.

She was a wonder that bewitched him all over again.

And then she tiptoed, slid her right hand around his nape and pulled his head down. She captured his lips, her kiss soft and accepting, stunning and humbling him. The darkness faded, but anger remained—anger that she hadn't run as promised.

Gratitude overshadowed it, quietening it as she kissed him, her lips barely brushing his. A kiss that made him feel light inside, that cast the shadows from him and warmed him right down to his soul. Gods, he was grateful that she had stayed with him, showing him that she didn't fear him, and proving that she wanted to help him.

The longer she kissed him, the quieter the darkness became, until he felt in control again. But it didn't disappear entirely. It lingered, whispering temptation in his ear that had him stealing command of the kiss from Persephone. He wanted her. Needed her. Right here.

Right now.

Both the man in him and the darkness craved her, ached to bend her to his will and lay claim to her. The hunger she roused in him reached a new height as her hands came down on his chest and she pressed closer to him, rubbing her body against his.

Making him ravenous for her.

Hades twisted with her and kept kissing her as he backed her towards the base of the statue, fevered with need of her, his veins on fire with wicked heat. He groaned as he peered beyond her to the raised black stone altar strewn with offerings of fruit and wine.

He wanted to set her down on it.

Hades gripped her waist.

Turning her into the most delectable offering there ever was.

He lifted her, tearing a gasp from her.

An offering he intended to devour.

CHAPTER 31

Persephone gasped as Hades lifted her and the sound of metal bowls striking the stone floor of the temple to spin away from them filled the silence together with their frantic, rasping breaths. His shadows tossed several bottles on the floor, the sound of them smashing ratcheting up her desire together with the drugging scent of ambrosia. Her heart galloped as he set her down on the altar and shoved her dress up her thighs.

A moan tore from her lips as he ripped her undergarments away and fell to his knees before her. That moan became a strangled gasp of pleasure and shock as he pushed her thighs apart and delved between them, his tongue stroking the length of her from her feminine core to her aching nub.

Her head fell back as he licked and laved her, as he wrapped his lips around her bead and sucked, sending a sharp thrill bolting through her and ripping another moan from her. Her gaze grew hooded as she rested on her elbows, her mind whirling and body aflame as he waged war on it, every hard flick of his tongue over her sensitive bead more drugging than the ambrosia that laced the air.

Persephone stared up at the statue that towered over her as Hades devoured her, feeling as if she was an offering to him, one he relished as he growled and moaned. She found the strength to move her head, tipping it upright again, and groaned.

The sight of his dark head between her pale thighs was wanton. Wicked. Incredibly erotic.

Incredibly delicious.

Another moan tumbled from her as he licked her harder. It felt too good. Far better than she had ever imagined possible. She watched him as he ran his tongue up her and sucked her again, her fingers itching to burrow into his hair and hold him to her. When he lowered his head and probed her with his tongue, the tethers holding her back frayed and snapped.

Persephone thrust her fingers into his onyx hair and gripped it hard as she rocked against his tongue, the ache building inside her stealing control and demanding she satisfy it. She rolled her hips against his face, moans falling from her lips with each stroke of his tongue as he took her higher. The fiercer he devoured her, the hotter the fire in her veins burned, and the less control she had.

Hades planted his hands against her knees and pushed them apart, his gaze dark as he drew back and stared at her. Not into her eyes. Not even at her face. He gazed at her cleft, dark fascination shining in his eyes, together with a ravenous hunger that called to her.

"Hades," she murmured, aching for him to continue, desperate to come.

"Such a pretty thing," he husked back at her and ran a finger down her petals.

She shivered and moaned, her thighs trembling from his light touch and his wicked words.

"You taste sweeter than ambrosia." His dark eyes met hers, black ringing his crimson irises and fire flickering in his pupils.

Was his darkness one with him right now? While he was taking her like this? The thought of it being at the fore in this moment should have stirred fear or anxiety. At the very least it should have made her feel she should stop him.

Instead, it ignited a wildfire so intense it scorched her and had her eagerly reaching for him, hungry for him to take her right that second, to fill her and pound into her, to drive her out of her mind until she shattered.

Hades only fanned the flames by idly running his finger up and down her cleft, his eyes never straying from her as he uttered, "I could drink from you for eternity. Feast on you forever, my little queen."

A shiver wracked her and she stared at him, silently challenging him to do it.

Only he wasn't done with taunting and arousing her.

He licked his lips and bent to his left to press kisses along her thigh, to nip at it with his fangs in a way that made those flames burn hotter still, his gaze still holding hers. He circled her opening, shortening her breaths with his teasing until she was on the verge of begging him.

"I like that look," he murmured, a slight smile curving his lips. "By the time I am done with you, you *will* be begging for my cock. You want to feel me filling you, sweet Persephone?"

She nodded, aching for it.

His eyes narrowed. "You want my seed in you."

It wasn't a question.

She groaned and nodded in response anyway, his wicked words setting her entire body aflame as her mind conjured visions of him coming in her, flooding her with his essence. She wanted to feel that. She needed it.

Hades swooped on her on a low growl, and she cried out as he stroked and teased her again, more vigorously than before, as if his own words had fanned the flames of his desire and he was as lost to it as she was to hers.

A scream burst from her lips as release crashed over her, her entire body quaking as her head fell back and she spasmed.

Hades didn't give her a moment to recover.

Metal hitting the stone floor rang out and then his fingers were digging into her thighs and his cock shoved into her. She cried out again, the fierce invasion both sweet and painful, bliss and agony at the same time. Her thighs shook against his as his left hand came down on her chest and he pressed her spine against the altar. His dark gaze held hers as he took her. Hard. Fast. Grunts burst from his lips with each meeting of their hips, each thrust of his cock that had him striking as deep as she could take him.

Hades had never been so brutal with her.

And she loved it.

Her hands scrabbled around, seeking something to hold on to as he plunged deeper. Harder. Rocking her with the force of each thrust. His eyes narrowed, shadows streaming from his shoulders, and his fangs flashed between his lips and they pulled taut. She moaned, the sight of him cranking up her temperature, until she was on fire for him.

She found something above her head and shoved her hands against it, stopping herself from moving each time he filled her. Her eyes shot wide as she felt the full brutality of his punishing thrusts, pleasure bolting through her to have her moaning and silently begging him for more, for that one push that would take her over the edge.

Hades growled, baring fangs at her, and took her harder, his eyes growing darker.

"Hades," she breathed, desperate.

Something flickered across his eyes, azure blue that bewitched her, and then he shoved deep into her.

His cock kicked and pulsed as he grunted, hot jets of seed bursting from him to fill her greedy body as it spasmed around him, milking him and hungry for all he had to offer.

Her cries echoed around the temple as release blasted through her, shattering her mind and her body. Every inch of her trembled and throbbed, warm waves of chills skittering along her limbs.

Hades eased back and then into her again, his thrusts slow, the feel of him pulsing inside her rousing her body.

His gaze seared her.

Filled with a wicked promise that he was far from done with her.

CHAPTER 32

Hades was now certain that in all his centuries, he had never felt like this. He would have remembered it, even in his darkest days. Light seemed to bathe his soul, holding the darkness at bay, and warmth was his constant companion, driving out the cold. He stroked his fingers through Persephone's hair as she lounged against him, occupying one side of the black chaise longue in his chambers, her back half-resting against his chest and her head on his shoulder.

"Your temple is rather beautiful," she murmured and stroked his fingers of the hand he had on her waist, a possessive grasp that he couldn't quite convince himself to loosen.

Far too many males had gazed upon her in his temple. Just as far too many males had looked at her during their visits to several villages, the barracks and even Tartarus. His little goddess had been curious about that place too, asking questions about it whenever they lazed together like this, savouring each other's company and the peaceful quiet.

She angled her head back so her gaze touched his face, her brow furrowing. "Hades?"

"Hmm?" He slid his gaze to meet hers and smiled to alleviate the concern growing in her eyes. "I am fine."

She twisted onto her front, her hands coming to rest on his chest as she pressed against it and frowned at him.

"You are not fine. I wish you would not shut me out." She sighed at him as she lifted one hand and feathered her fingers down his cheek. "Your eyes betray you. Speak to me, Hades."

"I do not like how every male in my realm looks at you." His arms tightened around her as his mood darkened again, veering back towards the abyss that beckoned him now. "You are mine, Persephone, and I will not share you with anyone."

She smiled, a sweet one that teased but soothed him. "I do not wish to be theirs, so you do not have to worry about sharing me with anyone."

Did she wish to be his?

He feared voicing that question, even when she had been his constant companion over the last ten days, never leaving his side whenever he was at home. The only time they had been apart was when he needed to handle business in Tartarus or help his men with unrest in the regions.

Unrest that had been decreasing each day now that he had finished hunting down the final dangerous and dark souls that had eluded capture and moved them to the new district he had set up for them.

And maybe also because he was growing lighter.

He could feel it.

The whole of the Underworld was a testament to the effect Persephone was having on him.

The land had settled, the volcanoes becoming dormant, and water had begun to flow where lava had once been. His throne room was the perfect example of how much he had changed, and the Underworld had changed with him. Beyond the smaller columned temple that housed his throne, deep in the canyon that bordered the plateau where they were now, a river cut a path between the flat bank and the steep sides of the mountains that enclosed it.

A river that had once flowed with lava.

The darkness remained though. His other constant companion. He wasn't sure he would ever be able to shake it. It was swift to seize him whenever a male neared Persephone or even glanced in her direction, rising within him to goad him into taking their head so they couldn't gaze upon his love.

Or steal her from him.

"Your eyes are changing again," she murmured softly and stroked her fingers across his brow, soothing that darkness with her light touch. Rather than snapping and snarling, it purred.

He had discovered in his temple that his darker side was just as possessive of Persephone as he was, that the side of him that craved bloodshed and violence and could so easily turn him into a mindless slave to it craved her too. She had tamed it so easily when she had faced him, driving it back far quicker than he had ever managed himself.

"Hades…" She hesitated, and he knew what she wanted to ask.

The same thing she had asked many times over the last few weeks.

She wanted him to speak to her about the darkness, to break down that final wall that stood between them and let her all the way in. Just as she had for him. She had told him of her pain. She had confided in him and shared the source of her darkness with him.

He gazed at her, his fingers pausing in her hair, nerves rising. It felt only right to do the same for her.

But he had never spoken of the darkness to anyone.

He frowned.

He doubted she had either.

She had hidden her pain from the world, concealing how deeply her mother's actions had wounded her. But she had told him.

He drew down a deep, calming breath as the darkness growled that she would use it against him. If he told her of it, she would fear him. Despise him. Hades shut it down and silenced it, refusing to listen to its fearmongering.

Persephone trusted him.

And he wanted to keep that trust between them, and strengthen it if he could.

He wanted to trust her.

"The darkness…" he started and her eyes lit up, the dull edge of resignation that had been filling them disappearing in a heartbeat. He cleared his throat and fought for the words, to find a way of putting it that wouldn't make her fear him or despise him. "The darkness is… My darkness is part of me… but in a different way to yours."

"An affliction," she murmured thoughtfully and when he frowned at her, her eyebrows rose and she gave a little shrug. "I have been studying you and how you change, and it always seems to me like you have to fight the change that comes over you, as if you have no control over it. It is not anger, nor rage, that makes you dark. It is something else, isn't it?"

Hades nodded and tried to push the words out, but it was harder than he had expected and they refused to come. He stared at Persephone. He could trust her. She wouldn't betray him. She wouldn't run from him.

She had proven that.

Telling her might lift the weight from his heart, and it might even help him master the darkness so it wouldn't take him again. Or at least it wouldn't take him as easily as it did now.

If he told her of it, she might be able to help him with it.

The thought of that was more than appealing. It was as bewitching as she was as she patiently waited, not pressing or pushing him to tell her. That soft look in her eyes spoke to him, telling him that even if he failed to tell her, if he couldn't find the words or the courage right now, that she wouldn't be upset. She would continue to wait, even if it took forever for him to find the strength to tell her.

"It is an affliction," he said, repeating what she had said in order to get the words flowing, and held her gaze, needing to lose himself in it in order to find his courage. "Many centuries ago, when I was given the Underworld to rule, I was bitter and angry. My brothers had betrayed me and condemned me to this dark place. I raged and I warred, and I spilled blood across the realm. With every drop, something grew inside me, feeding on the violence and the anger, and the hatred. I did not realise what was happening until it was too late. I created this darkness that overcomes me at times, and I must live with it."

Persephone stroked his brow again, her featherlight touch soothing him as he let it all flow out of him, feeling as if a dam had broken and he couldn't stop the surge.

"Rather than fighting it, I fed the darkness. I courted it. I wallowed in it. I realised my mistake when the blackouts began."

She frowned now, concern flickering in her eyes. "Blackouts?"

His eyebrows pitched low and he struggled to hold her gaze. "If the darkness takes me, I find it hard to recall things I have done. I can wake a great distance from the temple grounds, bathed in blood, surrounded by death."

Just as he had not long ago.

Hades didn't tell her that. There were some things she was better off not knowing.

"They happen infrequently and I would never harm you, my love." He threaded his fingers through her hair.

She smiled softly. "I know. What does it feel like?"

"When the darkness takes me?" He waited for her to nod before he continued. "Cold. Numbing. Like I am a prisoner in my own body. I am not in control. It poisons my mind, blackening it, and all I feel is an intense craving for violence—a thirst for bloodshed. I care little about anything when I am lost to it. It is… *debilitating*."

It was the first time he had ever called it that, admitting how terrible it felt and how he despised the lack of control in only a single word.

One that made him feel weak.

But Persephone made him feel strong as she held his gaze, silently listening to him with no trace of judgement in her eyes. There was only warmth and understanding.

Warmth and understanding that fuelled his courage and gave him the strength to continue, pushing another admission up from the depths of his black soul that was difficult and cranked him tight inside as he struggled to force the words to leave his lips.

"The darkness… is like a living thing. It… speaks to me. Whispers to me." He cast his gaze away from her, unable to look at her as he confessed something that made him feel weak and vulnerable, and he was sure would taint her opinion of him. "It tempts me, Persephone. It seduces… drawing me into its embrace as it feeds my fears to weaken me."

"Even now?" she asked softly.

Hades nodded stiffly, because it was hissing vile things at him, tormenting him with thoughts that Persephone might no longer want him if he said anything else about the darkness.

Rather than leaving him, Persephone shuffled closer, making blissful contact with him, and gently framed his face in her warm, soft palms. She angled his head towards her, her emerald eyes still filled with understanding, and then she lowered her mouth to his and tenderly kissed him.

A kiss that made him ache and yearn for more.

A kiss that was a balm to his weary soul.

She drew back and breathed against his lips, "Even now?"

"You wield such power, my love. Over me. Over the darkness within me. Power I do not understand," Hades whispered against her mouth. "It is often quiet when you are close to me."

"Then I shall endeavour to remain close to you always," she murmured, and pressed her lips to his, tormenting him with a far too brief kiss, and then pulled back again to study him as he stroked her hair, marvelling at how incredible she was. "You fight it so hard when it takes you."

He frowned and shifted his gaze to the lock of her hair that slipped over his fingers. "No one has ever noticed that before."

She smiled slightly. "I am not surprised. I think this whole world does not understand you, Hades."

His gaze slid to meet hers and the solemn, wounded look in it touched him. She didn't like that people judged him on the stories others told of him, or that they were blind to his true nature. She felt hurt on his behalf. His beautiful, gentle Persephone.

"Not the whole world," he husked and dropped his fingers to her cheek, holding it to keep her eyes on him as she gave him a puzzled look. "You understand me… and that is enough for me."

Her smile returned, brighter this time, and she pushed up his body and captured his lips in a sweet, tender kiss that bathed his soul in light and soothed the hurt from it.

It was strange talking to her about the darkness, but cathartic too. They had only scratched the surface, but already he felt better for it. More hopeful that he could one day overcome it and live without constant fear of losing control to it and harming his people.

It was also strange to feel so supported by someone, to have someone look at him as Persephone did as she drew back, her smile still in place. Her eyes shone with love. Love that had been there even when the darkness had taken him in the temple. How could she look at him like that when she had seen him at his worst?

The darkness whispered that it was a lie.

Hades shunned it and focused on her, using her light to cast it back into the depths of his soul.

He struggled to find his voice again, sure she wouldn't be satisfied with knowing so little about how he had come to have such a dark side and his fight against it.

"Oh, I just remembered!" she said, all false brightness and fake forgetfulness that had him frowning at her because he wasn't sure what she was up to, and then she added, "There was another word I wanted to know, and I thought perhaps you might teach me?"

It dawned on him that she was trying to change the subject and make him feel he didn't need to plumb the depths of the darkness to assuage her curiosity about it. Not yet anyway. He was sure that in time, he would have the courage to speak of it again, and would tell her more about it.

And then she would change the subject again, giving him some reprieve.

And they would repeat this until she finally knew all there was to know about the darkness that afflicted him.

And Hades was fine with that.

"What word is that?" He banded his arms around her, savouring the shift in the conversation towards a lighter topic, and breathed a little easier for the weight she had already lifted from his heart, lightening it in a way he felt only she could.

"Kiss," she said.

"Yes, please," he husked and captured her lips just as she frowned at him.

She melted into him, her hands coming to rest on his chest to tease and stir his passion as her lips danced with his.

When she drew back, her gaze was hooded and hazy, and he wanted to growl at the sight of her looking so satisfied—wanted to put that look on her face with more than just kissing.

"Illa," he said, and when a little crinkle formed between her eyebrows, he added, "Illa is kiss. I can use it in a sentence if it helps."

She nodded eagerly.

Hades raked a look over her and growled in the language of his realm, "I want to kiss every inch of you."

Her cheeks heated, as if she had understood him. She had probably understood his look more than his words, but in time she would come to know what he was saying when he spoke in this tongue. Now that she had finally asked him, she would find he was a good teacher on this subject too.

Very skilled in fact.

Almost as skilled as he was at teaching her all about pleasure.

She gasped, her eyes widening, as he palmed her backside and pulled her closer, his gaze falling to her mouth.

She kissed him again, harder this time, stoking the flames of his desire.

And then she shoved onto her knees beside him.

"Come, let us go for a walk." She beamed at him. "You can teach me more of your language while we are out."

Hades banded his arms around her and pulled her down onto his lap, eliciting a squeak from her as she crashed into him.

"Let us stay here." He tugged her up him and peppered her throat with kisses. "I can think of other ways to distract me from my dark thoughts."

She leaned into his lips, her fingertips pressing into his bare chest, and loosed a breathy moan as she angled her head, giving him better access to her throat. She had done that several times when he had been kissing her throat, giving him the impression she liked it, and rousing a wicked hunger to bite her and mark her as his.

Would she like that?

The blush of colour on her cheeks whenever he looked at her after lavishing attention on her throat, and the awkward edge to her gaze, made him believe she might.

For a moment, he thought he had won, but then she whispered.

"There is another place I would love to see."

And he was defeated.

What his love wanted, his love would always get.

He kissed her throat a little more, lingering there to steal more of the feel of her in his arms, attempting to settle the darkness that still ran rampant in his blood. His head filled with pleasing images of cutting down every guard and pilgrim who had dared to gaze upon Persephone, and he kissed her harder, drawing her closer to him to pin her against his body.

"Hades," she murmured, her light voice working its magic on him to calm the darkness and push it back.

She shifted in his arms, her mouth coming to meet his, and her kiss was soft, bewitching, and filled with love that stole his heart all over again. Even when he was close to raging, to losing himself to the darkness, she showed him affection. As if she loved that side of him too. The darkness slowly receded as he greedily kissed her, devouring her affection and claiming it all for himself.

She was his.

But she still hadn't said the words.

She still hadn't agreed to be his queen.

He was growing impatient. Each day that ticked past without her saying that she would be his forever was a day in which the darkness within him grew stronger, gaining ground against the light, and rose more easily to engulf him and snatch control from his grasp. He needed her to be his. Couldn't she see that?

Hades drew back and sought her gaze, and the way her brow furrowed as she met it and her emerald eyes warmed, told him that she could see it. She could see how badly he needed her and that she was everything to him, as vital as air in his lungs and a beat in his chest.

And he could see the flicker of fear in her.

One he had yet to vanquish.

Something was holding her back, and if he pressed her to tell him, she would clam up. She had in all the times he had tried to goad her into talking to him about Olympus and her remaining here with him.

Rather than pushing her to answer, he had decided to give her everything she desired, to do whatever she wanted, slowly stripping down her barriers one by one until she was defenceless against him—just as he had no defence against her.

"Where does my love want to go today?" He tried to smile, an act that was still strange and foreign to him but one she apparently adored, because her face lit up whenever he smiled and whatever troubled her seemed to dissipate, no longer clouding her eyes.

Or perhaps it was because he insisted on calling her his love.

She liked his pet name for her, one that betrayed his feelings.

She was his love.

His everything.

"The Elysian Fields," she said with a little smile of her own, one that wobbled slightly to reveal the nerves he could already sense in her.

Because the first time she had asked about visiting that place, he had denied her.

Far too many heroic souls resided there, and while he knew Persephone didn't want to visit that part of the realm in order to see the handsome males who were far more worthy of her than he was, he still despised the thought of taking her to that place. Her look was pure hope as she gazed at him though, that smile faltering on her lips as he remained silent.

Hades sighed. "Very well."

Her entire face brightened, her smile so wide and delighted that it struck him like a thunderbolt in his chest, knocking the wind from him. By the gods. If he had known she would look so happy at just the thought of visiting the Elysian Fields, he might have taken her to them when she had first asked. She was radiant as she pushed off him, a bounce in her step.

His beautiful goddess.

She began towards the bed and then hurried back to him, bent and captured his lips in the softest, warmest kiss he had ever experienced.

Hades wrapped his arms around her and gathered her to him, unwilling to relinquish this kiss, needing more of it. All of it. He wanted her to keep kissing him like this forever.

Someone banged on the wooden doors.

A male voice rang through them. "My god-king Hades. A visitor awaits you in the throne room."

Hades growled as he surrendered Persephone's lips. "What visitor?"

The male said, "Your brother, my god-king."

CHAPTER 33

Cold skated down Hades's spine and his hands tensed against Persephone, his gaze darting to her as awareness of the reason for his brother's visit struck him hard. She paled in his arms, her hands closing over his shoulders and fear flashing across her face.

Zeus would not dare take her from him.

He told himself that on repeat as he forced himself to release her and stand, but no part of him believed it. Each step he took across his room was heavy, an effort that tore at his strength and drained him, and the feel of her gaze on his back had him wanting to tuck her in his arms and teleport her far from this place, to somewhere Zeus would never find her.

Hades pushed down the cold that scoured his insides and chilled his heart, and stoked the fires of his rage, calling upon the darkness and tugging it to the fore, if only so this meeting with his brother would hurt less, his emotions dampened by the darkness. He methodically attached each piece of his armour, his mind numbed as he worked to dress, his heart growing heavier by the second.

When he turned towards the door, Persephone was there.

"I am coming with you." She tipped her chin up but there wasn't an ounce of confidence in her eyes as she clenched her fists and they shook. Her voice lowered, growing strained, and tears lined her lashes, tearing at his heart. "I am coming with you."

He nodded, unable to deny her—as always. Part of him wanted her there, so Zeus could see that whatever he believed was wrong, and that she wanted to be here. He wanted his brother to see the hurt he was causing. He wanted him to suffer.

Hades held his gauntleted hand out to her and she slipped hers into it. She pulled down a breath as he tugged her into his embrace. He meant to teleport, but as she pressed against his breastplate, a sniffle escaping her, he ended up holding her instead.

"All will be well, my love," he murmured into her silky scarlet hair, telling himself that too. Zeus couldn't take her from him. Zeus had given his permission after all. He had told Hades to take her. He stroked her hair, lingering, aware that there was only one reason Zeus had come to the Underworld, and it was in his arms. He wouldn't give her up without a fight. If he had to wage war against the entirety of Olympus in order to keep her, he would do it. He pressed a kiss to her hair and whispered, "All will be well."

She nodded stiffly, sucked down a breath and expelled it, and when she tilted her head back to gaze up at him, confidence and courage shone in her eyes, her tears and her sorrow forgotten. She looked like a little warrioress as she steeled herself, ready to do battle.

In order to remain with him.

It touched him, deeper than she would ever know, and he dipped his head and brushed his lips across hers, afraid it would be their last kiss as he teleported them.

As feared, it was Zeus who stood in the centre of the open-roofed black temple on the shores of the river, looking out of place in his white chiton and golden armour. His brother's golden eyes lowered from the statues that stood atop the stone entablature that ran around the tops of the fluted columns and landed on him.

Hades strode towards him, shadows writhing around his boots, and snarled, "What is this about?"

Zeus dared to look beyond him to Persephone where she lingered in the spot they had landed. Darkness consumed Hades and he growled, baring fangs as he closed the distance to his brother in a heartbeat and seized him by his gold breastplate, gripping it so hard he dented the metal.

"Do not look at her," he barked.

Zeus's calm golden eyes eased back to him. "She must return to Olympus."

Hades unleashed a feral growl and twisted with him, hurling him across the temple. Zeus hit the far wall near Hades's black throne with a grunt and dropped to the stone floor.

"Never." Hades advanced on his brother, his shadows rising now, growing restless as they snapped at the columns and some lurched towards his brother. "I will never return her. You gave your word. She is *mine*."

Zeus pressed his left hand to the flagstones, golden arcs of electricity chasing over his fingers, and pushed himself back onto his feet. He came to face Hades, and Hades wanted to strike at him again. How could he look so calm and unaffected as he destroyed his own brother's life?

Hades's happiness?

Zeus truly did not love him. Not even a little.

"Her mother, Demeter, knows you have her and is causing glacial weather across the mortal realm. Crops are withering. Thousands of people are dying. She has sworn she will not relent until her daughter is back with her." A flicker of emotion coloured his brother's eyes as they entreated him to listen. "If there was another way, Hades, do you not think I would take it?"

"Slay the goddess," Hades snarled.

Persephone gasped.

He flinched and looked over his shoulder at her, instantly regretting what he had said. He would apologise about it later, once this was resolved and she was back in his arms, his forever.

"Demeter has agreed to terms. They are reasonable, Hades. She understands I gave you leave to claim Persephone as your queen and will allow her to return to you part of the year." Zeus's words weren't the comfort his brother clearly thought they would be.

"Reasonable?" he spat and scowled at his brother as his chest hollowed and ached. He clawed at his breastplate with his talons. "It is not enough. I cannot be without her for that long."

Months without Persephone would be a torment he couldn't endure, and being with her in Olympus wasn't an option either. His presence would affect the realm, darkening it, and his duty was here, in the Underworld.

He looked back at her, pain beating inside him.

Regret flashed across her features, there and gone in a heartbeat, but he saw it and he knew.

She was going to do as Zeus wanted.

He growled and bared fangs at her now.

"No." He stormed towards her, shadows streaming from his back and darkness welling within him to steal control, to fill his mind with images of hunting her mother down to end her and stop her from taking Persephone from him. When he reached her, those violent needs suddenly flooded from him and his brow furrowed as he framed her face with his palms and silently pleaded her not to do this. He whispered, "No. I cannot lose you, my love. I cannot."

She lifted her hands and gently placed them on his, her emerald gaze soft and filled with love, and despair. "And you will not. But I am a goddess of life… and I cannot bear the burden of all those deaths. I cannot, Hades. Please do not make me do it."

The tears in her eyes wrenched at his black soul, bringing them to his own eyes too as he gazed at her, seeing how much this was hurting her. Not just parting from him, but the knowledge that her being here with him was causing a catastrophe in the mortal world. His beautiful goddess was too kind. Too gentle. Too good of heart. She cared so deeply about beings she had never met, the thought of their deaths and her part in them paining her.

If he selfishly made her stay, it would destroy her.

He would destroy her.

He couldn't do that. No matter how fiercely he needed to keep her by his side, within his reach. He didn't want to be the one who killed her smile and snuffed out her light. He didn't want her to become as dark as he was. She would if he forced her to stay.

He heaved a shuddering sigh and lowered his forehead so it rested against hers, his heart feeling fragile and as if it might shatter.

"Very well," he husked.

She lunged at him, wrapping her arms around him and squeezing him tightly, as if she had expected him to refuse and now that he had agreed, she didn't want him to let her go. He held her, silently cursing her mother for hurting her like this, deeply aware the goddess had done it on purpose to force him to release Persephone, and was manipulating Zeus and all of them.

Selfish goddess.

Hades drew back and looked down at Persephone, her distress carving a hole in his chest. Did Demeter even care about the pain she was causing her daughter? He doubted it. Demeter was controlling. Manipulative. She cared only about herself.

And now she was stealing his love from him.

Persephone remained with her face against his chest, clinging to him, and he palmed the back of her head to hold her to him as he looked across at his brother. Guilt and sorrow shone in Zeus's eyes, and for once, Hades felt he might actually care about him.

But then the emotions that coloured his expression were probably all about what this was doing to Persephone rather than what it was doing to Hades.

"Give me a moment longer with her." Hades held his gaze, not bothering to conceal his feelings from his brother, allowing him to see how badly he needed just a few more hours with her before she returned to Olympus and left him alone for months to wonder about her and crave her. "I will return her tomorrow at first light."

He thought Zeus might deny him, but then his younger brother dipped his head, and turned to leave.

And lingered.

He glanced back at Hades.

Looked as if he wanted to say something as his dark eyebrows furrowed slightly and his lips parted, but then he disappeared.

Hades lowered his head and rested his cheek against the top of Persephone's head. Her grip didn't loosen. She clung to him as tightly as he did to her, and he liked to believe she didn't want to let him go either and that she would be as miserable as he during their time apart.

He lightly rubbed her back, unsure how to comfort her, but wishing he could steal her hurt away and free her from it.

How he had changed.

How she had changed him.

By the gods, he loved her.

Would do anything for her.

Even bear months away from her.

Although he still wasn't sure he would be able to manage it, not without losing himself to the darkness again. Was his realm doomed to fall back into darkness and violence as the light she created within him guttered out during their time apart? Only to find balance and peace whenever she returned?

He wasn't sure the Underworld could take it. He didn't want his people to suffer because his only light in this world was far from him, too far to keep the darkness at bay for him.

If he told her how her leaving might cause death and cruelty and violence too, would she stay?

CHAPTER 34

Hades drew back and looked down at Persephone, his heart supplying the answer to that question. He couldn't tell her. He couldn't place her in that position, making her choose between bearing the deaths of mortals and bearing the horrors of what would happen to the souls in his realm. He would do his best to keep them from her and make her believe that his realm continued as it was now without her.

That he was continuing as he was now without her.

An impossible feat.

The moment she returned to him, she would see the darkness had taken him, and would be forced to draw him back into the light.

He smiled tightly when she emerged from his embrace and looked up at him, her eyes red and lashes still damp. She looked far too pale still. He carefully brushed the backs of his talons across her cheek, concern for her eclipsing the concern he felt for himself and his realm.

"Do you wish to go somewhere still?" he husked, willing to do all the things she wanted in the scant few hours they had together. Whatever she desired, she would have.

She nodded.

"To the Elysian Fields?" He focused on that part of the realm, preparing to teleport her there.

Only she stopped him with a small shake of her head.

He frowned. "Where then? To our chambers?"

He smiled wickedly, trying to lighten the mood and succeeding judging by the half smile she gave him and the way her gaze admonished him.

"The orchard." Her gaze left him to drift up to her right, towards the top of the plateau that towered above them beyond the sheer cliff of the canyon. "I would like to go to the orchard."

"The Elysian Fields are far more beautiful, my love." He cupped her cheek and canted his head, studying her distant gaze and not liking how far away from him she already looked.

She forced another smile as her gaze came back to lock with his. "And I will see them when I am… next here. I will see them when I am next here."

For a heartbeat, he had felt sure she would call his realm her home, and gods, it warmed his aching soul to know she thought of this place as her home now.

"Please, Hades. Take me to the orchard." Her emerald gaze backed up that plea, and he nodded, pulled her against him and into a teleport.

When they appeared in the orchard, she shoved out of his embrace, knocking him back, and hurried to the nearest tree. He followed her, his concern growing now, spreading confusion through him.

"Persephone?" He chased her through the trees as she raced through them, her gaze darting over their dark canopies, her behaviour verging on frantic. "What is this about?"

She came to a dead halt, her breath leaving her in a relieved sigh, and tiptoed, straining to reach something.

He looked up in time to see her pluck a pomegranate from the tree and his eyes widened as she wrenched it open, tipped her head back and shook the fruit, scattering seeds into her mouth. She cast the pomegranate aside as she lowered her wild gaze to meet his.

And swallowed.

Hades stood there, shock rolling through him as he fought to comprehend what she had done, and why she had done it.

She had chosen him.

It hit him hard.

She had bound herself to his realm—to him in a way—ensuring he could always call her back to him.

He couldn't believe it.

Hades swept her into his arms and kissed her, tasting the pomegranate on her lips, shaken by what she had done. Her kiss was fevered and demanding as she wrapped her arms around his neck, drawing him down to her, tugging a growl from him as she fought for control of it. He clutched her bottom and lifted her into his arms, pinning her to him as he teleported again.

Landing in their chambers this time.

She had chosen him.

Accepted him.

She might not have spoken the words, but her actions had screamed them loud and clear for him to hear. She wanted him. Needed him.

Loved him.

He was sure of it.

She loved him as deeply as he loved her.

He wanted to show her the depth of that love.

He slowly stripped the pieces of his armour off as he kissed her, keeping it gentle and unhurried, a kiss filled with the tender passion she awakened in him. When she realised what he was doing, she eased back to help him and he unfastened her dress. He groaned as it slipped down her body to reveal her lush bare curves, his cock hardening in response to the breathtaking sight of her.

Hades reined in his desire and held it in check, battling it as she smoothed his trousers down his legs. His gaze tracked her, hunger building inside him as she kneeled before him while he stepped out of his leathers. Her emerald eyes blazed with need as she tipped her head back, and as they lowered to his erection.

Later.

He would let her fulfil that desire to know the taste of him later, after he had made love with her.

Hades bent and swept her up into his arms, and carried her to the bed. He gently lay her down on it and covered her, easing between her thighs, and her lips captured his as she cradled him. She moaned as she kissed him, as he skimmed his hands down her body, teasing her nipples as he pressed his hard length against her slick cleft. He followed her, moaning as he rocked, losing himself in the electrifying friction.

But it wasn't enough.

He needed her.

And she needed him.

It was there in her eyes as they met his, a silent plea that begged him to fill her and make her forget what would happen in only a few hours. He kissed her again as he eased into her, slowly joining them, refusing to let his need to find release make him rush. This was more than sex. This was making love. Something they hadn't done before.

Something he had never done.

He had never believed in the spiritual connection many often spoke of when they talked of making love.

But by the gods, he felt it as he drew back and gazed down at Persephone, their bodies fused into one and his soul feeling as if it had melded with hers too.

He kept his eyes locked on hers as he rocked into her, his pace unhurried, each long press and withdraw filling him with warmth and light. Her eyes glittered at him, the love that shone in them telling him she was right there with him, feeling everything he was. Nothing had ever felt like this.

He felt soul-deep connected to her.

And she was all that existed in the world.

There was only her. Only him. Only their love.

She slid her hands over his shoulders and gently lured him down to her, and he moaned as she captured his lips, her kiss pure tenderness that spoke to him on a primal level, lightening his heart to chase the shadows from it with her love. He lengthened his strokes, curling his hips to hit the spot that had her moans growing louder, her body arching to meet his, and lifted his head, wanting to see the moment she found release. His own built inside him, a gathering storm that felt as if it might leave him forever changed, just as she had.

She cried out, his name a broken whisper on her lips as she spasmed, as release swept her up and took him over the edge with her, the feel of her body milking him propelling him towards his own climax.

Persephone angled her head to her left, revealing the smooth column of her throat, and his gaze snagged on it, the hunger to bite her that he had battled countless times over the last ten days seizing hold of him.

He swallowed hard.

Held himself back, even when every fibre of his being roared at him to mark her, so everyone in this world would know that she was his.

Her hand cupping his nape startled him and his gaze leaped to meet hers, the heated look in it beckoning him and wrenching control from him. He didn't resist her as she tugged him down to her. He hovered with his mouth above the curve of her neck, his fangs aching to pierce her tender skin.

"Hades," she murmured, his name a desperate plea, telling him that she wanted this.

She wanted his fangs in her throat.

He groaned and struck hard, sinking them deep. The taste of her flooded his mouth as she cried out and arched against him, as her body spasmed around his again, the feel of her climaxing from his bite pushing him over the edge with her.

He grunted and pressed deeper into her and spilled, clutching her to him with both his hands and his fangs, holding her in place beneath him.

When his heart stopped racing, and his body stopped trembling, he slowly released her throat and licked the marks he had made. He gazed at the twin puncture wounds, the sight of his mark on her warming the cold reaches of his heart. For at least the next few days, all in Olympus would know she was his.

His gaze shifted to meet hers and he drowned in the love that shone in her eyes.

She wrapped her arms around him and gathered her to him, holding him on top of her, with their bodies still joined. He banded his arms around her and rolled them over, so her light weight rested on top of him, and held her.

Just held her.

Minutes trickled past, becoming an hour before long, and a need built within him, an urgency that made him want to make the most of every second they had left. He framed her face and lifted her head from his chest, and kissed her again, stoking her passion until she was writhing on him, rubbing her body along the length of his to madden him.

He made love to her again, and again, until the stillness of night gave way to the dawn, and their time had run out.

No tears touched her eyes as she silently dressed, choosing the green gown he had given her, and his heart ached heavily as he paused halfway through fastening his trousers to watch her gliding around their chambers. Her green gaze was sombre as she took it all in, as if she was putting it to memory.

As if she feared she would never see it again.

She turned and looked over her shoulder at him, past her fall of scarlet waves, and that sensation grew as she stared at him.

Hades went to her and gathered her into his arms, banding one around her shoulders and clutching the back of her head with his other hand. He growled, "She cannot keep you from me, my love. No one in this world can. We shall be together again, and I will await that moment every day we are apart."

Persephone tipped her head back and seized his lips, her kiss desperate.

He kissed her back, slanting his mouth over hers to steal control of it, and swept her into a teleport that took them to the gate to Olympus. She pushed back and stared at it, tears glistening on her lashes, and then at him. The colourful light of the rings and glyphs that formed the circular portal washed over her fair skin, painting her in soft rainbow hues.

Hades palmed her face and kissed her again, needing one more moment with her to carry him through the dark days ahead.

And then he abruptly broke away from her as it became too much, and seized her hand and pulled her to the gate.

He had meant to make her walk through it, but he lingered before it, afraid to let her go and sure he would never see her again.

But it had to be done.

If he didn't return her to her mother, the whole world would suffer for it.

She would suffer for it.

It was better he suffered than she did.

"Go," he husked, his voice tight and low, and his eyes burned as she looked at him, love and fear shining in her eyes. "I will see you again soon, my love."

She nodded and tears spilled down her cheeks, and went to leave, and then she hurried back to him, gripped his hand and kissed him hard. He tasted her tears as he kissed her as fervently, desperate for it to continue even when he knew it couldn't. The kiss lasted all of a few seconds before she wrenched herself away and hurried through the portal.

Her hand lingering in his until the last moment.

It slipped from his grasp.

And she was gone.

The ground shattered in a circle around him, a thousand fractures breaking its surface to drop him by close to a foot, and the mountains around him trembled and split, hurling great rocks into the air as lava exploded from them.

Hades threw his head back and bellowed in rage and agony.

And the darkness devoured him.

CHAPTER 35

The moment Persephone crossed the threshold of the white temple she had once called home, something felt off. She frowned and looked over her shoulder, cold snaking down her spine to make her want to turn back the way she had come and run.

"Persephone, my child!" Her mother's voice rang out, startling her, and she turned back to face her.

Demeter hurried towards her, her gold diaphanous robes swirling around her delicate matching sandals, and her dark red curls gathered up and held with shining gold pins and braids.

Persephone frowned as her mother embraced her, wrapping arms laced with heavy gold bangles around her, and that feeling still didn't go away. This wasn't right. Something was wrong. Her mother grasped her waist and pushed her back, her forest green eyes raking over her and a frown flickering on her brow as she noticed Persephone's dress.

"This is not the gown you were wearing the day that vile male took you from me. And what is that on your neck?" Demeter's eyes darkened as Persephone's fingers flew to Hades's bite mark, and then softened as they leaped to meet hers, flooding with concern as she petted Persephone's face. "Oh, my child, pray tell me he was not cruel to you… that he did not take advantage of you."

Persephone slowly shook her head, but Demeter didn't look convinced.

"Such a wretched beast. Taking you like that." A look crossed her mother's face, one that chilled Persephone's blood as Demeter plastered on a bright smile that didn't quite cover the machinations of her mind. Persephone could practically see it churning as Demeter checked her over again, and the reason for her mother being swept up in her thoughts became apparent as she muttered, "All will be well. The wedding will go ahead tomorrow and Aristaeus will be none the wiser to your indiscretions. We only need to have a healer deal with that mark."

Persephone's fingers closed more tightly over the twin punctures as she backed away from her mother, shaking her head more vigorously now. "No. I will not be marrying Aristaeus, Mother."

She frowned at Demeter, that cold growing within her and spreading as realisation slowly dawned, and she couldn't believe it. Wouldn't believe it. Not until her mother confirmed it for her.

"You harmed all those mortals just to force Hades to return me to Olympus so you could marry me off as planned." Persephone searched her eyes, but she didn't have to look hard to see her mother had done just that. She threw her arms up, disbelief crashing over her, the levels to which her mother would stoop in order to have things turn out the way she wanted astounding her. "I cannot believe you!"

Persephone pivoted on her heel and stormed towards the patio.

"Where are you going?" Demeter snapped.

"Home. To Hades." Persephone tossed the words over her shoulder, biting them out as rage burned up her blood and a desperate need to return to the Underworld flooded her. "I am not marrying Aristaeus. I will not. Your fears are utterly unfounded, Mother. I have no desire to take your place or overshadow you. I love you and want you to be happy. I have only ever wanted you to be happy… but I will no longer do as you command. I will not let my happiness be destroyed in order for you to keep yours."

She had to get away from Olympus, before her mother did something foolish, and broke her heart.

The row of armed guards that stepped into her path, forming a wall to block her escape, said it was too late for that.

Her head whipped towards the white columns to her left, where a broad terrace overlooked the city, and more guards stood there beyond the sheer green drapes that hung in sweeping curves, anchored to the golden rings on the columns. She spun on her heel to face her mother, not bothering to conceal the hurt that flared in her heart or her anger.

"Let me go," Persephone barked. "I will not let you force me into wedlock to another. I love Hades. No one here understands him… No one here knows him as I do. I love him with all my heart, Mother. I will not marry Aristaeus."

"You will." Demeter lunged for her, seizing hold of her arm to grip it so tightly that it hurt. Persephone flinched as her mother dragged her towards her, and then along the corridor, towards her room. "Hades has brainwashed you, weaving spells to make you foolishly believe you feel something for him, and I will not hear it. You do not love him."

"I do!" Persephone wrestled against her mother's hold, twisting her arm in her tight grasp and not caring that her skin burned from the friction. "I love him."

Demeter scoffed and glared over her shoulder at her. "Foolish child. You only think you do. It only takes a look at you to know he seated himself between your thighs and took the only thing you had to offer in a marriage, and now you believe you are in love with him. Many a girl has fallen for a male's charms in the way you have, and found themselves thinking that meant the male loved them, and then—"

Persephone stopped dead, pulling her mother to a stop too as it hit her. "And then you find yourself with child and with no father for your baby."

Demeter glanced at her again, the anger and hurt in her eyes confirming it. Her mother had trusted a male, believing he loved her, and he had used and discarded her, saddling her with a daughter and no chance of wedding another.

"Hades is not like the male you trusted. He loves me, and I love him." She gripped her mother's arm and pulled on it, forcing Demeter to look at her. "Just give him a chance to prove it to you."

"No." Demeter wrenched free of her grip, her expression dark and unrelenting. "You will wed Aristaeus tomorrow and I will hear no more about it."

Hurt arrowed through Persephone, a cold dagger in her chest. Her mother meant it. She was going to force her to marry someone she didn't love, forsaking someone she did, all because she couldn't believe that Hades could love her, and that she loved him.

Or was it because marrying Hades would place her above her mother in the hierarchy of the gods?

That seemed the more likely reason. If a lesser god had taken Persephone, her mother probably wouldn't have cared. But it had been Hades who had taken her and desired to make her his queen, a god so far above Demeter in standing that her mother couldn't bear it, even though he made her daughter happy.

Persephone clenched her fists. She wouldn't stand for it. She had allowed her mother to control every aspect of her life for too long.

It was time she made her own decisions.

Starting with this one.

She pivoted on her heel, grabbing her skirts and lifting them at the same time, and ran at the guards. She felt Demeter turn behind her and everything seemed to slow as she sprinted towards her freedom. The guards drew their swords.

Persephone focused and summoned vines to hurl them out of her way.

And nothing happened.

Persephone turned horrified, wide eyes on her mother, struggling to believe that she would go as far as sealing her powers to trap her here and force her to do as she bid.

"Are you that desperate to ruin my life and destroy the only happiness I have ever known?" Persephone clenched her trembling fists, not feeling her nails biting into her palms as rage and hurt consumed her and she stared her mother down, needing her to see how much this was killing her and hoping to see she regretted what she had done.

But not a single drop of regret coloured Demeter's dark green eyes as she signalled the guards.

Two of the men marched forwards and grabbed Persephone, and she fought them, punching and kicking them, her heart thundering as she tried to escape their hold. More of the guards joined them, the four of them combined making them too strong for her to break free from.

All her fight left her as she realised she was trapped again.

In a prison far worse and more dreadful than the tower Hades had constructed for her.

She slid her mother a cold, hard look she hoped conveyed her raging emotions—all the hurt and the anger, and the dismay.

"Zeus will be furious with you," she hissed at Demeter. "You manipulated him. You have made him go back on his word to Hades. He promised me to his brother!"

Demeter's expression darkened further, her lips becoming a thin line as her eyes narrowed on Persephone, rage that might match Persephone's own anger blazing in them.

"He will find out what you have done. Mark my words," Persephone bit out and glared at her mother. "Zeus will have no mercy to show you, and Hades—"

"Lock her in her room!" Demeter snapped.

Persephone's gaze darted to the door at the end of the corridor, the one that led to her room, and the desperation that had been mounting within her became full-blown panic. No. She couldn't let them lock her away. She had to escape.

She had to get back to Hades.

She summoned all her strength and smashed her elbow into the face of the guard to her right, knocking him into a second male, and stomped on the inside of a third guard's ankle with enough force that he howled in pain and released her. She broke free of them, running towards her room, aiming for the corridor that branched off to the left near to it. There was another route out of the building there.

One of her maidens walked into view.

"Despina!" Persephone called to the young woman, her hope soaring as she finally spied an ally among a sea of enemies intent on destroying everything. "Help me."

Only the brunette refused to look at her.

She cut Persephone's heart to pieces as she turned away from her and went back along the corridor, disappearing from view again.

Persephone stumbled to a halt, her ears ringing as Despina's betrayal swept through her to rob her of her strength. Was no one in Olympus on her side?

She wrapped her arms around herself, feeling cold to her marrow, and alone. She had never felt so alone.

The guards caught her again, jostling her, but she was barely aware of them as they seized her and marched her towards her room. Her ears rang, numbness swallowing her as the last of her hope bled from her.

They pushed her into her room and the door slammed behind her, and she looked at it and then at the windows that had been boarded up, leaving her in near darkness, only faint light that seeped through cracks in the wood chasing it back so she could see.

The irony wasn't lost on her as she sank onto a chair and listened to her mother barking orders at the guards stationed outside the door and her boarded-up windows.

This room that she had been so desperate to return to felt more like a prison than the tower ever had.

And her mother had torn her down and shattered her faster than Hades ever could have managed.

She clutched her arms as she held herself, aching to see him and wishing it was his arms that held her so tightly, keeping her together when she was close to falling apart.

He wasn't the monster.

Her mother was.

And now, she would be forced to wed another.

CHAPTER 36

Hades stalked across the black lands, his dark gaze narrowed on the temple ahead of him and shadows streaming around his feet. His talons flexed, making the tired muscles in his arms ache, but he couldn't halt the action. His mood was too black. Too grim. The fight that had broken out in a region far from the temple had been a merciful reprieve from his torturous thoughts, and he had savoured crushing his foes with his bare hands and his bident, battling in close quarters with his enemies for the first time in a long time.

Seeking to satisfy the dark, wicked craving for bloodshed and violence that continued to roar inside him, and had his thoughts twisting down wretched paths that made him have to fight his own body.

His feet veered off course of their own will, and he was halfway to the main temple and the group of guards that waited outside it before he caught himself.

He growled and gnashed fangs at what he had almost done.

Fighting his own men now?

Persephone had only been gone a day, but he had sunk swiftly into the abyss during her absence, far quicker than he had anticipated. Instead of the slow slide into the darkness that he had thought would happen, he had plunged into it the moment she had disappeared from view, and it had been quick to seize him and drag him deeper still.

"Persephone," he murmured, breathing her name with all the love and the need that burned inside him, an inferno that seared him with constant thoughts of her.

With an undying need to see her right that moment.

Had he done enough to win her heart and ensure she returned to him now that she was back in her bright, warm city of Olympus?

He wasn't sure that he had.

He shifted course and headed for his chambers, his body and his heart feeling heavier by the second. He could have done many things better. He could have approached her differently, being gentler with her from the beginning. Warmer. He half-smiled and scoffed. If only he had been able to remember how to be such things back then.

He still wasn't sure he had ever known how to be gentle and tender.

In fact, he was sure it was Persephone who had taught him to be such things, showing him that it was all right for him to feel warmer emotions. He might be a king with a realm to rule and keep under control, but he was still a man. He could still love and be loved in a way all other men in this world experienced. Needed even.

He huffed as he trudged into his chambers, pushing the twin wooden doors open, and paused on the threshold of the black-walled room to look back beyond the columned terrace.

To the tower.

More of his strength left him as he slowly turned and drifted back to the edge of the raised flagstones to stare at it.

His heart ached, so he pressed his palm to the chest of his breastplate and dug his talons into the metal, filled with a strange need to claw it out in the hope it would stop it from hurting so. The feelings that twined with the darkness, threading it with ribbons of light, were still foreign to him. And a nuisance, he was beginning to discover. They caused him only pain now, when before they had given him so much pleasure.

Hades leaned his right shoulder against the fluted black column and gazed at the tower, the ache growing. He wasn't sure how people could live with such feelings, and he didn't want to feel their torment any longer, but he was well aware they wouldn't go away. They were only going to grow stronger. Deeper. Even while Persephone was away from him.

Perhaps because she was away from him.

He craved the sight of her, the scent of her. He needed to feel her in his arms again. He needed to hear her light, soft voice.

He needed her.

This feeling he had for her was deep. Permanent. Etched on his heart. She was the light in his soul and the moment she had left his side, the darkness had risen, a creeping tide that was smothering him.

It was too much.

Hades reached for her, using the fact she was now tied to his realm to draw her back to his side and vowing that he would return her again. He just needed a few minutes with her to see him through the next day. Surely her mother wouldn't deny him that?

Only Persephone didn't appear.

Hades growled and tried again, diving deeper into his connection to this world and to her through it.

And couldn't feel her.

Rage swelled inside him, laced with darkness, and his fangs punched long from his gums, the ground beneath his boots quaking as a feeling slithered through his mind, hissing and dripping poison in his ears.

She had tricked him.

She had somehow pretended to eat the seeds to fool him into letting her go, making him believe he could always summon her back to him. She had faked those tears and the pain he had read in her eyes, ravaging his defences to make him unaware of what she had planned.

She had pretended to be in love with him.

Had betrayed him.

The mountain to his right cracked and split open, lava exploding from it to shower the lands around him, and terrified screams rent the silence as pilgrims and guards scattered in all directions, desperately trying to avoid being struck by the missiles of rock that slammed into the ground.

One of them struck the tower, shattering it and hurling great chunks of black stone in all directions.

Hades didn't bother to move as one rocketed towards him.

He pivoted on his heel, turning his back to it, and stormed into his room.

His shadows that streamed behind him lashed at the rock when it came close to striking his temple, sending it flying into the mountain with such force it formed a crater in its face.

She had betrayed him. Played him for a fool. Everything had been an act. The darkness roared that at him, stoking his rage to keep it at boiling point and clouding his thoughts, blotting out the last rays of the light.

Hades plunged into the black abyss.

What a good little liar she had been too. She had made him believe she felt something for him, and in turn he had foolishly softened his heart towards her.

Not anymore.

He hardened it now, coaxing the darkness and surrendering to it, resolve flooding him as he drew it up like a shield.

No one would touch his heart again.

He sneered and crossed the room, his boots a heavy thunk and scrape as the pointed tips of them scratched at the stone floor. He glared at the bed they had shared. She had wanted to return home—to her world of beauty and light—and life. She had told him that to his face, and then she had told him what he had wanted to hear so she could fulfil her mission to escape this *dead realm* as she had called it.

Hades snatched his black bony helmet from his armour stand, gripping it by one of the twisted horns that flared up from the back of it. Smaller, smooth bones swept down to form a protective plate that reached the tip of his nose as he placed it on his head. They arched around to points that sat before his ears too, tipped with talons whose tiny claws clutched at his cheeks.

His helm of darkness.

The moment it sat snug against his head, a shimmering veil descended over the world. Power seeped over him like a cold caress. He glanced at his right hand and then his left arm, tracking the flow of it to his wrists. When it had covered all of him, and he was satisfied that he was now invisible to all eyes—even those of a god—he grabbed his bident, growled and teleported.

Landing near the gate to Olympus.

Persephone was his.

And no one would stop him from taking her back to the Underworld.

Hades stalked through the shimmering circular portal and stepped out into the white city of Olympus, slipping into it unseen thanks to his helmet. A storm rolled in behind him as his gaze tracked upwards, past the clusters of terracotta-roofed white buildings that lined the harbour and the lower quadrant, to the elegant columned temples that stood looking down upon them. Boiling black clouds blotted out the sunlight and the people around him cast fearful gazes at the sky. Waves lashed the shore, crashing over the harbour walls to douse the wooden stalls that extended from the buildings, and several people shrieked and ran out of their path.

His lips stretched in a cold grin that flashed his fangs as he savoured their terror, soaking it up as it fed the darkness that writhed within him, murmuring at him to make Persephone pay for what she had done.

To make the whole of Olympus pay.

He stormed along the broad avenue that led up the hill and spotted decorations on the white buildings. The city was preparing for a celebration. For Persephone's safe return?

Hades collared a passing male, digging talons into his neck and ripping a cry of pure fear from him as he hauled them towards him and growled, "What is this celebration for?"

The male turned wild, dark eyes on Hades. Eyes that only grew wider when he saw nothing, only the streets around him as people rushed back and forth, many of them ducking into nearby buildings to take shelter as great fat drops of rain began to fall, pelting the city and filling the air with the scent of earth.

"P-Persephone," the man stammered. "Her wedding."

"*Her wedding?*" Hades snarled, two words that cut him to his soul, unleashing darkness from it that poured through him to have him closing his talons and pressing them deep into the male's neck.

He cast the man aside as he choked on his own blood and a female unleashed a terrified scream. Several guards ran down the hill, all of them sweeping past Hades, not seeing him. Hades twisted and lodged his bident into the back of the skull of one of them, and the guard nearest him turned wide eyes on the male as he went down, blood bursting from the wounds as Hades ripped his bident free. He cut that male down too, and then another, and then two more as he stormed up the road, heading for the white and gold columned temples.

He growled, ceaseless snarls and rumbles escaping him as he seethed, as his shadows ripped at the decorations in his wake and tore into more of the people as they shrieked and tried to escape the wave of destruction that followed him.

Hades's onyx eyes scoured the temples, seeking the one that belonged to Persephone, and halted as they landed on a lush garden next to one. A garden far more beautiful than any other temple owned.

"Persephone," he snarled and teleported there, landing in the middle of that garden, a silent unseen predator who had just found his prey.

She stood on a pale stone patio among the vivid green bushes and colourful fragrant blooms that were as beautiful as she was as she gazed at the sky, her luminous emerald eyes fixed on the storm as thunder rumbled across the heavy black clouds.

By the gods, she was beautiful.

The sight of her arrested him right down to his heart, had his fury abating as he caught her scent and felt the softness of her power as it curled around him in this place born of her creation.

Hades growled and stoked his rage back into an inferno, refusing to be swayed by her, to be fooled again.

She started at the sound of his black snarl and turned, her eyes widening as they scanned the garden. Rain pelted her, soaking her pale dress so the white layers stuck to her skin and saturating her scarlet hair so it hung in ribbons like blood across her bare shoulders.

When her gaze grew desperate and she turned to leave, Hades snarled again and removed his helmet, revealing himself to her and ripping a gasp from her rosy lips. The fear that had been building in her eyes transformed into hope, into relief he refused to believe as she gazed at him.

"Hades," she breathed and hurled herself at him, wrapping her arms around his neck and burying her face there as she clung to him.

She had the audacity to sob.

Hades gripped her waist and shoved her away from him, the pain that welled inside him fuelling his rage as he glared at her. "I hear you are to be married. So, you were betrothed after all. Perhaps not everything you told me was lies."

"Lies?" Her brow crinkled as she frowned at him. "I have not lied to you, Hades. I am betrothed but—"

"And now you will be wed, on this very day… soon after you escaped me." He refused to listen to more of her lies, to let her addle his mind and placate him so she could wed another. "How pleased you must be to be home in your city of *light* and *life*. How pleased you must be to be marrying your beloved."

She shook her head now, a flicker of darkness crossing her expression even as it remained pleading and laced with desperation. "I tried to return to you. I tried. Mother stopped me. She keeps me under guard. She is not giving me a choice, Hades. She is forcing me to marry another, when I want only you."

He snorted at that. Who could want a male like him? Not someone as beautiful, and tender, and sweet as this goddess standing before him that was for sure. He had been a fool to believe she could come to love him and want him. He had been a fool to think he could make her his queen and find the happiness his brothers had.

"I see no guards, Persephone," he growled and cast a look around them.

Her eyes grew wild. "They were here. When the storm hit, they went to protect the temple. People were trying to find shelter in it and Mother was not—"

"Spare me your lies," he barked as thunder crashed and lightning branched across the clouds. "I came only to congratulate you."

He had come to take her back with him, but now he wavered, his heart aching so fiercely that he couldn't breathe. Persephone didn't want him. He was right. Everything had been a lie. A beautiful lie. One he had foolishly believed to be real, and had found happiness in.

He turned away from her, unable to bear the hurt any longer.

Her words lashed at him, her voice strained. "You will leave me to my fate then?"

Hades slowly closed his eyes and lowered his head, tears burning and heart shattering as he murmured, "You have made your choice."

"I did." She had never sounded so grave, and he almost looked back at her, needing to see if she looked as sad as she had sounded. "And now I will make another. If I cannot have the one I love, I will ensure the one I despise cannot have me."

Hades grimaced as her words plunged into him, as deadly as any blade, and couldn't stop himself from looking back at her.

Pain glittered in her eyes, hurt she couldn't mask, and grim resolve painted itself across her face. She trembled, her fear a palpable thing that reached out to him and made him want to soothe it.

He crushed that desire.

"I will not stop you. I will not keep you from your love," he husked, each word a labour as he wanted to say others, ones designed to wound her and hurt her as deeply as she had hurt him, but he couldn't bear the thought of her being unhappy.

It hadn't taken him long to realise something when he had been holding her in the Underworld.

He would rather she be happy—that she chose who she was with—than force her to be his.

She didn't move.

Hades glared at her and growled.

"What are you waiting for?"

CHAPTER 37

"You! I am waiting for you!" Persephone bit out as she shook her head, her emerald eyes holding his and frustration and fear sweeping across her delicate features as rain battered her and another peal of thunder rumbled overhead. "You are the one I love, Hades, but if you do not love me then I will embrace death."

Hades roared, his claws and fangs lengthening as pain engulfed his heart and tore down his strength, just the thought of her dying enough to make him feel as if he was.

He rounded on her, anger pouring through him, rage that had the storm growing fiercer and a jagged lightning bolt striking close to them.

"I will not allow you to die," he barked. "Never! I would refuse your soul." His voice hitched and his throat tightened, emotions closing it. "I would beg Zeus to restore it."

Persephone closed the distance between them, her gaze beseeching him as water rolled down the tangled strands of her hair and tears filled her eyes. She laid her small hand on his chest, her skin far too pale against his black breastplate, almost ashen.

Like death.

"Then free me from this prison." Her softly spoken words roused a dangerous beast within him, one that had his mind turning towards violence again.

That hunger only grew when he pulled her into his arms and tried to teleport her back to the gate to the Underworld.

And found he couldn't.

She hadn't been lying. She wasn't here by choice. Her mother was holding her against her will. Anger at Demeter morphed into fury at himself.

"Forgive me, my love," he murmured thickly, despising himself for being so quick to doubt her. He dropped his bident and his helmet, gently cleared strands of her hair from her cheeks, careful not to harm her with his talons, and framed her face, angling her head up to keep her eyes locked on his and filled with a need to hear her say she would. His eyes darted between hers, seeking absolution in them. "Forgive me for ever doubting you."

She brought her hands up, placed them over his, and smiled. "I forgive you… but you will be making things up to me for a time to come."

"Anything," he growled. "Whatever it takes to make you forgive me, I shall do it."

She stepped closer to him, shifted her hands from his to his cheeks, and stroked his face, the fear that had been in her striking eyes fading away, replaced by warmth, and tenderness, and hope.

"You can start by taking me home," she breathed.

"Home," he husked, liking the sound of that but at the same time needing to be sure she meant what he thought she did, mostly because he was still having a hard time believing she had really chosen him. "To the Underworld?"

She nodded.

Hades swept her into his arms and kissed her, pouring all the love he felt into it and savouring how desperately she kissed him, as if she couldn't get enough of him either. When he sensed people closing in on them, he released her and grabbed his helmet and bident. He handed the helmet to her and was tempted to order her to put it on, but the steely look in her eyes warned him not to dare.

"We do this together," she said and reached for his free hand. "As soon as we are free of the temple grounds, I should be able to use my powers to help you. It is not far to the gate."

She looked as if she was trying to convince herself of that when her gaze darted to the harbour.

"I will teleport the moment we are free, my love. You need not worry." Hades swept her into his arm, tucking her against his side, almost lifting her off her feet as he hurried from the garden, heading for steps that led down into a narrow street below them.

Three guards were running towards them when they reached it. The moment they spotted Persephone, they drew their swords and charged him. Hades tucked her behind him and blocked one sword with his shadows and another with his bident, and kicked the third male in his stomach to knock him back. He swept his bident around, unarming the first guard, and shoved forwards, impaling him with the two sharp prongs.

Persephone gasped.

Hades wrenched his bident free, twisted it and plunged the pointed end of the staff into the chest of the remaining guard.

He reached an arm out behind him for Persephone, summoning a teleport at the same time, only he wasn't free of the wards that dampened his powers yet and Persephone didn't take his hand.

Hades turned to face her.

And growled.

She was gone.

"Hades!" Her shriek was distant, and it struck him that her gasp hadn't been because she had been shocked by the sight of him fighting and killing.

It had been because someone had snatched her.

Another guard?

Hades sprinted after her, her scent of lilies faint in the rain. He felt it the moment he was free of the wards Demeter had used to imprison her only daughter and the urge to teleport was strong, almost overwhelming, but he tamped it down. It was the wyvern nest all over again. If he teleported, he might miss Persephone and lose her.

He sent his shadows out in all directions, seeking her.

Grinned when he found her a short distance to his left, heading towards the harbour.

Hades made a hard turn, slamming into the white wall of a building as his boots skidded on the slick dirt that formed the road in this area of the city. He growled as he spotted a flash of crimson and then she was gone.

He had seen enough though.

A male had her.

One who wore a white chiton with gold embroidery, and a gold breastplate.

Not a guard.

His clothing had been too fine.

If Hades had to guess, which he didn't, because every fibre of his being screamed the truth at him, the one who had Persephone was the male her mother had intended to marry her off to. He had come to claim his bride.

Hades's grin widened.

And so had Hades.

He sprinted harder, into a teleport that landed him ahead of the blond male.

The male's sandals skidded on the wet white stones of the main avenue as he tried to come to a halt, his hazel eyes flooding with fear as they landed on Hades. The wretched god slipped and fell on his backside, and Persephone grunted as she planted face-first into the road beside him.

Hades growled when she wriggled free of the god's grip, sank onto her backside, twisting to face him at the same time, and touched her bloodied lip.

His beautiful queen was hurt.

He had been settled on only terrifying and perhaps injuring the male in order to teach him a lesson, and so he didn't anger Zeus by slaying one of his pantheon.

Now, the male would die.

"Aristaeus, do not be a fool." Persephone picked herself up as the blond male reached for the sword in the leather scabbard that hung from his waist. "I never wanted to marry you. I would sooner die than be your wife."

Aristaeus.

Hades arched an eyebrow. Demeter had thought to marry her beautiful daughter off to a dull little god of low standing?

Persephone had been made to be a queen.

His queen.

Hades readied his bident and pointed it at Aristaeus. "You would be wise to heed her words."

Apparently, Aristaeus was as big a fool as Persephone had said he was, because rather than bending the knee as he should have, lowering himself before a god of Hades's stature and strength, the blond drew his sword.

Persephone pulled a face and hurled her right hand towards the male, and vines burst from the flagstones, cracking them as they erupted and shot towards the god. They snaked around his leg and wrist, holding him back as he went to swing his sword, and then hurled him to the ground.

Bloodying his lip as his face smacked off the pale stones.

"Do not touch my Hades," she growled, a fierce little thing that froze Hades's boots in place and had him staring at her, bewitched by the sight of her.

And painfully aroused.

"You will learn your place!" Aristaeus bellowed as he launched at her, a seething hunger for violence flashing across his face as he swept his hand up, the back of it aimed at her face.

Hades thrust his bident forwards before the male could strike her, lunging towards him, and the male grunted as it sliced across his forearm as it slipped between the two prongs, and then howled in agony as Hades continued driving forwards, until the twin spikes lodged into the white wall of a building.

And bone crunched.

"Dare strike my queen and you will not live to tell the tale," Hades boomed and shoved his hand against the male's chest, pinning him to the wall as he frantically struggled to free his arm.

Aristaeus's face grew dark and cold, and he brought his other arm up.

Hades barely dodged the tip of his blade, pirouetting away from him and pulling his bident with him. The male swung again, his blow cleaner this time, more skilled as he spun and put his weight into it. Hades blocked it with his bident and tried to twist the sword free of his grip, but Aristaeus withdrew it and stepped back, evading his attack.

And ran.

Right at Persephone.

"If I cannot have her, no one will!" Aristaeus yelled.

She shrieked and ducked beneath his arm, hitting the ground, and then resolve flashed across her face and she pressed her hands to the pale flagstones. Vines shot up around her and turned to thorny brambles that bent and rocketed towards the blond.

Aristaeus hacked at them.

His distraction cost him.

Hades twined his shadows with the brambles, lacing them around one as it attacked the god, and grinned as the male cut the woody stem, revealing the shadow. Aristaeus's eyes widened as it survived the blow and struck him in his chest, sending him flying backwards. The male hit one of the buildings, crashing through the wall, and a section of the tiled roof fell in on top of him.

Satisfied that the foolish god had learned his lesson, Hades extended his hand to Persephone.

Aristaeus reappeared, covered in splinters of wood and white dust that clung to his wet hair and armour, and bared his teeth as fury blazed in his eyes and he lunged for Persephone.

Hades swept his shadows around her to shield her and growled as he thrust his bident forwards, lodging one point of it deep in Aristaeus's chest and the other in his throat. The male gasped and choked, blood pouring from his lips as he staggered backwards, shock rolling across his face. Hades grinned as Aristaeus's horrified eyes slid to meet his, letting the male see in his gaze that he wasn't done with him.

When his soul entered the Underworld, Hades would be waiting for him.

He put his left foot against the male's stomach and kicked him backwards, pushing him off the prongs of his black-and-gold bident, and retrieved his helmet where it had tumbled from Persephone's grip. He kept his shadows around her, shielding her and stopping her from seeing Aristaeus as he fought his inevitable death, feebly struggling to hold on to life.

Hades pulled her to her feet and ushered her away from the scene, towards the gate in the harbour as the storm continued to rage, a heaviness growing inside him as he saw the destruction he had caused.

Several of the white single-storey villas lay in ruin, and the streets ran with blood as people desperately tried to aid the injured. They turned fearful gazes on him as he passed them. As his shadows fell away from Persephone to reveal her, she gasped and looked at him.

He struggled to meet her gaze, to tear his eyes away from what he had done.

His victory was a defeat in disguise.

Because he could already feel Zeus's anger and was sure his brother wouldn't let him have Persephone after all now that Hades had wrought carnage across his city and harmed its citizens.

The air charged with familiar power.

Zeus was coming.

Hades looked at Persephone.

Certain he was about to lose her.

CHAPTER 38

"Hades!" A powerful male voice boomed his name and beside Persephone, Hades locked up tight, his shoulders going rigid beneath his black plate armour as they came to a dead stop at the entrance to the harbour.

Persephone cast a glance at Hades, concern blooming inside her when she saw resignation and hurt in his steady crimson gaze. It remained fixed on the gate that stood only one hundred feet away now. A war erupted in his eyes as the power she had felt curled around them and pressed down on her, and she was sure he would teleport her to it and rush her back into the Underworld to escape his brother's wrath.

But then he released her hand and slowly pivoted to face the direction they had come.

Persephone turned too, surprise chasing through her as she saw the large crowd that had gathered to block the route back towards the temples of Olympus and to her left and right along the harbour road too.

The people ahead of her parted and Zeus strode towards them, his golden eyes unflinching and hard as rain pelted him, soaking his white chiton and rolling down the gold pieces of his armour.

Those eyes locked onto Hades.

And narrowed.

Lightning crackled in Zeus's hand as he closed the distance between them and murmurs ran through the crowd, whispers that had Hades growing even more still beside her and had her looking at him again. He looked calm, unaffected, but she could see through the façade to his true feelings now. He was bracing himself, attempting to steel his heart so whatever Zeus said wouldn't wound him.

"Leave this realm at once and never return," Zeus growled.

The murmurs grew louder, and she scowled at the gathered as they whispered how just their god-king was, how right he was to banish Hades from the realm, and how vile her love was.

How evil.

Their cruel words ignited her blood and had her stepping closer to Hades as a powerful urge to protect him surged through her.

"For the damage and death you have caused here today, you deserve far worse." Zeus held his brother's gaze. "You had no reason to attack this city. What you desired was given to you freely, and yet you came here and wrought this suffering, and have doomed the mortal world to a far worse fate by attempting to take Persephone before she is due to return to you, breaking our agreement."

Persephone looked at Hades, sure he would set his brother straight.

He remained mute, his crimson eyes verging on black as he stood his ground but made no move to defend himself. Why wasn't he fighting his brother on this?

She noticed the way the people were watching him, staring at him alone. They were waiting for him to act like the monster they all portrayed him to be, and he was trying hard not to be that male, even when his brother's words were hurting him. Not just his words. The fact Zeus had ordered him to leave and had banished him from Olympus had cut him deeply, almost as deeply as his regret over the damage and injuries he had caused while the darkness had him in its grip.

Everyone believed her love to be heartless and cruel, incapable of feeling any soft emotion, but they were blinded by the lies people spread about him, and saw only one side of him.

Because he hid the other too well.

But not well enough to fool her.

His fear was right there in his eyes as he glanced at her. There for his brother to see if he looked closely enough. But it wasn't Zeus or his banishment that he feared. It wasn't the opinion of those around them as they whispered about him.

He feared losing her.

He thought that if he reacted and defended himself that Zeus would take her from him.

She feared losing him too.

But she was damned if she would let Zeus believe Hades was the only one to blame and that he had come here without cause to take her to the Underworld and break their agreement.

Persephone stepped in front of him, moving to shield him and earning an arched brow from Zeus.

She balled her hands into fists and stared the god-king down, her heart thundering a hard rhythm that made it difficult to breathe as rage and fear collided inside her.

"Hades did not act alone," she snapped, and Zeus didn't need to raise his eyebrow even higher or their audience didn't need to gasp for her to know she was crossing a line by speaking to the ruler of Olympus in such a manner. But she refused to stand by and bear her love suffering in silence. "I fought too. I am responsible too. And Aristaeus's death is his own fault. Hades tried to spare him, but he would not be deterred. His desire to make me his wife was too strong."

"Hades's desire?" Zeus's brow crinkled and confusion washed across his tanned features.

"No. Aristaeus's. He wanted our wedding to go ahead." She shook her head. "He snatched me when Hades was trying to help me escape the wedding my mother had planned and Hades tried to let him live, but Aristaeus persisted, and then—"

Zeus held his hand up, silencing her, his look dark as he turned it on Hades.

"She speaks the truth?" Zeus growled, confusion morphing into anger as the lightning that crackled in his other hand grew brighter.

Hades dipped his head. "Always. Sometimes to a painful degree."

She scowled at him for that one.

Zeus looked around them, at the buildings that had remained intact along the seafront, and the decorations that had been hung on their fronts, and then he looked at her, and then at Hades, and then the air charged with electricity.

"You were not informed of the wedding." Hades stared at his brother, a flicker of surprise chasing the black from his eyes to leave them crimson as his expression slackened.

"I was away, consulting the Moirai. You have my word, brother. If I had known of it, I would have put an end to it." Zeus looked from Hades to her, regret in his golden gaze now.

He opened his mouth to speak, but someone pushed through the crowd behind him, shoving people aside and earning black looks from several of them. Persephone braced herself, the familiar feeling of power telling her who was heading directly for her, and she inched back towards Hades. He noticed it and moved forwards, closing ranks with her, and gently gripped her hand, the touch comforting and reassuring her. If things looked dire, she was sure he would teleport her to the gate and have her back in the Underworld before she could blink.

Demeter pushed the last person in her path aside, her look thunderous as her dark green eyes settled on Hades.

"I should have known a fiend such as you would steal my beautiful daughter a second time, going back on the terms of your agreement with our god-king Zeus." She moved to stand beside Zeus, her chin tipped up and a smug look entering her eyes.

Demeter thought she had won this battle.

Her poor, foolish mother.

"Aristaeus is dead," Persephone said and almost savoured the shocked look Demeter levelled on her. "Slain by my true husband."

Hades's gaze burned into the back of her head and his shadows twined around her legs, and she could feel his desire to turn her and see in her eyes that she had meant that.

That she had chosen him.

Finally.

She glanced back at him, not wanting him to have any doubts about her desire to be his wife.

His queen.

She held his gaze as she spoke to Zeus. "Mother manipulated you into asking Hades to return me, falsifying her grief and harming the mortals to force you to act. The moment I returned as promised, she used wards and guards to trap me in the temple and announced I would wed Aristaeus the next day—today. When she knew you were away from Olympus. She wanted to take me from the one I love."

Hades's gaze softened and searched hers.

"He does not love you, foolish child!" Demeter spat. "He only uses you to get what he wants, and he will—"

"She is my heart," Hades interjected, cutting her mother off, and lifted his free hand to cup Persephone's cheek as he gazed down at her and the crimson in his irises gave way to blue. "My light. My everything. I love her with all that I am, and I will not allow anyone to take her from me. She is mine."

His eyes lifted and narrowed, and his fangs emerged to flash between his lips.

"She is mine, Zeus," Hades snarled, his expression growing fierce, and he shifted his bident, raising it and setting it down on the pointed tip of the staff. He looked bewitching like that, dark and commanding, and stole her heart all over again. "Not because you gave her to me, but because the Fates made her for me. No man or god will stand between me and my queen… my Persephone."

Demeter spluttered.

"I love you, too, Hades," Persephone whispered before her mother could rail about this or make out it was all lies, and he searched her eyes again, as if he needed to hear her say it more than twice for him to believe it.

She smiled softly.

She would show him the depth of her love later.

When they were alone.

Back in the Underworld.

"I withdraw my banishment." Zeus moved a step towards them, his power buffeting her but held away from her too by Hades's own darker power, and Hades lifted his head again to look at his brother. Zeus's look turned sombre and serious. "I apologise for what has happened here this day. I will see to it Demeter is punished and will not stop you from taking your queen with you to live at your side in the Underworld."

Persephone twisted to look at her mother, half of her wanting to ask Zeus not to harm her and the rest of her glad that she would never interfere in her life again. The side of her that still cared deeply about her mother despite the things she had done and how she had treated her throughout her life began to win the war within her and sorrow teased at the edges of her heart.

Hades stepped up beside her, his hand falling to her shoulder, and his words sent warmth and surprise sweeping through her.

"I will put aside my anger towards Demeter, so there is no need to punish her now that she has accepted her daughter will be happy as my queen, and will abide by our agreement, brother." Hades didn't look at Persephone as her gaze leaped to his profile. His tone was sombre, almost grave as he added, "Persephone will spend spring and summer here in Olympus, and the rest in the Underworld with me."

Tears threatened to line Persephone's eyes as she gazed at her love, soul-deep aware how hard this would be on him. How hard it would be on them both. She didn't want to leave his side and be parted from him, but he was trying to be diplomatic and show Zeus and Olympus that he wasn't the monster many made him out to be.

A coldness grew within her, spreading inwards towards her heart as she realised something.

It wasn't autumn yet.

Hades was going to be forced to leave without her and she wouldn't see him for over a month, when she longed to go back with him and continue where they had left off, getting to know each other and strengthening their bond.

"Zeus—" Demeter started but he held up his hand, silencing her this time.

"And so it shall be," Zeus's tone softened and he half-smiled as he shifted his golden gaze to Persephone, "until such a time comes when you no longer wish to divide your time between this city and your home."

Her home.

She smiled at that.

"Perhaps the advent of your first child might be reason enough for you to remain in the Underworld throughout the year. I am sure your mother would not complain about losing your company once you have a family who needs your time and devotion." Zeus smiled slyly.

Children?

She looked at Hades, who didn't look enthralled by the idea of them having children. He looked rather unsettled by it. His gaze slid to her and heated, and she suddenly wasn't so sure that he didn't want children. Did he like the sound of a family with her?

She liked the sound of a family with him.

"I am young." She glanced at Zeus. "While I do not wish to leave my husband's side for even a moment, I would like to have him to myself for say… a few centuries?"

Hades growled, slid his arm around her waist and tugged her to him, telling her without words that he liked the sound of that.

A few centuries of just enjoying each other's company, savouring the moments they had together and falling deeper in love each day, and then maybe they would be ready for a family. Maybe. She couldn't imagine what their children would be like, but she knew they would have his courage and strength, and would be fierce warriors worthy of his name.

Zeus waved the gathered people away and then dipped his head to Persephone. "I shall expect your return in the spring."

"Spring?" She blinked and shook her head. "But it is only late summer now. If I return in the spring—"

"Your mother will not chill the mortal world while you are enjoying your honeymoon with your new husband, will you, Demeter?" Zeus levelled an expectant look at her.

Her mother's lips flattened, her look mulish, but then she huffed and muttered, "I will not."

Persephone had expected she would have to let Hades go back to the Underworld without her, but now she had seven months with him instead, and by the gods, she couldn't wait to get started.

She seized Hades's hand and pulled him towards the gate before Zeus could change his mind or her mother found the courage to protest. Hades must have been as surprised as she was by his brother's decision to allow them to be together until spring, because he stumbled along behind her, a blank look on his face.

But then it sank in.

Hades growled and swept her into his arms, and teleported with her, landing close to the gate. He cradled her in his arms as he carried her across the threshold between Olympus and the Underworld.

Taking her back to his realm.

To her home.

"Home," she breathed as the dark realm appeared around them, the sight of it no longer grim and frightening, but a comfort to her. She had come to love this realm almost as much as she loved its ruler.

Hades swept her into another teleport and landed with her in their chambers.

He gazed down at her, his pale blue eyes fierce and his deep voice laced with tender emotion. "I love you, Persephone."

"I love you, Hades." She slipped her hand around his nape and drew him down for a kiss, one she couldn't get enough of as he held her to him, warming her right down to her soul to chase all her fears away. "Nothing will part us again."

He opened his mouth, his look telling her he was going to contradict her by bringing up the terms of his agreement with his brother.

She pressed her finger to his lips to silence him and murmured, "Even when I am in Olympus, you will still be in here," she touched her chest over her heart and then shifted that hand to his, "and I shall still be in here."

He kissed her again, harder this time, stealing her breath and her heart with it.

And when he broke away this time, she smiled wickedly.

"And Zeus never said you could not visit me in Olympus." She toyed with his lips, feathering her fingers over them. "We could steal moments with each other."

He growled, evidently liking the sound of that, and captured her lips again, his kiss fierce and beautiful, and then rested his forehead to hers as he breathed against her lips, "Then expect me to steal a moment each day, for I do not want to be without you, my love. I never want to be without you. I meant what I said."

He pulled back and gazed down at her, his look pure adoration.

"You are my heart, Persephone."

She smiled and stroked his cheek, holding his gaze and sure her look was as soft and filled with love as his.

"As you are mine, Hades."

He peppered her lips with kisses as he carried her towards the bed, ones that slowly heated her blood and made her shiver and ache, and her mind leaped forwards to all the things she wanted to do to him—wicked things.

"My king," she murmured, meaning to tease him but it came out breathless and her heart added, "My forever."

Hades growled and reared back, his gaze searing and filled with love she knew would be eternal and unwavering, and happiness she knew she had caused, because he was no longer alone. She was no longer alone. He was right. The Fates had made them for each other—light and darkness—two hearts that balanced each other, and now they had found each other.

And nothing would tear them apart.

"My forever," Hades husked.

Lowered his mouth to hers again and breathed against her lips before he claimed them.

"My queen of the Underworld."

The End

ABOUT THE AUTHOR

Felicity Heaton is a New York Times and USA Today best-selling author who writes passionate paranormal romance books. In her books she creates detailed worlds, twisting plots, mind-blowing action, intense emotion and heart-stopping romances with leading men that vary from dark deadly vampires to sexy shape-shifters and wicked werewolves, to sinful angels and hot demons!

If you're a fan of paranormal romance authors Lara Adrian, J R Ward, Sherrilyn Kenyon, Kresley Cole, Gena Showalter, Larissa Ione and Christine Feehan then you will enjoy her books too.

If you love your angels a little dark and wicked, her best-selling Her Angel romance series is for you. If you like strong, powerful, and dark vampires then try the Vampires Realm romance series or any of her stand alone vampire romance books. If you're looking for vampire romances that are sinful, passionate and erotic then try her London Vampires romance series. Or if you like hot-blooded alpha heroes who will let nothing stand in the way of them claiming their destined woman then try her Eternal Mates series. It's packed with sexy heroes in a world populated by elves, vampires, fae, demons, shifters, and more. If sexy Greek gods with incredible powers battling to save our world and their home in the Underworld are more your thing, then be sure to step into the world of Guardians of Hades.

If you have enjoyed this story, please take a moment to contact the author at **author@felicityheaton.com** or to post a review of the book online

Connect with Felicity:
Website – http://www.felicityheaton.com
Blog – http://www.felicityheaton.com/blog/
Twitter – http://twitter.com/felicityheaton
Facebook – http://www.facebook.com/felicityheaton
Goodreads – http://www.goodreads.com/felicityheaton
Mailing List – http://www.felicityheaton.com/newsletter.php

FIND OUT MORE ABOUT HER BOOKS AT:
http://www.felicityheaton.com